I0590219

THE MASTERS CLUB
A Novel

by Olivia Savage

The Masters Club
A Novel by Olivia Savage

THE MASTERS CLUB
© 2025 Olivia Savage
All rights reserved.

This is a work of fiction. Names, characters, businesses, places, events, and incidents are either the products of the author's imagination or used in a fictitious manner.

First Edition

ISBN: 979-8-9999006-0-9

A Note from the Author

If you've ever doubted your place in the lane...
If you've felt too much, not enough, or feared it was too
late to begin again — this story is for you.

You are not behind.
You are not broken.
You are not done.

The wall isn't the end — it's your launch point.

To everyone swimming against the current: may you
always find your lane, your breath, and your people.

Welcome to The Masters Club.
— Olivia Savage

Acknowledgments

To everyone who's ever lost themselves somewhere between the hustle, the heartbreak, and the PTA sign-up sheet — I see you. This book is for the version of you who thought she was too busy, too tired, or too far gone to start again. Spoiler: you're not.

To my own Lane 4 — the fierce, funny, glitter-loving women who have cheered me on, called me out, and poured the wine when I needed it most — thank you for reminding me that friendship is its own kind of superpower.

To my family — for surviving the kitchen table chaos, and the mysterious appearance of swim goggles in the laundry. Your patience, love, and laughter are in every single page.

To you, reader: Thanks for grabbing this book, tossing it in your beach bag (or onto your nightstand), and letting me keep you company for a few chapters. I hope you leave these pages feeling braver, louder, and a little more like the main character in your own life. You were never behind — you were just waiting to find your lane.

Prologue: Nora

These things don't happen all at once. There's no thunderclap, no single final straw you can point to and say, *that's when I lost myself.*

It's slower than that. Quieter. The kind of erosion you only notice when you're standing at the edge, realizing the ground beneath you has been carried away grain by grain. It starts small. A laugh you swallow because it feels too loud in the room. A story you don't tell because you're not sure anyone cares to hear it. The shirt that once made you feel beautiful ends up shoved to the back of the closet after someone says it's "a lot."

You trade the songs that make you sing for silence. The food you love for whatever's easiest. The late-night talks for quiet that isn't peaceful. You tell yourself it's not erasure, just compromise. Choosing your battles.

It's just the way grown-ups love each other. You learn to file down the bright edges so you'll fit together better. But over time, those edges fade, worn down until you're nothing but a smoother, smaller version of yourself.

It doesn't happen with dramatic exits. No slammed doors. Just the steady, unremarkable unravelling of someone who once took up space. A laugh quieted here. A dream postponed there. Choices made smaller and smaller until they barely feel like choices at all and one day you wake up and realize you've been living in the outline of a life, the color slowly drained away.

Then one day, you catch your reflection in a bathroom mirror and, for a fleeting second, you recognize her—the woman you used to be. When she was brighter, sharper, more alive in a way you no longer are. Then the flicker fades. You go back to brushing your teeth, telling yourself this is fine. This is life. This is marriage. Except deep down—you know it's not fine.

Here's the cruel thing about fading: you don't notice how far you've gone until something—just one thing cuts through the haze. A smell that takes you back. A photograph you didn't remember existed. A voice in the dark asking a question you can't ignore. Something that cracks the veneer just enough for light to get in. Then you're left with an ache you can't put away. An ache that says you could try to find that light again, if you were brave enough to want to.

I didn't think I was. Not yet, but life has a way of shoving you toward the water, and sooner or later, you either sink quietly… or you learn how to swim.

Prologue – Simon

It's strange how you can build your entire life around something, pour every hour, every heartbeat into it— and still watch it slip through your hands.

For me, it was always the water. Early mornings before the sun came up, muscles aching in that clean, satisfying way. Lanes stretching ahead like promise. Coaches telling me I was built for this, teammates who felt more like family than my own blood. I believed them. I believed in *me*.

For a while, it was true. Until the sport I loved became the only thing I was. Until the friendships blurred into rivalries, and the people I thought would love me—through medals, through mistakes—made it clear their love had terms. Terms I couldn't keep.

When it ended, it wasn't with a bang. No scandal. No public collapse. Just an empty pool at the end of a season, my name already fading from the record board. My phone stopped ringing. The people who once swore they'd always be in my lane drifted to other currents.

I told myself I was fine. That I could still have the water, even if I couldn't have the life I'd imagined with it. Coaching seemed like a way back in—different role, same world. But it's not the same and neither am I.

So I stay on deck, stopwatch in hand, distance in place. Teaching other people how to chase what I couldn't hold onto. Keeping my guard up so nothing and no one can take more from me.

At least, that was the plan. Until she showed up—unexpected, unprepared—and somehow made me want more than the safety of staying on the shore.

The Dive

The house was too quiet. Not peaceful quiet—the kind that sinks into your bones and tells you you're safe. This was a brittle, echoing silence, the kind that made every creak in the floorboards sound like judgment. Nora sat on the edge of the couch, still in her work clothes, one shoe off and one on, staring at the envelope on the coffee table like it might bite her.

FINAL NOTICE – DIVORCE DOCUMENTS ENCLOSED

She didn't need to open it to know what it said. The logistics of being unloved. The invoice for the life she'd failed to hold together. With a sigh, she leaned forward and swept it into the drawer of the side table— right on top of the others she hadn't opened. It wasn't like she needed more proof that everything had officially, irrevocably ended.

Her eyes flicked to the far wall, where a gallery of frames still hung like nothing had changed. Wedding photos, vacation candids, a shot of David mid-laugh with his arm slung around her like they were solid. Like they were forever.

Nora stood, crossed the room, and stared at them. It took her a moment to realize she was holding her breath. With a trembling hand, she reached for the photo from their honeymoon in Venice—her smile radiant, his casual and practiced. She remembered that moment. She also remembered that she hadn't wanted to take the gondola ride because it felt cliché. He'd insisted. Said the point of romance was to lean into the cliché. She'd leaned, my God, had she leaned, but David had never really caught her.

Her fingers gripped the frame and before she could talk herself out of it, she pulled it off the wall, walked it straight to the kitchen trash, and dropped it in face-down. Then another and another. Until the wall was bare and her pulse had steadied.

In the emptiness, her reflection ghosted back at her from the glass panes. She barely recognized herself anymore. Not just the lines that had deepened over the last year. Not just the gray strands that had crept in when she wasn't paying attention. But the hollowness in her eyes. Her once-wavy hair was now pulled back in a limp ponytail, streaked with defiance-colored silver she hadn't bothered to dye. Freckles dusted her shoulders.

Her body, stronger than she gave it credit for—held the softness of grief, of comfort eating and restless nights. Her lips, unpainted. Her posture, a quiet question mark of someone still negotiating her space in the world. The weight of too many silences swallowed.

Her phone buzzed. She ignored it. She walked to the bedroom, peeled off her blouse, and caught sight of herself again in the mirror—The woman staring back wasn't weak. She was tired. Grieving. Bruised in the way only disappointment can bruise a person, but she wasn't done.

She walked into the closet to grab a sweater. The scent of lavender sachets had long faded, replaced with a faint mustiness of forgotten years. Shoes lined the floor like soldiers awaiting orders—heels she hadn't worn since networking mattered, flats she wore to every open house they never bought, sneakers with laces still knotted from that one half-marathon training app she abandoned after David said it was "too ambitious."

She crouched, pulled open a bottom drawer, and froze. A one-piece swimsuit lay folded beneath a stack of tank tops. Black with a faded pink stripe. She held it up. The fabric stretched loose, the elastic worn out, but it was hers from a time before things were complicated. When she felt joy, not shame.

She sat on the carpet, swimsuit clutched to her chest. Tears gathered, hot and sharp. She didn't cry loudly. Just enough to feel the salt sting her lip. Enough to release the ache curled tight in her ribcage. She laid the swimsuit in her lap and whispered, "I miss you," but she wasn't sure if she meant herself or the girl who used to wear it.

Nora changed into a pair of leggings and a zip-up jacket and moved into the kitchen, the coffee pot clicked off with a hollow pop. She moved on autopilot pouring a mug, wrapping her hands around the ceramic like it could anchor her. She leaned against the counter, staring through the window above the sink. There was nothing but gray sky and the brittle limbs of trees. No revelations. No dramatic signs.

Just a woman, standing in the wreckage of a life she hadn't planned to rebuild. She took a sip. It scalded her tongue. Good, she thought. At least that still hurts. She wrapped her sweater tighter around herself, the sleeves pushed up just enough to reveal a faint tan line from a watch she no longer wore.

The floor beneath her was clean. Too clean. Without the scuff of shoes or trail of clutter, the house felt sterile. Like a showroom. Like something waiting to be staged and sold.

She sipped her coffee and stared at the fridge, where expired coupons and half-faded photos clung to crooked magnets. Her eyes flicked to the calendar, blank squares stretching into next week like an empty promise. No reminders. No appointments. No shared notes or dry cleaner pickups. Just silence.

David was gone. Not in the explosive way people brace for. There were no slammed doors, no final fights, no dramatic ultimatums. He simply stopped being part of the story. Quietly, cleanly.

He had packed a single duffel bag and left a mug in the sink. Said he needed "room to breathe," and she had let him go. Not because she agreed. Not because she understood, but because by then, she had already stopped holding on. Not just to him. To herself.

The unraveling had started long before that morning. In the way she defaulted to what was easiest. The way she picked restaurants she didn't like and watched shows she didn't care for just to avoid the sigh he gave when she disagreed. In how she chose beige instead of bold. In how she wore quiet like armor.

It wasn't about him leaving. It was about how she had started to vanish. She didn't miss David. She missed the girl who used to paint her nails bright red just because it made her feel dangerous. The one who would book a weekend trip on a whim, who once danced barefoot in a fountain at midnight, tipsy on cheap sangria and summer. She hadn't been that girl in a long time.

Now she was a woman who forgot her own birthday until Facebook reminded her. Who ate microwave dinners over the sink and hadn't changed the burnt-out hallway bulb in four months. Who hadn't cried the day her marriage ended but had cried over a missing sock two weeks later.

The Masters Club

She turned from the coffee machine and walked toward the dining room, brushing past unopened mail, a brittle rosemary plant she kept forgetting to throw away, and a framed photo of her and David at someone else's wedding. She should have put it in a drawer, but she hadn't. Not out of sentiment, out of inertia.

She stared at the wilted plant on the windowsill, once lush, now brittle and browning at the tips. She'd meant to water it. To care. To notice. It had been a gift. Not with a note, not even wrapped. Just something her mom handed her in the kitchen last December, casually, like it meant nothing. "You need something that fights to stay alive," her mom had said, rinsing carrots in the sink.

Nora hadn't known what to say then. She still didn't but the words stuck. Echoed louder now in the quiet. She reached out and touched the dried stem. It crumbled under her fingers. She didn't throw it away. She just stood there, fingers full of what used to be something green and growing and let it ache.

Her phone buzzed again—some news alert she didn't open. She picked it up. Scrolled. Closed it. She thought of calling someone. Anyone, but didn't. Instead, she pressed her palm against the counter. "I'm not fine," she whispered to the stillness. "I haven't been in a long time." This time, the silence didn't feel peaceful. It felt like the only thing honest enough to answer back.

The grocery store was over lit and understocked, its fluorescent lights buzzing overhead like tiny, judgmental bees. Nora wandered the aisles in a daze, pushing a squeaky-wheeled cart that protested with every turn. Her haul so far looked like it had been assembled by someone coming off a three-day bender or starting a new life on Mars; frozen waffles, discounted wine in a bottle shaped like a swan, a candle labeled Morning Zen that smelled vaguely like lemon furniture polish and desperation.

She turned a corner toward the frozen foods section, already regretting leaving the house, when she froze for a different reason.

Down the aisle, past the bagged edamame and vegan meatballs, stood a woman in an aggressively matching workout set. Ponytail. Gold hoops. Holding a six-pack of sparkling water and looking far too put-together for a Wednesday afternoon. Nora squinted.

Janine, her old neighbor. The one who used to wave from her porch every time David mowed the lawn. Who organized block parties and once offered Nora her homemade hummus recipe like it was the Holy Grail. Who asked questions that weren't really questions, just polite probes wrapped in concern.

"Oh, hell no," Nora muttered, ducking so fast she almost ran over a kid in a dinosaur onesie. She made a beeline for the waffle case and hunkered down behind it like a civilian in a war zone. Her breath fogged the glass.

She waited. Prayed. Peered through the racks of frozen food like they were camouflage.

She wasn't ready. Not to make small talk. Not to smile and say Oh, I'm doing okay when everything in her life was covered in metaphorical smoke and ash. Especially not in baggy sweats and three-day-old dry shampoo and the faint mascara smear of someone who'd cried in a parking lot this week.

She backed away and ducked into the cereal aisle, heart racing. Twelve types of granola stared back at her, smug and clustered, like judgmental PTA moms. She picked one up. Put it down. Picked it up again. Pretended it mattered which one had flaxseed.

It didn't. She glanced over her shoulder, just in case. Coast clear. Still, she didn't move. It wasn't just Janine. It was the idea of being seen. Of someone recognizing her—really seeing her—and knowing what had unraveled. The failed marriage. The forgotten dreams. The woman who used to wear heels and book spa weekends and now couldn't get through a grocery run without emotionally hiding behind toaster waffles.

Eventually, Nora wandered back toward the freezer aisle, cart still pitiful. Her reflection ghosted across the glass of the ice cream case—dim, distorted.

She stood in front of the rows of mint chocolate chip, her favorite since childhood, and didn't move. The cold seeped through the glass. She pressed her fingertips to it. Let the chill anchor her. She whispered, "Am I a ghost?"

Not for anyone else to hear. Just to test the air. To see if the universe would echo back. It didn't. Only the buzz of the lights. The hum of the freezer and a toddler wailing in aisle seven. She stared at her own pale, flickering reflection and wrapped her arms tighter around herself. She wasn't ready to be seen but maybe, just maybe—she was tired of disappearing.

Nora sat in her parked car outside Target, one hand on the steering wheel, the other gripping a plastic bag that contained exactly three things: Sugar Babies, a rotisserie chicken, and a bottle of wine she wasn't even sure she liked.

It was 11:07 a.m. on a Wednesday and she had officially run out of excuses not to cry. The tears didn't announce themselves. No sobs. No cinematic collapse. Just a slow, quiet blur. A blink that lasted too long. Then another. The kind that slid down her cheeks while the radio played something aggressively cheerful, as if the world hadn't read the memo.

She scrubbed at her face with the cuff of her sweatshirt and opened her phone, pretending to check messages she didn't have. A text from her ex-sister-in-law sat unread, like a splinter she couldn't quite bring herself to dig out. Instead, she swiped to photos.

The first one in her "Holidays" album: her and
David in matching pajamas, mid-laugh, with mugs of
hot cocoa that had clearly been staged. She looked so...
sure. Or maybe just strained, in a way she didn't
recognize back then.

A sudden knock on the window jolted her so hard
she almost launched her phone into the rotisserie
chicken. She turned and blinked. A woman grinned at
her through the glass, cupping her hands like binoculars
and smudging the window with glitter-dusted fingers.

"Rina?" Nora mouthed.

Rina beamed like she'd just won something. "Roll
it down, baby. I come bearing chaos."

Nora lowered the window halfway. "It's been
years."

"And yet, here we are. Me, thriving in head-to-toe
leather. You, hiding from life in a Target parking lot.
Iconic."

Nora gave a breathy laugh. "It's not what it looks
like."

Rina cocked an eyebrow. "You're alone. Crying.
Clutching Sugar Babies like a woman on the brink. I'm
pretty sure it's exactly what it looks like."

Without waiting for permission, Rina yanked open
the passenger door and slid in, her oversized tote
thumping down between them. It smelled vaguely like
patchouli and chlorine.

"Okay," she said, poking at the plastic bag. "Is this your emotional support chicken?"

Nora wiped her nose. "More like my avoid-the-world chicken."

"Valid." Rina dug around in her bag, pulled out a mini tissue pack, and handed it over. "So... who broke your heart and how many times should I slash their tires?"

Nora sniffled. "David and I separated. A while ago, technically. But today it just... caught up to me."

Rina's face softened instantly. "Ugh. That sucks, I'm so sorry."

"Thanks," Nora whispered. "I haven't really told anyone. Everyone either tries to fix it or acts like grief has a deadline."

"Well, I suck at fixing things and I'm aggressively bad with time, so... I'm your girl."

Nora managed a laugh. "God, I forgot how much I liked you."

"You should be so lucky. So listen," Rina said, shifting to face her fully, "you need Lane 4."

Nora blinked. "Is that a secret underground support group?"

"Close. It's the adult swim crew at the rec center. We're all a mess. It's beautiful."

"I haven't swum laps since high school."

"Perfect. Come emotionally dog-paddle with us. It's like therapy, but cheaper and with better calves."

Nora gave her a look. "You always this subtle?"

"Never. But I am persistent and you, Nora Blake, are giving off major 'needs a fresh start and a well-fitted swim cap' energy."

Nora shook her head, smiling despite herself.

"I'm serious," Rina added. "Come once. If you hate it, I'll personally smuggle you out wrapped in a towel and dignity." Somehow, that was the first offer all day that didn't make Nora want to scream.

She didn't say yes. Not exactly. But she didn't say no either.

Which is how she found herself twenty minutes later tucked into a corner booth at a tiny café wedged between a dry cleaner and a nail salon. The kind of place where the blinds never quite closed, the posters were sun-bleached at the edges, and the mugs were probably washed more with hope than hot water.

The specials board listed something called a "glitter latte." Which, of course, Rina ordered. "Liquid sunshine for your insides," she called it. Nora got a chamomile tea she didn't really want, just something to hold so she didn't have to fidget with her sleeves.

Rina started talking immediately, her voice filling every dusty corner of the café. First, a story about a Bumble date who had used the phrase "alpha energy" unironically—twice. Then a saga about her dog, Sir Bark Twain, who had recently eaten an entire wedge of Brie and then thrown up on her houseplants "as an act of protest or performance art, unclear."

She was loud, unapologetic, and a little unhinged. Her eyeliner was smudged in a way that somehow looked intentional. Her earrings were the size of coasters. Her hoodie read "Emotionally Unavailable, Spiritually Feral."

Nora tried not to laugh but she liked her. She always had. Then Rina quieted. Stirred her drink like it had secrets.

"So really," she said. "How are you doing?"

Nora stared into her mug like it might offer answers. "I don't know," she admitted. "I feel like a ghost in my own life. Like everything's still moving but I'm not in it."

Rina nodded. "That's exactly how I felt before Lane 4."

Nora raised an eyebrow. "You keep saying that like it's a secret society."

"It kind of is. But with more leg hair and less Kool-Aid."

She pulled out her phone and flipped to a photo— Rina in goggles, flashing a peace sign next to three other women in various stages of post-swim dishevelment. No makeup. Damp swim caps. Giant grins.

"That's us. Vanessa's got three kids, a thriving tomato empire, and the patience of a saint. She could probably forgive a mosquito mid-bite. Lulu's basically a human disco ball with ADHD and no filter. Once wore a tutu to practice because it was 'on theme," and me, well, I'm the emotionally constipated chaos wrangler."

She looked at the picture, then back at Nora. "We're all mid-recovery disasters. Marriages, careers, identities, we all watched something blow up, but somehow, we found each other in Lane 4 and we swim. That's the deal. That's the hope."

Nora took the phone and stared. They didn't look like Instagram influencers. They looked... alive. Tangled and laughing and real. "I don't know if I can do that," she said.

"Sure you can. You don't even have to get wet at first. Just come watch. I'll sit with you. Or forcibly submerge you. Consent is a journey."

Nora smirked. "You're completely unhinged."

"I know. That's why you've missed me."

They sat for a moment in silence, mugs between them like truce offerings. Then Nora lifted hers. "Maybe." Rina clinked hers against it. "To maybe," and somehow, maybe felt like enough to start.

Back at home, the house was quiet again. Nora stood in the kitchen with her laptop open, the glow of the screen casting soft shadows on the granite countertop. The rotisserie chicken from earlier sat untouched in the fridge. The wine remained corked. She hadn't even changed out of the hoodie she wore to Target.

She was bone-tired, not from physical exhaustion but from the weight of herself. The kind of tired that seeps into your thoughts and makes simple choices feel like impossible decisions.

She took a sip from a mug of now-cold tea and stared at the Parks & Rec registration page open on the screen. Her mouse hovered over the list of offerings. Youth basketball. Senior tai chi. Indoor pickleball.

Then she saw it:

Masters Swim – Beginner Level
Thursdays 6:00 a.m.

Her finger froze over the touchpad. She could still hear Rina's voice. Lane 4 saved my sanity. Nora exhaled slowly. "What the hell am I doing?" Her hand trembled slightly as she moved the mouse. Each click felt like stepping onto ice—fragile, uncertain. The registration form blinked open. Click. Scroll. Submit.

Every motion thudded with a cocktail of doubt, fear, and something that might've been hope.

You're registered.

Plain. Bright. Final. Her stomach flipped—not with dread, not exactly with excitement. It was something in between. A friction of newness, of daring to want.

She closed the laptop gently, walked to the couch, and pulled a blanket over herself. For no reason she could explain, she opened YouTube on her phone and typed in Olympic swim relay.

She watched as sleek bodies cut through the water, powerful, purposeful, unbothered. The kind of women who didn't shrink to fit someone else's idea of acceptable.

David would've laughed. Swimming? That's adorable, Nora. You'll quit halfway through like everything else.

She could hear it so clearly. That smug tone. That barely contained smirk he used when pretending to care. He'd say it with a chuckle, like it was all in good fun. Like she was being overly sensitive. Again. *You're not built for this kind of thing. Be realistic. You're good at planning brunches, not pushing yourself.*

God, she hated how easily the voice returned. How it slipped into her thoughts like it belonged there and the worst part? He wasn't even here to say it but the voice still lived rent-free in her head.

She didn't turn it off. Not when her tea went cold. Not when her eyelids sagged under the weight of the day. Not even when the doubt returned—soft-footed and familiar, curling up beside her like it belonged. Because this time, she'd said yes. Not to him. Not to fixing anything or proving she could. She said yes to herself. To the quiet flicker of want that hadn't gone out. It was messy. Unsteady. Maybe even a little foolish, but it was hers and for once, she wasn't asking for permission to want more

Later, under a blanket with her phone glowing inches from her face, Nora opened the voice memo app. The light cast long shadows across the room, highlighting the stillness she'd grown used to—her kingdom of almosts and maybes.

Her thumb hovered above the red circle.

She wasn't sure why this felt scarier than the registration but it did. Because this? This would be her voice. Her truth. She tapped record. A beat of silence. Then, softly:

"I know no one will hear this. That's the point, I guess," she whispered, her voice a rasp of uncertainty. "But I need to say it somewhere. To someone. Even if that someone's... me."

She shifted beneath the blanket, the fabric rustling like waves.

"I don't even know what I'm doing," she admitted. "It's like—I've been holding my breath for a year. Maybe longer. Pretending that if I stayed still enough, quiet enough, the pain wouldn't find me." She swallowed. "I think I was wrong."

Her voice cracked, but she didn't stop.

"If I drown, it'll be my own damn choice. I don't want to be safe anymore. I want to feel something. Even if it hurts. Even if I fall apart."

A shaky breath. "At least I'll know I tried."

Her thumb hit stop.

Then play.

She listened. Winced at the tremble in her voice. At the rawness. Then she deleted it.

She stared at the screen for a long time. The cursor blinked like a heartbeat. She tapped record again.

"First swim Thursday," she said, voice steadier now. "I'm scared shitless, but I'm going anyway."

She paused, then added, barely a whisper: "Because I want to remember what it feels like to try."

She saved this one. She named it: **Start.** Then turned off her phone, rolled onto her side, and let the quiet wrap around her like a dare she was finally willing to accept.

Just Breathe

The parking lot of the rec center was half-full, the kind of Thursday morning mix that suggested retirees on treadmills, new moms in stroller fitness, and people who already had routines—knew where to go and how to belong.

Nora sat in her car with the engine still running, both hands on the steering wheel. Her fingers tapped out a jittery rhythm she couldn't quite still.

She was early. Or late. She wasn't sure. Time felt slippery lately, like everything had been slightly off-axis since David left. No one was expecting her. Not really. She could leave right now and no one would know the difference.

She stared at the rec center's entrance. Automatic glass doors. A few motivational posters in the window, one featured a smiling child holding a swim ribbon, another showed a woman lifting weights with perfect form and zero body fat. Nora pressed her lips together.

A woman walked by in leggings and a bright windbreaker, earbuds in, water bottle in hand. Confident. Focused. Alive. Nora shrank a little lower in the driver's seat. What was she even doing here? A masters swim team? She wasn't a master of anything.

Unless you counted eating toast over the sink and pretending not to cry in grocery store aisles.

Her phone buzzed in the cupholder.

Rina: *You better be walking in right now or I'm sending Lulu out to drag you in, and trust me, she'll make a scene.*

Nora let out a half laugh, half groan. Of course she would. Her hand hovered over the gearshift. For a breath, maybe two, she considered reversing. Going home. Back to safety. Back to stillness. Back to nothing but then another woman walked out of the center, hair still wet, cheeks flushed, towel slung over her shoulder like a victory banner. She was laughing at something someone had said behind her. She looked tired. But also… light.

Suddenly Nora ached for that. For the version of herself that used to feel light. She shut off the engine. The silence inside the car was immediate, total. "Okay," she whispered to no one. "Just walk in. That's it. Just walk in." She grabbed her bag from the passenger seat. The strap was frayed, the zipper bent. It had been in the back of her closet for years, but it was something. A beginning. Or at least the costume for pretending she belonged.

With one final glance at the doors, and the life she could still choose not to enter, she opened her car door and stepped out. The air smelled faintly like cold pavement and chlorine and she walked in.

The Masters Club

The automatic doors whooshed open with a hydraulic sigh, releasing a puff of chlorine and floor wax into the cold morning air. Nora stepped inside. The rec center was... clean. Bright. Unapologetically functional. A high-ceilinged lobby stretched in front of her, all beige tile and laminated signs; Zumba classes, open gym hours, community potluck night.

It smelled like bleach and rubber and, somehow, stability. Nora clutched the strap of her old swim bag tighter, suddenly aware of the coffee stain on her jacket and the fact that she hadn't worn mascara in three days. Her sneakers squeaked as she walked in, too loud in the lobby's polished hush. To the left: a bulletin board plastered with photos of smiling kids holding swim ribbons. To the right: a row of vending machines and a grim-looking water fountain.

Straight ahead: the front desk. She didn't move. She didn't even breathe for a second. It hit her how long it had been since she'd entered a place without a script. No agenda. No show to put on for others. No meeting to run. Just... herself and the silence inside her was deafening.

She glanced at the pool window and caught a flash of it—the water. Shimmering. Still. Not inviting, exactly, but familiar and suddenly, like a memory on a trigger wire, it hit her. The first time she swam in a meet. She couldn't have been more than ten. New team. New goggles that didn't quite fit her right. Her mom had kissed her forehead and said, "Just have fun," which was code for "don't embarrass me." Her heart had pounded so hard she was convinced people could see it through her Speedo but when the buzzer went off and she hit the water, it all went quiet.

Not the stands. Not the coach. Not even her mother's voice. Just her. The water didn't care if she was anxious or awkward. It didn't care if she was too much or not enough. It just held her. Let her push. Let her race. Let her be.

She hadn't thought about that moment in years. Now, standing on the sterile tile floor of a rec center in the middle of a midlife crisis, she almost laughed. What the hell was she doing here?

Trying to remember what it felt like to be herself. Maybe that was reason enough. She adjusted the strap on her shoulder and moved toward the desk.

"Hey! New girl!" Nora turned just as a blur of a person, tall, laughing, wrapped in a towel like a cape, appeared at her side.

"Rina sent me to keep an eye out. You must be Nora. I'm Lulu!" she said, offering a damp handshake. Her eyeliner was waterproof but dramatic, and there was a small glittery star sticker on her cheekbone.

"Hi," Nora said, overwhelmed.

"Don't look so nervous. We don't bite. Except maybe Vanessa, but only before coffee."

Right on cue, a tall woman in a perfectly pressed swimsuit and matching swim cap gave Nora a once-over from across the pool deck. Her arms were crossed; her vibe straight Wall Street meets lifeguard.

"That's Vanessa," Lulu stage whispered. "She's terrifying, but she'll die for you in three weeks, tops."

"Good to know," Nora said, trying not to bolt.

As Lulu led her to the bench near Lane 4, another woman in a rainbow swim cap and high ponytail called out, "If you're allergic to sarcasm, you should probably leave now."

"and you already know Rina," Lulu said. "Her bark's louder than her bite, but she's also, like, the team therapist. Don't tell her I told you that."

Nora smiled, a real one, small but stubborn. Her nerves didn't vanish, but they scattered slightly, like dust in the sun. For the first time in a long time, she felt something unfamiliar. She felt welcome.

The locker room was warmer than she expected—thick with steam, echoes, and the sharp scent of chlorine softened by lavender body wash. Nora hovered just inside the doorway, in her workout clothes, clutching her gym bag like it was the only thing keeping her from falling apart.

Her palms were already sweating. Not from the heat. From the fact that she was here, actually here. Too late to back out. Too early to fake confidence.

She took a cautious step forward. Flip-flops slapped against damp tile. The fluorescent lights hummed overhead, casting a sterile glow on rows of metal lockers and women in various stages of getting their lives together—pulling on swim caps, toweling off, laughing over inside jokes she didn't know yet.

Nora caught her reflection in the long mirror near the showers. She looked... fine. Not tragic. Not ready. Just a woman trying very hard not to look like she wanted to bolt. She adjusted her ponytail, even though it didn't need adjusting, and gave herself the kind of nod people reserve for cliff edges.

"You came," she whispered to the mirror. "Now don't run." and then she turned, opened the gym bag, and started to change—one piece of clothing at a time, like courage could be put on in layers.

Around her, women moved with the easy rhythm of routine. They dropped towels, stepped into swimsuits, adjusted goggles like they were brushing their teeth—normal, unremarkable. Nora, meanwhile, was acutely aware of every inch of her skin, every fold, every flaw the fluorescent lights seemed to spotlight.

She ducked into a changing stall, her heart thudding like she was about to give a speech naked. Which, in a way, she was. Stripping down in public felt like peeling off armor. As she pulled on her swimsuit, black, one size too snug—her mind drifted.

The Masters Club

A few years ago, after a long run on a too-hot day, she'd caught a glimpse of herself in the mirror—cheeks flushed, ponytail wild, sweat shimmering along her collarbone. She'd looked messy. Radiant. Real. For one fleeting second, she'd felt strong. Like her body belonged to her again. Like she was more than someone's wife, someone's plan B. She remembered that flicker. How rare it had felt.

David had walked by then, towel slung over his shoulder. He paused. Let his eyes rake over her, that familiar smirk tugging at his mouth.
"Damn. You look good."

She'd laughed. Because it felt like love. Because being seen—wanted—had felt like being valued. Like enough. What she didn't know then was how fragile that kind of power could be. How easily it cracked when it didn't come from inside.

Now, she stood in front of the mirror again, under unforgiving fluorescent lights, but the woman staring back wasn't flushed with life or glowing with effort. She looked pale. Tired. Eyes rimmed with something she refused to call sadness. Arms crossed tightly, like she was holding herself together from the outside in.

Not tragic. Not ready. Just bracing for the day, for the voices in her head, for the version of herself she didn't recognize anymore. She met her own gaze in the mirror.

"You don't get to define me anymore," she whispered. And this time, she didn't look away.

Rina leaned around the corner like a sitcom entrance. "You still breathing, or did the spandex claim another victim?"

Nora stepped out, adjusting her suit with the grim dignity of someone who'd just survived a small war. "Barely. There was a moment I saw the light."

Rina smirked. "You look hot. In a 'go get 'em, tiger' kind of way. Not a creepy gym guy kind of way."

They walked out together, towels slung over their shoulders, flip-flops smacking against tile with each step. The sound echoed under high ceilings. Chlorine hung in the air. The pool stretched out ahead—ridiculously blue and far too public. Swimmers sliced through the lanes with the ease of people who didn't second-guess their bodies.

Laughter echoed from the far end. The whole room buzzed with movement, with life. It felt like stepping into someone else's story. Her heart banged against her ribs. Not from exertion but shame. Old, sticky shame that clung to her skin more than the humid air.

She adjusted her goggles for the third time and glanced down the lane where others were already mid-stroke—controlled, efficient, focused. The opposite of what Nora felt.

She stepped in slowly, the water biting at her calves. Then her thighs. She took a breath and ducked under, emerging with a gasp that wasn't about temperature at all. Nora gripped the wall. The tile felt cold against her fingertips. She was supposed to swim one lap. Just one.

Her muscles felt foreign, like they belonged to someone else. Her breath came too fast, too shallow. The hum of water in her ears made it hard to think. Hard to ground and then, just like that, she was back.

Not in the pool, but in a memory. It had been late on a Tuesday. David had gone quiet, again. One of those nights where every word felt like a risk, and silence was the only way to avoid the inevitable sigh.

She'd slipped out without telling him. Grabbed her old goggles, a towel, and the keys. Drove to the community pool that stayed open until ten. No music. No plan. Just the need to be anywhere but in that house with its eggshell tension and empty rooms full of noise.

The pool had been mostly empty. She'd stepped into the water slowly, shivering, until she ducked under and pushed off.

She swam lap after lap, hard and fast. Not to train. Not to win. Just to forget. The rhythm of breath and burn gave her something to hold onto. Something that didn't feel like failure.

For forty minutes, she'd felt free. Then she went home and David was in the same place on the couch, scrolling. Same glass of wine, half-full. Same blue glow of the TV painting shadows on the wall.

He didn't even glance up. No "Where were you?" No "Are you okay?" No "I missed you." Just, "Hey, can you grab more granola next time you go out?" As if she hadn't just tried to come back from the edge of herself. She'd gone upstairs. Shut the bathroom door and cried so quietly the steam from the shower masked the sound.

Now, standing poolside, that version of her felt both distant and dangerously close. She blinked back the memory. Her eyes stung—chlorine, she told herself. What if she wasn't different now? What if this was just another version of quiet sadness in a different location?

Someone brushed past her humming under her breath. Vanessa adjusted her cap nearby, focused. Rina offered a wink from the lane. They didn't know her. Not yet, but they saw her. Nora took a breath. The kind that wasn't just for her lungs but for her life.

She swam forward. The water wasn't warm. It never was. As it wrapped around her calves, then her thighs, she remembered what it had felt like that night—not the sadness that came after, but the part when she moved through the water and felt, if only briefly, like herself.

She moved faster this time, when she came up for air—gasping, clumsy, heart racing—someone cheered from the next lane over. She smiled, water dripping into her mouth. Not because it felt perfect, but because she didn't do it alone.

Nora kicked off the wall again. It was awful. Her legs didn't sync with her arms. She inhaled a mouthful of water on her second breath. Her kick felt like flailing. Midway down the lane, her chest burned but she didn't stop.

She pulled, kicked, coughed, pushed. She reached the wall and slammed her palm against it like it owed her something. One lap. She clung to the edge, chest heaving, eyes stinging, muscles trembling. It was a mess and it was hers.

She looked down the lane. No one had stopped to laugh. No one was judging. Nora clung to the wall, lungs heaving, arms like wet spaghetti noodles, heart thudding loud enough to drown out the ambient splash of the pool.

One lap. She'd made it one damn lap. Not gracefully. Not confidently. But fully, stubbornly and that had to count for something.

She pressed her cheek to the cool tile, breath coming in short, uneven bursts. Her body was screaming. Her ego was bruised. But deep inside, something small and defiant stirred. You didn't drown. You didn't leave. You're still here. Her fingers flexed against the wall. That's a start.

She tilted her head, cheek still resting on the tile, and looked across the lanes.

Rina was already halfway through her second set, talking to Lulu between strokes. Vanessa floated on her back like she was born buoyant. They laughed. They splashed. They moved like they belonged to the water and to each other.

Nora watched them, something tight twisting in her chest. She wondered—not for the first time—if she could ever be part of something like that. Not just tolerated. Not just present, but known. Missed when absent. Rooted in something more than survival.

You don't have to know the ending to take the next step. The thought startled her. Not something David would've said. Not something her inner critic would've allowed. Maybe it belonged to someone new. Maybe it belonged to her.

She glanced down at her trembling hands. Her body had betrayed her in so many ways over the past year—fatigue, shame, tension knotted in her back like ·grief that had hardened but it hadn't quit and neither had she.

A splash nearby drew her out of her thoughts— Vanessa had made her way back down the lane and offered her a thumbs-up, cheeks flushed with effort, hair plastered to her face.

Nora raised a hand in return. Not quite a wave. But not nothing. She wasn't ready to laugh with them yet. Wasn't ready to banter or belong, but maybe—just maybe—she was ready to try.

She gripped the wall. Took another breath. Kicked off
again. When she surfaced at the shallow end, lungs
burning and limbs heavy, the chatter of Lane 4 drifted
over the water like music from a room she hadn't yet
been invited into but could almost imagine entering.

They hovered nearby, magnetic in their ease. Rina
stood tall and sharp at the edge of the lane, adjusting her
swim cap with the kind of precision usually reserved for
scalpel work. She wore her authority like a second
skin—posture perfect, expression unreadable. She didn't
stretch. She aligned.

Vanessa sat on the bench, gently tying her hair into
a braid. She wore a cozy terrycloth wrap and the
peaceful smile of someone who had learned to take up
space without apology. A canvas tote next to her
overflowed with snacks, kid art, and—Nora was almost
certain—a hardcover novel wrapped in a Ziploc bag.

Lulu lounged sideways across two chairs like a
Greco-Roman pool goddess in fluorescent pink. Her
swimsuit was cut just a little too high and glitter
shimmered in her ponytail. She was telling a story with
full body enthusiasm, complete with dramatic gasps,
sweeping hand gestures, and absolutely no sense of
volume control.

They were loud. Beautiful. A little unhinged and,
somehow, already a unit. "Don't stress," Rina said
beside her. "When I joined, I thought a breaststroke was
something you needed stitches for." She looped her arm

through Nora's with a casual confidence that made the panic in Nora's chest feel almost… manageable. "Come on. Lane 4 doesn't know what hit it."

Nora climbed out of the pool and followed Rina. Her brain screamed. Her lungs forgot how to expand. Every single cell in her body begged her to turn around and hide, but she didn't. Not this time and somewhere beneath the fear, something else stirred. Hope. Or maybe rebellion. Either way—she kept walking.

They walked to where Lane 4 stood stretching, chatting, adjusting their goggles with the kind of comfort that made Nora feel like she'd shown up to a play without knowing her lines.

A man stood just past the lane rope, clipboard in one hand, a whistle slung around his neck like it had earned tenure. Tall. Broad shoulders beneath a faded rec center sweatshirt. Athletic in a way that didn't ask for attention but held it anyway. His dark hair was slightly disheveled, damp at the edges like he'd just climbed out of the water and hadn't bothered to tame it.

He wasn't smiling but he wasn't stern either. He looked… engaged. Like someone who noticed things. Like someone who expected effort, not perfection. His gaze flicked across the swimmers with quiet precision, mentally cataloging posture, form, energy. He didn't command the space but the space bent toward him anyway.

Nora felt her stomach do a small, inconvenient flip. Not attraction exactly. Recognition, maybe. That startling jolt of being near someone whose presence hums on a slightly different frequency.

He glanced past her, not quite at her. But close enough to make her breath catch. Just a coach, she told herself. Just another person in this new world. Then why did it feel like something had shifted?

Their eyes didn't meet. He didn't even glance her way but Nora noticed him.

"Morning, Lane 4," he called out, his voice calm but commanding like someone used to being listened to. "Welcome back—or welcome for the first time."

She followed Rina to the edge of the pool, heart thudding louder than her footsteps. Around them, swimmers slipped into the water, adjusted their goggles, moved like they belonged here. Nora clung to the edges of herself.

The coach—Simon—crouched beside a plastic bin brimming with gear. He had the kind of ease that came from repetition, but his gaze flicked briefly across the group, pausing—for half a breath too long—on her. "If you're new," he said, offering the faintest half-smile, "grab a kickboard and a pull buoy. If you're not, pretend you know what those are." It wasn't flirtation. But it wasn't nothing and Nora's pulse tripped anyway.

Rina grabbed a kickboard and pull buoy like she was born doing it, then handed a set to Nora. "The floaty things," she stage-whispered.

"Very technical." said Nora, "Thank you. I'm basically an aquatic shaman."

Vanessa appeared at her side, cherry blossom tattoo peeking over her towel. "Look at you, already geared up. I panicked my entire first week. You're ahead of schedule."

"I'm currently faking confidence and mild hydration," Nora said. Vanessa nodded solemnly. "Excellent. That's Lane 4 energy."

From across the pool, Lulu lounged sideways on a bench, chin in hand, watching them like it was a soap opera. "You didn't drown. You didn't bolt. She's one of us now." She raised a water bottle in salute, glitter shimmering in her ponytail.

"I'm not sure I passed the vibe check," Nora murmured.

"You passed the survival check," Rina said. "That's more important."

Vanessa grinned. "Trust me, vibes are overrated. But snacks? Essential."

Nora clutched the kickboard, her knuckles white with tension and something else flickering beneath. A thread of possibility. She wasn't part of it yet. Not really. But for the first time in a long time, she wanted to be.

Vanessa leaned in. "It's mostly oversharing and the occasional snack-fueled existential crisis." Nora let out a breath she didn't realize she was holding. They weren't just welcoming, they were ridiculous, magnetic, alive and somehow, they'd made space for her.

"She's not kidding," Rina added, now adjusting her cap in the lane. "Lulu once told a story about a wax appointment during warm-up laps."

"It was relevant," Lulu insisted. Nora laughed—genuinely, unexpectedly. Somewhere deep in her chest, something unclenched.

Simon clapped once, drawing their attention. "Alright, Lane 4, easy warm-up: 100 free, 50 kick, then we regroup. No heroics. This is not the Olympics."

Lulu pushed off first, clean and efficient. Vanessa followed, cheerful and splashy. Rina lingered beside Nora, adjusting her goggles.

"You good?" she asked. "No. But I'm here." "That counts."

Nora pushed off the edge, heart pounding, and slid into the water. Then, one breath. One stroke. Another. She kicked—ungracefully, unsure, but forward. The water didn't exactly welcome her. It slapped. It shocked. It stole her breath, but it didn't reject her either and for now, that was enough.

She kicked with more determination than technique and made it halfway down the lane before her body started filing complaints. Arms aching. Lungs burning. Legs doing something that could generously be called freestyle.

By the time she reached the far end, she was clinging to the wall like it might float her to safety. Her heart pounded. Her goggles fogged and her left calf threatened mutiny.

Rina popped up beside her, grinning like she lived here. "Still breathing? Or did your soul exit your body mid-lap?"

"Unclear," Nora panted. "Is death by chlorine a thing?" "No, but public humiliation is. You passed that phase." From the other side, Vanessa spoke without looking up, adjusting her goggles with mechanical precision. "It doesn't get easier. You just get better at tolerating the discomfort."

"Super comforting," Nora muttered. "You did great," Rina said, floating in like a mermaid who also packed granola bars. "Way better than I did my first day. I panicked, hyperventilated, and kicked Simon in the chest. He was very professional about it."

Lulu cackled. "That's why he flinches every time someone does a dolphin kick." "He forgave me eventually," Rina said. "But only after I brought cookies."

Vanessa smiled. "Oatmeal chocolate chip. Never underestimate the power of baked goods." Nora huffed a laugh and rested her cheek against the cool tile. The ache in her shoulders was real, but so was the buzz in her chest—that strange, electric flicker that maybe, just maybe, she'd stumbled into something she hadn't even realized she needed.

She was still catching her breath when Simon appeared beside the lane. No whistle, no clipboard flourish. Just him. Quiet. Observing. His voice was low enough that only she could hear it. "You looked like you were fighting it," he said, eyes on the water, not her. "Then you let go."

Nora blinked, startled—not by the words, but by the way he said them. Like he hadn't just seen her swim. He'd seen her struggle and he wasn't judging it. "I didn't know I was," she admitted.

He gave the faintest smile. "Most people don't. Until they stop." Then he stood, already turning to call out instructions to another lane, like he hadn't just cracked something open in her with a handful of words.

Nora watched him go, her heart knocking a little harder—not from attraction, exactly, but from something quieter. The thrill of being seen without performance.

From further down the lane, Vanessa called, "You okay over there, champ?"

Nora turned, still gripping the wall. Her arms trembled. Her goggles fogged, but her smile—small, crooked—held. "Yeah," she said. "I think I am," and then she pushed off again. Not gracefully, but with something like hope.

By the end of the session, Nora's muscles trembled, her hair clung to her face in wet ropes, and her lungs ached like they'd been filed down to their last breath but she was still swimming.

Simon called for one last drill—an easy 50 freestyle. "Not fast," he said. "Just smooth." Nora nodded, slid her goggles back on, and pushed off the wall. This time, she didn't fight the water. She let it hold her. Let it push and pull. She moved like someone not trying to escape—but someone trying to stay.

When she touched the wall and turned around, the rest of Lane 4 was scattered nearby—some chatting, some gasping for air, all of them grinning like they'd just done something brave… and maybe a little stupid.

Rina reached across the lane and slapped her hand. "You did it. Officially not a pool noodle."

Vanessa raised an imaginary trophy over her head. "Most Improved Newbie. No blood, no tears, minimal splashing." Nora laughed, really laughed and the sound startled her. Not because it came out of nowhere, but because it felt like hers.

Simon crouched at the edge of the pool, clipboard forgotten. His gaze found hers, steady, unreadable, with just the edge of a smile tugging at his mouth. "Should I save you a lane next week… or would that ruin the mystery?" The words were casual, but something in his tone lingered—like he saw more than just her stroke technique

The deck buzzed with chatter and dripping towels. Lane 4 was already dispersing. Lulu making a glittery exit with a dramatic "toodle-oo," Rina digging for her car keys, Vanessa debating snack priorities with herself. Nora stood at the edge, toweling off, limbs shaky but alive.

She reached for her bag just as she sensed him. Close now but not looming. No clipboard, no whistle, just a steady presence and an unreadable look in his eyes.

"Hey," he said, voice low, like this moment wasn't for anyone else. Nora startled, then offered a breathless smile. "Still vertical." He smiled. Just barely. "You looked different by the end."

She blinked. "I did?" He nodded. "Yeah. First few laps, it was all fight. But then…" His gaze softened. "You stopped bracing. Let the water carry you." A quiet beat passed. Nora's fingers tightened on the edge of her towel. "I wasn't sure I could."

"You did." A pause. Then: "That's the shift I wait for. Not perfect strokes. Not endurance. Just… trust." Something flickered in her chest. Not crush-level butterflies, just the startled warmth of being seen clearly and kindly. She cleared her throat. "Thanks. That means more than I expected."

Simon gave her one last look—not flirtatious, not impersonal. Just something steady and knowing. Then he turned, already calling out shoulder cues to another swimmer as he walked off.

Nora stood there, towel wrapped like armor, heart thudding like it wanted to remember this. Not because it was romantic. Because it was real. Because someone had seen her in motion and didn't ask her to be anything but herself and for the first time in a long time, she didn't apologize for being a work in progress. She wasn't just surviving. She was surfacing.

Nora exhaled. Her muscles ached. Her heart thudded too fast for how still she stood. But under it all, something glowed—steady, quiet. She'd been seen. Not for what she used to be, or who she'd failed to stay. But for a flicker of who she might still become and she wasn't the only one who noticed.

"Come on, spandex survivor," Rina said, appearing at her side like she'd been there all along. "Before you melt into a puddle." Nora blinked, then gave a wobbly smile.

The rec center doors sighed shut behind them, leaving a trail of damp footprints across the concrete. The air outside was cooler than Nora expected, and the fresh hit of it made her skin prickle beneath her hoodie. Her towel was slung over one shoulder, her wet hair dripped steadily onto the asphalt, and her limbs felt like overcooked linguine.

Beside her, Rina walked with the loose-limbed ease of someone who did this all the time, like her body knew its way through discomfort and didn't bother making a fuss about it.

They reached Nora's car, Rina leaned against the driver's side door. "So," she said, crossing her arms. "Scale of one to soul-crushing, how bad was it?"

Nora let out a hoarse laugh. "Somewhere between mild drowning and emotional whiplash."

"Solid," Rina said, grinning. "That's actually above average for a first-timer. You didn't cry in your goggles. Lulu might promote you."

They both chuckled and Nora let her bag slide off her shoulder with a satisfying thud.

"You were good," Rina said after a beat, her voice softer now. "Not because you were fast. But because you didn't leave."

Nora looked down at her waterlogged sneakers. "I wanted to. About forty-five times."

Rina shrugged. "Yeah. Me too. My first practice, I stood in the locker room for twenty minutes debating whether to fake a phone call or pretend I had a sudden rash."

"What stopped you?"

She tilted her head toward the pool behind them. "A woman named Michelle. Sixty-two. Breast cancer survivor. She floated the entire practice on her back, humming ABBA under her breath. Told me, 'You don't have to be fearless. Just stubborn.'"

Nora smiled. "I think I like Michelle."

"She wore leopard print goggles and once slapped a lifeguard with a kickboard for talking too loudly."

"Definitely like her."

They stood there for a moment, the laughter fading into a comfortable hush. The sky was a dusky lavender, parking lot lights flickering overhead like stars that didn't quite commit.

Nora opened her car door halfway, then hesitated. She looked at Rina—really looked—and said, voice quiet but steady, "Thanks for not letting me disappear."

Rina's expression softened. "You don't seem like the disappearing type."

"I didn't used to be," Nora said.

"Well," Rina said, nudging her shoulder gently, "maybe you're on your way back."

Nora nodded, throat tight, emotions pulling taut behind her ribs.

She got in, started the engine. Rina backed away, giving a mock salute. "Same time next week?"

Nora met her gaze. "Yeah. Same time." As she pulled out of the lot, her muscles still sore and her heart a strange mix of heavy and light, she realized something. She was already looking forward to it.

Lane 4 - Take 2

The locker room was still loud—still steaming up the mirrors and echoing with the clash of flip-flops on tile but it didn't feel like a battlefield this time. More like a proving ground.

Nora stood at her locker, swimsuit already on, goggles looped around her wrist, towel folded with purpose. Her pulse still hummed, but it wasn't panic, it was anticipation.

Around her, the chaos was more familiar. Someone was blow-drying their hair with the force of a leaf blower. Another woman was debating post-swim brunch out loud while shimmying into compression leggings. There was a smell of lavender body wash and something vaguely citrus. It was chaos. Real. Alive.

She didn't feel invisible this time. Just… peripheral. Still figuring out where she fit, but not entirely outside the frame.

A stall door creaked open behind her. Another woman emerged—mid-thirties, hair slicked back, shoulders tight like she'd been holding her breath for years. Her eyes were rimmed red. She clutched her towel like a lifeline.

Their eyes met and just like last time, Nora didn't look away. She didn't smile, didn't rush in. She just nodded. A quiet, steady I see you.

The woman nodded back. That was it. That was enough. Nora turned back to the mirror. Her own reflection met her more steadily this time. Still damp. Still nervous, but upright and awake.

She whispered, "You're doing it. Not perfectly. But still." Then she grabbed her bag and walked toward the pool.

The glass doors sighed open, releasing Nora onto the pool deck in a breath of warm, chlorinated air that wrapped around her like memory. The sharp scent of disinfectant, the muffled slap of water against tile, the distant whistle, it all hit her at once. Familiar, but not yet hers, yet.

She hesitated for a beat, goggles clutched in one hand, towel draped over her shoulder like a question mark. Lane 4 was already gathering—stretching, adjusting swim caps, chatting like this was their living room and not a slightly damp rectangle of chaos.

Rina stood at the edge of the lane like she owned it, posture sharp and purposeful. Her swimsuit was black and severe, her hair pulled into a braid so clean it looked airbrushed. She looked like someone who could write a thesis and win a bar fight in the same afternoon.

She caught sight of Nora and arched a single eyebrow. "You came back," she said. Not a question. A statement of fact. A marker laid down. Nora shrugged, pretending her heart wasn't pounding with the effort of showing up again. "Glutton for punishment?" Rina smirked. "Or hope. We're big on both around here."

From the bench, Vanessa waved her over, already ensconced in her cozy floral towel that looked like it had lived a previous life as a vintage curtain in a seaside cottage. She was braiding her hair in practiced motions, a trail of sunscreen along one collarbone. "Nora! I brought extra snacks today. Peanut butter pretzels. They cure all sins."

Lulu burst into view like a confetti cannon in human form. "Also," she said, eyes wide with mock gravity, "you've been officially christened."

Nora blinked. "I have?" Lulu nodded solemnly, looping an arm through hers. "Spandex Phoenix."

Nora tilted her head. "Because I rose from the ashes of my first practice?"

"No," Lulu said, completely serious. "Because your suit is black and red, and we're really into metaphors before sunrise."

Nora laughed. Not the polite, deflective kind. Not the brittle, overcompensating laugh she'd trained herself to deliver in meetings and awkward dinners. A real one. It snuck up on her and rolled out full-bodied, warm and startled. Like her ribs had been waiting for it.

The noise of the pool faded a little. The echoing whistles and sloshes and overhead lights all dimmed behind the hum in her chest. Because in this small, ridiculous moment with peanut butter pretzels and pre-dawn metaphors—something in her cracked open and this time, it didn't snap shut. It softened. It made room.

She was still smiling when she noticed him. Simon stood near the shallow end, clipboard in one hand, his other adjusting lane ropes with the practiced ease of someone who never had to raise his voice to command attention. His hair was damp again—messy and maddeningly good at it—and he wore that usual expression: unreadable, focused, like he was constantly five seconds ahead of the rest of the room.

Their eyes met. This time, he did see her and something flickered. Recognition. Maybe approval. Maybe something more subtle. She couldn't quite tell. He walked toward her, not hurried, just deliberate.

"Back for more?" he asked, voice low enough that only she heard it. Nora gave a one-shoulder shrug, trying to match his tone. "Either I'm committed... or I have a short memory."

Simon's mouth tipped into something that might have been a smile. Not the full thing, but enough. "Let's go with committed."

He held her gaze a beat longer, then gestured toward the kickboards. "Warm-up's the same. You remember what to grab?"

"I think so," she said.

"You'll be fine." He said it like a fact, not a compliment. Like he'd already seen her do the hard part and now he was just waiting to see what she'd do next and somehow, that meant more than any cheerleading ever could.

The pool looked different this time. Not because anything had changed. The same harsh lights buzzed overhead. The same damp air curled her hair at the edges. The same cracked tile marked the edge of Lane 4 but something in her had shifted.

Nora smiled—easier now—and slipped into the water without needing a second breath. This time, she didn't flinch at the cold. She pushed off, arms slicing through the still surface, stroke clumsy but determined. Her lungs burned by the second lap, but the panic didn't follow.

At the wall, she paused, gasping, and wiped water from her face. Beside her, Rina surfaced like a mermaid-turned-assassin. "You're breathing too shallow," Rina said. "Fix it. Or drown trying."

It was said without cruelty. Just fact. Nora nodded, coughing a little. "Got it."

Simon's voice echoed from the far end of the pool. "Nice adjustment, Nora. Keep your chin tucked next round." She blinked. He'd noticed. Again.

When practice ended, she clung to the wall longer than necessary, catching her breath. Her arms ached.

Her thighs trembled but under the physical exhaustion was something sharper—something stubborn.

"I did it again," she whispered.

From the deck, Vanessa tossed her a towel like it was a medal. "Still alive?"

"Barely."

"Good. That's the sweet spot."

They walked in loose formation toward the locker room, wet footprints trailing behind them like ghostly signatures. Chlorine clung to the air, to their skin, to the ache in Nora's limbs that somehow felt earned this time. Her towel was wrapped tight around her shoulders, half for warmth, half for armor. Each step squelched softly against the tile, echoing in the quiet way that only shared exhaustion could.

Vanessa walked beside her, close but not crowding. Her tote bag bounced gently against her hip, a floral blur of snacks, swim caps, and mystery mom magic. She was humming some 90s song Nora vaguely recognized—off-key but unapologetic.

"Hey." Vanessa's voice cut gently through Nora's thoughts, like a hand brushing her shoulder without ever touching it. "We're heading to the café across the street. Nothing fancy. Just caffeine and carbs and probably Lulu reviewing someone's horoscope out loud. You in?"

Nora's instinct kicked in fast and sharp. Decline. Retreat. Smile politely and vanish before anyone noticed the crack in her voice or the tremble in her fingers. She opened her mouth to say something—anything safe— but then she caught herself.

The look in her own eyes after that final lap floated back: Awake. Not invincible. Not even confident, but undeniably present. Still tender. Still figuring it out. But not numb.

She swallowed. "I—" She stopped. Tried again. "Yeah. I'm in."

Vanessa's grin spread slowly, warm as the steam rising off their skin. "Good. Lulu already called dibs on the glitter latte, whatever the hell that is, so you might have to settle for a boring cappuccino."

"Damn," Nora said softly. "Guess I'll survive."

As they pushed open the locker room door together, a gust of cooler air kissed her damp skin, and Nora felt it, real, almost defiant: She didn't want to disappear. Not today and maybe that was enough.

The café across from the rec center smelled like roasted beans and nostalgia—warm and a little chaotic, like it belonged to the kind of people who didn't apologize for tracking in water. All mismatched mugs, overstuffed chairs, and houseplants thriving on miracles.

Nora slid into a chair at the end of the table. Her hair was still damp. Her sleeves tugged low. Her whole body ached but the women around her buzzed with energy like they hadn't just swum laps, they'd survived something.

"So," Lulu said, leaning dramatically across the table. "Tell us your deepest fear, your worst date story, and your favorite bagel topping. Go."

"She's kidding," Vanessa said.

"Am I?" Lulu blinked innocently.

"She's not," Rina added, unwrapping a blueberry muffin like it had wronged her personally. "I once told her I preferred cream cheese over butter and she staged an intervention."

Vanessa sipped her coffee. "I'm still recovering from the time Lulu asked a waitress what her star sign was before ordering."

"Listen," Lulu said, "it matters. An Aries can't be trusted with oat milk foam."

Nora laughed too loudly, too easily and just like that, she felt it again. The flicker. Not safety. Not certainty. But possibility. There was a pause, just long enough to let the moment breathe.

"You know," Rina said, uncharacteristically gentle, "when I first joined, I didn't think I belonged either. Total disaster. Cried in my goggles. Didn't even own a proper swimsuit. Just some sad tankini situation with flamingos on it."

"You?" Nora asked, eyebrows lifting. "Miss Intensity-In-A-Speedo?"

Rina cracked a smile. "Yep. Post-divorce, lost as hell. I needed something that didn't feel like a chore. Something that reminded me I was more than paperwork and property division. Swimming helped me find my edges again."

Nora stirred her coffee, the spoon clinking against ceramic. "You really think swimming can do that?"

"I think being around people who let you show up messy helps," Rina said. "And Lane 4? We specialize in messy. Graceful's optional."

Vanessa nodded, resting her chin in her hand, a gentle smile playing at her lips. "When I joined, I had just left my job. Burned out, barely holding it together. I thought I was just signing up for a swim lane and some exercise. Didn't realize I was signing up for people who'd text me to check on my tomatoes. Or bring me soup when I got the flu."

"And harass you into singing karaoke," Lulu added brightly, stirring her glitter latte with a tiny pink straw. "Very important part of the healing process."

Vanessa rolled her eyes fondly. "I'll never forgive you for that ABBA medley."

"You're welcome," Lulu said, not even pretending to be sorry.

They all laughed—easy and unforced. Nora wasn't sure when she'd last sat with a group of women and not felt like she was being graded. She wasn't performing. She was just... here.

Then Rina pulled out her phone with the gravity of someone initiating a secret society. "Alright. I'm adding you to the group chat."

"Oh no," Nora said, immediately wary.

"Oh yes," Rina replied. "It's called Masters Club. There will be memes. There will be panic about swim sets. There will be unsolicited skincare recs and shows to binge and hot takes about waterproof eyeliner."

Vanessa reached into her tote and handed Nora a granola bar like it was a sacrament. "Also, Lulu made a shared Google doc for snack rotations."

"And themed playlists," Lulu added, eyes gleaming. "I take requests. I do not take criticism."

Nora's phone buzzed. She looked down.

Masters Club (173 unread messages).

Her jaw dropped. "Oh my god."

"We're very emotionally available," Rina said with a wink.

Vanessa clinked her coffee mug lightly against Nora's. "You're one of us now."

Lulu leaned in, stage-whispering like they were plotting a jewel heist. "Welcome to the deep end."

That evening, Nora curled up on the couch with a fleece blanket, a lukewarm bowl of leftover pad Thai, and her phone balanced on her knee. The lamp cast a soft pool of light across the room, the kind that made shadows gentle and everything feel a little more forgiving.

The Masters Club

She hadn't meant to check the Masters Club thread again, but the notifications were relentless and weirdly welcome.

It was chaos. Glorious, glitter-soaked chaos. There were memes—dozens. A dolphin with false eyelashes. A Barbie diving in slow motion. A looped gif of a swimmer flailing wildly with the caption: *Me trying to look graceful when my cap starts sliding off mid-lap.* Someone, probably Lulu—had turned a clip of Vanessa doing her warm-up stretches into a slow-mo highlight reel set to Celine Dion's My Heart Will Go On.

Rina had posted a picture of her golden retriever wearing swim goggles and a swim cap, with the caption: *She's training for doggy paddle nationals. She's very serious about her taper.*

Vanessa replied with a blurry photo of her garden, mid-sunset, her caption reading: *Tomatoes are thriving. I, however, am one minor inconvenience away from spiraling.*

Then: *That's paws-itively adorable,* followed by eight tomato emojis and a GIF of someone dramatically watering plants with a wine bottle.

The chat had already cycled through four new names. It was currently titled: **Masters of the Splashverse**, but earlier that day it had been **Swim Shady & the Backstrokers**. Rina seemed to take her renaming duties very seriously.

There were polls about brunch locations. A Google form for sunscreen brand rankings. A heated debate about whether waterproof mascara was a scam or salvation.

Vanessa had suggested a Secret Santa exchange with a *"glitter optional, snacks mandatory"* theme. Lulu, naturally, had volunteered to host. *"I own six disco balls,"* she wrote. *"It would be unethical not to."*

Nora should have felt overwhelmed. A week ago, she might've. Too many texts. Too many opinions. Too much... everything, but instead, she felt looped in. Like she wasn't watching the world from behind glass anymore.

She scrolled back through a picture Rina had posted, Lane 4, post-practice, huddled together on the pool deck, towels draped like armor and laughter frozen in motion. Nora was in the frame too, not posed or posed-upon, just mid-laugh, eyes squinting, cheeks flushed. She didn't even remember the picture being taken, but it was her. The her she hadn't seen in a long time. Unpolished and alive.

She set her phone down and let her head fall back against the cushion. The hum of the fridge, the soft tick of the wall clock, the faint chlorine scent still lingering in her hair. It all settled around her like proof. She was in it. Not fixed. Not finished. But here, part of something. Wanted. Without needing to shrink or sparkle to earn it.

Her phone buzzed again.

The group chat was still going strong.

Vanessa: *Everyone bring a fun fact to practice tomorrow. I'll start: I once went on a second date just to get my Tupperware back.*
Lulu: *Good strategy.*
Rina: *That's the kind of emotionally intelligent pettiness I aspire to.*

Nora snorted into her blanket, her fingers already moving before doubt could catch up. She didn't need to be someone else to belong. For the first time in years, being herself felt like it might be enough.

Her phone buzzed again.

Vanessa: *@Nora How's the soreness? Want my Epsom salt rec? It smells like a lavender spa and only slightly like old people.*
Rina: *She's aggressively pro-bath. Prepare to be wooed.*
Lulu: *If Vanessa offers you snacks and bath salts, say yes. That's basically a love letter.*

Nora smiled. Her thumbs hovered. Then she typed:
Nora: *I'll take the spa bath, minus the old feet. Thanks for letting me in, guys. Really.*

A flood of heart emojis followed. Then a gif of a dolphin clapping in goggles and finally, a glitter explosion sticker from Lulu with a caption that read:
Lulu: *Baptized by chlorine. Officially one of us.*

Nora tucked the phone against her chest and sank deeper into the couch. The hum of the quiet house felt different now, less like a vacuum, more like a space waiting to be filled. She didn't know what was coming but for the first time in a long time, she was ready for whatever came next.

Later that night, Nora sat on the floor by her bed, knees tucked to her chest, journal resting in her lap. A half-melted candle flickered on the nightstand, casting long, golden shadows that danced across the floorboards. The flame bent with every small breath, like it, too, was trying to hold steady.

The room was still except for the ticking of the old wall clock and the occasional creak of the house settling into night. The kind of quiet that used to make her anxious. Now, it felt like a clean slate. Or maybe a soft pause.

She uncapped her pen. The ink was low, of course it was. She hadn't written anything just for herself in months. Maybe longer. Not since everything fell apart and she'd thrown all her energy into pretending she was okay.

The journal prompt at the top of the page stared back at her:

What's something you've left behind that you're still grieving?

Her fingers hesitated. Then began.

Me.

I left her somewhere between "I'm fine" and "Don't worry about it."

She used to dance in the kitchen. She used to make wishes at 11:11. She used to be louder.
She blinked. The candle wavered again.
She laughed with her whole face. She believed people when they said they loved her. She dreamed big and cried over songs and planned spontaneous road trips to nowhere in particular.
She wasn't perfect, but she was real and I abandoned her. Slowly. Quietly. In favor of being palatable.
The pen stopped. Her hand trembled like it wasn't sure it wanted to keep going but it did.
And now? She folds instead of fights. She overthinks before she speaks. She apologizes for taking up air.
She stared at the last line, the words smudging slightly under her thumb. Something stung behind her eyes, but she didn't blink it away this time. She drew a slow breath. Exhaled. Then added, beneath it:
But maybe she's not gone. Maybe she's just... waiting. For me. To stop surviving and come find her.
She let the pen fall softly onto the blanket beside her, the ink tip still wet. Her hand ached from writing. Her chest ached from the truth of it. She ran her palm over the page as if to seal it in. This quiet agreement between who she'd been and who she might still be.

Not a declaration. Not a plan. Just a promise to stop disappearing.

The candle flickered again, and she reached over to blow it out. The room dimmed, but inside, something had been lit. She closed the notebook gently like a truce and for the first time in a long time, she didn't feel like she was ending the day with regret. She felt like she was beginning something.

She stayed on the floor, spine pressed to the side of her bed, eyes tracing the faint patterns of candle smoke curling into the ceiling. Her mind drifted, not forward, but back.

To a night when she hadn't been quite so quiet. When her laugh had echoed off the tile and her feet had skimmed the bottom of the pool in the dark. When being alone didn't feel like being lonely.

The memory surfaced uninvited—but not unwelcome. A few months ago, a night like this would've ended with wine straight from the bottle and scrolling through old text chains she should've deleted. Not reading them, really—just watching the blue and gray bubbles like they might flicker back to life. As if she could rewind a conversation and find the version where he stayed.

She thought of one night in particular. Cold. Gray. The kind of quiet that seeps into your bones. She'd sat on the kitchen floor, back pressed to the dishwasher, the hum of the fridge the only sound in the house. The dinner she'd made, some hopeful Pinterest recipe involving lemon and dill—sat congealing on the table. David had canceled. Again. Work thing. Something came up. His voice smooth, apologetic. His tone so kind it almost covered the fact that she wasn't worth showing up for.

No fight. No yelling. Just... absence, softened with pleasantries.

She hadn't even had the energy to be mad. Just folded herself in half, face buried in a dish towel, tears soaking through the fabric while the overhead light buzzed faintly above her. She'd cried quietly, like she was trying not to disturb the furniture. Like admitting she was that lonely would make it real.

The worst part? No one had done anything wrong. It wasn't betrayal. It wasn't drama. It was slow erosion. The kind that hollows you out from the inside until there's nothing left to argue about. Until even grief feels like too much effort.

Now, sitting on the floor of her bedroom the quiet felt different. Not hollow. Not punishing. Just... open. She closed her eyes and let the memory fade. It didn't disappear. It was part of her, but it didn't own her anymore. Maybe that was what healing started to look like. Not erasing the pain but finally being able to set it down without apology.

The quiet held. For once, she didn't rush to fill it. Nora leaned back against the side of the bed. She hadn't moved in what felt like hours—until her body reminded her she was tired, in the deepest way. Bone-tired. Soul-tired, but not the kind of tired that begged for escape. This was the kind that came after letting go.

She pulled herself up off the floor, slid between the sheets, and clicked off the light. Sleep didn't arrive all at once. It crept in, soft and unhurried and somewhere between one blink and the next—

She was standing at the window. Not quite awake. Not quite dreaming. Caught in the stillness between. The curtain moved in her hand as if pulled by a breeze that didn't exist. Outside, the world was silver-washed—moonlight painting the quiet streets in cool brushstrokes. Leaves glimmered like glass. Rooflines curved like gentle waves and in her dream—she saw it. A pool. Empty. Lit only by stars.

Not the rec center, not some Olympic facility—just a rectangle of water surrounded by silence and soft blue shadows. She stood at its edge barefoot, wrapped in something weightless. A robe? A dream version of herself? The water shimmered, black and inviting. She stepped in.

It wasn't cold. It wasn't warm. It was perfect, the kind of perfect that had nothing to prove. It welcomed her without expectation.

No whistles. No lane assignments. No time to beat. No past chasing her heels. She slipped beneath the surface, and everything slowed. Her limbs moved with grace she didn't know she had. Not for performance. Not to earn rest. Just for the joy of being in motion. The water didn't resist her. It held her. Buoyant. Forgiving.

She twirled once underwater, arms sweeping wide like wings. Her hair floated around her face, and for a moment she opened her eyes, saw nothing but the silver light filtering through and the quiet bubbles that danced past her cheeks.

This wasn't a dream about swimming. It was a dream about being. Being alone without being lonely. Being seen without being judged. Being free—utterly and unapologetically—in her own body and when she surfaced, she laughed. Loud and breathless and real. Not for anyone. Not for anything. Just because she could.

Her body didn't ache. Her breath didn't burn. Her arms stretched forward and the water made room. She dove deeper, and the world dimmed to soft silence. Her hair floated around her like a halo, and her heart—her heart—didn't hurt.

Here, there was no David. No broken pieces. No pretending. Only her. Moving freely. Fully herself. The stars shimmered like they knew her name and in that impossible, liquid silence, she whispered to no one:

"I'm still here."

And the water whispered back:

"Yes. You are."

Nora stirred. At first, she couldn't tell where she was. Her skin still felt wet, like moonlit water clung to it. Her breath was steady, deeper than usual. The softness of the pillow beneath her cheek was almost jarring too solid after the weightless grace of the pool.

Her eyes fluttered open. The room was quiet, save for the soft whir of the heater and the occasional creak of old pipes settling, but something was different. Not the room. Her.

Nora pressed a hand to her chest. Her heartbeat steadily beneath her palm—no panic, no weight pressing down, just... presence. She didn't remember the dream in full, but she felt it in her bones. The shimmer. The silence. The certainty.

She sat up slowly, blanket falling from her shoulders, and looked out the window. The world was still dark, just a hint of dawn graying the sky.

A thought rose in her, gentle but insistent.

You're still here. She didn't need to write it down. This time, she believed it. A buzz from her phone broke the silence—a message lighting up the lock screen.

Vanessa: FYI, Lulu says today's swim set is "spicy but survivable." That's either a warning or a dare. You in?

Nora smiled, her thumb already moving.

Nora: Spicy sounds better than sleepwalking. I'm in.

She set the phone down, stood, and stretched—
muscles sore but somehow eager. The fact that she was
starting to believe was its own kind of magic.

Nora blinked into the stillness. No alarm. No rush. Just
the hush of early daybreak and the unfamiliar sense that
maybe—just maybe—she wasn't dreading what came
next.

She shuffled into the bathroom, bare feet cold on
the tile. As she brushed her teeth, she caught her
reflection and paused. Eyes a little puffy. Hair wild from
sleep but there was a hum beneath the surface, a
whisper of something warm that hadn't been there
before.

She hummed without realizing it. A tune she didn't
quite know, but that felt like it belonged to her anyway.
Her sweatshirt was oversized and soft, sleeves
swallowed her hands. She tugged on a pair of clean
joggers, rolled the waistband once, and stood barefoot
for a beat before the mirror.

Still soft. Still unsure, but her shoulders didn't
hunch this time. Her spine had found its length again.
There was a steadier rhythm to her breathing like she'd
remembered how to take up air without apology.

She braided her hair loosely, fingers working
through the strands with surprising gentleness. No tight
bun. No need to pull everything into place. Just a braid.
Just her.

She moved through the small motions packing her towel, goggles, and a slightly smushed granola bar into a tote bag that still smelled faintly of sunscreen and summer.

She added her water bottle. Her flip-flops. Her phone charger. Then paused. She looked back at the mirror, half expecting it to reflect the version of herself she used to brace against. But the woman staring back looked different. Not fixed. Not fierce. Just... here. Awake.

There were still cracks. Still sore spots. Still pieces that didn't quite fit together but something had shifted, and whatever this was—this almost-confidence, this flicker of forward motion—it was hers.

She slung the bag over her shoulder. "Let's go," she whispered to herself. Not a command. A nudge and then she walked out the door.

The New Ritual

The third practice didn't hurt less. Her arms still ached, her kick still wobbled, and her breathing hitched every third lap—but something had shifted. The sting of chlorine felt like a welcome. The wet slap of feet on tile, once disorienting, now sounded almost like applause and the hum of voices, splashes, whistles, it no longer overwhelmed her. It anchored her.

The chaos was still there. The humility of starting over hadn't vanished. But the fear? It was quieter.

"Alright, Lane 4," Simon's voice rang out, calm and clear. "200 warm-up, then 3 x 50 drill. Pick your poison." There was no whistle. No barked orders. Just that quiet authority again—voice like river stone: smooth, unshakable, quietly strong.

Simon paced the deck with that same easy confidence, clipboard in hand, strides long and steady. The kind of man who never had to raise his voice to command a room or a pool. His black tee clung damp along the collarbone, hinting at the lap he'd swum before practice. His hair curled slightly at the edges, still drying, and his jaw was shadowed in just enough stubble to make her think maybe he didn't care how he looked… and maybe that was why it worked.

The Masters Club

Nora didn't mean to watch him. Not really, but it was hard not to notice the way he moved—unhurried, observant, like he saw more than just swim technique. Like he paid attention to how people carried themselves, not just how they swam.

When his eyes landed on her? It wasn't with judgment. Or pity. It was quieter than that. Intent. Noticing. It made her skin prickle. Not with shame this time, with possibility.

She pushed off the wall, and for the first time, the water didn't feel like a test. It felt like something she might—eventually—learn to love again. The rush of cold wrapping around her like armor, sharp, bracing, necessary. She didn't glide but she didn't panic. Her kick was uneven. Her breathing, jagged. Her stroke, messy at best. But she kept going. Stroke. Gasp. Kick. Repeat.

Out of the corner of her eye, Nora saw him pacing along Lane 4 like a man who had all the time in the world and none of it to waste. Clipboard in one hand, whistle swinging like a lazy metronome, he moved with that maddening, effortless calm that made her want to both impress him and throttle him.

"Drive the elbows, Rina," he called.
"That's it, Lulu—less splash, more pull. You're not trying to water the plants."

Then, right beside her lane, voice pitched just low enough to slide under her skin—
"Relax your neck. Breathe. Don't force it."

Her arms faltered mid-stroke. Relax her neck? Was she supposed to be clenching it? Was that a thing? Her thoughts ricocheted like ping-pong balls in a dryer. Was her jaw locked? Shoulders scrunched? Did she look constipated?

She adjusted, flailing somewhere between grace and survival, and somehow—miraculously—she made it to the wall. When she surfaced, heart pounding and water cascading down her face, Simon was still there, crouched just slightly, clipboard tucked under one arm.

He met her eyes. No critique. No smirk. Just a nod, quick, real and the faintest curve of a smile. Not cocky. Not performative. Pleased, and then he turned like it meant nothing, calling out something to another swimmer as casually as if he hadn't just short-circuited her central nervous system.

Nora blinked, gasping softly.

"What the hell was that?" she muttered.

From halfway down the lane, Rina called, "Girl, if you bite your lip any harder, he's gonna file a swim report!"

Lulu popped up beside her with a mischievous grin. "Blink twice if you need CPR. Preferably from Simon."

"I'm fine," Nora lied, yanking her goggles down to hide the shade of crimson currently consuming her face.

"Sure you are," Rina said. "Just try not to melt next time he gives you a compliment disguised as a coaching cue."

"He said relax your neck." "And your soul tried to leave your body," Lulu added.

Nora groaned and shoved off the wall, lungs burning, face flaming, and her entire body one giant, traitorous nerve ending. The water didn't help but at least under the surface, no one could hear her scream.

By the time Nora reached the wall after her third 50, her lungs were tight and her arms felt like wet noodles. She clung to the gutter, catching her breath, when Simon crouched beside her lane, clipboard tucked under one arm.

"You're overthinking your arms," he said, voice low and smooth—like velvet with just a hint of gravel. "You're muscling through the water instead of moving with it."

"Overthinking is my cardio," she panted.

His mouth twitched. "Try focusing on your exhale. Let your breath lead. Everything else will follow."

She raised an eyebrow. "That sounds dangerously like yoga."

"I contain multitudes," he replied dryly.

"You don't look like someone who owns a yoga mat."

"I don't. I borrow other people's and leave before the gratitude circle."

Nora let out a short, surprised laugh.

Simon didn't move. Just watched her with that steady gaze that made her feel like she was being read, not looked at. "You're fighting the water," he said, softer now. "Try listening to it instead."

Her smile faded, not in a bad way. Just... recalibrated. "I thought the goal was to beat it."

He shook his head once. "It's not a fight," he said. "It's a conversation." Just like that, the air between them shifted. Quiet. Charged. The pool faded, the chatter around them dissolved, and for a moment, it was just his voice, her breath, and the slight tilt of his mouth like he was trying not to let on just how much he noticed her.

Then, because of course he had perfect timing, he stood up with casual grace. "Nice work today," he added, walking backward with maddening calm. "You're getting stronger."

She didn't say anything. Couldn't, really. Her brain was still busy translating what the hell had just happened.

He turned, calling out something to Lulu like he hadn't just rearranged her entire circulatory system.

Nora sucked in a breath and pushed off the wall again. Stroke. Kick. Breathe. But this time—God help her—it actually felt smoother. The panic ebbed. The rhythm settled and just for a few precious yards, her body remembered how to move without apology.

When she surfaced again, Simon was there. "You felt that, didn't you?" he asked.

She blinked up at him, water dripping from her lashes, her pulse still skittering.

"Yeah," she said, breathless for reasons she would not examine too closely. "I think I did."

He nodded once, satisfied, but his gaze held hers a beat too long. Not inappropriate. Just… observant and something else. Something that made her stomach tighten in a way that had nothing to do with core strength.

"You're listening to your body," he said, quieter now. "It shows."

Behind them, a sharp whistle of a splash broke the moment.

"Jesus, you two," Rina called from halfway down the lane. "If this were a rom-com, we'd be in the slow-motion montage right now."

"Does anyone else feel like we're all extras in their sexual tension movie?" Lulu added.

Vanessa cackled. "Ten bucks says she offers to help him stretch by next week."

"Twenty says he asks her first," Rina fired back.

Simon chuckled under his breath and straightened, glancing down at Nora. "They're relentless."

She pushed wet hair from her face. "They're not wrong."

His lips quirked again. "No. They're not."

With that, he walked off, calm, unhurried, clipboard swinging at his side like he hadn't just cracked her open in a 90-second emotional deep dive.

Nora leaned back against the wall, floating just enough to feel weightless. Her body ached, her cheeks burned, and her chest buzzed with something wild and giddy and so *not* allowed. It wasn't love, but it was definitely the beginning of trouble. The good kind. The kind that lingered in your limbs after practice. That buzzed in the quiet moments when your brain should've moved on but didn't.

She noticed things about him now. The calm way he moved between lanes, like nothing rattled him. The confidence in his voice, not loud or showy, but steady and earned. The way he gave feedback without making it feel like failure. How he actually listened when someone spoke. How his corrections made her want to improve, not shrink.

He didn't fill the silence with performance or dominance or sarcasm. He just was. Steady. Present, and then there were the smiles. Quick, real ones, like when Rina cracked a joke and he actually laughed, not politely, but like he couldn't help it. Once, when Lulu challenged him about pacing drills, he said, "You're not wrong, but you're not right either," and the corner of his mouth twitched just enough to make Nora grin beneath her towel.

It was a quiet kind of humor. The kind that caught her off guard. The kind David never had. David had been sharp, polished, clever in that *look how smart I am* way. Praise always came with strings. Smiles were strategic. Nothing about him ever felt unguarded, not even with her.

But Simon? He didn't ask for attention and somehow, that made her notice him even more. She hated how disarming it was. How unfamiliar it felt to be seen… and not immediately second-guess what was being seen. Something was shifting. Not fast but undeniably and it terrified her—just a little less than it thrilled her.

When practice ended, Nora lingered at the edge of the pool, legs dangling in the water, towel draped loosely around her shoulders. Most of Lane 4 had already trickled into the locker room, their laughter echoing faintly against the tiles. Someone dropped a bottle. Someone else shouted about the brunch, but it all blurred into background noise.

She stayed still, breathing in the chlorine and the ghost of adrenaline, her body humming from effort. Her muscles throbbed, but in a way that felt earned. Her heart did, too.

Simon walked by clipboard in hand, scribbling something that looked important. He was in that zone again, coach mode. Focused. Efficient, and then, without fanfare, he paused beside her.

"You coming Wednesday?" he asked, not looking down right away.

Nora glanced up. The lights haloed off the water behind him, giving him this unintentional glow she refused to find attractive. His gaze met hers, steady, clear, but with that unreadable undertone she was starting to recognize. The kind that made her feel like she was being seen, not scanned.

"Yeah," she said, voice low but sure. "I think I will."

He nodded, started to turn—then hesitated.

His eyes flicked to her towel, then lower, just for a beat.

"Bright blue suits you," he said. Voice quieter now. Not performative. Not flirty in the usual way but intimate in a way that sent heat crawling up the back of her neck.

Nora blinked. "Oh."

That was it. That was all she managed, because her brain had short-circuited. By the time she remembered how to function, he was already moving away, calling something to a swimmer in Lane 2.

She stared after him, lips parted, pulse thudding in her ears like she'd sprinted a 400 IM.

"You okay there, Ariel?" Rina appeared beside her, slick with water and smirking. "You look like a Disney princess who just made eye contact with her land-bound crush."

Nora groaned, laughing despite herself, and nudged her with an elbow. "Stop."

Rina wiggled her brows. "I'm just saying, he's never noticed anyone's swimsuit before. We're talking historic levels of fluster-worthy."

Nora leaned back on her hands, letting her heels skim the surface of the pool. Her laughter faded into a slow, exhale-like smile. Something had shifted. Not huge. Not loud. Just enough to crack open something quiet inside her. A flicker of warmth in a place that had gone cold. A tether to something beyond the routine.

The ritual wasn't just survival anymore. It was starting to feel like living.

***

Simon didn't usually linger after practice. Clipboard tucked under one arm, routines etched into muscle memory, he moved from swimmer to swimmer, stroke to stroke, week to week.

But tonight… he paused. Nora sat at the edge of the pool, legs swaying just beneath the surface, her towel slipping off one shoulder. Bright blue against her skin. Calm in her posture. Something quieter in her eyes.

He almost hadn't said it. *Bright blue suits you.* It wasn't protocol. It wasn't necessary, but it was true and he'd meant it more than he should've.

He kept walking after, kept his tone even, his gaze forward. But his brain? It was still a few paces behind. Back at the edge of Lane 4. Back on the slight lift in her mouth when she smiled. The spark of disbelief, like no one had told her she looked good in a long time. Or maybe she hadn't believed them when they did.

Simon exhaled through his nose. Rina's voice floated up from behind him, teasing and sharp. He didn't turn around, but he heard every word.

Historic levels of fluster-worthy.

He allowed himself one brief smile, small, involuntary. Yeah. That about tracked. He made a mental note to erase that compliment from the clipboard of his brain. Too late, of course. It was already there. Along with the way Nora was starting to show up not just in the pool, but in the quiet corners of his thoughts.

He wasn't sure what that meant yet but he was sure of this: he'd be looking for her on Wednesday.

***

The locker room buzzed with the soft rustle of towels, the hiss of showers, and the sound of women letting their guards down.

The Masters Club

Nora sat on the bench toweling off her legs when Vanessa plopped down beside her, already halfway through a protein bar and dramatically recounting a tale.

"So there I am," Vanessa said, wrapping a towel around her head like a turban, "giving this PTA presentation, right? I'm in full mom-mode—blazer, printed agenda, everything. I get home, go to change, and realize I've had my nursing bra unclipped the entire time. One boob was just... freelancing."

Lulu choked on her water. "Did no one tell you?"

"Apparently not," Vanessa said. "I guess my left tit gave a hell of a keynote."

Rina doubled over. "Honestly? Iconic."

"Could be worse," Lulu said, toweling off with. "I once did an entire hospital orientation with spinach in my teeth, and a pair of my kid's Paw Patrol undies static-clung to the back of my scrubs."

"Chase is on the case," Lulu muttered, and they lost it.

"You want chaos?" Rina cut in. "I taught a beginner boxing class once. Threw a punch, ripped my leggings clean down the butt. Just—hello, world."

Nora gasped. "No!"

"Oh yes, and I kept going. Finished the combo, called for cooldown, walked out like a queen with half my ass on display. The new guy tipped me."

Vanessa wiped tears from her eyes. "That's not fitness. That's feminism."

Lulu flung her locker open dramatically. "ANNNND I once matched with my OB-GYN on Bumble. After he delivered my second kid."

Everyone screamed.

"Oh my God," Nora laughed. "Did he recognize you?"

"He sent a message that just said, 'You look familiar.' I deleted the app and burned my phone."

Vanessa deadpanned, "Honestly, that's grounds for a support group."

"Lane 4 is the support group," Rina said, snorting. "We're just wetter." They all cracked up again, laughter bouncing off tile, wrapped in steam, damp towels, and each other and somewhere between the boobs, the Bumble, and the butt-rip, Nora realized she wasn't just included. She was in.

Rina leaned over to Nora. "This is the real reason we swim. So we can earn our place in the post-practice confessional."

"I thought it was for cardio," Nora said.

"That too, but mostly this."

Lulu sat on the bench and began braiding her damp hair. "Funny thing is, no matter what crap I see during the day; emergency surgeries, broken families, late-night calls—this place? This crew? It steadies me."

Vanessa nodded. "It's like we shed the rest of our lives when we dive in. No one's judging your job title or your laundry pile. Just your kick turns."

"And even those we judge lovingly," Rina added with a wink.

Nora smiled, towel tucked tight around her. She wasn't used to this—women showing up for each other without pretense or performance. It wasn't about perfection. It was about presence and slowly, she was beginning to understand the difference.

Later that evening, Nora lay on her couch, wrapped in a blanket with her feet tucked under her and a half-watched documentary playing in the background. Her hair was still damp, curling around her shoulders, and her muscles thrummed with exhaustion, but the good kind, the kind that meant she'd shown up for herself.

She scrolled past emails from HR, a marketing webinar invite, and a 20%-off sale for a brand she didn't remember subscribing to.

Her phone buzzed

Group Chat: *MASTERS CLUB*

Lulu: *Okay but CAN WE TALK ABOUT THAT POOLSIDE FLIRT?*

Vanessa: *Are we calling it a flirt? A flirtation. A flirt-adjacent moment.*

Rina: *He complimented her suit. Simon. Complimented. A suit. I've been wearing neon leopard print for three months and got nothing.*

Lulu: *It wasn't the suit. It was the energy. Chemistry so thick you could backstroke through it.*

Vanessa: @Nora You good? Do we need to fan you with a kickboard?

Nora: STOPPPP …It wasn't like that.

Rina: Girl. He paused. Simon does not pause.

Lulu: He paused. He spoke. He gazed. We're talking WOAH levels of tension.

Vanessa: I'm making a new spreadsheet called "Swim Meets Where Nora and Simon Should Just Kiss Already"

Rina: I'll start the betting pool: First kiss happens after she nails her 100 IM.

Nora: I hate all of you.

Lulu: You love us. Almost as much as you love swim-coach compliments.

Vanessa: It's okay. We support your love story. We're just going to narrate it in real time with memes and unnecessary GIFs.

Rina: Speaking of…

Attached: Gif of two dolphins doing synchronized flips with the caption: "When Coach Notices Your Kick Technique"

Nora: I'm blocking this group.

Lulu: Too late. You're one of us now. There's no unswimming into the glittery deep end.

She was about to toss her phone aside when a new message popped up:

Simon: Remember to keep your fingertips relaxed when you enter the water. Think of reaching, not punching.

That was it. No emojis. No greeting. Just a quiet correction that somehow felt more intimate than any "great job" she'd gotten in years.

Nora stared at it. It was helpful. It was technical, but it was also… personal. She could picture him sending it, deliberate, measured, thinking it through before hitting send. Like he wanted her to know he'd noticed. That he saw her.

Her lips curved before she could stop them. Her fingers hovered over the keyboard.

Be cool, she told herself. Be breezy. Be normal.

Instead, she typed:

Nora: *Got it. Thanks, Coach.*

She hit send, heart thudding like she'd just swum a 500 IM. A beat passed.

Then her phone lit up again.

Simon: *You're doing great. See you Wednesday.*

She blinked at the words. Re-read them…and again. There was nothing overt. Nothing inappropriate, but God, something in her chest still flared like a struck match. Not because he said she was doing great, but because he meant it, and because it mattered to her that he did.

She didn't answer. Just set the phone down slowly, her smile impossible to suppress. It wasn't a date. It wasn't anything, really. Except… maybe it was the beginning of something she hadn't let herself want in a very long time.

Her phone buzzed once more, and for a moment, her breath caught, but it was just a calendar reminder. Still, her pulse stayed elevated. She set the phone down and leaned back, heart still fluttering like the last few kicks of her freestyle set. The house was quiet except for the low hum of the fridge and the faint whir of the ceiling fan, but somehow, it didn't feel lonely.

Her eyes drifted to a half-finished vision board she'd started the week after the separation. A piece of corkboard littered with clippings, quotes, and hopes she hadn't fully admitted yet. One square in the middle had read: **Be seen. Even if it scares you.**

She remembered when she'd pinned it up, still feeling raw, directionless. Like maybe if she stared at that phrase long enough, she'd believe it and now, somehow, it was starting to happen. Not because a man texted her, but because she was letting herself be visible again. Vulnerable. Present.

Something in her chest loosened. She pulled the blanket tighter around her and let herself sink into the softness of the couch, into the quiet buzz of maybe. Someone was seeing her again. Really seeing, and for the first time in a long while, she wasn't scared of what they'd find.

She reached for her phone again, typed a message, then paused with her thumb hovering over 'Send':

Nora: *You make it easier to show up.*

She stared at it for a breathless beat. Then she deleted it. Not yet, but soon.

***

The rec center had emptied out an hour ago, but Simon remained in the coach's office, feet propped on the desk, clipboard on his lap, and a protein bar half-eaten beside him. The only sound was the occasional metallic groan of the water heater and the low hum of the vending machine down the hall.

He liked this hour. The quiet after the splashing stopped. When the pool was still and the fluorescent lights didn't feel so harsh. When he could think.

Usually, he used this time to update swim logs, write up drills, or tweak the week's schedule. Tonight, the clipboard sat idle. Instead, he found himself replaying the morning's practice. Nora and the way she'd hesitated at the wall, breath ragged, face flushed and then pushed off again anyway.

She was raw. Not inexperience, though she had plenty of that—but something underneath. A kind of stripped-down honesty. Most beginners tried to mask their fear with bravado or deflection. Nora just... showed up with all of it. The nerves, the self-doubt, the shaky strokes. It made him notice her more than he should.

He'd watched her out of the corner of his eye—how she laughed when Rina teased her, how her strokes sharpened with every lap, how she paused before each push-off like she was daring herself to believe she could do it.

Simon exhaled slowly and set the clipboard down on the bench beside him. It wasn't that he had a strict rule. Not exactly, but over the years, he'd learned to keep a certain distance. Not because he didn't care—he cared too much, sometimes. But because caring led to complication and complication, in his experience, rarely helped anyone.

He liked order. Routine. Measurable progress. Laps were clean. Feedback was actionable. The pool was the one place in his life where everything made sense. Until Nora. She didn't burst into his world. She wasn't loud or flashy. She didn't ask for extra attention, but there was something about her—a kind of quiet unraveling beneath the surface. Like she was trying to hold her pieces together long enough to find out who she was without someone else's voice in her head.

He recognized that more than he wanted to admit. It wasn't attraction, not at first. It was curiosity. Recognition. The way she showed up anyway shaky and unsure, but present. The way she kept trying, even when every part of her seemed to whisper that she didn't belong here.

That whisper—that was what got to him. Because it sounded an awful lot like his own voice years ago, back when everything in his life had fallen apart in ways no one saw coming. He'd rebuilt himself on discipline and distance. Kept his world tight, controlled, safe and now, this woman—this stubborn, unsure, brave-as-hell woman—was showing up and making him feel things he hadn't allowed in a long time. Not desire, exactly. Not yet, but awareness. Pull, a flicker of something he didn't have a name for.

Simon ran a hand through his damp hair, let out a soft laugh under his breath. This is not the plan, he thought. This is not the deal. But plans shifted. Currents changed and Nora wasn't just another swimmer.

He picked up his phone. Typed the message. Read it twice before hitting send.

Simon: *Remember to keep your fingertips relaxed when you enter the water. Think of reaching, not punching.*

No emojis. No overthinking. Just a line. A piece of encouragement. He told himself it was just a coaching note. But the truth was, it mattered if she replied back and he wasn't sure what that said about him anymore.

He didn't know her story. Not really, but he could see the outlines of it in how hard she tried to pretend she wasn't unraveling and how stubbornly she kept showing up anyway.

Simon glanced down at the clipboard again. He should really finalize the Saturday set. Instead, he picked up his phone, again thumb hovering over his messages. No. Not yet. Keep it clean. Keep it professional. He set the phone aside.

Just one more swimmer, he told himself, but the lie didn't sit right. Because somewhere between her first shaky lap and that moment she surfaced laughing after her last drill, he'd stopped seeing Nora Blake as just another swimmer and that, he knew, was exactly where the trouble began.

***

That night, sleep came slowly. Nora lay in bed, eyes fixed on the ceiling fan, replaying the day in shimmering fragments; Rina's laughter, Vanessa's dry wit, Lulu's splashy high-fives... and Simon's voice low beside her lane.

Then there was the text. She felt it again, that spark igniting somewhere below the surface. Not just attraction. Not even hope. Something broader. Something alive. Presence.

In that tiny, measured text about finger placement, she realized someone had seen her. Not as a project or a challenge. Just her, and he'd spoken to her like she mattered.

Maybe, she thought, slowly letting her gaze drift off the ceiling and into the dark corner of the room, maybe she was starting to belong to more than just the pool.

Piece by piece. Stroke by breath. She let herself feel it. Because for the first time in a long time, she wanted more than comfort. Slowly. Quietly. Fiercely real, and the next practice couldn't come soon enough.

Deep End Friendships

The pool was still. A flawless sheet of blue, glassy and undisturbed, it reflected the overhead lights like a mirror holding its breath. Faint ripples of color shimmered across the ceiling—silver, aqua, ghostly yellow like the building itself was dreaming. Chlorine hung in the air, sharp and familiar. The scent had lodged itself into her skin by now, into the seams of her towel, into the strange new rhythm of her week. She didn't mind it anymore.

Nora stood at the edge, arms wrapped around her torso, towel hanging loosely from one hand like a flag she hadn't decided whether to plant or drop. Her hair was damp, not from swimming yet, but from an unhurried shower she'd taken before leaving the house. She'd blow-dried her bangs. Worn her good hoodie. For once, she wasn't late. She wasn't rushing or apologizing or fumbling with goggles while muttering excuses.

She was here early on purpose. The quiet before practice felt almost holy. No splashes. No whistles. No chaos. Just the hum of industrial lights, the soft squeak of sneakers on damp tile, the steady inhale-exhale of a space waiting to come alive. The pool didn't intimidate her this morning. It didn't loom. It welcomed.

She took a breath. Let it fill her lungs, slow and deep. She didn't know exactly when the water had stopped feeling like a threat. Maybe it hadn't completely but something had shifted. The fear had softened, or maybe she had. The pool wasn't an enemy anymore. It was a mirror and in it, she caught glimpses of herself. Not the version from before, not quite the one she was becoming, but something in between. Fluid. Forgiving.

When she swam, she didn't think about David. Or her resume. Or the stillness of her kitchen. She didn't have to be productive or poised or likable. She just had to move and for once, movement felt like peace.

A breeze of motion swept in beside her. "Double shot latte, half a donut, and zero judgment," Rina said, holding out a coffee cup and a napkin spotted with powdered sugar. "Swimmer's fuel."

Nora took them like they were sacred offerings. "You know you're my favorite person, right?"

"I get that a lot. Usually right before people realize I talk through movies and forget to text back."

Nora smirked. "Sounds like you and I would thrive in a toxic group chat."

"Oh please, we'd dominate. You'd be the one sending long, thoughtful check-ins. I'd be replying with a meme of a raccoon eating Cheetos in the rain."

"That's... weirdly accurate."

They settled onto the bleachers, legs stretched out, the soft slap of feet on tile and the distant echo of showers filling the quiet around them.

"Did you hear about the Halloween Masters meet?" Rina asked after a moment, brushing sugar from her leggings. "It's ridiculous. Relay teams. Costume heats. Someone swam the 200 fly last year in a full Batman cape. It was both inspiring and deeply upsetting."

Nora raised an eyebrow. "I've been swimming for, like, two weeks. The only costume I could pull off is 'Drowning Civilian.'"

"Oh, honey." Rina grinned. "That's the whole point. We lean in. Embrace the ridiculous. You haven't truly lived until you've breaststroked next to a woman dressed as a haunted chandelier."

Nora laughed, the sound bubbling out of her before she could help it. "I'm pretty sure I'd just trip over my own cape and sink."

"Then we'll float down together. Lane 4 ride or die."

Nora shook her head, still smiling. "You're completely unhinged."

Rina took a proud sip of her coffee. "And yet, here you are—voluntarily sharing a bleacher with me before sunrise. Don't act like you're not impressed."

Nora bumped her shoulder lightly. "Okay, fine. A little."

Rina leaned back against the wall, her grin softening. "You're showing up, you know. That's kind of a big deal."

Nora glanced at the water, then back at Rina. "Feels like it," and it did. Not dramatic. Not loud. But real. Quietly real.

The stillness around them began to ripple, towel snaps, locker room laughter, the thump of gear bags hitting the floor. Morning had arrived.

Rina stood and offered Nora her hand like they were about to walk into battle. "Come on, partner in chlorine. Let's go survive the IM ladder."

Nora took it. "Define survive."

"With flair," Rina said, tossing her hair like a shampoo commercial. "Always with flair."

They walked toward the lanes side by side, two mismatched pieces from different puzzles that somehow fit perfectly in this one.

Simon's whistle sliced through the morning hum like a starting gun. Sharp, commanding, impossible to ignore.

"Alright, Lane 4!" he called out, clipboard in hand. "IM ladder. Start at 25, build to 100. Fly, back, breast, free."

Nora blinked. "Wait, what's an IM ladder again?" she whispered to Rina as they shuffled toward the blocks.

Rina adjusted her goggles, completely unfazed. "Pain. Alphabetized. You'll love it."

Nora's stomach dropped. Alphabetized pain? That sounded both accurate and entirely above her skill level. She tugged her cap over her ears and tried to steady her breath.

Butterfly. Backstroke. Breaststroke. Freestyle.

She remembered those terms. Vaguely. Butterfly was the one where you flailed like a wounded bird. Backstroke involved staring at the ceiling and praying not to smack into the wall. Breaststroke always made her sink like a stone. Freestyle… well, she could sort of survive that one. Sort of.

The first 25 meters went by in a chaotic splash of limbs. Her butterfly was more panic than propulsion. By the second round, her arms felt like sandbags. She flopped through backstroke like an unstrung puppet, misjudged a turn, and coughed up half a lung of chlorinated water.

Rina touched the wall beside her, breathing hard but laughing. "You alive?"

"Barely," Nora managed, clinging to the gutter. "Do we have a safety word?"

"Yeah. It's 'Simon, I regret everything.' But you only get to use it once."

Nora grinned, then winced as she peeled her goggles up. Her eyes stung. Her lungs burned. Her pride felt like it had been put through a blender. She glanced down the lane and caught Simon pacing alongside them. Clipboard tucked under one arm, stopwatch dangling from his hand, he moved with the calm confidence of someone who'd lived inside a pool longer than on dry land. Focused. Unrushed. Like nothing ever surprised him and nothing slipped past him, either.

He crouched near the edge of her lane just as she surfaced from a rough breaststroke.

"You okay?" he asked, voice low and even.

"Define okay," she panted.

"You're doing better than week one." His eyes scanned her stroke, then settled back on hers. "You're not flailing anymore."

"Just floundering gracefully?"

His mouth quirked. "Something like that."

She gave a shaky laugh, then dropped her chin to the edge of the pool. "Still feels like I'm always half a lap behind."

Simon was quiet for a beat. Then he said, "Why'd you start swimming?"

The question hit with a thud she didn't expect. It wasn't casual. It wasn't light. It was intentional, like he wasn't asking to make conversation but to understand something essential.

Nora hesitated. The water clung to her skin. The echo of voices, of movement and whistles and shouts, dimmed for a moment.

"To stop disappearing," she said quietly.

His gaze didn't shift. Didn't flicker. Just held hers with a quiet stillness that felt like safety.

"That's a good reason," he said. "One of the best, actually."

She wasn't sure what to say to that. Her throat felt tight, not from exertion this time, but from the unexpected weight of being seen.

Simon rested one forearm on his knee. "You're not disappearing here." That did it. That cracked something open, like a soft shell she'd grown used to carrying.

For a few seconds, neither of them moved. It wasn't dramatic. It wasn't cinematic, but it was real. She could feel the difference. The weight of the water. The beat of her heart. The heat that crept up her neck had nothing to do with exertion.

Before she could answer, a loud splash erupted behind them. "Hey!" Rina yelled. "If someone doesn't return my kickboard, I will start hexing people!" Laughter followed from the other lanes, rippling across the water.

Simon straightened, the spell of the moment breaking, but not disappearing. "Next set—start at the top!" he called, returning to coach mode with a practiced ease.

Nora let go of the wall and pushed off again. Her limbs were heavy. Her lungs felt firelit, but something inside her had shifted. Not just recovery. Something closer to awakening.

She sliced through the water, her rhythm still imperfect but more grounded, more hers. The strokes weren't easier but they weren't foreign anymore either. With each kick, she felt something return to her. A sense of place. A flicker of belief. Maybe this wasn't just about fitness. Maybe it never had been.

Nora reached the wall at the end of the next set, arms trembling, chest heaving. She yanked her goggles up, blinked the water from her lashes, and tried to catch her breath.

Rina popped up beside her, grinning like she'd just discovered something juicy.

"So…" she said, drawing the word out like a piece of gossip. "You and Coach Whisper-Voice having a moment over there?"

Nora groaned, resting her forehead against her arm on the wall. "Please don't."

"Oh no, I insist." Rina flicked water at her. "You were floating like a damn swan afterward. Graceful. Ethereal. Emotionally compromised."

"I was swimming," Nora argued, but her cheeks were already warming.

Rina shrugged. "Sure. Swimming. With extra eye contact and vulnerable truth bombs."

"God," Nora muttered. "Do you watch everyone this closely?"

"Just the ones who blush like a Jane Austen heroine when Simon crouches nearby."

Nora splashed her, fully this time. "You are the worst."

"And you, my friend," Rina said, flipping onto her back like a smug otter, "are so obviously into him, it's a wonder the chlorine hasn't started bubbling from tension."

Before Nora could reply, Simon's whistle blew again. "Let's go, Lane 4! Round two—same strokes, but cleaner this time. Think smooth. Think control."

Rina rolled her eyes and pushed off the wall. "Yeah, yeah, coach," she muttered under her breath. "Think fewer feelings, got it." Nora laughed, a real one this time, and dove back into the set. Heart still pounding but lighter now. This team was chaos but it was hers.

The locker room buzzed with steam and noise— slamming lockers, dripping swimsuits, the distant drone of a hair dryer. Nora was juggling her towel, a half-zipped swim bag, and a buzzing phone when disaster struck.

One slick patch of tile. One distracted glance at a text. Her heel slid out from under her like a cartoon banana peel.

"Whoa—whoa—!"

Before gravity could claim her, two sets of hands shot out—Vanessa from the front, Lulu from behind, catching her mid-flail like synchronized lifeguards.

"You good?" Lulu asked, steadying her with a firm grip and zero judgment.

"Define good," Nora muttered, heart thudding, dignity somewhere near the drain.

Vanessa looked her up and down, grinning. "Honestly? That was the most elegant slow-motion wipeout I've seen since Rina tried to floss in fins."

"Thank you," Nora deadpanned. "I do all my own stunts."

"Girl, that wasn't a stunt," Lulu said. "That was a graceful collapse. Like a Victorian heroine about to faint."

"Waterproof dignity," Vanessa added. "Limited edition. Only sold in Lane 4." Nora couldn't help it, she laughed. A real, belly-warming, unfiltered laugh.

"God, I needed that," she said, still breathless. "You guys are ridiculous."

"Please," Vanessa said, bumping her hip. "We're Lane 4. Ridiculous is our brand."

"And catching you mid-wipeout?" Lulu added. "Part of the starter kit."

Nora grinned, slumping against the lockers. "For the record... if I had hit the floor, I wouldn't have cried. I would've just stared dramatically at the ceiling and reevaluated my life choices."

"Ah yes," Vanessa said solemnly. "The swimmer's existential crisis pose. A classic."

"Usually performed after butterfly sets," Lulu nodded. "Or spotting Simon in damp joggers."

They all howled, the sound echoing off the tile and cutting through the post-practice fatigue. Nora clutched her side, laughing so hard she had to sit down on the bench. She looked at them; Lulu with her eyeliner still perfect somehow, Vanessa braiding her own hair mid-roast and felt something settle in her chest. A click. A truth.

This was more than friendship. It was a net. A pact. A messy, hilarious safety net that caught her not just when she slipped on tile, but when she faltered in herself.

"Thanks for catching me," she said, quiet now, but sincere.

Lulu winked. "You fall, we catch. That's the Lane 4 creed."

Vanessa nodded. "Also; never trust the tile, always double-knot your suit, and don't date anyone who calls butterfly 'the one where you flop around.'"

Nora laughed again, but this time, her eyes stung just a little, because this wasn't just about swimming. It was about showing up and being seen. About slipping and knowing someone would reach for you anyway, and with her towel askew, hair a frizzy chlorine mess, and cheeks flushed from laughter and almost-faceplanting, Nora realized something: She didn't just belong. She was home.

Group Text: *Lane 4 Maniacs*

Rina: *Just reviewed the security cam footage in my head. Nora, 10/10 dramatic slide. Full points for flair. Docked half a point for no jazz hands.*

Lulu: *I still think she was aiming for a viral TikTok moment. #FallingForLane4*

Vanessa: *Honestly? Olympic-level recovery. If Lulu and I hadn't caught you, you would've ghosted through the wall like a chlorine-soaked Kool-Aid Man.*

Nora: *Glad to provide post-practice entertainment. Should I start wearing a helmet?*

Rina: *No. But you should wear that bright blue suit again. It's clearly enchanted. Got Coach Smoothbrain actually giving out compliments.*

Lulu: *Yeah, what was that?? "Bright blue suits you"?? Boy was practically whispering sweet nothings in front of the gods and everyone.*

Vanessa: *It was so tender I almost proposed on his behalf. We were ALL blushing and he wasn't even talking to us.*

Nora: *STOPPPP*

Rina: *We would, but the chemistry was LOUD.*

Nora: *Pretty sure my ears are still ringing from Lulu shouting "Just kiss already!"*

Lulu: *You're welcome. I'm here for chaos and truth.*

Vanessa: *And snacks. Don't forget snacks.*

Rina: *Okay but real talk—Nora. You belong here. Like, officially. Post-fall initiation complete.*

Lulu: *Lane 4 caught you. That means you're one of us.*
Nora: *Thank you. Seriously.*
Vanessa: *No getting rid of us now. We know where you swim.*
Rina: *And where you trip.*
Nora: *Noted. I'm never showing weakness again.*
Lulu: *Too late. You already bared your soul via floor-slip. We saw inside you. It was sweaty but noble.*
Nora: *I hate you all. (Not really.)*
Vanessa: *Love you too, Princess Fallington.*

Nora's hair was still damp as she curled up on the couch, oversized hoodie wrapped around her. A half-eaten bowl of cereal sat beside her, forgotten, spoon balanced precariously. The TV was off. The house was quiet. Too quiet, the kind that used to press in on her, sharp and echoing, but tonight, it felt… softer. Like the silence was holding space instead of closing in.

The only light came from the soft glow of her laptop screen, its blank document blinking like a dare. She stared at the cursor.

Blink. Blink. Blink.

There was a familiar tightening in her chest, the same one that usually had her clicking the window shut and disappearing into social media or online shopping or busywork that looked productive but wasn't. But tonight, her fingers didn't flinch away. They hovered. Then dropped.

A word. Then another. Not a report. Not a résumé. Not a grocery list or a breakdown of monthly expenses. Just a sentence. A thought. Something small and quiet and true. Then another, and another. The words weren't brilliant. Her internal critic stirred, ready to judge, but she ignored it. The sentences didn't have to dazzle. They just had to breathe.

She paused and let herself feel the silence again. Let it settle into her skin like bathwater. This wasn't for anyone else. Not a pitch. Not a cry for validation. Just... her. She typed until the radiator clinked and the air shifted in that way it always did near midnight, when the world held its breath and everything felt just a little more possible.

When she finally sat back, blinking at the tiny patch of words on the screen, something fluttered in her chest. Not pride. Not yet. But a tiny, persistent pulse of possibility.

A whisper: *You're still in here.*

She didn't need a masterpiece. She just needed a moment. She closed the laptop gently, like sealing a secret.

Her phone buzzed on the coffee table.

Simon: *You nailed that last 100. You in for Friday morning?*

Nora stared at the screen, heat blooming across her cheeks, not from the compliment, but from the fact that it felt like one. Specific. Not obligatory. Seen. Her thumb hovered, heart doing that ridiculous skip thing it hadn't done in a long time.

Nora: *Wouldn't miss it. Especially if you're timing.*

She hit send before she could overthink it and then she waited, pretending she wasn't.

A moment later, another buzz.

Simon: *Then I'll be there. Lane 4, 6:15. Don't be late.*

Her smile stretched, lazy and a little wicked. She sank deeper into the couch, warmth blooming from somewhere beyond the fleece of her hoodie. She didn't know what Friday would bring—probably more laps, more mistakes, more flailing butterfly attempts that looked like interpretive drowning.

But also… maybe more of this. This slow-burn something. This undercurrent. This way her pulse kicked at the sound of his voice. The way he saw her trying, not just performing. Not just surviving.

She stretched her legs along the couch, letting the blanket fall to her waist, staring up at the ceiling like it might whisper back all the things she hadn't dared to imagine. Her body ached in places she'd forgotten had muscles, but the soreness wasn't punishment—it was proof.

The words she'd written still hovered in her chest, fragile and alive and so did that smile, the one she wasn't even trying to fight anymore. For the first time in a long time, she wasn't just getting through the week. She was looking forward to it.

The house had gone silent again. She stood barefoot by the window, the streetlamp outside casting a soft amber glow across the floor. The neighborhood was quiet, just the occasional dog bark, the hum of a passing car. The kind of stillness she used to dread.

Now it felt like a pause. A breath between chapters. She hugged the sleeves of her hoodie tighter, staring out at nothing and everything. For months, she'd been treading water in a life that looked passable on the outside—smiling when she didn't mean it, saying yes when she wanted to scream no, answering "I'm fine" when she was anything but.

Something was different now. Not louder. Just deeper. She wasn't swimming laps to escape anymore. She was swimming toward something. Even if she didn't know what it was yet. Her reflection shimmered faintly in the glass and for the first time in a long time, she didn't look like someone drowning in fine. She looked like someone learning how to breathe again.

Beyond the Lanes

The air after practice always felt different. Less like a weight, more like an exhale. They didn't rush to the showers or bolt for their cars. Instead, Lane 4 lingered—soaked, spent, a little breathless. Not from the laps, exactly. From the release. Not long, just long enough for their legs to stop shaking and their hearts to return to something human. Nora found herself on the bleachers again, towel draped around her shoulders like a cape, arms resting on her knees. Her hair was still damp, her limbs pleasantly heavy. The burn in her shoulders hadn't faded yet, but it no longer felt like punishment. It felt like proof.

Lane 4 trickled in around her one by one; Rina stretching her calves against the rail, Vanessa dramatically flopping down beside her, Lulu perched like a smug cat on the top bench with a half-eaten granola bar in hand.

The deck was quieter now. No splashes. No whistle. Just the soft buzz of overhead lights and the occasional rustle of swim bags being zipped. It felt like the world had exhaled with them.

"Remind me why we do this again?" Rina groaned, swinging her arms in slow circles like she was trying to reattach them.

Vanessa answered without opening her eyes. "Because we're masochists with high hydration needs."

Lulu peeled off her cap and fluffed her curls. "Because the pool is cheaper than therapy and wetter than spin class."

That got a laugh from the group. Even Nora, who let her head tip back against the cinderblock wall and grinned up at the ceiling.

This was becoming her favorite part. The aftermath. The in-between. The sweaty, unfiltered, slightly unhinged decompression where no one was pretending to be fine. They didn't have to. They were past fine. Past pretense. Still—they were here.

She stretched out her legs in front of her, flexing her toes. Her calves ached. Her arms felt like noodles. Her lungs had finally stopped gasping and somewhere beneath all that—beneath the burn and the banter and the low hum of fluorescent lights, there was something else. Pride. She glanced across the pool deck and her breath caught in her throat.

Simon stood near the lifeguard stand, clipboard in hand, curls damp and messy. He was scribbling notes with a mechanical pencil, the kind of focused calm that made him look carved from still water. He didn't posture. Didn't command attention, but it found him anyway.

A swimmer called something out, and Simon answered with a quiet smile. Not the polite kind. The real kind. It curled at the corners of his mouth just enough to expose the traitorous dimple Nora had absolutely not been noticing.

She turned away quickly. Too quickly. Rina, of course, noticed.

"Oh my God," she whispered. "You're blushing. Are you blushing?"

"No," Nora said, very convincingly.

"You're blushing," Vanessa confirmed. "Confirmed blush. Lane 4, we have a sighting."

Lulu cackled from the top row. "Blush and a dimple? This is basically a rom-com trailer."

Nora rolled her eyes, trying not to smile. "I was just looking. You're allowed to look at people. In public. Like a human."

"You were looking like you wanted to lick," Rina said.

"Rina!" Nora gasped, scandalized and laughing.

"What? I'm just saying. Some of us flirt with words. Others flirt with proximity to lane ropes."

Vanessa raised a hand. "This feels like it's turning into a team meeting. Motion to nickname him Coach Dimple?"

"Seconded," Lulu said with zero hesitation.

Nora groaned. "Please stop."

"Too late. It's official now."

She tossed her towel at Rina, who caught it with a wink and flung it dramatically over one shoulder like a cape. Nora shook her head but the smile stayed, tugging at her lips, stubborn and warm and underneath the jokes, the teasing, the ache in her muscles and the echo of her own laughter, something was shifting.

She wasn't holding her breath anymore. Not waiting to disappear. Not trying to blend into the bleachers. Part of the rhythm. Part of the mess. Part of the team and maybe, just maybe, part of something else that hadn't fully taken shape yet. She could feel it. Like strength coming back in waves.

"So, since we're practically bonded by chlorine now," Rina said, her voice echoing slightly in the cavernous space, "can I admit something super embarrassing?"

Vanessa sat up like she'd just been offered popcorn at a movie. "God, please. Do. We live for that."

Rina, stretched out like a starfish on her towel, propped herself on her elbows. "Alright. Post-divorce, I signed up for a tap class. I thought it would be... healing. Like, I don't know, rhythmic empowerment. Eat Pray Love, but with jazz hands."

"Oh no," Nora murmured, already grinning.

"I had exactly zero rhythm," Rina said. "But full commitment. I went all in. Custom shoes. Sequined leotard. I even named my character, Rhonda Rhythm."

Vanessa snorted. "You did not."

"Swear on my Costco membership. Anyway, I got kicked out of the spring recital for improvising the finale of 42nd Street. Apparently, you're not supposed to moonwalk during a time step."

Lulu let out a cackle. "Total fascists."

Nora was laughing so hard she had to brace herself on the bench. "That's art. They didn't deserve you."

Vanessa wiped a tear from under her eye. "I would pay actual money to see that footage. Like, subscription-level."

Rina grinned but then shrugged. "Truth is... I wasn't trying to dance. I was trying not to come home to an empty house."

That stilled the air. Vanessa exhaled slowly, picking at the corner of her towel. "Yeah. I feel that. After I burned out, I signed up for every PTA committee I could find. Science night, fundraising, freaking shoelace awareness day. If it had a clipboard, I was there."

Nora raised a brow. "Why shoelaces?" Vanessa smiled faintly. "Because crying over ziti in your car feels less pathetic when you have a name tag." A hush fell. Not heavy, just honest.

Then Lulu, quietly: "I started swimming because I needed something that was mine. Not borrowed. Not assigned. Just mine. I was tired of being everyone else's something. Daughter. Employee. Disappointment."

Rina reached over and bumped her foot. "You're nobody's disappointment."

Lulu gave a one-shouldered shrug. "Try telling my mother that."

The silence held. Warm. Spacious. Unafraid.

Nora stared at her hands, the knuckles faintly red from chlorine. "I didn't even know I was disappearing but I was. In my marriage. In my job. In my own damn skin. I got in the pool and it was like—oh. There I am. I'm still here."

Vanessa nodded, slow and reverent. "It's wild, isn't it? How we forget we matter until our lungs burn and we touch the wall." No one spoke for a while. They just sat in the ache and the comfort of being seen.

Then Rina cleared her throat. "This is the part where we start a girl band or a commune, right?"

Lulu smirked. "Only if there's a glitter clause in the charter."

Vanessa laughed and leaned back on her elbows. "You know what? Forget therapy. This right here—this stretch and spill—this is the good stuff."

Rina raised a finger. "With better outfits and more nudity."

"Speak for yourself," Nora said, tugging at her fraying towel. "Mine's one spin cycle away from becoming a dish rag."

Lulu smiled. "Doesn't matter. You're still one of us."

The words landed like a wrapped gift. Unexpected, undeserved, and absolutely needed. Nora blinked, then smiled back, something loosening deep in her chest. For the first time in a long time, she wasn't alone in the after. Not holding herself together with duct tape and denial. She was surrounded by women who had shattered and rebuilt and laughed anyway. Not just teammates. Something more.

A beat passed. Then Vanessa stood and stretched like a cat. "Alright, emotions released, secrets spilled. Time for coffee and pastries that fully cancel out the laps. Who's in?"

Everyone raised a hand. As the group gathered towels and flip-flops, Nora lingered behind for just a second. She glanced at the puddle forming beneath her and then at the space these women had created, raw, ridiculous, real.

She felt it in her chest. That click. That truth. They weren't just swim teammates. They were the kind of women who caught you mid-fall, laughed at your pain, and passed you coffee afterward and suddenly, she wasn't drowning in "fine" anymore. She was swimming in something better. Belonging.

Simon was at the storage cubbies, bent at the waist as he stashed a mesh bag of fins and paddles, his shirt clinging damply to his back. Water glistened along the curve of his neck, catching the light in a way that made it hard to look anywhere else. He moved like someone who belonged to the space entirely. Not in an arrogant way, but with that quiet, elemental confidence of a person who had spent more time underwater than on land. Like the pool knew him. Like it listened when he moved.

Nora didn't mean to stare. She told herself that. But then, he looked up. Their eyes caught. No words. No smile. Just… awareness. The kind that pins you in place. It wasn't a long moment. A breath. A heartbeat, but it lingered—charged, steady, unflinching. The noise of the pool receded into something soft and far away, and for a suspended second, she wasn't a woman with damp hair and sore shoulders and a fraying towel—she was simply seen. Entirely, unsettlingly seen.

The heat crept in slowly. Not embarrassment. Something deeper. Something that settled low in her stomach and curled her fingers slightly against her thighs.

His gaze didn't flick away. It held anchored and unhurried. Not demanding. Just there. Steady in a way that made it hard to breathe. It wasn't flirtatious, not exactly. It was something else. Something deeper. Like recognition. Like he saw the version of her she was only just beginning to rediscover. The one who showed up early. The one who didn't laugh when everyone else did.

The one who swam like she was trying to find her way back to herself.

There was no smirk. No teasing tilt of his head. Just quiet awareness. A look that said, I'm paying attention. It wasn't a question. It was... almost a promise. Her breath caught. Her throat tightened. She glanced down—too fast, too obvious—but she couldn't hold that look a second longer without unraveling...and damn it, she was smiling.

Not wide. Just a tilt of her mouth. The kind that came from being known without effort. From being seen without having to wave her arms and explain herself. From knowing—suddenly, undeniably—that whatever that was? It wasn't nothing. It wasn't her imagination. Not anymore.

The group filed toward the exit—tired, damp, glowing. Chlorine lingered in the air, clinging to skin and hair like a badge of effort. Flip-flops slapped against the wet concrete; towels draped over shoulders like battle flags. Hair still dripping, shoulders loose with fatigue, they moved like a pack—disjointed but connected.

Someone cracked a joke about post-swim bagel priorities. Rina snorted. Vanessa groaned about needing to re-enter the real world. Lulu performed a dramatic shiver and declared war on whoever had stolen her favorite parka. The laughter bounced off the tile, easy and unrehearsed, as the locker room door swung shut behind them.

Nora lingered just a beat longer, the cool morning air brushing against her damp calves as they stepped outside. Steam curled off her skin. The sky was still gray-blue with the early hour, the sun not quite committed to the day yet. But something inside her had already woken up.

She glanced around at the women beside her— Rina looping her goggles around her wrist, Vanessa squeezing water from her braid, Lulu pretending not to watch her reflection in the glass. They weren't just teammates. They weren't just women who swam. They were women who showed up.

Who laughed loudly and swore generously and caught you when you slipped, literally and otherwise. Who made space at the edge of the lane and didn't care how long it took you to find your rhythm. Who let you be new, messy, and learning without flinching and maybe—just maybe—she wasn't just relearning how to swim. She was relearning how to belong.

For the first time in too long time, she didn't feel like she was drowning in fine. She felt like she was finally starting to breathe.

The Masters Club

***

Simon stood at the far end of the pool deck, clipboard in hand, but he hadn't written anything for the past five minutes. He was watching them—Lane 4. Laughing, stretching, towel-snapping their way out of practice like a roving band of misfits he hadn't realized he needed in his orbit and in the middle of it all, like the eye of a storm she didn't know she was calming—Nora.

She moved differently now. Still tentative in the water, sure, but something in her body language had changed. Less apology, more presence. She wasn't just participating anymore. She was in it. Finding her place. Holding her own.

He watched as she nudged Lulu's arm, rolling her eyes at something Rina had said, and then tossed her head back in a full-bodied laugh. Unfiltered. Unpracticed. It caught him off guard—how good it felt to see that sound come from her.

When was the last time someone's laugh had hit him like that? He exhaled slowly, forcing himself to look away, pretending to jot something on his clipboard. Useless. His brain was still tracking her every movement—how she tucked her towel tighter, how her damp hair curled at the nape of her neck, how she walked out not behind the others, but with them.

She hadn't looked at him when she left. Not really. But there was that one glance—brief, almost accidental—where her eyes flicked toward him and lingered.

It was enough, and it shouldn't have been. Simon knew how to compartmentalize. He was good at it—had to be. Feelings had guardrails. Lines you didn't cross. People you didn't let in too far. He'd built a life on that kind of structure. Clean. Contained. Safe.

Nora was undoing that. Not with declarations. Not even with intent. Just… with her. With the way she looked when she wasn't trying to impress anyone. With the rawness she didn't seem to know she carried. With the way she laughed now, like it surprised her.

He told himself not to read into it. Not to want more than what this was, but that look—brief, accidental, charged—slipped past every wall he thought was solid, and for the first time in a long time, he didn't want to shut the feeling down.

He just didn't know how to let it in. Not just the attraction—though yeah, there was that, too—but something deeper. The kind of thing he recognized because he'd felt it before. That ache of someone rebuilding themselves one practice at a time.

He'd seen swimmers fight for speed. Fight for medals. Fight to beat someone else. But Nora? She was fighting for herself and damn if that wasn't the bravest thing he'd seen in a long time.

He stayed there as the last of them filed out, the sounds of the locker room fading. The pool returned to stillness, only the gentle slap of water against tile and the echo of his own heartbeat filling the silence. He closed his clipboard without writing another word. Tomorrow, they'd do it all over again and he'd be here. Watching. Coaching. Trying not to fall. Too late for that, probably, but he could pretend a little longer.

***

Lane 4 Group Chat – *Wet and Wild*

Vanessa: *Just found a swim cap in my laundry. Smells like victory and sadness. Mostly sadness.*

Rina: *You're welcome. That cap's from my glitter stash. You've been baptized in fabulous defeat.*

Lulu: *Some people collect stamps. Rina collects swim caps like a sparkly swamp witch.*

Nora: *Pretty sure I pulled a muscle sneezing after practice. That's cross-training, right?*

Lulu: *Only if you ice your ribs with a bag of frozen peas and cry in a plank position.*

Vanessa: *Where's our medal for "Showed Up and Didn't Drown"? I want it engraved.*

Rina: *Participation trophy but make it sexy.*

Vanessa: *"Lane 4: Equal Parts Effort and Delusion."*

Nora: *I'd wear that on a t-shirt.*

Lulu: *Don't tempt me. I have a Cricut and no boundaries.*

Rina: *If this team had a motto, it would be "Hydrated, Slightly Unhinged, Always Show Up."*

Nora: *Add "Wobbly but willing" and it's basically my dating profile.*

Vanessa: *Same. Except mine also includes: Has strong opinions about granola bars.*

Lulu: *Honestly, I love us. We may suck wind in breaststroke, but emotionally? We're elite.*

Rina: *Lane 4: Where the real flex is vulnerability.*

Nora: *And glitter. Don't forget glitter.*

The group chat exploded. Memes. Glitter cap jokes. Lulu threatening to rename the thread **"Coach's Crushes."** Nora laughed so hard she nearly dropped her phone in the sink. When it finally went quiet, no new notifications, no Rina chaos—she sat back and stared at the ceiling.

She reached for her phone again.

[Private Text – Nora → Simon]

Nora: *You survived another Lane 4 storm.*
Honestly, I'm impressed.

Simon: *Low-key fearing for my life but hiding it well.*
Should I ask what I survived specifically?

Nora: *Let's just say your name came up.*
Repeatedly. With… strong opinions.

Simon: *Should I be flattered or concerned?*

Nora: *Both. Apparently, you give off "brooding poetry-writing swim coach" energy.*
Also someone said you alphabetize your foam rollers.

Simon: *Outrageous.*
They're arranged by density.

Nora: *Exactly what we said.*

Simon: *So… are you saying you think about me when I'm not around?*

Nora: *Only when I'm not too busy gasping for air or plotting your downfall.*

Simon: *Sounds like a healthy dynamic.*

Nora: *Mmm. Or a dangerously effective one.*

(A pause.)

Simon: *You looked good in the water today. Comfortable. Strong.*

Nora: *Careful. Say one more nice thing and I might start showing up early on purpose.*

Simon: *You already do.*

Nora: *Are you… keeping track?*

Simon: *I notice things.*

Nora: *That sounds suspiciously like flirting.*

Simon: *Only if you're reading between the texts.*

Nora: *What if I like reading between the texts?*

(Longer pause.)

Simon: *Then maybe I'll stop waiting for practice to find reasons to talk to you.*

Nora: *Well now I'm the one gasping for air.*

Simon: *Hydrate Blake.*

Nora: *Yes, Coach.*

Nora set her phone down but didn't move right away. The smile lingered this small, stunned thing that felt too new to trust but too warm to ignore. The room was quiet, except for the ticking radiator and the rustle of wind through half-cracked windows, but inside her, something was shifting. Not loud, but real. She wasn't just looking forward to the next practice. She was looking forward. Full stop.

Somewhere in the echos, a group text chimed again—Vanessa announcing that tomorrow would be Lane 4's official *"Glitter Ceremony,"* whatever that meant. Nora shook her head, laughing softly. Of course it would involve glitter and for once, she couldn't wait to show up for it.

It happened in the parking lot. The sun had just crested over the tree line, casting long golden shadows across the rec center's damp asphalt. Steam curled lazily from travel mugs. Hair was still wet, shoes squeaked with every step, and gym bags were flopped onto trunks like tired toddlers.

The usual post-practice buzz had faded into a warm, bleary hush—until Lulu skidded into the circle like a chaotic comet. She was, naturally, already dressed like a highlighter that had mated with a disco ball. Neon hoodie, galaxy leggings, metallic scrunchie threatening to become sentient. A few pine needles were stuck to her shoe. No one asked why.

"Important announcement!" she called, leaping onto the nearest curb like it was center stage at the Tony Awards.

Nora, still half-asleep and clutching her coffee like it was a life source, instinctively took a step back. "Oh no."

"Shhh." Lulu held up one finger, commanding silence with the gravitas of a slightly unhinged prophet. "This is a sacred moment. Ceremonial, even."

Rina straightened. "Wait. Is this... the thing?"

Vanessa's eyes lit up. "Oh my god. It's happening. It's finally happening!"

"Someone film it," muttered someone (probably Lulu, to herself).

From her Mary Poppins gym bag, Lulu produced a ziplock bag coated in sparkles—like a crime scene at an arts and crafts store. With reverence, she reached in and pulled out a glitter-covered scrunchie the size of a croissant, bedazzled within an inch of its life and, possibly, humming with chaotic energy.

"Behold!" Lulu declared, holding it aloft. "The sacred Scrunchie of Lane 4. Handcrafted from the shattered dreams of swim team past, sealed with Mod Podge, and blessed under the light of a full moon."

Rina squinted. "Is that... hot glue?"

"And ambition," Lulu replied solemnly.

Vanessa wiped an invisible tear. "I've never been prouder."

Lulu turned to Nora. "You, my brave and waterlogged friend, have survived initiation. You've laughed. You've swam. You've cried in the locker room while pretending to fix your goggles. You've earned this."

"I feel like I should kneel," Nora said, half-laughing, half-horrified.

"Too much moisture on the asphalt," Lulu said, crouching instead. With great ceremony, she slid the scrunchie around Nora's wrist. "Rise, Lady Nora of Lane 4. May your stroke rate be snappy and your suit wedgie-free."

Nora blinked at the ridiculous thing on her arm. "I don't know whether to cry or exfoliate."

"It stays on," Lulu said, "until you cry or admit out loud that you love us."

"She already cried during week two," Rina said helpfully. "I caught her hugging her towel like it owed her money."

Vanessa nodded, serious. "Then it's official. You're one of us now."

"Do we chant or something?" Nora asked, deadpan.

Lulu stepped back. "No chanting. We save that for the solstice swim. But you will be added to the group text under your new name."

Nora raised an eyebrow. "Which is…?"

Rina grinned. "Spandex Phoenix, or course."

Nora let out a laugh that startled even her. Loud, unfiltered, unguarded. The others joined in, a tangled braid of chaos and affection. "May your strokes be smooth, your flip turns functional, and your snacks plentiful," Lulu intoned.

The group broke like confetti into the morning, everyone peeling off toward their cars, tossing jokes and post-practice plans like confetti. Nora didn't move just yet. She looked down at the absurdly sparkly scrunchie hugging her wrist. Sticky. Bright. Unapologetic…and somehow… perfect.

It wasn't just decoration. It was a marker. A moment. A memory. A ridiculous, beautiful, unsolicited proof that she belonged. Not because she was the best swimmer, but because she kept showing up and that was enough.

Her heart felt lighter. Her wrist, a little heavier and for the first time in a very long time, Nora Blake felt claimed. Fully. Absurdly. Joyfully. By a group of glitter-wielding mermaids in discount goggles and it felt exactly right

They took over a corner table at the local café, the kind of place with mismatched chairs, indie folk music on repeat, and muffins the size of regulation dodgeballs. Their towels peeked out from unzipped gym bags under the table, and the unofficial dress code was damp ponytails and post-swim glow.

Nora sat between Rina and Vanessa, her hands curled around a latte big enough to require a lifeguard. She wasn't sure if it was the caffeine, the sugar, or the residual endorphins from the glitter scrunchie ceremony, but everything felt slightly electric. Their table buzzed with overlapping conversation and too-loud laughter, the kind that made nearby patrons glance over and then smile despite themselves.

"New rule," Vanessa announced, holding up half a dismembered blueberry muffin like a gavel. "No talking about husbands, ex-husbands, or current disappointing men for the next thirty minutes."

"Seconded," Rina said, raising her iced coffee like a solemn offering.

"Thirded. Or is it thrice'd?" Lulu asked, flopping into the seat across from Nora. She was carrying a cinnamon roll that could double as a flotation device and had already managed to get frosting on her sleeve.

Rina pointed a straw at her. "We're going to pretend that shirt was clean when you left the house."

"It was clean. Just… pre-decorated," Lulu replied, licking frosting off her knuckle.

Vanessa leaned in, narrowing her eyes like a bloodhound catching a scent. "So. Can we talk about hot swim coach crushes instead?"

Nora inhaled sharply and nearly aspirated her latte.

Rina slapped the table. "Oh my God, that was involuntary. She choked. She choked."

"I did not," Nora coughed, dabbing at her mouth with a napkin and waving them off. "Nothing is happening."

"Yet," Lulu said, eyes sparkling as she tore her cinnamon roll in half with reverence. "But the tension is chlorinated and certified organic. I felt it from five lanes away."

"Simon's basically a Greek statue in board shorts," Rina said. "Like, hello, have you seen his shoulders? That man *is* upper body day."

"Stop," Nora groaned, cheeks flaming.

Vanessa winked. "We're just saying, we'd support it. Swim team hookups make for excellent gossip and team morale. Like, solidarity through sexual tension."

"I am not hooking up with my coach," Nora said firmly. "I barely know what I'm doing *in* the water."

"Exactly," Lulu said. "You're vulnerable. It's romantic."

Rina snorted. "You've been reading too much fan fiction."

"First of all," Lulu said, holding up a finger. "There's no such thing. Second of all, this whole friend group has main character energy. Don't fight it, Nora."

Nora laughed, hiding her blush behind her mug. They were relentless, but underneath the teasing was something warmer. Something that didn't require her to defend herself, or explain, or shrink.

She hadn't told them much. Just a casual mention of the divorce, like dropping a name in passing. She hadn't shared the spiral that came after. The silence of the house. The way she'd stopped playing music. How she used to fill time with noise just so she wouldn't have to hear her own thoughts. None of them pressed. None of them poked or pried. They just... made space. Loudly. Clumsily. Hilariously. With cinnamon rolls and rule-making and unsolicited commentary about Simon's traps.

She glanced around the table; Rina with her neon scrunchie slipping halfway down her bun, Vanessa licking sugar off her fingers while trying to Google a new dry shampoo, and Lulu humming something vaguely unhinged as she built a frosting tower with a stir stick.

They were chaos and comfort. Weird and wild and wonderfully unfiltered and somehow, against every expectation, they were hers. Nora smiled into her cup, warmth spreading from her fingertips to her chest. This, whatever this was—felt like beginning again. Not alone this time. Just surrounded and maybe, for once, that was enough.

Her phone buzzed by her coffee cup.

Simon: *Friday's set is brutal. You still in?*

A slow, unexpected warmth unfurled in her chest. Not butterflies, too soft, too teenage. This was something sharper. Older. Like remembering her body wasn't just for surviving, it was for feeling things again.

She wiped a smudge of cinnamon sugar off her thumb and typed back:

Nora: *Can't wait. Bring it on.*

She hit send. Looked up. All of the women were watching her like she'd just announced a royal engagement. Rina's chin was resting on her palm, grinning like the cat who'd swallowed an entire aquarium. Vanessa had paused mid-bite of her muffin, one brow lifted with suspicion and glee. Lulu was already pulling out her phone like she was live-tweeting the moment.

Nora froze. "No. Whatever this is—don't."

"Too late," Lulu said. "I already started a betting pool. Odds are on Simon offering to 'adjust your form' by next week."

"I genuinely hate all of you," Nora said, grabbing her muffin like a shield.

Rina was typing at light speed. "New name for the group chat: Siren + Coach: Forbidden Lane Love."

"Oh my God," Nora groaned.

"There's a glitter emoji," Vanessa added. "And a dolphin. For... thematic consistency."

Lulu leaned in closer. "Can we talk about how he complimented your backstroke and your swimsuit in the same week? That's like the swim team version of forehead kisses and holding hands."

"I swear," Nora said, holding up her hands, "if one of you actually prints merch—"

"Tank tops are already in the prototype phase," Rina deadpanned. "Yours says 'Lane 4 Lust' in cursive. Limited run."

"Someone save me."

Vanessa patted her knee. "We would, but this is way more entertaining."

Laughter rolled across the table—wild, unfiltered, full of something Nora hadn't realized she missed this much: joy without strings.

And then her phone buzzed again.

Simon: Hope you're not letting them gang up on you too hard. Want me to assign them extra kickboard sets as revenge?

Nora bit her lip.

Nora: You'd be doing them a favor. Vanessa says you're swim coach second base if you compliment my swimsuit again.

Typing bubbles.

Pause.

Disappear.

Then:

Simon: Noted. I'll stick to backstroke technique. Probably.

She didn't even try to hide her grin this time.

Rina caught it first. "Look at her! That is a full smile. A swim-crush smile."

"I'm not smiling," Nora lied, cheeks warm.

Lulu clapped. "Ladies, we have movement in Lane Flirt!"

"I will throw this muffin."

"Don't you dare," Vanessa said. "That thing cost six dollars and part of my dignity."

More laughter. Easy, loud, unfiltered. The kind that wrapped around her like a towel straight out of the dryer. In the middle of it all amid the espresso steam, glitter jokes, and simulated scandal—Nora felt something shift. Not just acceptance. Belonging. Real. Undeniable. Hers, and when she glanced at her phone again, at Simon's name glowing on the screen, her smile deepened. She wasn't just swimming anymore. She was surfacing.

Later that night, Nora sat on the edge of her bed, fingers laced in her lap, the glittering scrunchie still snug around her wrist like a quiet promise. Her house was quiet—the kind of quiet that didn't soothe. It pressed in from all sides, thick and underwater, like the moments right before surfacing.

The glow of the bedside lamp cast soft shadows across the walls, and somewhere in the hallway, an old pipe ticked. She hadn't turned on music. Couldn't bring herself to fill the silence.

Her phone buzzed once. Then stopped. She didn't check it. Instead, she stared at the jacket hanging from the closet door, a soft blue one she hadn't worn in ages. It still held the faintest whiff of cologne. His cologne. Musky, sharp, familiar.

It was enough to crack the seal. The memory crashed in—vivid and violent in its quiet.

David had been sitting at the kitchen table, hands folded, shoulders squared like he was bracing for impact.

"I feel like we're just... roommates," he'd said. No anger. Just exhaustion. Like the end had already happened, and they were just catching up to it. She had stood in the doorway, groceries still clutched to her chest. Apples, she remembered. Gala. Her favorite.

"You don't even look at me anymore," he'd said. "We go through the motions, but there's no... us."

She had put the bag down too fast. Too hard. Apples spilled, bouncing across the tile like accusations. One rolled under the fridge and she hadn't had the energy to retrieve it.

She didn't reply. Not that night. Not for many nights after.

He moved out two weeks later.

She kept functioning. Walked the dog. Sent emails. Paid bills, but when she looked in the mirror, all she saw was static. Blurred edges. A woman-shaped outline with no one in it. She remembered whispering to her reflection, voice trembling like glass: "I don't even know who I am anymore."

Now—sitting on the edge of her bed, hair damp from swim practice, heart unsteady—she reached for the scrunchie. Thumbed the glittery fabric like it was a talisman. She wasn't that woman anymore. Not exactly. She wasn't healed. Not whole, but she wasn't hollow either. Something was shifting. The laughter in the locker room, the ache in her muscles, the group chat full of snark and support—it was more than distraction. It was a rebuilding.

Nora exhaled, shaky but deliberate. "I'm figuring it out," she said aloud, voice barely above a whisper but she meant it. Even if only a little. Even if only just tonight. As she crawled beneath the blankets, scrunchie still hugging her wrist like a ribbon of resilience, she thought—not of David, not of what was lost—but of the glimmer of something new. Something hers.

She lay back on her pillow, eyes tracing the ceiling shadows. There were cracks still, sure—but there was also light coming in.

Two days later, that light followed her to the pool. It drifted in on the steam rising from the lanes. It lingered in the clatter of flip-flops on wet concrete, in the sharp tang of chlorine mixed with the sweeter scent of coconut conditioner hanging in the heavy morning air.

Lane 4 was already in rare form. Vanessa was stretching like she was auditioning for Broadway. Full jazz hands, exaggerated lunges, and the kind of dramatic hair flip that warranted a backup dancer.

"Ma'am," Rina called from the pool, deadpan. "This is a municipal swim practice, not Chicago: The Revival."

Vanessa blew her a kiss. "Just trying to stay limber. You never know when someone might film a documentary about our greatness."

Lulu was off to the side fiddling with her goggles, squinting at her phone. "My horoscope said to avoid chaotic water energy, which feels targeted."

Rina, already half-submerged, grinned. "Too late. You swim with us." She kicked up a splash and called out, "Last one in buys post-practice muffins!"

Vanessa bolted. "Absolutely not, I have a mortgage."

Lulu shrieked. "I'm not made of bagel money!" and took off behind her, waiting until the very last second before launching into the water with a cannonball so aggressive it earned a shout from a lap swimmer in Lane 2.

Nora stood at the edge, watching them—their messiness, their mischief, their joy and something in her chest bloomed. Not from fear. Not this time, but from the rush of choosing to stay. Of showing up not because she had to, but because she wanted to. Because maybe there was something here worth returning to. She tugged on her cap, adjusted her goggles, and took a breath. Then dove. Not away from anything, but toward.

The water opened around her, cool and clear, like a promise. Her arms cut through clean, her legs kicked strong, and when she surfaced—lungs full, heart pounding—she was laughing, and so were the others. She swam to the wall where the team was treading water, voices overlapping in gleeful chaos and from the deck came a familiar voice—dry, amused, just loud enough to reach them.

"Nice form, Lane 4."

Nora turned toward the sound.

Simon stood near the lifeguard stand, clipboard tucked under his arm, one brow slightly raised and he was watching her.

Not the team. Her, and this time, she didn't look away. She let it land—the acknowledgment, the weight of it—and let the corner of her mouth curl, just slightly, before pushing off the wall and disappearing beneath the surface.

***

Simon blinked and she was gone, just a splash and a shimmer trailing behind her. He exhaled through his nose, slow and deliberate, like the breath might carry away whatever that moment had stirred.

The team had just started drills, the pool echoing with splashes, laughter, and the occasional curse muttered into water but he barely heard any of it. She'd looked at him. Not just glanced. Not the polite nod swimmers gave their coach. She'd looked—really looked—like she saw something in him that wasn't clipboard-deep and she didn't flinch. She smiled. Small. Quiet. Real.

He wasn't used to that. Not anymore. Most people saw the whistle, the stopwatch, the calm surface. The guy who used to be something and now taught other people how not to drown. But Nora? She didn't look at him like a warning sign. Or a crush. Or worse, a disappointment. She looked at him like she understood something about the weight he carried. Like maybe she carried some of it too.

Simon stood there, the clipboard forgotten. He watched her dive—not like a coach clocking split times, but like a man watching something he didn't realize he needed until it showed up and refused to blink.

She didn't swim pretty. Not always. But she swam honest. Like someone clawing her way back to herself. He exhaled, and with it came something unfamiliar. Not guilt. Not regret. Hope, and maybe—just maybe—he didn't have to keep his story locked behind perfectly timed sets and quiet detachment. Maybe someone could see the cracks and not turn away. Maybe she already had.

The Masters Club

***

He didn't say her name, he didn't have to. That look—steady, unreadable to anyone else—had landed like a hand on her skin. She felt it even now, long after she'd slipped out of her suit and into dry clothes, long after Lane 4 had dissolved into the night with promises of muffins and sore shoulders. She felt it in the car. In the shower. In the soft ache behind her knees and the stubborn flush across her chest. It followed her home like heat clinging to skin.

Now, curled on her couch in an oversized hoodie and nothing else, Nora scrolled absently through her phone, pretending she wasn't waiting for something.

Then, it came.

Simon: *You dove in today like you meant it. Thought you should know.*

No emojis. No fluff.

Her breath hitched, because it wasn't nothing. It was a breadcrumb. A flare. A thread. She stared at the message, thumb hovering, pulse ticking like a metronome just behind her ribs. Part of her wanted to overthink it—craft a clever reply, deflect with humor, play it safe.

Instead, she told the truth.

Nora: *It finally feels like mine.*

She hit send.

A pause.

Not long, but long enough to imagine him reading it. To imagine him feeling it.

When her phone buzzed again, the response was simple:

Simon: *Good. I see you, Nora.*

That was it, but it landed hard.

She sank deeper into the cushions, blanket slipping from her thighs, the ghost of a smile tugging at her lips. She didn't know where this was going. Or what tomorrow would bring, but for the first time in too long, she wasn't waiting to be chosen. She had chosen herself and somehow… someone else had noticed.

Off Deck, On Display

Rina plopped onto the bench, flipping her hair out of her cap with a dramatic sigh. "Okay, real talk. Are we even friends if we've never seen each other outside of goggles and chlorine stank?"

Vanessa slung her towel around her neck. "I mean, I've seen Lulu's elbow in my face and Rina's butt in a swim mirror. That feels intimate."

"Not that kind of intimate," Rina groaned. "I mean, real clothes. Real food. Maybe even, brace yourselves, lip gloss."

Nora blinked, mid-way through shoving her suit into a plastic bag. "You want to hang out? Like... socially?"

"Groundbreaking, right?" Lulu said, perched like a gremlin on the counter, already scrolling through her phone. "I'm talking margaritas. I'm talking neon lighting. I'm talking dancing badly in public and pretending we're not middle-aged."

"Speak for yourself," Vanessa muttered. "I'm in my prime. Like an avocado with exactly one good day left."

Nora shook her head, chuckling but her stomach did a weird flip. She hadn't done a girls' night out in... years. Her wardrobe consisted of Target loungewear and business-casual compromise. What if she didn't fit? What if this version of her—the one outside the pool—wasn't someone they'd want to keep?

"I don't know," she hedged. "I've got—"

Lulu launched a hair tie at her. "Nope. No excuses. You've been officially claimed by Lane 4. That comes with mandatory glitter bonding time."

Vanessa nodded solemnly. "You swam the 100 fly with Lulu and lived to tell the tale. That's friendship-level trauma. You're in."

Rina leaned closer, waggling her brows. "Also... we should totally invite Coach."

Nora nearly dropped her water bottle. "Wait, what?"

"Oh come on," Rina said. "He's always so serious. Let's see if the man even owns jeans."

Lulu was already typing. "On it."

"Lulu, no—" Nora started, but it was too late.

Lulu grinned wickedly. "Text sent. 'Coach, we're going out Friday. You in? Promise no tequila butterfly drills unless requested.'"

There was a collective pause.

Vanessa gasped. "You didn't."

"I absolutely did."

Nora groaned. "He's going to ignore it. Or worse—reply with a dry, dad-level emoji."

Three seconds later, Lulu's phone buzzed.

She blinked. "Guys. He said yes."

"What?" Rina screeched.

"He said: 'Sure. Just don't make me wear glitter.'"

Vanessa stood up, fist in the air. "This is historic. Lane 4 is going to rage—with supervision!"

Lulu cackled. "Oh, he's so getting glittered."

Nora just sat there, half-laughing, half-panicking, towel in her lap and heart pounding. A night out. With the team. With Simon. She swallowed hard. This was happening and somehow, she was excited and terrified in equal measure.

Nora's bedroom looked like a tornado had touched down in her closet. Jeans hung from the doorframe, two dresses lay crumpled on the floor like they'd fainted from rejection, and a pile of maybe shoes teetered dangerously on the edge of her bed.

She stood at the mirror in her underwear and a sports bra, cold air prickling her skin. Half her wardrobe was either too young, too tight, too beige, or just too not her anymore.

She held up a slinky black dress, turned sideways, and sighed. "Who am I trying to be?"

That's when it came—his voice. Smooth. Icy. Burned into her ribcage. "You always do this," David had said once, watching her from the bed as she rifled through hangers. "You agonize over outfits and still end up looking like you're trying too hard."

She'd frozen, the zipper halfway up the side of her dress.

"It's not a runway, Nora. It's dinner. Can we not make it about you?"

That night, she'd taken off the red lipstick she'd just put on. Wiped it off with a tissue until her mouth was bare and colorless. She'd worn a gray blouse. Quiet. Safe.

Now, years later, standing in a soft pool of lamplight, that memory punched the air from her lungs. She sank onto the edge of her bed, the old shame prickling like static under her skin. She'd spent so long swallowing herself—making herself palatable, pliable, quiet, but that woman was gone. Or at least, she was trying to be.

Nora stood. Crossed to her dresser. Opened the top drawer and pulled out the tube she hadn't touched in years: **Red Alert**, the same shade she used to wear when she felt like the main character of her own damn life.

She rolled it open. Bold. Brazen. Fire-engine confidence in a $9 tube. Her hand trembled slightly as she applied it. *You're too much*, David's voice whispered.

She pressed her lips together and stared herself down in the mirror. "No," she whispered back. "I'm finally enough."

She chose a rust-red blouse with a subtle drape and a neckline that said I see you seeing me. Paired it with high-rise jeans that made her feel like a woman with opinions and an ass that didn't apologize for existing. Gold hoops. Stacked rings. A spritz of perfume that smelled like citrus and rebellion.

She wasn't dressing for Simon. She wasn't dressing for revenge. She was dressing for the version of herself who used to get excited about nights out before she learned to make herself small, and when she stepped into her shoes and grabbed her keys, her heart kicked with something sharp and alive.

She didn't know what the night would bring, but for the first time in a long time, she was showing up as all of herself and that felt dangerous—in the best possible way.

Setting: The Dented Keg — a cozy, slightly divey bar with exposed brick, flickering string lights, and a jukebox stuck on moody 80s ballads. There's a pool table in the back, a "Don't Ask, Just Drink" cocktail board, and a bartender who clearly doesn't believe in measuring pours.

The place had the kind of soft chaos Nora liked in theory but usually avoided. Tonight though, the low hum of laughter, clinking glasses, and the faint scent of lime and wood polish felt oddly like home.

Nora stood just outside the front door, hand still on the handle, when Simon stepped up beside her.

He wore dark jeans, a fitted t-shirt under a zip hoodie, and a look that was... disarming. Less coach, more man. The kind of man who knew how to blend in until suddenly, he didn't. His hair was still damp, curls slightly unruly like he'd fought the mirror and lost—just enough imperfection to make him look achingly real.

They both paused, startled by the unexpected synchronicity. Simon looked át her. Really looked. His breath caught—just slightly, just enough for him to notice. She wasn't in swim gear or damp from the pool. She was in jeans that hugged her hips, a soft top that dipped just enough to tease, and a red lip that hit him square in the gut. Not because it was bold, but because it was intentional. A flare shot into the night. A woman daring to be seen.

"Ladies first," he said, voice quieter than usual, his hand curling around the door to open it for her.

Nora looked up, met his gaze and held it. For just a moment. A breath suspended in time. The kind that thickens with electricity. That hums under the skin like a warning—or a promise.

"I'll allow it," she murmured, stepping through.

He watched her go, slow blink, jaw tight and for the first time in a long time, Simon forgot to breathe.

Inside, the rest of Lane 4 was already in full volume. Lulu had taken over a high-top table like she was hosting a talk show. Vanessa was at the bar flirting shamelessly with the bartender—something about needing a cocktail named after her. Rina was deciphering the jukebox's ancient touchpad.

"There she is!" Lulu shouted, throwing both arms in the air when Nora approached. "And look who she brought!"

Simon raised an eyebrow. "I wasn't aware I was being brought."

"You were summoned," Vanessa corrected, slipping a neon pink drink into his hand. "Now hush and sip."

Lulu dug into her massive tote bag, because of course she brought a tote—and pulled out a tangled pile of glow stick bracelets.

"These," she said with all the gravity of a TED Talk, "are for safety and sparkle. Lane 4 does not go unmarked."

She handed one to each of them, cracking them with a flourish. Rina instantly snapped three around her wrist like cuffs.

Simon hesitated.

"Coach," Lulu said, narrowing her eyes. "Do not disappoint me."

With a quiet shake of his head and the smallest of smiles—Simon slid the glowing green bracelet onto his wrist. Nora bit back a grin.

"Ladies and Coach," Lulu said, raising her glass, "to questionable decisions, aggressive friendship, and the fact that none of us have drowned yet."

"To Lane 4!" Vanessa shouted.

"To inappropriate group texts!" Rina added.

"To glitter, bad life choices, and the resurrection of Nora's social life!" Lulu finished.

They all whooped and clinked glasses, a cacophony of chaotic joy.

Nora looked around the table, at their flushed cheeks and unapologetic laughter, at Simon sipping something citrusy while trying not to smirk, at the pulse of music vibrating through the floorboards—and felt it again.

That hum in her chest. That spark in her ribs. Not just from the drink or the dress or the way Simon's gaze occasionally landed on her like a hand but from being part of this. Seen. Claimed. Lit up from the inside out and the night was just beginning.

The group sat at two tables pushed together. Empty glasses, crumpled napkins, and glow sticks litter the space like remnants of a wild art project. The jukebox hums in the background, and they're several rounds into whatever hybrid drinking game Lulu has invented.

"Alright," Rina said, slamming her glass down. "We've officially reached the part of the night where poor decisions are made and remembered forever."

"Truth or dare, but make it feral," Lulu grinned, draping glow sticks like battle medals over her shoulders. "Vanessa, you're up."

Vanessa didn't even blink. "Truth. I'm too old to get dared into licking bar floors."

"Boo," Rina said. "Okay—what's the weirdest thing you've ever cried over?"

Vanessa took a long sip of her drink. "A YouTube video of a duck hugging a golden retriever. Like, full-body, shoulder-shaking sobs."

"I remember that video!" Nora gasped. "That duck was emotionally fluent!"

Simon, perched at the end of the table, chuckled into his beer.

Rina pointed a dramatic finger. "Coach. You're not off the hook. Truth or dare?"

He raised an eyebrow. "Seriously?"

"Seriously," Lulu said, tossing him a glow stick bracelet like a gauntlet.

Simon sighed. "Fine. Truth."

Nora grinned. "What's your most embarrassing swim moment? National-level humiliation preferred."

Simon gave her a slow look. "You want National?"

"Give us the goods," Vanessa said, already leaning forward.

He took a breath and leaned back in his chair. "Alright. 2012 Nationals. Semi-finals. I was doing the 100 backstroke and feeling cocky—like, peak twenty-two-year-old energy. Tight start, clean turn, crowd's on fire. I go for the final wall... and mid-kick, I feel it."

"Feel what?" Lulu asked, wide-eyed.

Simon deadpanned, "My jammer. Splitting. Dead center. Right down the back."

Gasps. Wheezing laughter.

"No!" Nora clapped a hand over her mouth.

"Oh yes," Simon said. "I finished the race like a damn professional. Came out of the pool holding my suit together with both hands like I was protecting national secrets. Footage still lives on Reddit, probably."

Rina wheezed. "Freedom stroke!"

Vanessa wiped tears from her eyes. "That's it. That's the best one."

Nora leaned toward him, laughing. "That's not even embarrassing. That's heroic."

Simon smiled, that rare, reluctant kind. Then Lulu—who had clearly hit her tequila truth limit asked the next question.

"Okay, Coach," she said, less teasing now. "Have you ever thought about quitting? Like, for real?"

The table quieted.

Simon's eyes flicked down to the rim of his glass. He rolled it between his palms, the glow stick on his wrist catching the light, eyes distant.

"I lost the Trials. Olympic year. Everything had been building to that race. I was seeded second. I had a real shot."

He paused, breath shallow. "But I choked. Missed the wall on the turn. Came in sixth."

The table quieted.

"No medal. No team. No second chance. Sponsors backed out within a week. Agents stopped calling. Coaches I'd known for years didn't return texts." He let out a humorless laugh. "Some of them had the decency to ghost me. Others made sure I knew exactly how much of a disappointment I was."

Even Lulu didn't crack a joke.

"I spent that summer pretending I didn't care. Hooked up. Drank too much. Trained with no one. Hated everyone." He shrugged, but it was the kind of shrug you make when there's a bruise under it.

"Eventually, I stopped going to the pool. Thought if I stayed away long enough, the ache would go quiet."

A pause.

"It didn't."

The silence that followed wasn't awkward. It was reverent.

"I didn't just lose a race," Simon added, softer now. "I lost the version of myself I'd spent a decade building and once that cracked, everything else did too. People. Trust. My own damn compass."

Nora's voice was quiet. "So what made you come back?"

He glanced up, meeting her eyes.

"A rec center job. Coaching beginners. Lane drills and kickboards. It was supposed to be temporary."

He looked around the table, at the women laughing, glowing, messy and alive. "But it's the only thing that's ever felt honest since."

Nora's gaze didn't waver. "I'm glad you stayed."

His eyes lingered on hers—longer than polite, quieter than flirtation. Just real.

Lulu raised her drink like it was a glow stick. "To sixth place and second chances."

The table erupted with laughter, but Nora kept looking at him because for the first time, she didn't just see the walls. She saw the man behind them.

Vanessa coughed loudly. "Well. Now that I'm emotionally compromised, someone pass me the fries and the number of your therapist."

Lulu tossed a glow stick bracelet in the air. "To broken swimsuits and broken hearts—may they both make us faster." They all raised their glasses. Nora raised hers a second later, her smile catching the glow of the light and Simon's eyes still quietly, steadily on her. The laughter slowly faded. Their drinks were lower, voices softer, like the night had shifted into that late-hour haze where confessions came easier and walls felt thinner.

Someone queued a slow, nostalgic track on the jukebox—Fleetwood Mac or maybe The Cure—and Lane 4 started drifting. Rina went to flirt with the bartender. Vanessa pulled Lulu toward the dance floor in a fit of tequila-fueled inspiration. The circle broke, not apart—just looser, more fluid, like teammates after the final relay.

Nora stood to stretch her legs, weaving through chairs toward the bar, craving a refill and a moment of air. That's where she saw him. Simon, alone at the bar, swirling the last of his drink in his glass like it held answers. His head turned just slightly when she neared—like he'd felt her presence before he saw her.

Just like that, the world narrowed. Music faded. Voices blurred and it was just the two of them again, in the kind of silence that buzzed with possibility.

Nora slid in beside him, hip brushing his. She didn't speak at first. Just stood there. Present. Still. It was an intimacy that didn't ask permission. He glanced at her, and for once, he didn't mask the look. There was no coach-face. No careful neutrality. Just tired eyes and something quietly exposed.

"That story," she said finally, voice low so only he could hear, "you didn't have to share that."

"I know."

"But I'm glad you did."

He nodded once, slowly. "I don't usually talk about it. Especially not with a table full of glitter."

That got a small smile out of her. "They're a lot," she said, gesturing toward Lane 4 who were currently arguing over whether Lulu could legally carry three margaritas at once.

Simon's mouth curved. "They are."

"But good," Nora added. "In the way you don't know you needed until you're already in too deep."

He looked at her then. Really looked. "You feel like that?

"Like I showed up for a swim workout and accidentally joined a therapy cult?" She shrugged, playful. "Yeah. Kind of."

A beat passed.

"You're different in here," he said.

Her brows lifted. "Different how?"

He looked down at the bartop, then back at her. "You let yourself take up space."

She blinked. "Is that a compliment?"

"It's the highest one I give."

Nora studied him, this man who watched everything and said little, who wore his reserve like armor but still managed to make her feel... seen. Truly seen. She leaned in slightly, not enough for anyone to notice, but enough for him to feel the shift.

"I like this version of you," she said.

Simon tilted his head. "What version is that?"

"The one who lets people in."

Their eyes locked. Heat curled between them, slow and simmering. A question neither of them quite asked. An answer neither could quite give.

Then Lulu shouted from across the bar, "NORA! SHOTS OR BETRAYAL—CHOOSE!"

Nora sighed. "They don't let you be mysterious for long."

Simon smiled. "Good."

She lingered one beat longer, just long enough to let her fingers graze his forearm. Just a brush. Just a whisper of contact. Then she turned and walked away and for the first time in a long time, Simon didn't feel like retreating behind his walls. He just watched her go, with something dangerously close to hope in his chest.

The bar lights dimmed as the DJ (aka the bartender's Spotify playlist) transitioned from 90s pop bangers to something with a deeper beat and a little more bass. The kind of music that dared you to move—badly, boldly, or both.

Lulu was the first to shriek. "Dance floor! Let's go, you beautiful sea witches!"

Rina groaned. "Oh god, not again."

"Shut up, you love it," Vanessa said, already dragging her by the wrist.

Within seconds, Lane 4 was in the middle of the small, sticky dance floor. Vanessa and Rina launched into what could only be described as synchronized chaos—part cheerleader, part interpretive dolphin.

"Is this a routine?" Nora called out over the music.

Rina shouted back, "It's performance art! Respect the vision!"

Lulu tossed a glow stick bracelet into the air like it was confetti. "Welcome to the splash zone!"

Nora laughed, the kind that cracked open her ribs a little. She didn't even realize she was dancing until her feet were moving—half a sway, half a step. Just enough to count. Then he was there. Not on the edge, not coaching from a distance. But next to her. Moving. Barely. Just a subtle shift of shoulders, hips angled toward hers like muscle memory brought him here and he'd decided not to fight it.

They weren't touching. Not quite, but the space between them crackled like a live wire—close enough to feel the heat, not close enough to feel relief.

"I didn't take you for a dancer," Nora said, her voice low, meant only for him.

Simon leaned in—just a fraction—but it was enough for her to catch the scent of soap and something earthy, something him. His breath brushed her cheek when he spoke.

"I don't usually," he murmured. "But tonight felt like a... show-up kind of night."

She tilted her head, a soft, crooked smile playing on her lips. "You always watch the water like it holds secrets."

His eyes locked on hers, the air tightening.

"Sometimes it's the only place people don't hide," he said, voice rougher now. Throatier. Like he wasn't just talking about swimming anymore.

Her pulse tripped. She didn't look away. Instead, she moved—just a shift, subtle but deliberate. Her arm grazed his, her chest a breath away from brushing his. The warmth of him curled around her like gravity.

He didn't step back. His hand twitched at his side like he was debating whether to reach for her. The music thudded around them. The bar blurred, nothing but her mouth, his breath, and the question hovering between them.

She could feel it—his restraint. The quiet war in his body and still, he didn't look away.

Neither did she.

One more inch and she'd be in the orbit of something unstoppable. Then—laughter cut across the dance floor, loud and ridiculous. Lulu had dragged Rina into a failed attempt at a spin, and Vanessa was cheering like it was the Olympics.

The moment broke but didn't vanish. It pulled back like a wave, waiting. They didn't kiss. Not yet, but they were close enough to feel the possibility of it and in that breathless space, with pulse and promise tangled between them, something sparked. Something real. Something beginning.

The night had splintered into hugs, glittery goodbyes, and Lulu yelling, "Nobody eat your feelings unless they're waffle fries!" as Rina dragged her toward a waiting Uber.

Vanessa was already texting blurry selfies into the group chat with captions like ***"Synchronized Swim Queens"***, ***"Lane 4 or Bust,"*** and one unfortunate photo of Simon mid-blink labeled ***"Coach caught in the wild"***.

Nora laughed as she scrolled, keys clutched in one hand, a breeze tugging at her loose curls.

"You parked over here?" Simon asked, falling into step beside her. She glanced up, surprised. "Yeah. I'm good though. You don't have to—"

"I know," he said. "But I want to."

They walked in silence for a few steps, the clink of her keys and the low hum of cicadas the only soundtrack. Streetlights cast soft pools of gold across the lot, and their shadows stretched long behind them.

"You handled that dance floor like a pro," she teased.

He smirked. "I was just trying not to step on Lulu."

"Fair," she laughed, then glanced at him. "Thanks for coming tonight. I know it was... not your usual scene."

Simon stopped at her car, hands tucked into the pockets of his hoodie. "It wasn't bad."

"Oh?" she said, unlocking the door with a chirp. "Just *not bad?*"

His eyes met hers, and it hit her again—how different he looked under streetlights instead of fluorescents. How easy it would be to fall into this. Into him. "I didn't mind being off-duty," he said softly.

Nora's breath caught. Not in surprise, but in something else. Something warm and delicious that curled down her spine like a secret.

"Me neither."

There was a beat. That lingering kind. That almost. Then she opened the door and slid inside, not trusting herself to linger longer.

He stepped back, gave her a little wave. "Goodnight, Lane 4."

She smiled. "Goodnight, Coach."

***

She drove off with the windows cracked, the sound of her laughter still lingering in his ears. Simon stood there for a moment, watching the red taillights fade. The buzz of the night still thrummed through his chest—not the bar, not the noise, but her. The way she'd looked at him. The red lipstick. The way she said *"me neither"*.

He exhaled and walked to his truck. The cab was dim, the only light coming from the faint blue glow of his phone screen. The post-bar quiet wrapped around him like a second skin—familiar, comfortable, but different now. He opened the Lane 4 group chat, expecting chaos. It delivered.

Lane 4 Group Chat: ***Chaos Queens***

Vanessa: *I demand a glitter-themed brunch.*

Lulu: *I just found glow stick goo in my bra. Worth it.*

Rina: *Nora and Simon had major "we almost kissed but didn't" energy. Discuss.*

Nora: *Logging off now, thank youuuu.*

He laughed softly, thumb hovering above the screen.

Then he paused. Hesitated. Scrolled back to that last message from Nora. Read it again.

Nora: *Logging off now, thank youuuu.*

His thumb moved.

Simon → Nora: *I didn't mind being off-duty tonight.*

A beat. Then:

Nora: *Me neither. We clean up okay.*

He smiled, head resting against the seat.

Typed again.

Simon: *I think you'd look good in any lane.*

He didn't overthink it. Just hit send because some things don't need coaching. They just need courage.

***

Her house was quiet, save for the hum of the fridge and the faint rustle of sheets as Nora curled deeper into bed, phone still in hand.

She reread the message.

Simon: *I think you'd look good in any lane.*

Her smile was slow and surprised. The kind that sneaks up on you when you're not looking. She tapped the screen to turn it off, and for a moment her reflection stared back—soft, lit only by the moonlight filtering through the blinds. Hair slightly tousled, cheeks still warm, red lipstick smudged at the corner of her mouth.

She barely recognized herself, but in the best way. That face—this version—wasn't careful or polite or trying to disappear. She looked... happy. Buoyant.

Maybe you don't need the water to feel weightless. Maybe sometimes, belonging finds you dry, barefoot, laughing, a little buzzed and it still counts.

She set the phone on the nightstand, lips quirking as she reached for her water bottle. Maybe, just maybe...it was only the beginning.

Buoyancy

Friday morning hit like a brick. Music pulsed through the speakers, too loud for the hour, and Simon stood on deck wearing a smugness that should have been illegal before 7 a.m. The whiteboard behind him was covered in a scrawl that looked like it had been designed by a sadist.

"IM pyramids?" Nora squinted up at him. "Who hurt you?"

Simon leaned against the stack of kickboards, arms folded, a smirk curling his mouth. "They build character."

"They kill spirits," Lulu muttered from behind her. "And bladders."

Nora slid into the water, immediately questioning every life choice that had led her here. Her body ached, her suit was staging a quiet rebellion, and her hair had surrendered to the humidity—but still, there was a flicker in her chest. She wasn't just surviving anymore. Frizz and all, she belonged here.

The first hundred meters went down easy. The second set of butterfly, not so much. Her lungs burned, shoulders screamed, and each stroke felt like betrayal.

From the deck, Simon's voice cut through the chaos—low, calm, maddeningly effective.

"Relax into the catch. Don't muscle it. Let the water carry you."

It worked. She hated that it worked. More than that, she hated how much she liked hearing it from him.

By the time she slammed into the wall, gasping like she'd been reborn, Simon was crouched beside her lane. Clipboard forgotten. His expression softer than usual.

"You lived," he said with a small grin.

"Questionable. I think I lost my soul on lap three."

He laughed—actually laughed—and it hit her low and sharp, like the sudden drop of a roller coaster. "That looked strong. You've been putting in the work."

"Or slowly dying," she panted.

"But still here." The words came quick, too quick, like they meant more than he'd intended.

Water dripped from her lashes as she blinked at him. There was something in his eyes—steady, unfiltered—that saw past her exhaustion to the grit underneath. The woman she was trying to rebuild.

"I told myself I'd give this three practices."

"And?"

She smiled, small but certain. "I'm still here, aren't I?"

Something flickered in his face—approval, yes, but something warmer too. Something that made her want to float in this moment, suspended between breath and something more.

"Good. Lane 4 would mutiny if you left."

She laughed, slipped her goggles back into place, and pushed off. This time, her strokes found rhythm, her breath settled, and her heart moved to a new beat. She wasn't just swimming to prove something. She was swimming toward something.

The locker room buzzed with post-practice energy. Steam curled into the air, mingling with the sharp tang of chlorine that clung to hair, towels, and tile. Nora wrung out her swimsuit when Rina dropped beside her with a groan.

"I need coffee and validation," Rina declared. "Possibly a priest."

Vanessa flopped down nearby, flipping her wet hair like she'd been hired for a shampoo commercial. "That last hundred nearly killed me. I saw my ancestors. They waved."

Nora laughed. "Is it bad that I liked it? Not the part where I couldn't feel my arms, but the rest."

"There's something twisted in you," Rina said, nudging her. "But in a good way."

"It's just—there's this moment after you push off the wall, when it's quiet. Like my brain finally shuts up."

"Yeah," Vanessa agreed. "Underwater is the only place I don't overthink."

The door swung open and Lulu burst in, headphones draped around her neck, humming Broadway. "Did we survive? Are we stronger? Are we sexy?"

"Only in the way limp spaghetti is technically flexible," Vanessa said.

"I'll take it." Lulu grinned, tossing her towel over her shoulder. "Look at you, newbie. Almost looking like an athlete."

It was meant to tease, but the word *almost* landed hard. David used to say that. When she cooked. When she had an idea. When she wanted more.

"Almost impressive."

"Almost worth the risk."

"Almost like you knew what you were doing."

Always with that half-smile that pretended to be kind.

Her hands stilled on her towel, pulse spiking. Rina noticed. Of course she did. She slid an arm around Nora's shoulders. "Careful. This one's a shark now. Glitter goggles and everything."

The banter moved on, but the word stayed lodged under her ribs, heavy and damp. She dressed on autopilot, laughed in the right places, and carried *almost* with her into the hallway, the cooler air making her shiver.

The drive home was quiet except for the tick of the cooling engine. Damp hair clung to her neck, the scent of chlorine rising from her skin. Out the windshield, two kids lugged swim bags nearly bigger than they were—one giggling, one grumbling.

Almost.

It was a joke in the locker room. Harmless on the surface, but her body didn't buy it. Somewhere under skin and muscle, memory stirred—the kind that lives in the shoulders, in the set of the jaw. The instinct to flinch before the words even land. The slow folding inward to take up less space. The bracing for the laugh that turns sharp at the edges.

Her hands tightened on the steering wheel, tendons pulling white at her knuckles. She was tired of it. Tired of having to *earn* a place she already belonged. Tired of pretending not to notice when the sting came wrapped in a smile. Tired of shrinking in gratitude for being allowed in the room at all.

The thought pressed against her ribs until it felt too big to contain. She took a breath, deep enough to hurt. Not a release yet. Not forgiveness. Just the beginning of something that refused to fold.

Steam fogged the bathroom mirror as the shower blasted hot, almost too hot. She stood under it, still, as if heat could burn the word off her skin.

David's voice rose uninvited. "Almost sexy... if you didn't try so hard." She'd smiled, put down the lipstick, changed the dress. Each small edit shrinking her just enough to fit the version he preferred.

Soap lathered over her arms, her neck, as if she could scrub down to something untouched by him.

"Almost impressive."

"Almost worth the risk."

"Almost someone."

Her hands stilled. Not anymore. She pressed her palms to the tile, tears coming—hot, quiet, determined. Not collapse. Release.

When the shaking finally passed, she stood there for a long moment, palms still braced against the tile, letting the steam wrap around her like a second skin. It felt different now. Lighter. As if the air itself had been wrung free of something heavy.

She reached for the towel, the rough cotton grounding her as she stepped out of the shower. Droplets slid from her hair, trailing down her spine, and pooled at her feet.

In the mirror, the fog clung stubbornly to the glass. She swiped a wide streak clear. The face staring back wasn't smaller. Wasn't tentative, and it wasn't *almost*.

Her cheeks were flushed from the heat, eyes sharp and unflinching, mouth set in something that wasn't quite a smile but was damn close. This was her—carved out of everything she'd endured, still standing, still looking herself in the eye.

Not perfect.

Not finished.

But her.

Later, curled on the couch, her skin still warm from the shower, Nora stared at the shadows shifting on the ceiling. The ache in her muscles felt earned. Alive. The word was still there, but dulled now, softened by the quiet.

Her phone buzzed.

Simon: *Did you survive the IM pyramid?*

She smiled before she typed.

Nora: *Still twitching from the fly sets, but technically alive.*

Simon: *Lane 4 standard: twitchy, mildly traumatized, and secretly proud of it.*

She laughed—full, unguarded.

Nora: *Be honest—am I actually getting better? Or is this a legally required pep talk from Coach Charming?*

Simon: *You're getting better and you keep showing up. That matters.*

It landed deep, in the spaces *almost* had tried to hollow out.

Simon: *Flip turns next week. Don't say I didn't warn you.*

Nora: *Should I stretch… or draft a will?*

Simon: Why choose? Stretch while the lawyer draws up your aquatic last rites.

Nora: Good to know my inevitable underwater cartwheel will be coach-approved.

Simon: You'll land it. I have a feeling.

Nora: Professional assessment or personal faith in my flailing?

Simon: Let's call it informed curiosity. Bordering on fascination.

Her breath caught.

Nora: Careful. That's dangerously close to flirting.

Simon: Almost?

She stared at it. The word hit differently now.

Nora: Not almost. Full send.

Simon: In that case... I hope you keep showing up.

Her chest tightened, not from doubt, but from want. She set the phone down, smiling the kind of smile that stayed.

***

Simon sat on the edge of his bed, a towel draped around his shoulders, damp hair curling at the ends from his own post-practice shower. The lamp on his dresser cast a warm pool of light across the room, the hum of the ceiling fan steady as his pulse—until her last message lit his phone again.

Not almost. Full send.

The words made something shift in him. Not a jolt, not a shock, something slower, deeper. It was the difference between curiosity and gravity. Between noticing her and being pulled toward her.

He hadn't meant to text her in the first place. Just like he hadn't meant to track her stroke all morning or notice the way she kept showing up even when the sets were brutal, or store the sound of her laugh somewhere it would keep him company later, but here they were.

He scrolled back through the thread, the corners of his mouth tugging upward without permission. She didn't hedge. Didn't play coy. Just stepped into the space between them and stayed there like she meant to, and that terrified him.

Because the last time he'd let someone in—really in—it had cost him more than he thought he could afford. Olympic trials. Missed qualifying by fractions of a second. Silence from people who'd promised to be there. A girlfriend who loved him in the glow but not in the shadows.

So he'd built walls. Kept close things casual and deep things out of reach. Coaching was safe. Laughing was safe. This—Nora—wasn't safe at all, but he wanted it anyway.

He picked up the phone again, thumbs moving before his brain could talk him out of it.

Simon: *In that case… I hope you keep showing up.*

The Masters Club

He stared at the words for a moment before hitting send. Watched the bubbles appear, disappear, reappear. Then nothing. Silence.

He let it sit, leaning back against the headboard, the quiet stretching between them like the space before a race start. It wasn't comfortable, but it was alive and maybe he was done protecting himself from that feeling.

***

The next afternoon, he hadn't planned to linger after the meet. Show up, fill in for a few heats, hand off the clipboard, ghost out. That was the plan.

Instead, he found himself leaning against the bleachers, watching steam rise off the pool. Coaches called times, kids dragged heavy wet bags, parents juggled medals and snacks.

"Still out-coaching everyone like it's penance?"

He turned. Erica. Same sleek hair, same unreadable eyes. Once, that voice had whispered *I love you* in hotel rooms. Now it cut through the tile-and-chlorine air like a blade.

"I didn't know you were in town," he said, keeping it even.

"Weekend visit," she replied. "My niece's first meet. Thought I'd catch a few races... and see if you were still pretending not to care."

He forced a half-smile. "Some things don't change."

Her gaze swept over him, assessing. "You always had the best instincts on deck. But emotionally?" She shrugged. "Blind spot."

He thought of that night after trials—her voice soft, saying *I just don't think I can do this version of you,* while she zipped her suitcase. The way she left like it was logistics, not loss.

"I've learned a few things since then," he said.

"I'm sure. Hard not to, when you hit rock bottom."

He almost laughed. "Funny. I don't remember you staying long enough to see it."

Her expression flickered. "We both knew what that was, Simon. You loved the sport. I loved the shine."

"And when the shine faded—"

"You stopped showing up," she said.

The words hit, but he didn't flinch. "I show up now. For the people who matter."

"Good," she said, tilting her chin. "Took you long enough."

They held each other's gaze a beat too long. Then she gave a small smile, turned, and walked away, heels clicking against tile.

Later, when the pool was quiet and the lights shimmered across the surface, he stood alone on deck. Her voice still echoed—*You stopped showing up.*

Maybe he had, but not for the reasons she thought. He thought of Nora. Her raw, unpolished stroke. The steadiness in her eyes when she said she'd keep showing up. The way she never asked for shine, just truth.

He'd built his life to avoid this exact risk. And yet, with her, the risk felt less like drowning and more like surfacing.

Crossing the parking lot toward his car, he spotted her—twenty yards away, laughing with Rina, arms full of a towel bag and enough glitter to violate pool codes. Hair damp, face bare, smile unguarded.

She saw him and waved. Casual. Effortless. Real.

He lifted a hand back, the tightness in his chest loosening just a little. Not healed. Not whole. But maybe—just maybe—he wasn't sinking anymore.

Buoyancy. It wasn't always about soaring. It wasn't medals or perfect form or winning the lane. Sometimes it was the stubborn art of staying afloat when the weight tried to pull you under.

It was refusing to fold when the old voices whispered *almost*. It was scrubbing the residue off your skin and meeting your own eyes in the mirror. It was showing up for another practice, another lap, another conversation that might matter.

It was keeping your head above water, not because it was easy, but because you'd decided you were worth the effort.

The Masters Club

Tonight, that was enough—two bodies in the same tide, neither ready to let the other go under.

Flip Turns and False Starts

Monday's workout was a new level of aquatic chaos. Simon had written two ominous words on the whiteboard: **Flip Turns.**

Nora stared at them like they were written in Sanskrit.

"Don't worry," Simon said, catching the collective panic radiating from Lane 4. "We'll start slow. It's more like a somersault than a spin. Less grace, more guts."

Rina raised her hand. "Is there an option for 'panic and sink'?"

Simon didn't miss a beat. "That's called freestyle without breathing."

Laughter rippled through the group. Even Nora cracked a smile, until it was her turn. She swam hard to the wall, heart hammering. Kicked. Flipped too early and surfaced with a loud gasp, one goggle full of water, the other clinging for dear life.

Simon crouched at the edge, clipboard forgotten, a slow grin tugging at the corner of his mouth.

"Not bad," he said, eyes tracking her. "You rotated too soon. Try again. Slower. Let the wall come to you."

Easy for you to say, she thought. You probably flipped out of the womb. He mimed the motion from the deck—arms sweeping, torso pivoting in one fluid motion. Nora wasn't watching the technique anymore. She was watching him. The way his brows furrowed with focus. The precision in his movement. The relaxed confidence that made everything about him seem so… grounded and maddeningly attractive.

She tried again. Failed again and came up sputtering.

"Jesus," she muttered. "I have a PhD in face-planting."

Simon laughed under his breath and knelt lower, hand outstretched. His fingers brushed her elbow, firm but careful. Not lingering but not rushing, either.

"Feel your core tighten," he said, his voice dipping just enough to turn the air electric. "That's your center. That's where your power is."

His eyes held hers. Steady. Focused. Unblinking. Something fluttered under her ribs. A low, unmistakable hum. She nodded once, barely breathing. Then flipped again. This time, her feet hit the wall. Her push-off was crooked and her exit splashy but she'd done it. When she surfaced, Simon was still there. Still watching and smiling.

"Nice," he said.

Nora's chest was already tight from the effort, but the way he said it? That pushed her pulse into overdrive. She smiled back, goggles askew, water dripping down her neck.

"Guess I found my center," she said. Simon's smile twitched wider. "Told you it was there."

The moment lingered like the last echo of a lap, breathless, suspended, before the real world crept back in. The whistle blew, a chorus of groans rippled down the lane lines, and the spell broke under the churn of water and the slap of palms against the wall.

After practice, the pool deck looked like a battlefield. Kickboards abandoned like fallen shields, swim caps dangling from lane ropes, water bottles knocked sideways in puddles of defeat. Lane 4 was sprawled across the benches, breathing hard, towels draped over heads like war survivors.

"Whoever invented flip turns is a sadist," Rina groaned, dramatically sliding to the floor like a mermaid who'd given up on land.

"Actually," Vanessa said between gulps of Gatorade, "I think it was a Hungarian Olympian in the 1950s."

"Whatever," Lulu muttered, wringing out her glitter-dipped swim cap. "May their flip turn ghost haunt me forever. I nearly drowned in four feet of water."

"You didn't drown," Nora said, peeling off her cap with a wet snap. "You did, however, somersault directly into the lane line like a caffeinated seal."

Lulu pointed at her. "Oh, I'm sorry, Doctor Perfect Form. You only swallowed half the pool."

Nora grinned. "Progress."

Vanessa threw a towel over her face. "My soul left my body on that last set. It waved goodbye and everything."

Someone launched a rogue Goldfish cracker across the bench. It landed with a damp plop on Lulu's shin. She picked it up solemnly. "I accept this as an offering for my sacrifice."

Nora laughed so hard she had to lean forward, elbows on her knees, breath catching in the warm, chlorine-heavy air. The ache in her shoulders had settled into something good. Earned. The kind of sore that said: You showed up. You didn't quit.

Beside her, Rina was braiding glitter into Lulu's wet hair while Vanessa tried to sync up their post-practice playlist with a speaker that kept skipping.

It was chaos. Messy, loud, perfect chaos. Nora sat back, watching the swirl of movement, of friendship, of unfiltered presence and caught her reflection in the glass panel of the pool office window. Her hair was plastered to her cheeks. Her eyes were bright. Her skin flushed from effort, but more than that—she looked *there*. There was nothing *almost* about this version of her. Not faded. Not hiding. Just… real. She smiled, quietly this time. There was something about belonging here that didn't just feel good. It felt earned.

The pool had emptied. Just Nora and Simon remained, fluorescent lights buzzing low overhead, casting shimmering patterns across the still surface. The water held a quiet, heavy calm, like it knew something was about to shift.

Nora pulled herself onto the deck, feet dangling in the water, cheeks flushed, breath coming fast. She was smiling, but it wasn't just endorphins, it was adrenaline and something else she didn't dare name.

"You're doing great," Simon said as he crouched beside her, his voice pitched low, like it was meant only for her.

"You have to say that," she replied, brushing hair from her eyes.

He tilted his head, half-smile playing at his mouth. "No," he said. "I really don't."

He offered her a towel, their fingers brushing, just a moment, just enough. Then he stood, gaze steady. "Want a few form tips? One-on-one?"

There was something in his tone, casual, sure, but threaded with heat. Like this wasn't just about drills and technique anymore. Nora nodded before she fully meant to. "Yeah. Sure."

He extended his hand. She took it. His grip was warm and rough and grounding, and yet the second their palms met, a jolt shot up her spine. She let him pull her to her feet, close enough that the heat of his body cut through the humid air. They walked to the shallow end in silence, the distance between them feeling both measured and magnetic.

Simon stepped out of his sneakers, then peeled off his shirt in one clean motion. Nora's breath hitched—just barely, but enough. He wasn't flashy. Just solid. Strong. The kind of strength earned, not sculpted. There was a pale scar near his collarbone, a quiet story she didn't know yet. His presence had always commanded the deck, but here, shirtless and unguarded, he was something else entirely. He met her gaze as he slid into the water. "Come on in."

She stepped in slowly, the warmth of the water nothing compared to the heat beneath her skin. Her pulse quickened as she moved closer.

"Here," he said, voice low, eyes on her shoulder. "Let me show you."

He reached out, his fingertips skimming the bare skin of her forearm, then guiding her through a slow, deliberate stroke. His touch was firm, anchoring her in the moment.

"Relax here," he said, adjusting the curve of her wrist. "And pull through here. Let the movement carry you. Don't force it."

The pool was quiet except for the soft lapping of water between them. His chest brushed her shoulder once, accidental, maybe, but the contact lingered in her bones.

"Better," Simon murmured, his mouth just inches from her ear. "You feel that?"

She did. Every inch of it. The way his attention wrapped around her like gravity. The way his eyes never wavered. The way his voice coiled low and warm. Nora nodded, too breathless to speak.

"You're stronger than you think," he said, but the way he said it... it wasn't just about swimming. It felt personal.

Their eyes locked. Close. Closer. The space between them buzzed, charged and trembling.

Then—

A splash echoed from down the hallway. A door. Voices. Someone entering the locker room. Simon blinked, his hand dropping away.

"We'll work more next week," he said, voice back in neutral, but the shift was too late. The air still crackled. Nora drifted back a step, heart hammering as she tried to remember how to breathe again.

She pressed a palm to the water's surface, then let it fall away. She was learning more than just technique in this pool. She was waking up—stroke by stroke, breath by breath, and Simon? He wasn't just teaching her to swim. He was becoming the reason she wanted to fly.

***

Simon sat in his office long after the last swimmer had gone. The echo of the pool had faded hours ago, but the damp smell of chlorine clung to everything—his clothes, the towel draped over the back of his chair like a flag he'd never flown.

He'd showered, changed, logged the day's notes. There was nothing left to do but leave, and yet he stayed.

Her face kept surfacing—focused, flushed, curious. The sound of her laugh lingered in a place he'd long since bricked over. He told himself it was harmless, that coaches notice these things the way they notice a swimmer's breathing pattern or stroke efficiency. Observation, not indulgence. But even in his own head, the lie felt thin.

He hadn't meant to get in the pool with her. That was never the plan. But something in her expression—hope and hunger woven together—had pulled him in before he could think better of it. He told himself it was about form, about giving her what she needed to improve, but he knew it was also about something else.

He could still feel the tremor in her muscles when he guided her arm, the way her skin felt impossibly warm under the water. It wasn't the touch itself that unsettled him—it was the way the space between them seemed to shift, as if the water had carried them closer than he'd meant to be.

Simon leaned back, staring at the ceiling until the muscles in his neck ached. He reminded himself why the line mattered. Why it had to stay intact.

He tightened the line in his mind, pulling it taut. Still, it felt a little looser than it had this morning.

***

Later that evening, Nora stood in front of her bathroom mirror wrapped in a thick gray towel, steam curling up the walls. Her skin glowed pink from hot water and effort, and her damp hair clung in soft waves around her face.

She studied her reflection—not with critique or disapproval, but curiosity. Her eyes were bright. Her shoulders, a little more defined. Her cheeks, flushed with something that wasn't just heat.

She touched the spot where Simon's fingers had rested on her arm earlier. It was silly but the memory sent a spark through her nerves, as if she were waking up piece by piece.

Her body didn't feel foreign anymore. It felt… hers. Capable. Beautiful, even. She pulled the towel tighter around her chest and let herself smile. It wasn't about Simon, not really. Or not just about him. It was about remembering what it felt like to be wanted and more importantly, to want. Not out of obligation. Not out of performance. But for joy. For thrill. For the pulse just beneath her skin that said: You're still alive. You still matter.

She stepped away from the mirror, caught a glimpse of her scrunchie on the counter, and slid it back on her wrist. No more disappearing. Tonight, she'd remember who she was becoming and for the first time in a long time, she didn't dread what came next.

Unscripted Encounters

It was supposed to be a simple errand. In and out of the juice bar, maybe a protein shot for good behavior. No emotional turbulence. No ghosts. Nora had just finished a recovery swim—hair still damp, skin flushed, and hoodie half-zipped. She was digging for her wallet when she heard it.

A laugh. Familiar. Too familiar. Effortless in that curated way she used to mistake for charm. David, was near the pickup counter, leaning against it like it was home base. Same easy grin. Same navy pullover—the one she used to steal when their house was cold and she couldn't sleep.

Next to him: a woman. Brunette. Glossy hair, long legs, manicure that probably matched her calendar. She was holding two smoothies and smiling up at him like they shared secrets.

Nora froze, her instinct said to duck, hide behind the protein bar display. Or fake a call and bolt, but that was the old version of her—the one who'd shrink to make space. This version? The one with a scrunchie on her wrist and chlorine still clinging to her skin? This Nora wouldn't shrink.

She squared her shoulders and stepped forward. "Hey," she said, voice calm. Cool. Perfectly neutral, like she'd been training for this exact moment. David looked up. Blinked. Then smiled. "Nora. Wow."

The woman turned with polite curiosity. "This is Jenna," David said. "Jenna, this is Nora."

Jenna extended a hand like they were all part of some civilized cocktail party. "Nice to meet you."

Nora shook it. "You too." Her fingers were steady, but her pulse tapped out a furious beat in her throat. David glanced at her again, longer this time, eyes scanning like he couldn't quite place her. "You look… good," he said. "Different."

"I am," she replied, voice sharper now. Clearer. "Different, I mean."

He nodded slowly, as if trying to translate her words in real time. A silence stretched. Not friendly. Not hostile. Just… loaded.

Jenna took a polite sip of her smoothie. "Well, we should—"

"Yes," Nora cut in. "Enjoy the drinks," and before anyone could say more, before her strength could turn brittle—she turned, pushed through the door, and stepped out into the sunlight.

The air hit her like a wave—fresh, open, real. She exhaled. Not shaky. Not weak. Just done. Let him be charming. Let him have smoothie dates and effortless mornings and women who didn't know what it meant to fall asleep wondering where the light in you went.

He could keep the sequel. She wasn't flipping back to that chapter. This one would move forward—slow, steady, and hers.

As she walked back toward her car, she caught sight of her reflection in the darkened window. Her cheeks were flushed, hair messy, and her sweatshirt was damp around the collar. In her eyes, there was something steadier there.

Her phone buzzed.

Simon: *I owe you a smoothie. Post-practice? No pyramids this time. Promise.*

Nora stared at the message, then smiled. She didn't need to erase her past to feel whole. She just had to keep swimming toward the version of herself who already was.

Nora didn't rush home after the juice bar. Instead, she drove with the windows down, letting the air wash over her. Somewhere between a red light and a half-sipped iced coffee, she realized she wasn't thinking about David anymore.

Not really. She was thinking about Friday's practice. The way Simon's hand had guided hers in the water. The pulse of something she hadn't let herself feel in a long time. The sound of Rina's laughter echoing in the locker room. The absurdity of glitter scrunchies and post-lap pastry runs.

The new rhythm of her life was louder than the old one and it was starting to drown it out. She tucked her phone into her hoodie pocket and let the corner of her mouth lift—not a grin, not yet, but the start of one. She didn't text back. Not yet. Instead, she drove to the one place that made her feel like herself than anywhere else. Chlorine and chaos. Laughter and laps. Lane 4.

The first thing she heard when she entered the pool was Rina declaring war on a lifeguard's attention span. If swimming was cardio, flirting was Rina's contact sport. She checked her lip gloss in the reflection of her hydroflask, smacked her lips once for luck, and capped it with a smug little snap.

There was a new lifeguard today. Tall. Tan. Beard scruff that screamed, "I own artisan surfboards and an oat milk subscription."
Rina gave herself two laps to make him smile.

"Lane 4, you're up!" Simon called.

Rina slid into the water like a Bond girl—if Bond girls wore waterproof mascara and glitter nail polish. She offered a lazy wave toward the lifeguard stand.

No response. Yet. Challenge accepted. She kicked off the wall with zero urgency. This was not about speed. It was about strategy. Hair mostly dry. Eye contact at the turns. A smirk that said, I know I'm ridiculous, but you love it.

Nora groaned from the next lane. "Is this going to be one of those practices?"

"If by 'those' you mean invigorating and inspirational, yes," Rina replied, breaststroking like she was cruising the Amalfi coast.

Vanessa called from the deck. "You're going to get kicked out again."

"That was one time, and I was invited to leave. There's a difference."

"I seem to remember glitter being involved," Lulu added. "And a strategically placed pool noodle."

"Allegedly," Rina said, flipping her hair and doing a slow, deliberate dolphin kick.

Nora leaned against the lane line, the water lapping softly at her shoulders, watching Rina work the pool like a stage. It was ridiculous. Absurd and exactly what she needed. She wasn't dissecting every syllable David had said. She wasn't wondering if she looked composed or pathetic or if Jenna's hair had been more salon-fresh than hers. She wasn't analyzing. She was here.

Her arms floated at her sides, loose and tired. Her legs drifted in the water. The fluorescent lights buzzed overhead, but not in a way that felt harsh. Just present. Around her, Lane 4 dissolved into glittering chaos; Rina executing her slow-motion seduction strokes, Vanessa pretending not to care but absolutely tracking the lifeguard's reaction, Lulu humming something from a Broadway soundtrack between backstroke sets.

Nora? She was laughing. Not because she was supposed to. Not to soften a moment or smooth tension or perform lightness for someone else's comfort. She was laughing because the ache in her shoulders reminded her she was strong. Because her cheeks were warm and her chest was open and the water—this whole world—felt like it was making room for her. For the first time in longer than she could remember, she wasn't trying to belong. She already did. Wet. Laughing. Whole.

Simon blew the whistle. "Focus, Lane 4."

Rina gave him a wink. "I'm focused on expanding my cardio options."

Simon crouched down beside the pool, dry sarcasm at the ready. "I swear, one day you'll show up for a workout that's not part of your dating agenda."

"Don't threaten me with personal growth," she shot back, grinning.

He tried to look stern but failed spectacularly. "Just try not to cause a workplace incident."

"No promises."

She reached the wall, glanced up casually and there it was. The lifeguard smiled. Victory. Rina emerged from the water like she'd just closed a major deal, goggles perched stylishly on her forehead and swam over to the others.

"Well?" Vanessa asked, towel in hand.

"He smiled," Rina said, smug and soaking.

"Of course he did," Nora muttered. "You're practically a sponsored hazard."

"Confidence, ladies," Rina declared, wringing out her ponytail with a flourish. "It's a muscle and mine is thriving."

Simon passed by, tossing her a fresh kickboard without breaking stride. "Then let's put that muscle to work."

She caught it, winked again. "Coach, you flirt almost as hard as you coach."

"I'm not flirting," Simon said, deadpan.

"But if you were…" Rina teased.

He didn't answer. Just kept walking with the tiniest shake of his head and a barely concealed smile, and just like that, she slid back into Lane 4—lip gloss intact, heart lighter, and hair only slightly damp.

After practice, Nora lingered, not just to towel off or stretch or avoid the cold air but because the idea of walking into her house, turning on the light, and hearing nothing but the hum of the fridge felt… heavier than usual.

Her muscles ached in the best way. Her hair was damp beneath her hoodie. Chlorine still clung to her skin like a secret. But her heart? It felt full in places that had been empty for too long and hollow in others she hadn't quite figured out how to refill.

She sat on the bench beside her gym bag, watching the team filter out in clusters—laughing, teasing, pulling on sweatpants and dragging duffels. The buzz of belonging. This was the part she never used to stay for. Back then, she always had an excuse. A meeting. A deadline. A man waiting at home who didn't understand why she needed other people to feel whole.

Now? She had nothing to rush toward and for once, that didn't feel like a failure.

Her phone buzzed.

Vanessa: *First round's on me. Don't make it weird.*

Nora stared at the screen, a smile tugging at the corner of her mouth. Vanessa's version of a hug. Slightly aggressive. Deeply effective.

She was tired. She was sore but maybe showing up didn't always have to look like pushing through the pain or delivering the perfect comeback. Maybe it wasn't about proving anything. Maybe sometimes, it was just about saying yes to the invitation. To the people who made you laugh until your sides hurt. To margaritas the size of bathtubs and stories that didn't need polishing. To being seen. She stood, slinging her bag over her shoulder, and texted back:

Nora: *I'm in.*

For the first time in a long time, the next few hours didn't feel like something to survive. They felt like something to look forward to.

They were only supposed to grab one drink. That was the rule. The excuse, the gentle peer pressure wrapped in a casual group text.

Vanessa: *Post-practice debrief? First round's on me. Don't make it weird.*

For a moment, they'd all assumed her phone had been hacked, but here they were—packed into a booth at a loud, sticky-floored Mexican joint that smelled like lime, salt, and bad decisions. The salsa was too spicy. The booths were cracked vinyl. The margaritas came in goblets large enough to bathe a toddler and it was perfect.

Vanessa sipped hers with clinical precision, still in her sandals and a hoodie that smelled faintly of tomato vines. Her phone lay face-down on the table like it had annoyed her. She didn't say much, but she didn't need to.

Rina was mid-story, gesturing wildly with a chip in one hand and a half-empty glass in the other. "...so I turn around, right? And there's this woman holding my yoga mat like she's about to propose—"

"Oh my God," Lulu gasped, already wheezing.

"—and long story short," Rina continued, grinning, "I may be engaged to a woman named Darlene. I said yes mostly out of fear."

They erupted in laughter. Nora leaned back, shoulders still warm from practice, throat sore from laughing too hard, too often.

The restaurant doors opened just as Lulu strutted in twenty minutes late—combat boots, glitter eyeliner, and a frozen yogurt cup held high like a trophy.

"You brought dessert to a restaurant?" Vanessa asked, deadpan.

"I brought balance," Lulu replied. "And vibes. You're welcome."

They all cheered like she'd returned from war.

At one point, Nora found herself squished between Lulu and Vanessa, watching them argue over whether ghosts could drive Teslas. She didn't jump in. She didn't feel the need to perform. She just... existed. Present. Warm. Held. It felt like slipping into a scene that had already started, but no one cared she'd arrived late.

Then Lulu turned to her, all wide eyes and wild sincerity. "You good?"

Nora blinked. "Yeah. I think I am."

"Cool," Lulu said, tapping her arm. "You have very empathetic eyebrows. I like that about you."

Vanessa snorted into her drink.

Nora glanced sideways and caught something rare—Vanessa, laughing. Not the polite, practiced kind she usually rationed out, but a full-bodied laugh that crinkled her eyes and softened the edges she wore like armor. Her shoulders dropped. Her phone stayed in her bag.

"Don't get used to it," Vanessa said, catching Nora watching her. "I'm still terrifying."

Nora bumped her shoulder, a grin tugging at her mouth. "Please. I wouldn't survive crossing you." Vanessa smirked but didn't disagree.

Around them, the table buzzed—chips crunching, drinks clinking, Rina belting out a song no one else knew. Glitter caught the light on Lulu's cheekbone, someone's elbow knocked over the salsa, and the air felt loose and alive.

In the middle of it—lime-sticky napkins, off-key harmonies, the messy joy of women unguarded— something shifted. Not with fanfare, but with the quiet click of a lock turning from the inside. She wasn't looking in anymore. She was here. At the table. In the circle.

She belonged—not because she'd earned her way in or proved herself worthy, but because sometimes, if you're lucky, the right women make space beside them, tip their chins toward the empty chair, and say without saying: *Stay*.

Treading Deeper

Wednesday morning arrived swaddled in steam and the sacred scent of chlorine. Lane 4 was already alive— trading sleepy insults and splashy greetings like a team that had earned their chaos.

Nora tugged her cap over damp hair, the laughter from last night's margarita-fueled mayhem still tucked in the corner of her smile. Her phone buzzed.

David: *Didn't peg you for the spandex-and-self-discovery type. Hope it's working out.*

Just words. Polite. Nonchalant, but somehow, they landed like an old bruise she'd forgotten was still there. She locked her screen and shoved her phone into her swim bag. Not now. Not here.

Vanessa stood on deck, holding up Tupperware like a prize. "Guess who brought cinnamon muffins?"

"Was world peace baked in?" Rina asked, surfacing beside Nora with a dramatic flip of her goggles. "We already solved leggings and lifeguards. Needed a third win."

Nora grinned, her breath catching from the cold shock of the water and the warmer jolt of belonging. "Sorry I'm late. My bed tried to hold me hostage."

The Masters Club

Laughter rippled through the lane. It wasn't just the jokes—it was the rhythm. The ritual. The feeling of being folded into something real.

Yet—David's message sat like silt in her chest. *Hope it's working out.* He meant it as an observation. Maybe even a compliment, but it carried that same undercurrent she'd grown used to—like her glow-up was an inconvenience. Like her happiness should come with an apology.

He didn't get to do that anymore because the Nora he used to know—the one who minimized, who softened herself to stay safe...she wasn't here. The one here, now? She was damp, exhausted, a little sore—and alive.

She kicked off the wall with a little more force than usual, her legs slicing through the water. Every stroke shook something loose. Every breath said: Not his to define.

Between intervals, someone from Lane 3 called out, "You all swimming the Masters meet next month?" The energy shifted like someone had dropped a starter pistol into the pool.

"Oh God," Rina groaned. "We're really doing this again?"

"Competing?" Vanessa blinked, like someone had just suggested synchronized skydiving.

"It's optional," Rina said. "Unless Simon starts assigning mandatory fun."

Nora let the words roll over her. Competing? In public? With timers and spectators and nerves? Her stomach twisted but not entirely from dread. Something else stirred. Not quite confidence, not yet, but curiosity.

Could I?

She didn't answer. Just dunked her head and pushed off again, cutting through the water with a sharper kick and the quiet thrill of becoming someone new.

That feeling stayed with her through the rinse of the shower, the buzz of the locker room, even into the evening. She was halfway through folding laundry when her phone lit up.

Simon: *You mentioned mornings were quieter. Want to work through pacing before practice?*

No emoji. No pressure. Just calm. Steady. Sure, and for a long moment, Nora just stared at the screen. Then she smiled— Not because she needed to, but because she wanted to.

Yes, she typed back.

See you then.

It was earlier than usual when Nora arrived the next day. The pool was still, bathed in pale morning light that shimmered across the surface like glass. The quiet wrapped around her like a held breath.

Simon was already there, crouched near Lane 4, clipboard in hand. Damp curls clung to his forehead, and his t-shirt stretched in all the right places. When he looked up and saw her, his smile wasn't just professional, it was warm. Direct. Like he'd been waiting for her.

"Morning," he said, voice low and rough from disuse.

"Is it?" she asked, rolling her shoulder.

"Depends who you ask," he said, eyes scanning her face with a flicker of something more than coachly concern. "Let's work on your stroke pacing today. You're still leading with too much shoulder."

She stripped off her sweatshirt and stepped to the edge. His gaze tracked the movement. Just for a beat. Just long enough. She slipped into the water, coolness enveloping her skin like a jolt. "Warm up with a 200 free," he said. "Then hold."

She moved through the water with purpose, aware of her form, her limbs, her breath—and of Simon, watching. Always watching. When she reached the wall, he was there, crouched low, forearms resting on the pool's edge.

"You're stronger than when you started," he said, voice quieter now. "But you're still forcing it. Let's make it clean. Efficient."

Without another word, he stood, peeled off his shirt, and slid into the water beside her.

The moment snapped. Shifted. The air thickened. The distance closed. They swam a few strokes together—synchronized, close, his body cutting clean through the water beside hers. When he stopped, she stopped too, treading water. Breathless, but not from the workout.

"Watch my wrist," he said, lifting his arm between them. "Keep this angle straight. That's where you stop wasting energy."

She reached out to mirror him, but he caught her wrist first, his hand warm in the cold water, his grip sure.

"Like this," he said, guiding her hand in a fluid arc. His fingers trailed along her forearm, deliberate. Not possessive. Not clinical. Just... connected.

"Feel that?" he asked.

God, yes, but she nodded instead. A slow, careful nod. Her eyes held his.

Then his hand slid down her forearm, across her waist—adjusting her position with the lightest pressure but it might as well have been a match to dry tinder. Her body lit up, nerves buzzing like the water had turned electric. Her breath caught.

"You okay?" he asked, voice just above a whisper, closer now. So close she could feel his breath warm against her cheek, smell the faint salt of chlorine and something that was just... him.

"I'm fine," she said, barely audible. "Just...
recalibrating."

His mouth quirked, half smile, half something
darker. "You're doing more than that."

Neither of them moved. Not really but everything
shifted. The moment was alive. Breathing between
them.

Then, slowly, Simon swam backward, just a few
strokes—never breaking eye contact. Letting the
moment stretch. Letting it linger. His retreat wasn't
distance. It was invitation.

He pulled himself out of the pool in one smooth
motion, water sheeting off his chest and shoulders.
Nora blinked, heart hammering. She watched him towel
off, watched him glance back one more time. There was
no smirk. No wink. Just heat and certainty. Something
had changed. Not subtly. Not slowly, and Nora? She
wasn't flustered. She was ready. This wasn't just
swimming anymore. This was foreplay and she was all
in.

As she toweled off near the deck, her skin still tingling
from the water and from the electric charge Simon had
left in his wake—Nora felt lighter. Flushed. Open in a
way she hadn't been in years.

Then her phone buzzed inside her swim bag. She
reached for it, still smiling, her fingertips slightly pruned.

David: Just wanted to say I'm seeing someone. It's serious. Thought you should hear it from me.

The words didn't make sense at first. Her brain lagged, still caught in the afterglow of movement, of being wanted, of almost. Then they landed—like a slap she didn't see coming and the air left her lungs.

The heat she'd carried from the pool—Simon's gaze, his hands, that nearly-there moment—drained fast, leaving a chill in its place. She stared at the message. Her lips parted, but no breath came out. Just a tightness in her throat that threatened to bloom into something worse.

She sat down hard on the bench, phone still in her hand. The hum of the pool—the splashes, the whistles, the distant chatter—faded to static.

What did he want from her? Approval? Closure? Control? This was David in a text: cold, polished, delivered with just enough plausible kindness to gut her cleanly. *It's serious.* Like she needed reminding she'd been disposable. Like his happiness needed her acknowledgment.

She swallowed the lump rising in her throat, jaw locking with the effort to stay composed. The moment with Simon—his touch, his voice, the way he looked at her like she wasn't a project but a presence—had felt like something real. Something slow-building and solid.

Now this? A ghost of her old life, crashing in like a careless wave. David's text wasn't love or longing. It was the same lazy superiority he'd always worn like cologne—clinging, suffocating, hard to wash off. A drive-by reminder of the version of her he'd never really seen.

She slipped the phone back into her bag, fingers unsteady. Then she stood. Spine straightening. Breath steadying. Not out of spite. Not to prove anything, but because she could.

He could keep his smooth exits, his curated life, his leggy distractions. She had something better: A lane. A team. A body that remembered how to fight for itself and a man who met her in the deep end—not to rescue her, but to swim beside her.

Nora slung her towel over her shoulder like a banner. The sting lingered, sure. Old wounds had a way of whispering but this time, they didn't get the last word. She did.

The locker room buzzed with the usual chaos—zippers, dripping suits, the slap of bare feet on tile. Nora stood at her locker, towel clutched tight around her chest, staring blankly at the screen of her phone. The text still hovered there, glowing like a wound.

She didn't move until someone nearby—maybe Lulu—cursed at her stubborn locker. The moment snapped. Nora shoved her phone into her bag, pulled on her hoodie with damp hands, and tried to blink the sting from her eyes.

Behind her, the familiar rhythm of Lane 4 played on: Rina humming off-key, Vanessa muttering about missing tomato seedlings, someone launching a stray hairbrush across the bench.

It should've grounded her. Instead, her breath caught. "You okay?" The question came soft. Unnamed. Maybe Vanessa. Maybe Lulu. Maybe all of them.

Nora hesitated. Then lied. "Yeah. Fine."

There was a pause—thick, unhurried. Then the voice again, calm and certain: "You don't have to be fine. Not with us."

That undid her a little. She sat down hard on the bench, elbows on knees, towel damp against her thighs. "It was my ex," she said finally. "David. He texted."

Someone nearby stopped rummaging. The room shifted, subtle and still.

"What'd he want?" Vanessa asked, not nosy—just ready.

Nora swallowed. "To let me know he's dating someone. That it's serious. That I should hear it from him, not someone else."

A snort. "How considerate."

A pause. Then a quieter echo: "How cruel."

Nora smiled, thin and bitter. "I know it's not supposed to matter. I don't want him back. But it still hit like... like a memory I didn't want."

"It's okay to grieve the version of love you thought you had," Rina said gently. "Even if it was never real."

"I don't even miss him," Nora admitted. "I just... miss being chosen. Or feeling like I was."

A beat of silence. Then, Rina whispered "Loneliness can sound a lot like nostalgia. Don't believe everything it says."

Nora's throat tightened. She stared down at her hands, damp and trembling in her lap. She didn't say anything. They all moved and sat down beside her. Close enough to lean against. Close enough to steady her.

"You're not alone," they said, just loud enough to reach the softest part of her. "Not in here. We see you." She didn't answer. Just let the words settle. Let herself be seen.

When she finally stood to go, the ache was still there, but it wasn't sharp. It had softened at the edges, and when Vanessa tossed her a fresh hair tie and said, "Saturday. Come early. We'll warm up together," Nora nodded.

She wasn't okay. Not yet, but she wasn't pretending anymore and that felt like the start of something stronger.

That night, Nora stood at her bathroom sink, towel wrapped loosely around her body, damp hair leaving a trail of water down her spine. The mirror reflected someone new. Or maybe—finally—someone real.

Her eyes were bright, cheeks flushed. Not just from the swim or the steam, but from something deeper. Something blooming and not because of a man.

Because of them. The women in Lane 4. The way they held her in the locker room earlier without smothering her. The way they let her ache without demanding she snap out of it. Their laughter. Their warmth. Their belonging. She hadn't even known how lonely she'd been until they shattered it.

Nora pressed a palm to her chest, grounding herself in the quiet. She wasn't okay. Not entirely, but she wasn't unraveling anymore either. She was stitching herself back together, one messy lap at a time—with scrunchies, sass, and the solidarity of women who saw her. Chose her. Kept showing up.

Still, beneath all that grounded grace, there was another current. One that made her stomach flip and her pulse skip.

Simon.

The ghost of his touch still lingered—his fingers guiding her wrist, his hand resting just a beat too long at her waist. Not invasive. Not arrogant. Just... deliberate. A hum of possibility.

David had stopped touching her like that long before the end. Not cruelly. Just with indifference, like she'd become part of the furniture. Expected. Faded.

Simon didn't make her feel like furniture. He made her feel like friction. Nora picked up her phone before she could second-guess it and typed:

Nora: *Thanks for the tips today. Didn't know my wrist could do that.*

The dots appeared almost instantly.

Simon: *You're welcome.*

There's a lot more your wrist can do.

She let out a startled laugh, covering her mouth as if the girls might hear her from across town. That was... bold. But also? Hot. She didn't let herself overthink it. Just typed:

Nora: *Is that part of Thursday's workout?*

A pause. Then:

Simon: *Only if you're feeling brave.*

Her fingers hovered. She could play it off. Pivot. Cool it down, but she didn't want to.

Nora: *Brave enough.*

A longer pause this time. The kind that made her skin prickle.

Simon: *Then yeah. Lesson plan confirmed. See you Thursday, Lane 4.*

She swallowed hard, smiling. A response danced on the tip of her fingers, something clever, something wildly inappropriate—but she didn't send it. Instead, she set the phone down, the last words glowing like a secret in the dark.

This wasn't a rescue story. She wasn't waiting to be saved. She had her girls. She had herself and maybe, if things kept building like this, she'd have something else too. Not a replacement. Not a new version of the old story but something entirely different. Something she got to choose.

***

Simon sat on the edge of his bed, phone still warm in his hand, the thread with Nora glowing back at him.

Nora: *Brave enough.*

Simon: *Then yeah. Lesson plan confirmed. See you Thursday, Lane 4.*

He read it again and again. Like the words might anchor him in something real. She wasn't coy. She wasn't playing a part. She was… present. Brave in the kind of way that didn't need an audience. Brave just for herself, and damn if that didn't knock something loose in him.

He leaned back against the wall, head tipped up toward the ceiling like it might have answers. His pulse still hadn't settled. Not since the pool. Not since her. The feel of her wrist in his hand. Her breath catching. The way she didn't flinch. She let him touch her—not just physically, but with trust and that scared the hell out of him. Because once, a long time ago, Simon let someone in like that too.

When he failed to make the Olympic team, she didn't just walk away, she disappeared like he'd embarrassed her. Like his worth had been tied to the podium he never reached.

She'd said she loved him, but what she'd really meant was: as long as you're winning. So he learned. Love was conditional, and being good wasn't enough unless you were great. Gold-medal great.

Since then, he'd kept it surface. Work, training, coaching. Women who didn't want more than casual. Women who didn't look at him the way Nora did—like she saw past the stats and into the quiet ache he thought he'd buried.

He should be careful, but when Nora smiled up at him in the water—uncertain but open—he felt something crack. A seam. A breath. A possibility. She wasn't chasing perfection. She was chasing herself and that was the bravest damn thing he'd ever seen.

Simon ran a hand down his face, the ache in his chest a dull thrum. He wanted her. Not just in his bed—but in his orbit. In his silence. In the raw, quiet places he didn't let people touch anymore.

Simon: *Stretching's good. But I'll make sure you're warmed up.*

He sent it before he could overthink.

No follow-up. No winks. Just heat and truth. The line between them wasn't just flirting anymore. It was an invitation. One they were both getting closer to answering.

Thursday couldn't come fast enough.

Pajamas & Permission

The invitation had started as a joke. Lulu had sent a group text titled **Operation: Lane 4 Lock-In**, accompanied by more emojis than actual words— sparkles, wine glasses, a tent, three mermaids, and what appeared to be a screaming possum. The image attachment was a blurry photo of glittery face masks arranged in a circle like an occult summoning.

No one responded for ten minutes. Then Rina simply texted: *I'm in. What should I bring besides unprocessed trauma and candy?*

Now, Nora stood in her kitchen staring down at a tray of store-brand snacks and two lukewarm pizzas, wondering if she was hosting a sleepover or a coven ritual. The dining table was covered in a chaotic spread of magazines, glitter glue, string lights, and one very intimidating craft bin Lulu had dropped off "just in case the mood struck."

Vanessa arrived first, naturally punctual and serene, dressed in a cashmere cardigan over her pajamas and carrying what looked like a coordinated care package. She had a bottle of Red wine, a basket of homemade scones wrapped in a linen cloth, and a lavender-scented eye mask that looked medically engineered.

"I didn't know the vibe," Vanessa said, stepping inside and slipping off her shoes, "so I brought options."

"You look like you're here for a bougie wellness retreat," Nora teased.

Vanessa smiled. "Good. That means I'm blending in."

Next came Rina—trailing a giant turquoise beanbag, a karaoke mic that was already on and crackling with static, and a plastic bag of gummy bears so enormous it could've doubled as a flotation device.

"This is either going to be epic," she declared, barging in with glitter eyeliner already halfway smudged, "or a crime scene."

Then Lulu burst through the door wearing fuzzy unicorn slippers, heart-print pajama pants, and a hoodie that read **Chaos Queen** in sequins. She had a rainbow pillow under one arm and a gallon-sized Ziploc bag labeled "Emergency Snacks & Emotional Band-Aids."

She flung her arms around Nora like they were long-lost sisters reunited on a reality show. "I've already claimed the left side of the couch and all emotional breakdowns after 10 p.m.!"

"Noted," Nora said, laughing.

"Also, I brought three different face masks, one bottle of rosewater spray, and a tarot deck," Lulu added, already tossing her stuff onto the couch. "Because you never know where the night might take us."

The Masters Club

By the time the living room filled with blankets, glitter, throw pillows, and mismatched wine glasses, it looked less like a grown-up gathering and more like a teenage fever dream—which, somehow, was exactly the point.

Someone queued up a playlist that bounced between nostalgic girl power anthems and moody indie folk. Rina started doing warm-ups for karaoke. Vanessa was slicing her scones into perfect halves on a little bamboo cutting board she'd brought from home.

And Nora? Nora stood at the edge of the room and let the sound of it all wash over her. Laughter, overlapping voices, the occasional shriek from Lulu. The clink of glasses. The sound of belonging.

She hadn't realized how quiet her house had been until now. How hollow it had felt—even when David was still there, sitting across the table with his pointed silences and watch-checking disinterest.

But this? This noise? This chaos? This was joy and she was in the center of it.

The night unfolded in layers—first with board games that dissolved into storytelling, then with cocktail experiments that went terribly wrong. (Lulu's attempt at a "Strawberry Basil Explosion" ended with a sticky mess and the blender nearly catching fire.) They danced in socks on Nora's hardwood floor to a '90s playlist that somehow knew every one of their high school anthems and launched into a full-on debate over which boy band had aged the best.

"It's clearly NSYNC," Rina declared, twirling a glittery pen like a gavel. "Justin's still got it."

"Excuse me," Vanessa said, eyebrow arched. "Have we forgotten about AJ from the Backstreet Boys? That man is a silver fox now."

"Wrong," Lulu shouted from under a blanket fort she'd made on the couch. "It's Hanson. I don't care what anyone says. That middle one? Peak lumberjack energy."

Nora couldn't stop smiling. Her cheeks ached from it. The good kind of ache.

Eventually, they sank into a tangle of throw pillows and laughter, the music softening to a hum in the background. The string lights Nora had haphazardly pinned along the windows cast a warm, forgiving glow across the room.

"Okay," Lulu said, flopping back onto a floor cushion, a bowl of popcorn balanced on her stomach. "Time for real talk. Who here has cried in their car in the last month?"

All four hands went up.

Vanessa, surprisingly, spoke first. She sat cross-legged, back straight like she was about to deliver a boardroom presentation, but her voice cracked. "Sometimes I look in the mirror and don't recognize the woman staring back. Not because she's older—but because I don't remember choosing her."

Silence.

Then Rina leaned over and gently squeezed her hand. "You're still in there," she said softly. "You're just under construction."

Vanessa smiled, watery but real.

Lulu cleared her throat dramatically, wiping a single theatrical tear from her cheek. "Okay, my turn. I once broke up with a guy because he ate string cheese like a monster—sideways, like a psychopath."

The room exploded into laughter. Loud. Cathartic. The kind that carried grief and joy in the same breath.

Rina, cheeks flushed from laughing, added next. "I got let go from my job last year. Told everyone it was 'a personal sabbatical for creativity,' but the truth is, I was crushed. I felt useless. Swimming was the first thing that didn't make me feel like a failure."

The air shifted again. Not heavy, just honest.

Finally, Nora spoke. Quiet at first, unsure if the words would land right, but something about the glow of the lights, the swirl of cheap cocktails, the permission in their presence made her feel safe.

"I stayed in a marriage too long because I didn't want to disappoint everyone else," she said. "And because I thought being loved meant being small. Less noisy. Less needy. Less me."

Lulu sat up, eyes fierce. "Screw. That."

Rina raised her glass. "To taking up space."

Vanessa added, "And filling it with exactly who we are."

Nora blinked fast but didn't look away. "To finally becoming the main character."

They clinked glasses. Not just cocktails—but truths. Tiny toasts to the pieces they were gathering and reassembling.

Outside, the wind rustled through the trees. Inside, there was nothing but warmth, safety, and a feeling that maybe—just maybe—they were healing. Together.

Sometime around midnight, the living room was a pastel battlefield of face mask packets, empty scone plates, and glitter confetti that no one remembered opening.

Nora was lying on her stomach with her chin on a throw pillow, trying not to fall asleep to the soft hum of a '90s slow jam. Vanessa had claimed the armchair and was dutifully knitting something indeterminate with hyper-focus. Rina was mid-karaoke, dramatically crooning into her Bluetooth mic, while Lulu draped herself across the couch like an exhausted Greek goddess in unicorn slippers.

Then, without warning, Lulu sat bolt upright and pointed a neon-pink fingernail toward her tote bag. "We need a charter," she declared, eyes wide like she'd just discovered gravity. "Every cult—I mean, club—needs one."

Vanessa looked up from her knitting, deadpan. "Do cults normally wear this much glitter?"

"Yes," Rina answered, still holding the mic. "Glitter is canon."

Lulu rummaged in her bag like a raccoon on a mission and emerged victorious with a spiral-bound notebook covered in holographic cat stickers and what might have been a smear of lip gloss. She grabbed a marker, already uncapped, and flipped to a clean page.

"Okay, founding rules. Yell them out. No filter. No regrets."

"I regret nothing," Rina said, flopping dramatically onto the beanbag.

"Rule one," Lulu said, writing in loopy cursive. "No apologizing for crying. Ever."

"Especially not during slow-motion Olympic montages," Nora murmured.

"Or animal rescue TikToks," Vanessa added solemnly.

"Rule two," Lulu continued, "no judging swimsuit choices. Bikinis, tankinis, sports bras—we embrace the full spectrum of aquatic fashion."

"Even the ones with ruffles?" Rina asked.

"Especially the ones with ruffles," Lulu replied. "It's called texture."

Nora giggled, her cheeks still glowing faintly from the glitter peel-off mask that hadn't quite come off in one piece.

"Rule three," Vanessa said softly, "vulnerability points are real...and earned."

"Yes!" Lulu shouted. "And redeemable for snacks or unsolicited pep talks."

"Emergency glitter is always allowed," Rina tossed in.

"Clarify that," Vanessa said. "Glitter bombs are banned. Glitter support is encouraged."

"Add that. Important distinction," Lulu noted, scribbling.

"Rule five," Nora said, her voice quiet but sure. "We show up. No matter what."

The marker paused for a beat, her words lingering in the air.

"Damn," Lulu whispered. "That one gets a heart."

Rina reached over, plucked the pen from Lulu's hand, and drew a star at the top of the page. **"Lane 4: Where the mess is welcome."**

They all sat there for a beat, absorbing it. The quiet felt different now—not heavy, not hollow, but full. Like something sacred had just been said out loud and sealed with purple ink and a glitter sticker.

"Okay," Rina said, clearing her throat. "Now who wants to play M.A.S.H. and manifest a wildly unrealistic future with Jason Momoa and a pet llama?"

They all raised their hands at once.

Hours later, most of Lane 4 had drifted off—Rina curled up on the beanbag, one hand still loosely clutching her karaoke mic; Lulu snoring softly beneath a mountain of throw pillows with a tiara askew on her forehead. Vanessa had claimed the corner of the couch with military precision, blanket tucked just so, knitting still looped around her fingers.

Nora couldn't sleep. She padded softly into the kitchen, the hardwood cool beneath her bare feet. The silence buzzed with the kind of peace that only came after a night of laughing too hard and saying too much. She filled a glass with water and leaned against the counter, letting the hum of the fridge fill the space.

A moment later, footsteps. Vanessa appeared in the doorway, wrapped in a navy robe with a constellation print that made her look like she'd stepped out of a quiet galaxy. She didn't say anything right away, just joined Nora at the counter and reached for her own glass.

"You okay?" she asked gently, voice rough with sleep but laced with curiosity, not concern.

Nora looked down at her hands, still smudged with a bit of glitter glue. "I am now," she said softly. "I think I forgot what this felt like. Being seen and not having to perform."

Vanessa nodded, exhaling through her nose. "Yeah," she murmured. "Me too."

They stood in companionable silence, sipping water like it was sacrament. The moonlight slipped through the kitchen blinds, catching in the shimmer still clinging to Nora's cheekbone.

"I've spent so long keeping it together for everyone else," Vanessa said after a long pause. "My kids, my husband, my coworkers. I didn't even notice how much of myself I'd packed away. Like emotional Tupperware, sealed tight."

Nora gave a quiet, breathy laugh. "And tonight we popped the lids off."

Vanessa smiled. "With glitter cannons."

They both chuckled—soft, tired, and real. There was no need for big declarations or promises. Just the quiet knowledge that something had shifted. That in a house full of mismatched wine glasses, crumpled throw blankets, and broken-open hearts. They had built something that would last. A team. A sisterhood. A revolution in pajama pants.

Women who'd been told—by the world, by men, by their own reflections—that they were too much, or not enough. Women who had been left, overlooked, underestimated. and yet, here they were.

Not just surviving but saving each other. In the most ordinary, extraordinary ways. With laughter. With glitter. With space to fall apart and still be invited back in. Come morning, they'd lace up again—maybe still tired, maybe still healing—but stronger. Together.

The Masters Club

Before Lane 4

Nora: Three Hundred and Twelve Days Before Lane 4

The toast burned, but Nora didn't notice until the scent curled into her nose—sharp, acrid, like something unraveling. She blinked. Pulled the slices out with a fork and stared at them. Blackened. Ruined. Useless.

She scraped them into the trash and started over. The house was silent. No background podcast. No clink of dishes from upstairs. Just the hum of the refrigerator and the soft drag of the butter knife against ceramic.

She hadn't spoken to David in days. Not really. A mumbled "hey" when he got in late Tuesday night, carrying the scent of cologne she didn't recognize. A grunt when she asked if they needed anything from the store. Then nothing. Not even the sound of him coming to bed last night—because he hadn't.

She stood barefoot on the cold tile floor, waiting for the toaster to pop. Her hand hovered above a plate, mind drifting through a list of errands she wouldn't do and emails she wouldn't answer.

Behind her, the door opened. She didn't turn around. David moved to the fridge. The suction-pull pop of the door sounded too loud in the quiet. Then, without warning—without weight—he said it:

"I think I'm going to move out for a while."

No anger. No preamble. Just seven words, dropped like a glass onto concrete.

Nora didn't move. She buttered her toast. Slow. Even. Her hand shook once, but only once.

David leaned on the counter like he was commenting on the weather. "This isn't working. You've... changed. We both have."

She turned to look at him. Not surprised. Not even sad, not exactly. Just... hollowed out by how unsurprising it was.

He looked back at her, searching for something—guilt, regret, maybe even a fight.

She didn't give him one. Instead, she nodded once. A tiny, barely-there movement that said more than any plea ever could.

"Okay," she said softly.

That was it. No dramatic monologue. No suitcase hurling. No last-ditch effort to salvage what had already rotted beneath them because somewhere along the way, he had stopped choosing her—and she had stopped asking to be chosen.

He left an hour later. Packed two bags, grabbed his records, and paused in the doorway like he might say something important.

He didn't. The door clicked shut behind him.

Nora didn't cry. Didn't scream. She just stood in the kitchen, hands resting on the counter, feeling the silence swell like a bruise.

The toast had gone cold. She ate it anyway.

Vanessa – 189 days before Lane 4

The morning started with a cough. Then two. Then three.

By 7:42 a.m., all three kids were piled on the couch, flushed cheeks, glassy eyes, and a symphony of sniffles playing in the background. The baby had a fever. The twins were fighting over the iPad. Somewhere in the distance, the dryer buzzed like a warning siren she didn't have time to heed.

Vanessa balanced a thermometer in one hand and her phone in the other, texting her boss with one thumb while pouring orange juice with the other. Her hair was in a half-fallen bun, yoga pants covered in oatmeal, and a cold cup of coffee stared at her accusingly from the microwave.

"Mom! He touched me!"

"She started it!"

"Where's my hedgehog shirt?"

"Everyone just—breathe," she muttered, more to herself than to them.

At 9:00 a.m., she logged onto Zoom with one hand while holding a sobbing toddler in the other. She faked a smile, nodded through marketing updates, and dropped "circle back" into the conversation just enough to seem present. Meanwhile, the baby sneezed directly onto her keyboard.

At 12:15 p.m., she burned the grilled cheese. At 12:16, she remembered the laundry from two days ago, now a sad, mildewed lump in the washer. At 12:30, she scraped half-melted crayons off the wall while nursing the baby and microwaving mac and cheese for the third time that week.

At 4:00 p.m., Ballet. Addy's 4:00 ballet class. Pickup was 5:15.

At 5:42, Vanessa's phone buzzed. Ballet Studio: Addy is waiting at the front desk. Please let us know if someone is coming to pick her up.

Her stomach flipped. Ice water down her spine. "Oh my god." Shoes. Purse. Keys. No coat. She barely remembered to turn off the stove. The ballet studio was fifteen minutes away. She made it in eleven, heart pounding, teeth clenched, cursing every red light like it was personal.

When she pushed open the door, she saw her daughter—pink leotard, glittery hair bow drooping— curled in the arms of the instructor, tear-streaked cheeks and hiccupping sobs.

Vanessa crossed the room too fast, too loud.

"I'm so sorry," she gasped, scooping Addy into her arms. "I'm so, so sorry."

Her daughter clung to her, silent now, but heavy with disappointment.

"It's okay," the instructor said gently. "These things happen."

Vanessa nodded. Smiled. Thanked her. Promised it wouldn't happen again. She held it together until they got home. Until Addy was tucked into bed with extra stories and too many apologies.

Only then—when the house was finally quiet—did Vanessa slip into the bathroom, lock the door, and slide down the wall until her knees hit tile.

She didn't sob. Didn't wail. Just let the silent tears fall. No one knocked. No one called her name. No one asked where dinner was, and as she sat there, cheeks damp, head resting against the cold wall, one thought lodged itself in her chest like a splinter:

She couldn't remember the last time someone asked her if she was okay.

Rina – 103 Days Before Lane 4

She wore glitter eyeliner that morning—not because it matched her mood, but because it was Friday and she needed something to believe in.

The office smelled like burnt coffee and stale air conditioning. Her inbox was a nightmare, but Rina had already half-checked out, planning which rooftop bar she'd hit that evening. She spun in her chair, sipping iced coffee and typing aggressively into Slack about whether or not to make her dog an Instagram account. Her coworkers laughed. She played the part well—too well. Always a mood, always the energy.

So when the HR rep tapped on her doorframe, face tight and voice too gentle, she didn't flinch. Just grinned and said, "What's up? We finally getting those standing desks?"

The meeting lasted exactly six minutes. Budget cuts. Realignment. It's not personal. Rina cracked a joke. Something about being honored to be sacrificed to the gods of Q1. The HR woman didn't even smile. They gave her a branded box to pack her things.

Outside, the sun was mocking her—way too bright for the kind of day this was. She sat down hard on the curb, skirt wrinkling beneath her, heels digging into concrete.

Mascara smudged when she wiped her eyes with the back of her hand. She didn't care. She opened her phone and did something she'd told herself she wouldn't do again—texted her ex. *You were right. They let me go. I don't know what I'm doing. Can we talk?*

Three dots appeared.

Then vanished.

Then nothing.

Rina let out a half-laugh, half-sob. A sound that made the woman walking past her flinch and speed up. She sat there for a long time, the box of her life beside her, her reflection caught in the mirrored glass of the building she no longer belonged to.

When she finally got home—past the doorman who avoided her eyes, up the elevator that took forever—she dropped her bag by the door and stood in the middle of her apartment, uncertain what to do with her hands.

The silence was immediate. Vast. Unforgiving. She turned on music, then turned it off. Sat on the couch. Stood again. Walked into the kitchen and stared into the fridge like it might offer a plan, but the stillness just pressed harder.

The silence was so loud it made her want to scream.

Lulu – 58 Days Before Lane 4

The diner smelled like waffles and heartbreak. Lulu sat across from her friend Jenna in a red vinyl booth that squeaked every time someone shifted. Her coffee was already cold, her eggs untouched. She was scrolling Instagram, pinky finger stained from the glitter nail polish she'd slapped on at midnight the night before because "hot mess but make it festive" was all she had left in the tank.

Jenna was mid-rant about her boss when Lulu stopped listening. Her thumb froze. There it was. A diamond that looked like it had its own mortgage.

She said yes

Lulu stared at the screen, heart snagging on the caption like a sweater on barbed wire. The photo was filtered within an inch of its life—rose petals, champagne, a beach proposal at golden hour. Perfect. Effortless. The kind of staged magic she used to dream about when she still believed in timing and twin flames and being someone's first choice.

The caption didn't mention her name, of course. Why would it? People didn't tag the ex-girlfriend they dated for eight years before suddenly deciding they "weren't the marrying type."

Her hand started to shake.

"Holy hell," she muttered, flashing the phone to Jenna. "Look who just leveled up in delusion."

Jenna blinked. "Oh. Wow. Are you okay?"

Lulu snorted. "Please. I hope they name their first kid Tax Write-Off."

She tossed the phone onto the table like it burned, but her laugh was too loud. Her smile too tight. She didn't touch her coffee again.

Later, in the car, it all fell apart. She climbed into the driver's seat, slammed the door shut, and just sat there. Breathing fast. Not blinking. The silence of the car was too much—too honest.

Then it hit her. A sob ripped from her throat like it had been waiting for permission.

And then another.

And then another.

She slammed her hands against the steering wheel, forehead pressed to the leather and screamed. Full-body, primal, hiccuping heartbreak.

"It was supposed to be me," she choked out between gasps. "It was supposed to be me."

She didn't know how long she sat there. The sun dipped lower. Her mascara bled into the corners of her mouth. Her phone lay somewhere in the backseat, flung there in a moment of rage, a casualty of the truth.

That night, she drove home, took off the hoodie that still smelled like him, and dropped it in the trash. Then she bought glitter sneakers on clearance at 2 a.m. and decided to start over.

Because if she was going to break, she'd at least do it loud, messy, and covered in sparkle.

Simon – 39 Days Before Lane 4

The pool was empty but Simon walked its edge like it still had something to answer for.

Chlorine clung to the air like a memory he couldn't shake—sunrise practices, torn calluses, the sound of his own breath echoing inside his swim cap. It wasn't just a sport. It had been everything…and then it wasn't.

He stopped at Lane 4. Looked down at the still water. Flat. Deceiving. It looked peaceful, but he knew better. Water could pull you under and make it look like grace.

He could still feel the sting of it. The Olympic Trials. Final heat. One blink too slow. One breath too long.

The race had lasted mere seconds and yet, it managed to undo an entire decade of sacrifice. He'd given the water his body, his time, his future. Missed birthdays. Missed funerals. Pushed away friends. Watched the woman he thought he'd marry pack up her life and walk out the door while he sat icing his shoulder, too obsessed with his next split time to notice she was already gone.

When his father got sick, Simon hadn't gone home. He'd sent flower and a message that said, "I'll visit after the Trials." His dad died three weeks later. He never got the chance to say goodbye. The hardest part wasn't the loss. It was what came after.

The silence. His girlfriend didn't wait. His mom barely spoke to him now. His teammates stopped calling when he stopped winning. No dramatic blow-up. No betrayal that screamed in Technicolor. Just people slipping away, one quiet exit at a time—until he was the only one left, staring down an empty lane with a name on the board that no longer meant anything.

He hadn't been in the water—really in it—in almost four years. Not more than a few laps. Not without feeling like the pool might swallow him whole.

Not since everything he loved turned into a graveyard
for the version of himself he couldn't bring back.

He told himself he became a coach to give back.
But the truth? He needed the pool to need him. To
pretend he still belonged. To stay close to greatness
even if he couldn't reach it anymore.

"Coach?"

Simon turned.

Marcus, the night janitor, leaned on his mop near
the bleachers. His brow furrowed. "You alright?"

Simon paused. "Yeah."

His voice sounded foreign. Thin.

Marcus offered a wry smile. "Just you and your
ghosts again, huh?"

Simon forced a breath through his nose.
"Something like that."

He didn't say that his ghosts had names. Didn't say
that sometimes, when he woke up in the middle of the
night, he still reached for a body that wasn't there.
Didn't say that when he heard the splash of a relay start,
it felt like being punched in the chest. He just nodded
once, sharp and tight, and walked away.

The pool didn't look back but it didn't have to. It
had already taken everything and he'd let it. Because he
didn't know who he was without it and no one had
stayed long enough to help him figure it out.

Back then, they hadn't known. Not when Nora stood barefoot in the driveway, her breath fogging the cold morning air, the echo of David's words still stinging like a slap.

Not when Vanessa apologized to her crying daughter with a voice too calm to be real, then locked herself in the bathroom and crumbled behind the door.

Not when Rina sat on the curb outside her old office, hugging a cardboard box like it was armor, her phone a silent witness to her invisibility.

Not when Lulu screamed in her car, mascara streaked and heart cracked, hurling her phone and her pride into the dark.

Not when Simon stood on the pool deck for the last time, spine straight but soul sinking, the silence so loud it felt like judgment.

They hadn't known that while their lives were splintering, the center was already shifting. That there were others—just like them—cracking in private, braving it in public, holding themselves together with stubbornness and sarcasm and a desperate kind of hope. They hadn't met yet. Hadn't seen each other, but the undertow had already begun pulling them to the same shore.

Now—they know. Now they recognize the ghosts behind each other's smiles. They know the tone of forced cheer, the silence that hides a scream, the armor worn in plain sight. They've seen the versions of themselves that fell apart and they've witnessed the ones who chose to begin again anyway.

Lane 4 didn't save them. They did that themselves, but it gave them the space to be broken and brave at the same time. To swim through the wreckage, not away from it. To find something like healing in the wake of everything they lost.

They hadn't known, back then. That something new was coming. That they weren't alone, but they know now, and that changed everything.

Stirring the Surface

The sun crept through the blinds with a smug sort of confidence—like it knew a secret she hadn't quite admitted yet. Nora stretched beneath the covers, the sheets sliding over skin still warm from sleep and soreness. Not pain—the good kind. The kind that reminded her she'd earned every ache. That she was changing.

Her thoughts wandered instantly—inevitably—to him. Specifically, Simon's message.

There's a lot more your wrist can do.

A breath hitched in her chest. Her mouth curved slowly, secretive. She should probably be embarrassed. She wasn't. Instead, she let herself feel it: the zing of desire, the unexpected thrum of wanting. Not just attention, not even validation. Craving. Play. Chemistry. Connection.

The kind that made you choose your swimsuit like it mattered, and today? It mattered.

She stepped in front of the mirror, still in her sleep shirt. Her hair was chaos, and there was a faint crease across her cheek, but her eyes—her eyes were alive. Curious. Lit from somewhere inside.

Nora didn't reach for her usual grab-and-go gear. Today, she slipped into her deep navy one-piece, the one with the low back and just enough mesh to raise an eyebrow. Modest enough to swim. Bare enough to make someone lose focus. She tugged a hoodie over it and tossed her wet hair into a loose knot.

Let him notice. Let him look. She'd damn well look back.

Sliding into the driver's seat, her phone buzzed. Right on cue.

Simon: *You sleep okay?*

Nora: *Eventually. Took a while to come down from that lesson.*

Simon: *Funny… I was thinking about your form all night.*

Nora: *You mean my flip turns? Or the part where your hand was on my waist?*

Simon: *Yes.*

Nora: *Bold answer, Coach.*

Simon: *You didn't seem to mind.*

Nora: *I didn't say I did.*

Simon: *Good. Because I've got a few more techniques in mind for today.*

Nora: *Is that part of the official training plan?*

Simon: *Let's just say Lane 4 is about to get… intense.*

Nora: *Mmm. Guess I better warm up.*

Simon: *Don't. I like you a little breathless.*

Nora: *Careful, Simon. Keep that up and you just might end up in my next story.*

Simon: *Just promise I get the witty dialogue and a happy ending.*

She tossed the phone into the passenger seat, but the hum in her veins didn't settle. This wasn't just texting. It was foreplay, with words, with power, with possibility and God, it felt good to want again. The pool might be cold. But she was already burning. Today wasn't just practice. It was a spark and she was ready to let it catch fire.

The pool was already bustling when Nora arrived, the humid air buzzing with movement and the slap of feet on wet tile. Lane 4 was mid-warmup, and the energy was sharp, charged.

"Perfect timing!" Rina called. "Coach is making us race for bragging rights today."

Simon stood at the whiteboard, scribbling relay groups and heat times. His whistle hung loosely from his neck, and his hair was still dripping from his own laps.

When he looked up and caught Nora's eye, there was a flicker—a half-smile paired with a slow, deliberate once-over that made her stomach flip. She raised a brow at him.

He didn't look away.

Instead, he mouthed, "Distractions, remember?"

She bit back a smile and gave him a subtle shake of her head, equal parts warning and invitation.

"Relay drills today," he announced, turning back to the group. "We're breaking into two teams. Lane 4 versus Lane 3."

Groans and mock cheers erupted.

"Don't act like you're not into it," Simon teased. "Best overall time wins the good towels."

"Finally, the high stakes we deserve," Rina deadpanned.

They paired up. Nora ended up first in her lane. Simon walked over, crouched at her side, his hand bracing on the edge of the pool. Close enough for her to smell the sharp clean of chlorine on his skin and that cedar note she'd started to associate with mornings that made her pulse race.

"Keep your breathing tight and stroke long. You've got the strength—you just need the rhythm," he said, voice low and deliberate.

His shoulder brushed hers as he leaned in, as if by accident. It wasn't.

"Also," he added, his voice dipping just for her, "I rearranged the heat order so you'd race against Lane 3's loudest trash-talker. Figured I'd give you a little extra motivation."

She gave him a smirk. "Careful, Coach. Keep whispering sweet swim notes like that and I might start thinking you're flirting."

Simon's gaze didn't flinch. "Wouldn't want to confuse your pacing."

She tilted her head. "Who says I'm the one getting flustered?"

He chuckled, low and warm. "Then bring that same fire to the starting block—unless you need me to distract you a little more."

Her eyes narrowed, playful. "You'd like that, wouldn't you?"

He leaned in just a hair. "Only if it works."

The whistle blew, and she dove.

The water wrapped around her like silk this time. Not hostile, not overwhelming. She moved with it, not against it. Each kick felt powerful. Each stroke intentional.

She touched the wall and popped up, gasping but exhilarated.

"You crushed it," Vanessa yelled.

Simon clapped slowly from the deck. "Nice work. Clean form, and no splash. You're showing off now."

Nora tried to play it cool, but the praise sent a rush straight to her cheeks. She met his eyes just long enough to feel the heat again—just under the surface.

After the full set of relays, Simon gathered them around.

"That," he said, "is the energy I want at the Masters meet. You're all officially invited. No pressure, but if you want to prove how badass you really are…"

"Wait, wait," Rina said. "You're actually serious?"

"I'm always serious," he replied, grinning. "Especially when I'm out of good towels."

Laughter broke out, but Nora stayed quiet, her pulse still racing. The idea of racing in public still scared her, but when Simon looked her way, his expression lingered—not just proud but inviting. Like he wasn't just challenging her to race. He was daring her to keep showing up.

As the group disbanded, Simon approached her again, this time without a clipboard.

"Nice job out there," he said, voice softer now.

"Thanks," she said, still catching her breath.

He stepped just a little closer. "Next time, I want to see you anchor the relay. All eyes on you."

She swallowed. "That sounds... intense."

His lips quirked, and he leaned in slightly closer than strictly professional. "It is, but I think you can handle intensity."

Her pulse kicked. "I think I can too."

Simon's gaze dipped briefly—lips, collarbone, back to her eyes. A low hum of tension crackled in the space between them.

He straightened, just enough to reset the moment, but his voice stayed low. "Good. Because I'm not going easy on you, Lane 4."

Nora grinned, breath catching. "Wouldn't want you to."

The air in the locker room was heavy with steam, lavender body wash, and the high of a workout well survived. Nora wrapped a towel around her waist and sank onto the bench between Rina and Vanessa, her pulse still racing from the relay win.

Vanessa leaned in, all mischievous eyes. "Okay, are we going to talk about it or pretend we didn't all see it?"

Nora blinked. "See what?"

Rina snorted. "You two had more chemistry in lane four than I've had in my last three relationships."

Nora tried to laugh it off, but the blush on her cheeks was impossible to hide. "It's not like that."

"Yet," Vanessa sing-songed. "But it could be. And honestly, we support it."

Lulu pulled her wet cap off, letting her curls spring free. "He's cute. Steady. Has a whistle. What more could you want?"

"A time machine," Nora said under her breath. "To warn past me how complicated feelings get after divorce."

The words surprised her and silenced the others. Vanessa reached for her hand. "That's fair. But also? You're allowed to want something new. Or someone new."

"I don't even know if I'm ready for... anything," Nora admitted. "And it's not just about Simon. I spent years swallowing things—my needs, my opinions, my joy—just to keep the peace, and now, even the idea of letting someone close again makes me feel... brittle."

Rina nodded slowly. "It's not weakness. It's scar tissue. It tells the story of where you've been but it doesn't have to decide where you're going."

"I don't want to lose myself again," Nora whispered.

"You won't," Vanessa said firmly. "Because this time, you're not building your life around someone else. You're building it around you."

They sat in silence for a beat, the soft clatter of lockers and distant hum of hair dryers the only soundtrack. Then Lulu added, "If Simon breaks your heart, we'll hold him underwater until he sees the error of his ways."

Nora laughed, the tension cracking like sun through fog. They all laughed with her, the kind of laugh that closed wounds and opened doors. "I mean it," Vanessa added, eyes soft now. "Whatever happens, you've got us."

Nora smiled. Big. Genuine. She wasn't alone in this. Not anymore and even if she wasn't sure what came next, she knew who had her back, and that made all the difference.

That night, after a dinner scraped together from leftovers and the tail end of a Pinot Grigio, Nora curled up on the couch under her favorite threadbare blanket—faded floral, soft with time. Her body ached in that delicious way that meant she was doing something real, something that made her muscles and her life feel earned.

She reached for her phone, intending to scroll mindlessly before bed. But the screen lit up with a name she hadn't seen in weeks, David. The message was short.

David: *Saw a photo of you on that swim club page. Didn't know chlorine could fix everything.*

Her breath caught—sharp, involuntary. Not hello. Not how are you. Just that signature blend of sarcasm and cruelty, tossed like a dart with a grin behind it. He'd seen the picture, probably Rina's doing—of Lane 4, soaked and beaming, their arms slung over each other after practice. Nora was in the middle, wet hair slicked back, grinning like she'd won something. Maybe she had.

David… He couldn't stand seeing joy he didn't cause. He never had.

Her thumb hovered over the screen. The old muscle memory of typing something appeasing or disarming. A joke, maybe. A shrug. Anything to keep the peace, but peace with David had always meant silence. Shrinking. Smiling when she wanted to scream.

Didn't know chlorine could fix everything.

That wasn't curiosity. That was a reminder of who she used to be. Of how easily he expected her to fold.

She locked the phone. Let it fall to the blanket beside her.

Then sat there, motionless, as the heat of the text crawled up her spine and turned into something else. Resolve.

She reached for her journal—the old one, the one she hadn't opened since the night she stopped asking herself if she was too much. Flipped to a clean page. Wrote:

When he saw joy, he laughed. When I saw it, I stayed."

She paused. Then added:

I don't belong in his past anymore. I belong in my own future.

The ink pooled slightly at the edge of the word belong. Like it meant it. For the first time all day, her hands stopped shaking, because that was the difference now: He could still try to dim her light, but she'd finally learned how to keep it on.

***

Simon sat on the edge of his bed, sweat still cooling on his skin from the lap set he'd forced himself through after practice. The apartment was dim—just the glow of the streetlight bleeding in through half-closed blinds, the soft whirr of the fan working overtime in the corner.

He should've been asleep. Or reviewing tomorrow's training schedule. Or literally anything other than thinking about Nora, but here he was…again.

His phone buzzed once. Her name lit up the screen.

Like it always did lately—right when he started convincing himself to draw a line.

Nora: *Couldn't sleep.*

He let the message sit there, pulsing. Everything in his body reacted before his brain had a chance to reason it down.

He replied:

Simon: *Can't sleep either. Probably your fault.*

Nora: *Probably?*

Simon: *Definitely.*

The way you looked at me today? Dangerous.

There was a pause.

Long enough to make him think maybe she'd tapped the brakes.

Then:

Nora: *It wasn't just a look.*

Jesus.

He stood up, crossed to the window, needing the cool glass under his hand. His heart was racing and they hadn't even touched outside the water in days.

Simon: *You're not making this easy.*

Nora: *I'm not trying to.*

I don't want easy. I want real.

He closed his eyes. That did it. That opened something deeper —because it wasn't just about heat anymore.

It was the way she saw him. Past the coach. Past the control. Past the history and he wanted to see her back. All of her.

Simon: *Tell me something real then.*

Something no one else knows.

Nora: *I used to sleep facing the door, just in case he came home mad.*

His breath left him. It wasn't flirtation anymore. It was intimacy. He sat down hard on the bed, chest tight. Typed. Deleted. Then sent:

Simon: *Four years. That's how long it's been since I let anyone get close. Since I stopped believing people actually stay.*

Nora: *You deserve someone who stays.*

He stared at those words like they were a balm and a dare.

Like they'd reached past his ribs and touched something still bruised.

Simon: *You're getting under my skin, Nora.*

And I'm not sure I want you to stop.

She didn't respond right away.

And when she did—

Nora: *Then don't stop me.*

That was it. No games. No coyness. Just truth, typed in a dark room by a woman who wasn't scared to want more.

Simon set the phone down slowly. His heart was pounding. His palms were hot. But his mind? Clear. He wasn't falling anymore. He was choosing and when the next practice came, it wouldn't be about the stroke or the laps or the line they weren't supposed to cross.

It would be about them. Two people scarred and surviving. Wanting more and finally brave enough to reach for it.

Namaste and Nonsense

Vanessa stood outside the squat stucco building, arms crossed, eyes narrowed at the wooden sign like it had personally offended her.

Zen on the Hill: Recharge. Realign. Reimagine.

She scowled. "Is this a spa or a cult?"

"I try not to label things," Lulu said breezily, swanning past in a flowing tunic and a headscarf that made her look like a wellness influencer who churned her own almond milk and saged her inbox. "Let's just be open to the energy."

"I'm open to regretting this already," Vanessa muttered.

They'd signed up for the 'Elevate & Unwind' retreat mostly as a joke. Lulu had sent the link in their group text with too many sparkle emojis, Rina had impulsively Venmoed the deposit while wine shopping online, and Nora... Nora had been too emotionally exhausted to say no.

Now here they were—forty-five minutes outside the city, no Wi-Fi, no caffeine, no escape. They arrived in waves; Rina, in galaxy-print leggings covered in tiny cats doing yoga poses, balancing two matcha lattes in direct defiance of the "cleanse your vessel" morning juice ritual. Vanessa, gripping a venti Starbucks with both hands like it was life support. Nora, already wondering how she'd ended up trading chlorine and lane lines for chakra alignment and essential oil diffusers.

Lulu met them at the check-in table, somehow already glowing.

"Okay," she chirped, handing out small pastel name tags. "Instead of your name, write your intention for the day."

"My intention is to not pull a groin muscle," Vanessa said flatly.

"Perfect," Lulu beamed. "Write that."

Rina scribbled **World Peace (but make it cute)** in glitter gel pen.

Nora hesitated, then wrote *Be here.*

She wasn't sure she meant it yet. But it felt like a start.

Within minutes, they were ushered toward the lawn for the first session: 'Heart-Opening Goat Yoga.'

"I don't trust any activity with that many adjectives," Vanessa hissed.

They were handed yoga mats, essential oil mists and a warning to avoid stepping in goat poop, which apparently was abundant and unbothered by intentions.

Halfway through cat-cow, a brown goat named Nugget launched herself onto Vanessa's back like a tiny four-legged acrobat in a trust fall gone rogue.

"What the hell!" Vanessa shouted, tipping sideways and knocking over Rina's water bottle.

The instructor, who wore a shirt that said Namaste, Bitches—didn't blink. "That's Nugget. She senses resistance and offers support."

"She's about to sense my foot in her—"

"Vanessa," Nora wheezed, laughing so hard she nearly face-planted into child's pose.

Meanwhile, Rina was trying to take selfies with a goat named Bubbles and Lulu was attempting to "channel her inner alignment" while a third goat gnawed serenely on her scarf tassels.

A baby goat peed on someone's mat. Someone else shrieked. Vanessa was muttering curses under her breath in downward dog while still holding her coffee.

It was bedlam. Earthy, smelly, giggle-stained bedlam. Nora didn't feel broken. Or behind, or like a woman half-drowning in the mess of her own life. For the first time in a long time, she just felt… here. Present. Silly. Alive. When they were finally corralled inside—hair askew, leggings dotted with hay and questionable footprints—for their next session, she was still smiling.

The laughter still clung to the walls as they filed back inside—looser now, lighter. Goat yoga had delivered: pure, ridiculous chaos. A baby goat had knocked over Rina's water bottle, another had pooped on Lulu's mat (to her great delight), and everyone had fallen into fits of uncontrollable giggles at least once. It had been absurd and freeing.

Even Vanessa, usually composed and curated had laughed so hard she snorted, then covered her face in mock horror.

Now the mood shifted. The lights dimmed. The music softened to a hum you could feel more than hear. Cushions replaced yoga mats. Journals and pens were passed out with reverence.

"Write down what you're carrying," the instructor said gently, "that no longer serves you." Silence settled like fog. Nora held the journal in her lap. The cover was soft, the paper thick and forgiving.

What are you carrying?

She thought of the goat that had jumped onto her back and the way she'd laughed without flinching, without shrinking, without caring if she looked foolish. How rare that was for her to let go like that.

The pen hovered.

She wanted to write:

The feeling that I need to be small to be loved.

She almost did.

But instead, she wrote:

The idea that I'm too late to begin again.

Her breath caught. The words sat there, exposed and unapologetic because naming it made it real, and releasing it—if she dared—meant stepping into something unknown. Something that could become hers.

She drew a soft line beneath the sentence. Then, smaller:

I want to take up space.
I want to be the main character.
I want to want more and not apologize for it.
I want to stop asking for permission to matter.

Her eyes lifted for a moment. Vanessa sat cross-legged, head down, scribbling fast and sharp like the truth might outrun her if she didn't pin it down. Rina had stopped writing and was just staring at the page, unmoving. Lulu was unusually still, her brows knit, fingers tapping the pen against her lips as if uncertain where to begin. Each of them, silent in their own unraveling.

Nora looked back at what she had written. It wasn't everything, but it was a crack in the wall. A sliver of light and for the first time in a long, long time, it didn't feel like too much. It felt like finally—enough.

Nora closed the journal slowly, her fingers resting on the cover like it might still breathe with the weight of what she'd written. Around her, the others moved quietly, their moods softened, edges worn down by truth and whatever lavender-scented vulnerability had just cracked open in that room.

There were a few murmured jokes. A half-hearted plan to sneak out for brunch. Rina swore she smelled cinnamon rolls somewhere, which might have been a hallucination. Vanessa was already searching for an escape route on Google Maps.

Someone suggested mimosas. Lulu countered with a green juice toast. Chaos threatened to bubble back up, and Nora welcomed it grateful for the levity, even as her heart still thrummed with the emotional residue.

Just as they were plotting their escape and debating whether mimosas technically counted as electrolytes, a shadow crossed the doorway.

Simon stepped in like a gust of clean air—cool, quiet, impossible to ignore. Dark joggers hung low on his hips, a navy tee hugging the breadth of his chest and stretching just enough across his shoulders to suggest intention behind the "accidental" sex appeal. His hair was still damp from a shower, tousled like he'd just run a hand through it and his mouth—damn him—was quirked in that low key smirk that said he knew exactly what he was doing. He carried a drawstring bag and the kind of energy that made everything else in the room fade out like background noise.

"This is for Coach Joy," he said, placing the bag on the reception desk. His voice was smooth, quiet, but it landed with weight. Then, almost as an afterthought, he turned toward the room. "Didn't know you were all here."

The room snapped to attention, like someone had just turned the volume and the temperature up by ten degrees.

Vanessa raised an eyebrow, practically purring. "Oh, come on. You just happened to be delivering gear to a mountaintop retreat full of glowing women in sports bras?"

Simon didn't flinch. "I have GPS," he said, deadpan. But his eyes had already found Nora and they did not move.

That gaze—dark, direct, and completely unbothered by anyone else in the room—landed on her like a hand against bare skin. It burned. It lingered.

Her breath snagged in her throat. The hoodie she was wearing suddenly felt too warm. Too close. Her pulse kicked up, a flutter just beneath her collarbone. The rest of the room fell away.

"You're welcome to stay," Lulu offered, raising her green smoothie like an invitation to mischief. "We're doing trust falls and soul excavations next."

Simon's mouth curved, slow and wicked. "Tempting," he said, eyes still locked on Nora. "But I should probably go before I get talked into goat yoga and a group cry."

Still, he didn't leave. He stepped closer—just enough for her to catch a hint of clean soap and something darker beneath it. His voice dropped, low and intimate, pitched just for her. "You doing okay?"

God, he was close.

Nora swallowed hard. "Better now."

His eyes dipped just briefly, to her mouth and then back up. A pause. A beat that cracked open something reckless in her.

Then he nodded, slow and deliberate. "See you back in lane four."

And just like that, he was gone.

But her body didn't believe it. Her pulse was still racing. Her skin still tingled, like the air was holding onto the shape of him.

The others went back to their drinks and jokes, the spell broken for them. Not for her, because that wasn't just a delivery. That was a spark dropped in dry brush and she wasn't sure what scared her more— How much she wanted the fire…Or how close it already was to catching.

She needed air. Stillness. A place where her thoughts could catch up with the wildfire her body had just lit.

Nora wandered toward the edge of the property, drawn by a pull she couldn't name. A worn path led her past a vegetable garden, a row of prayer flags strung between trees, and finally to a weathered split-rail fence overlooking a small valley below. Morning mist still clung to the grass, softening the gold-tinged hills. The silence was deep, not empty, but alive with birdcalls, the rustle of breeze, the quiet rhythm of breath.

She pressed her palms to the cool wood of the fence and exhaled. Not just to calm down but to feel herself again. To stretch into this unfamiliar, thrilling awareness humming just beneath her skin.

Simon. His voice. His gaze. The way he looked at her—not with pity, not like she was a project or a problem or a woman past her prime. He looked at her like she mattered now. As she was and it shook something loose.

It had been years since she'd felt that kind of pull. Not the polite affection she used to barter for safety. Not the numbness she'd grown used to calling "enough."

This—this was raw. Present. Dangerous, and it wasn't just about desire, though God, her body wanted him like a flame wants air. It was about being seen.

When Simon looked at her, it felt like he recognized the battle she was in—the slow, brutal one of coming back to herself and wasn't scared off by the mess of it. He didn't want to fix her. He just wanted her. That scared her and thrilled her.

The wind picked up, brushing a strand of hair across her cheek. She didn't tuck it behind her ear. Just let it dance there, wild and untamed. She stood like that for a long moment—bare, rooted, breathing.

Then, soft and certain, she whispered to the valley:
"I want more and I'm not afraid to want it."

The words didn't echo. They didn't need to. They
were for her and for once—finally, fiercely, that was
enough.

***

He should've just dropped the bag and left. That was
the plan. Drive up, deliver the gear, wave hello to Coach
Joy, maybe grab a protein bar and some fake-healthy air
before heading back to the pool. Simple. Clean, but then
he saw her.

Suddenly nothing was clean or simple or remotely
safe. She was standing a little behind the others, arms
crossed over a worn hoodie, looking like she wasn't sure
whether to join the group or vanish into the mist. Her
hair was loose. Her cheeks still pink from the sun—or
maybe from something that had been said, or admitted,
or unearthed.

She didn't look polished. She didn't look guarded.
She looked real and it damn near floored him. There
was something about her in that moment, something
raw and unedited, like the version of herself she didn't
usually let out into the light. The woman she kept
tucked beneath sarcasm and apologies and the tight
schedule of a life that always seemed to be lived for
everyone else.

But here she was, all edges softened. Eyes wide
open and when their eyes met...

Hell. Time didn't stop. It locked in. The room went
fuzzy at the edges. His pulse hitched in that low,
dangerous way it hadn't in years and suddenly it wasn't
about the delivery, or the others, or the fact that this
was entirely the wrong time and place to feel anything.

It was just her.

When Lulu offered him a smoothie and an
invitation to stay, he should've cracked a joke and made
his exit, but he lingered. Long enough to ask if she was
okay. Long enough to hear her say, "Better now,' and
long enough to see it was true.

He left. Eventually. Got in the car. Started the
engine. Made it all the way down the gravel drive before
pulling over like some idiot in a rom-com with
unresolved feelings and no plan. He told himself he was
just clearing his head but ten minutes later, he found
himself circling back on foot—quiet, careful, staying just
beyond the property line. Like a ghost. Or a coward. Or
maybe just a man who couldn't walk away from
something that had already begun to matter more than it
should.

Then he saw her again. Alone by the fence at the
edge of the property. Her hands pressed to the
weathered wood. Her head slightly bowed, hair dancing
in the wind. She didn't know he was there. Didn't know
she was being watched and she looked... luminous.

Not in a soft-filter, retreat-glow kind of way, but like a woman on the edge of claiming something. Or someone. He watched as she lifted her chin and whispered something to the open valley. He couldn't hear the words. He didn't need to. He felt them like a current, running straight through him. The kind of vow that didn't need an audience to be real.

He should've walked away then. Left her to her moment. Let it be sacred, but he stayed, because some part of him needed to see it. Needed to see her. This wasn't a crush. Wasn't infatuation. It wasn't even about attraction anymore—though God knows he wanted her. It was more dangerous than that. Because he didn't just want to touch her. He wanted to be trusted by her. He wanted to be let in. He knew—knew—that if he wasn't careful, she wouldn't just undo his walls. She'd rewrite them

***

Later That Night – In the Yurt of Vulnerability (That's what Lulu had started calling it, and unfortunately, it stuck.)

They were strewn across floor cushions like the final act of a very niche off-Broadway play. The lighting was low. The vibes were... questionable. Someone had lit a candle that smelled vaguely like patchouli and unresolved trauma.

Lulu was upside down against the wall, legs in the air like a yogic bat. Rina was face-down in a blanket, groaning intermittently. Vanessa was sitting ramrod straight in a corner, sipping cucumber water with the energy of a woman who deeply regretted her life choices.

Nora was still wearing her hoodie, despite the rising temperature and the full-body spiritual exfoliation she'd apparently just undergone.

"I'm not saying today broke me," Rina said into her blanket. "But if one more goat tries to realign my chakras, I'm going to bite it."

"It licked your ear," Lulu offered gently.

"It whispered secrets," Rina said.

Vanessa sighed. "I came here for relaxation and maybe a light ego boost. What I got was emotional whiplash, exposure therapy, and Simon showing up like a lost Hemsworth."

"God," Nora muttered, dragging a pillow over her face. "Can we not?"

"We cannot… not," Rina said, lifting her head. "He looked at you like you were a croissant he wasn't allowed to eat in public."

"I don't want to be a croissant."

"You want to be the main course," Lulu said serenely. "And I support that."

There was a pause. A long, luxurious silence that felt heavier than any essential oil in the room. Then

Nora said it. Softly. Honestly. "I feel like... part of me is waking up and she's kind of a lot. I don't know if I like her yet."

Lulu reached out, fingers brushing Nora's ankle. "I think she's been locked in the basement too long. She's a little weird. She deserves snacks and sunlight."

Rina nodded solemnly. "And probably a rabies shot."

Vanessa lifted her water. "To basement Nora. May she rise like a phoenix who's had a really confusing few years."

They clinked mugs and bottles and whatever was within reach. Nora laughed, full-bodied and unfiltered. Not the polite kind of laugh, this one came from somewhere deeper. Somewhere honest. She looked around at the mess of them, all soft and feral and too much and exactly enough.

Maybe she was still figuring herself out. Still unlearning the rules. Still trying to stop apologizing for wanting more. But maybe, just maybe, this was what it looked like to begin again.

Outside, a goat screamed into the night, Vanessa sat bolt upright. "I swear to God, if that thing is inside the yurt—"

A thump. A pause. Then a head poked under the canvas flap. Everyone froze.

"Don't move," Rina whispered. "It can smell fear."

The goat sneezed and chaos exploded—Rina flailing into the curtain, Lulu clapping like it was a blessing from the divine, Vanessa hurling her sandal with deadly accuracy, and Nora—Nora laughing so hard she nearly cried.

Maybe that was the point. To cry. To laugh. To want. To want more, and to be fully, gloriously alive in the mess of it all.

Spark and Smoke

Nora woke later than planned, blinking at the bright numbers on her phone and the unexpected flurry of notifications. Texts from Rina. A message from Vanessa, and of course the unread one from David, still sitting like a landmine in her inbox.

She bypassed it. Instead, she tapped into the group chat, where Rina had shared the official flyer for the upcoming Masters Swim Meet.

Rina: *Look who made the cut! Lane 4 is FAMOUS.*

The image showed their team mid-huddle, half-drenched, half-laughing, all limbs and chaos and Simon standing just behind them, arms crossed and proud. Nora's face was turned toward the others, grinning. Joyful. Alive.

Her thumb hovered. She almost shared it to her Instagram story. Almost. Instead, she saved the photo and slid the phone facedown on the bed. She let her eyes fall closed for a beat, breathing in the stillness of the morning. The version of herself in that photo was not a fluke. That grin wasn't borrowed. It was earned length by length, lap by lap.

She reached for her journal, flipped past pages filled with grief, self-doubt, old to-do lists, and silent confessions.

At the top of a clean page, she scribbled:

I'm not trying to be someone else anymore. I'm just trying to be someone I recognize.

She tapped the pen on her lips, staring at the words.

"Okay," she whispered. "Let's see what today brings."

Simon was already at the pool when she arrived— whiteboard crowded with drills, stopwatch slung around his neck, hair still slick from a warm-up swim. Nora paused in the doorway, watching him move. He was all control and precision, a rhythm of muscle and focus that made her mouth go dry.

"You're late," he said, still facing the board.

"Only fashionably," she replied, slipping out of her hoodie, aware of every inch of her exposed skin.

He turned and looked. Really looked. "You wore the suit," he said, voice lower now.

She shrugged, but there was heat in her cheeks. "Felt bold."

"Damn," he murmured, the word more breath than voice. "That's the kind of bold that ruins a man's focus."

Her lips parted to say something clever, to cut the moment with a joke and retreat behind it but it fell away.

"I almost didn't wear it," she said instead, voice quieter now. "But I think I was tired of hiding."

His eyes didn't leave hers. "Don't."

She blinked. "Don't what?"

"Hide." It wasn't a suggestion. It was a vow. Like if she started to shrink again, he'd stop her.

He handed her a kickboard. Their fingers brushed. Just a second, but it was enough to detonate something under her skin. She didn't flinch. Neither did he and that—that—was more dangerous than anything he could have said.

The warm-up was basic on paper, but in her body, everything was different. Her pulse pounded in places she hadn't felt alive in years. Her awareness narrowed to water, breath, motion, and him. The way his gaze tracked her through every turn. Calculated. Controlled. Barely.

"Let's run the ladder again," he said.

His voice had a rasp to it, like he wasn't just talking about laps.

She nodded, throat dry. This time, she dove in with something feral in her chest. She wasn't just swimming. She was claiming. Owning. Daring. Her body sliced through the water like it belonged there. Fast. Sharp. Unapologetic.

They swam hard. No words. Just the churn of limbs, the echo of breath, the building tension that felt like it was begging for a breaking point.

When they both slammed into the wall at the final set, gasping, their shoulders broke the surface at the same time. Simon rested his forearm beside hers, close enough that their slick skin almost touched. Close enough that Nora could feel the heat radiating off of him, even through the water.

"You could win your heat," he said, voice low—hoarse—like he hadn't fully caught his breath.

She looked over, chest rising, the air between them tight and electric. "You really think so?"

"I know so." His eyes dragged down her face, slow and deliberate. "You've got strength. Precision." His gaze dipped—to her lips. "Fire."

She swallowed, the heat in her chest threatening to become something she couldn't contain. "Sometimes I feel like I'm faking it."

He leaned in, just slightly, until his shoulder grazed hers, wet skin against wet skin, a current between them.

"We all are," he murmured. "The trick is to fake it long enough to become it."

His breath was warm on her cheek now. His voice so close it curled around the inside of her ribs.

Their faces were inches apart. The kind of close that collapsed excuses. The kind of close that begged for surrender. She let her hand drift, slow and sure, until it found his under the water—just a brush. Intentional and he didn't move.

His jaw flexed. Neither of them breathed.

"I should—" she began, voice barely a thread.

"Yeah," he said, voice rough but he didn't move either. Not an inch.

They stayed there, pressed between heat and hesitation, soaked in chlorine and want and everything they weren't yet ready to say. It wasn't just tension anymore. It was ignition.

The spell broke with the sound of the lane rope clattering as someone pulled it from the water. Voices rose, the clink of kickboards stacking, the low hum of the filtration system taking back the air. They stepped apart—casual on the surface, anything but underneath. A quick nod. A half-smile.

By the time Nora left the rec center, the afternoon sun was too bright, the air thick with summer. She drove home with the windows down, letting the wind do what it could to cool the burn in her chest.

Later that afternoon, she lay on her bed, the ceiling fan whirring softly above. The day clung to her skin— chlorine, sun, steam, and something else. Something that still hummed beneath her ribs. She closed her eyes, but all she could see was the edge of the pool. Simon's voice in her ear. The way he hadn't moved back.

There was space between them now—hours, miles—but the tension hadn't cooled. If anything, it had grown teeth. Her phone buzzed. A single message lighting up the screen.

Simon: *Pool's free tonight after hours. Want another one-on-one lesson? Just you and me. No distractions.*

Her stomach flipped. A slow, deliberate somersault. She didn't hesitate.

Nora: *What time?*

The pool was cloaked in shadows, the overhead lights dimmed to a soft glow that shimmered across the still water like silk. The echo of Nora's footsteps bounced off the tile as she entered, towel slung over her shoulder, nerves humming louder than her heartbeat.

Simon was already there, leaning against the wall at the deep end, one hand braced behind him, the other loose at his side, hair curling at the edges, and a look that made the space between them feel shorter than it was.

She closed the distance slowly, deliberately.

"Looks like I'm not the only one who couldn't wait," she said.

He straightened, eyes skimming over her. "You came."

"I said I would."

He gave a half smile. "Suit looks even better under these lights."

She tried not to blush but failed. "We swimming, Coach? Or was the lesson something... less aquatic?"

Simon stepped toward her. "Depends on how brave you're feeling tonight."

Nora's breath hitched. She dropped her towel. "Try me."

The moment stretched, dense and electric until Simon broke it by diving cleanly into the water. She followed, the splash echoing behind her like a starting pistol.

They swam. Fast. Hard. A silent competition neither had declared but both understood. When they reached the wall at the same time, they stayed close, chests heaving, water trickling down bare skin, their breath mingling in the warm, chlorine-scented air.

Simon reached for the ledge behind her, one hand on either side, caging her in without laying a finger on her, but she felt him everywhere. The air between them pulsed humid, charged, laced with chlorine and want.

"Your timing's sharper," he said, voice rough. "But you still pull wide on the back half."

She tilted her head, eyes locked on his. "Guess I need hands-on correction."

His jaw tightened. His gaze dipped to her mouth and back up again slow, deliberate.

"You sure about that?" The rasp in his voice was not about swimming.

She didn't look away. "I wouldn't be here if I wasn't."

A beat passed. Long enough for her breath to hitch. Long enough to feel the burn low in her belly. Then, slowly like giving her every chance to stop him, his fingers brushed her wrist. The same move he'd made during drills but this time, he didn't stop.

His hand slid up, tracing the inside of her forearm, slow and reverent. Skin to skin. Like he was memorizing her by touch. Her body arched slightly toward his, unthinking.

"You're strong, Nora," he murmured. "Not just in the water."

She swallowed, heat pooling between her hips. "I'm trying to believe that."

He leaned in, his breath dancing across her lips, his eyes so close and locked in that it stole her equilibrium.

"Then let me help you remember."

Her restraint snapped.

She surged forward, and their mouths collided hard, hungry, real. There was no teasing now. No slow burn. Just fire meeting fire. His hand slid to the back of her neck, anchoring her as her fingers curled into his curls, dragging him closer, deeper.

They kissed like people who'd waited. Who had tried to be good. Tried to be professional. Tried to pretend this wasn't inevitable. When they finally broke apart, breathless, lips swollen, his forehead rested against hers.

"This is wildly unprofessional," she whispered, smiling against his mouth.

His eyes were dark, heavy with want. "I'm off the clock."

He kissed her again slower now, deeper. The kind of kiss that didn't ask for permission. The kind that claimed. His hand skimmed down her back, stopping just at the edge of the suit. Her pulse jumped. She didn't stop him.

"And you," he breathed against her skin, "are the only thing I want to work on tonight."

She laughed soft, wrecked, wrecking. Their mouths found each other again. Water lapping at their sides, hearts pounding like war drums, and in that charged, rule-breaking, world-tilting moment, Nora wasn't rebuilding. She was someone burning bright. Alive. Wanted and ready for whatever came next.

By the time she'd dried off and dressed, the kiss still echoed through her body like a struck bell, low and resonant, vibrating in places she'd forgotten could feel this alive.

She walked the dim hallway alone, towel-damp hair curling at her neck, the soft squeak of her sneakers the only sound. The fluorescent lights buzzed overhead, too bright, too ordinary, against the extraordinary thing that had just happened.

Her fingers brushed her lips once testing. Remembering. Confirming. The feel of his mouth on hers, the heat of his hand at her lower back, the way the world had narrowed to just the space between their breaths. It hadn't been planned. It hadn't even felt like a choice. It was a collision of everything they hadn't said finally catching fire and now she was walking out into the night like nothing had changed, when everything had.

She stepped into the cool air and let it bite at her flushed skin, grounding her. Her phone buzzed in her bag, but she didn't check it yet. Not yet. She wanted to hold the moment a little longer, untouched, unnamed, hers.

The parking lot was nearly empty. Just her car, tucked under the one flickering streetlamp. She slid into the driver's seat, pulled the door closed, and let the quiet wrap around her.

Her hands trembled lightly on the steering wheel— not from the cold, but from whatever this new thing was. Whatever they'd just stepped into. It was too fresh to label. Too alive to ignore.

What they'd shared in the pool tonight hadn't been just heat or chemistry, it had been a spark lit on something already smoldering beneath the surface for weeks. That kiss had broken something open in her. Or maybe… maybe it stitched something back together.

She pressed two fingers to her lips, then let them fall to her lap, a smile ghosting across her face. She wasn't just returning to herself anymore. She was becoming someone new and she wasn't afraid of it.

***

Simon sat behind the wheel of his car in the empty parking lot, gripping the steering wheel like it could anchor him to reality.

Her taste was still on his lips. Her voice still in his head. The kiss had burned through his resolve, through every reason he'd told himself to keep his distance. It wasn't just that she'd let him in, it was that she kissed him like she meant it. Like she wanted more than just the safety of flirting.

He had answered. With his mouth. With his hands. With all the heat and hunger he'd been holding back since the first time she made him laugh poolside.

He dropped his head back against the headrest and groaned. It was fire. All of it, but it wasn't reckless. It had clarity. In that kiss, there wasn't just lust. There was permission and something more dangerous:

Hope.

He could still feel the shape of her body against his. The way she'd curled into him, bold and unsure and open. He didn't want to ruin it by moving too fast or worse, by overthinking it, but he knew one thing: He wasn't letting go. Not now. Not after that, He took a steadying breath and finally turned the key. It was going to be a long night and an even more complicated morning.

***

Back home, Nora moved like she was underwater. Everything felt suspended by her heartbeat, her thoughts, the steady pulse of something new humming beneath her skin. She showered and pulled on her coziest sweatshirt, though she still felt warm all over. Electrified.

The house was quiet except for the buzz of her fridge and the occasional creak of the floorboards. She poured a glass of wine and curled onto the couch with her journal in her lap. The pages felt heavier than usual. As if they were waiting.

She flipped to a fresh one.

I didn't know I still had this in me. The wanting. The thrill. The hope.

Her pen hovered.

David never made me feel like this. Not even in the beginning. The thought startled her. She sat back, letting it settle. She wasn't angry, not in this moment. Just... aware. Of how little she'd asked for. How much she'd

accepted. How long she'd gone untouched, unseen—
not just by someone else, but by herself. Her phone lit
up on the table.

Simon: *You made me forget the set times.*

Her lips curled, heart stuttering.

Nora: *You made me forget the water was cold.*

A beat. Then another buzz.

Simon: *You made me forget the rules.*

She stared at the words, pulse ticking up.

Nora: *You made me forget myself. In the best way.*

Three dots blinked. Then stopped.

Then blinked again.

Simon: *Then let's not forget this happened.*

There it was. The line. The choice. She felt her
breath catch in her chest, fingers hovering over the
screen.

Nora: *I won't.*

He didn't reply right away but the silence felt full,
not distant.

Then:

Simon: *Dinner?*

Two syllables, but they hit like a match to dry
leaves. She stared at the message, heat curling in her
stomach. It wasn't just about food. It was about more.
More wanting. More risk. More of him.

She didn't answer, not yet. Instead, she picked up
her pen, the journal still open in front of her, the pages
still warm from her earlier truth.

She wrote:

I'm not fixing something broken.
I'm choosing something new.

She underlined it. Twice, and then she smiled, slow
and sure. This wasn't the end. It was just the beginning
and this time; she was the one writing it.

The next morning, reality reasserted itself with the
clatter of lockers, the scent of wet towels, and the
unmistakable chaos of Lane 4.

Nora stood in front of her locker for a beat longer
than usual, fingers lingering on the combination dial.
Her muscles ached in that delicious way not just from
the workout, but from everything that had unfolded
afterward.

Her body still hummed with the memory of last
night. The heat of Simon's breath. The way his voice
had dropped when he said her name. The moment his
mouth claimed hers like it had always been meant to.
That kiss hadn't just scrambled her brain. It had
rearranged something deeper, and now... she was
supposed to just toss on a swim cap and pretend like
nothing had happened?

She exhaled and opened the locker.

Around her, the team swirled in their usual storm
laughter, loud opinions, wet footprints, and a rogue
Bluetooth speaker blasting Lizzo. Someone snapped a
towel. Someone else screamed. Someone was trading

compression socks for dry shampoo like it was an underground economy.

Nora blinked. How was this the same world? Her thoughts flickered, traitorously, to Simon. Had he felt it too? Or was she the only one still walking around like her skin remembered him?

Then she caught her own reflection in the mirror on the locker door. Flushed cheeks. Shower-damp hair and a smirk tugging at the corner of her mouth that hadn't been there yesterday.

Nope. Not in her head. It was real and now she had to figure out what the hell to do with that. She turned toward the bench, where Lane 4 was already in full pre-practice pandemonium. Lulu was applying under-eye patches like she was prepping for war. Rina was dramatically unpeeling a muffin from its wrapper. Vanessa was scrolling through her phone and muttering about an ex who had the audacity to post inspirational quotes while still being garbage.

"Morning, mystery woman," Lulu sing-songed. "Someone's got a glow."

Nora froze mid-lace-tie. "What glow?"

"That glow," Rina said, pointing with half a muffin. "You're either in love or you found good coffee. Which is it?"

"She's got bedhead and secrets," Vanessa added without looking up. "Ten bucks says it's a swim coach."

"Twenty says it's Simon," Lulu whispered dramatically.

Nora flushed, but it was too late. The sharks had scented blood.

"I knew something was up at the retreat," Rina declared. "There was chemistry. Like, visible steam. I was sweating and it wasn't just the goat yoga."

"Guys," Nora warned, but she was laughing now blushing, but laughing. Because somehow, this wild, loud, slightly unhinged group made it feel... okay. Less terrifying. More like the start of something instead of the unraveling of everything. She plopped down on the bench, accepting a muffin and the inevitable interrogation.

Whatever she'd felt the night before heat, hunger, maybe even something more was now layered under the vibrant, messy noise of women who swam hard, loved harder, and knew how to ask the real questions in between sprints and snacks. Suddenly, Nora didn't feel like she was holding something fragile and secret. She felt like she was holding something worth keeping.

Ripple Effects

The diner buzzed with early morning energy. Clinking mugs, the hiss of an overworked espresso machine and the low murmur of a nearby run club debriefing over pancakes. The windows were fogged from the kitchen heat, and the scent of syrup and bacon hung in the air like comfort.

Vanessa waved from a corner booth, already halfway through her first cup of coffee. Her mug read *One Tough Mother* in bold red letters, and she wore it like armor.

"You're late," she said, not looking up as she stirred a creamer into her refill. Her tone was casual, but her smirk was loaded.

Nora slid into the seat across from her and shrugged off her jacket. "Is this a new tradition? Quoting Simon at me before caffeine?"

"Only when it fits," Vanessa said, lifting a brow. "And right now, it fits real well."

Nora reached for her water, trying to hide the small, involuntary smile tugging at her lips. "Blame the post-swim noodle legs. Recovery is a journey."

Vanessa topped off her coffee with the practiced hand of a woman who believed breakfast was sacred.

"Mmm. Sure. Could also be that someone's been swimming with extra incentive."

Nora choked. "Is that PTA-speak for 'you're glowing like someone got kissed breathless against a pool wall'?"

Vanessa gave her a look—equal parts smug and sisterly. "I call it like I see it."

Nora leaned back and stared out the window, suddenly unsure what to do with the warmth blooming in her chest. "It was just a kiss."

Vanessa snorted. "Right, and I run marathons for fun."

Nora didn't respond. Her fingers toyed with a sugar packet, folding and unfolding it until it nearly tore.

Vanessa's voice softened. "Nora. Come on. You don't have to explain it, but don't downplay it, either. You're lit up like a damn sunrise."

"I don't know what this is," Nora said finally. "And I think part of me doesn't want to. Not yet."

Vanessa nodded, setting down her mug with the kind of finality that always preceded a truth bomb.

"That's fine. You don't need a label. You just need a gut check." She looked Nora dead in the eye. "Does it feel like something that wakes you up, or something that puts you back to sleep?"

The question hit hard. Clean. Sharp. No dressing. Nora blinked.

"It feels… real," she said quietly. "And terrifying."

"Good," Vanessa said. No hesitation. "That's where all the interesting shit happens."

They sat in silence for a few seconds, the noise of the diner folding around them like background music. Outside, a dog barked. Someone dropped a fork. Life went on.

At the corner booth, the two women sat shoulder to shoulder in the shifting in-between—one with a heart still racing, the other holding space like a goddamn pro. Nora smiled, small and grateful. Vanessa smiled back. No more words were needed.

The pool was alive with echoing whistles and the rhythmic splash of arms cutting through water by the time Nora arrived. Lane 4 was mid-warmup, synchronized but fierce, like a school of sleek predators.

Simon stood at the far end, stopwatch in hand, calling out intervals with a voice that somehow managed to cut through the noise and curl under her skin. His hair was damp, curls pushed back in a way that made her stomach flutter. His shirt clung slightly to the line of his torso and peeked a hint of his hips when he lifted his arms.

Nora adjusted her goggles and slid into the lane beside Rina, heart already hammering. "Late night?" Rina asked under her breath, a devilish smile twitching on her lips as she floated through her kick set.

Nora smirked, trying to sound casual. "Just had a... private lesson."

"Oh, I bet you were working on your stroke," Rina purred.

Vanessa piped up from the other side. "She means your freestyle, right?"

Nora ducked underwater before they could see her grin. When she surfaced for air, Simon was watching. Not just noticing. Watching. His gaze tracked her every movement, calculated and slow, like he was memorizing the way her body moved through the water. Her pulse quickened under the weight of it.

After one particularly strong set, he crouched near the edge as she surfaced. "Nice pacing," he said, voice pitched just for her. "You're holding steady. Strong pull. Controlled... but not too controlled."

Nora met his gaze, chest heaving, breathless in more ways than one. "You saying I should let go a little?"

He gave the barest smile. "I'm saying you've got more in you. I've seen it."

The next round, she swam like her body was lit from within. The water wrapped around her like silk. When she touched the wall at the end, he was already there.

"Alright, Lane 4," Simon called, pulling back just enough. "100-meter build sets. Every 25 should turn the dial up. Last length—make it fire."

Groans echoed from the team, but Nora didn't complain. She wanted the burn. At the wall, lungs burning and eyes bright, Nora surfaced once more. Simon leaned in again, closer this time. Close enough to feel his breath.

"That's the stroke of someone who knows exactly what she wants," he murmured.

Nora didn't smile this time. She just held his gaze, heat simmering in her eyes.

"I'm learning to ask for it," she said softly.

Simon's lips parted slightly, the corner of his mouth twitching, somewhere between restraint and hunger.

Behind them, Vanessa whistled. "Alright, alright, break it up! Some of us are trying to swim, not melt."

Laughter erupted around them. Simon stepped back, his voice steady but his eyes still fixed on Nora.

"Get back to it," he said.

Even as she pushed off the wall, her fingers slicing into the cool blue, the heat between them didn't fade. It only deepened.

Practice ended with the usual blur of splashing limbs and tangled equipment, but Nora couldn't shake the energy humming beneath her skin. Her muscles ached in that delicious way, earned, pushed, tested and her body still remembered the heat of Simon's gaze like a phantom touch.

At the shallow end, Lane 4 had clustered in the familiar post-swim sprawl half-exhausted, half-alive. "Vanessa's going to lap us all in backstroke," Lulu declared, wringing out her hair like she was auditioning for a shampoo commercial.

Vanessa snorted. "Only if you all swim backward. Blindfolded and half-asleep."

Rina pulled her towel tighter and turned toward Nora with a sly glint. "Breakfast burritos? There's a food truck outside."

"I'm in," Vanessa said. "If only to make peace with my thighs."

Rina raised a brow. "Unless someone else has a better offer…" Her gaze slid, pointedly, to Simon, who was still at the whiteboard, jotting notes like the clipboard might catch fire if he looked up too fast.

He didn't hesitate. "I was actually thinking of grabbing a drink later," he said, casually. Too casually. His voice cut through the locker room noise like a current. "Something not chlorinated, Nora?"

The pause was electric. Rina dropped her cap. Vanessa dropped her jaw. Nora's heartbeat pounded in her ears, but she didn't flinch. She met his eyes. Steady. Intimate. The air felt hotter all of a sudden and not just from the chlorine.

"Sure," she said, voice low. Controlled. "Why not?"

There was a beat. Then Rina let out an unmistakable "oof", and Vanessa fanned herself dramatically with her towel. Lulu leaned over and stage-whispered, "Get the spicy margarita."

Nora turned, amused. "Why?"

Lulu grinned wickedly. "It's a personality test. If he sweats but still orders another round, you keep him."

Simon didn't comment, but his lips twitched, just enough to suggest he'd heard every word.

As the women wrapped up in towels and scattered toward the exit, Nora lingered.

Simon looked up from his clipboard. Their eyes locked. No teasing this time. Just something hungry. He tipped his head. "See you tonight, Lane 4."

She didn't answer. Just smiled, because she was already imagining what would happen when the water wasn't between them anymore.

***

Simon stayed behind at the whiteboard longer than necessary. He made a show of logging drills and heat splits, but his eyes kept drifting, following her. Towel slung over her shoulder, hair damp, skin glowing from the workout and something else. Satisfaction. Maybe even anticipation.

She laughed at something Rina said. Bit her lip. Looked back over her shoulder once, just briefly and caught him watching. The corner of her mouth lifted.

Simon exhaled slowly. He should've looked away. Should've returned to his clipboard. Should've done a lot of things that didn't involve memorizing the curve of her smile or wondering how long it would take to taste the salt of her skin.

He didn't. He just watched, because the way she moved now—confident, relaxed, even a little smug, was entirely different from the woman who'd first stepped onto the deck.

Lane 4 had lit something in her and now, she was lighting something in him he hadn't let himself feel in years. Not just want. Hope.

She disappeared around the corner with her friends, laughter echoing off the tile. Simon finally looked away but the image stayed with him. Tonight was going to change everything.

***

The text came through before she'd even made it up the steps to her place.

Simon: *I meant what I said. Let me buy you that drink tonight.*

Nora leaned against the banister, her heart already kicking.

Nora: *You sure you can handle me outside of chlorinated environments?*

Simon: *No. But I'm willing to drown trying.*

Her stomach flipped.

She bit her lip. Then sent her address.

An hour later, they were tucked into a corner booth of a low-lit bar that smelled like citrus and sin. The kind of place where secrets got whispered and rules bent for the right smile. Nora wore black denim that hugged just enough and a soft, slouchy top that slipped off one shoulder like it had been waiting all night to do exactly that. Her collarbone gleamed in the amber light, and Simon, holy hell, looked like he was trying very hard to behave.

"Spicy margarita?" the server said, sliding two glasses onto the table.

Simon raised an eyebrow. "Bold choice."

Nora's lips curved as she lifted her glass. "Figured I'd match the company."

He watched her over the rim of his drink. The way she sipped slowly. The way her eyes didn't break from his. The way her knee pressed against his under the table and didn't move.

The conversation started safe. Swim meet logistics. Training sets. Favorite post-workout meals. Then the words started to thin. The space between them thickened.

Her fingers brushed his on the table. He didn't pull away. When she leaned in close enough that he could feel her breath on his neck his pulse stuttered.

"You keep looking at me like that," she murmured, voice like velvet, "and I'm going to forget this is just a drink."

Simon didn't answer. He reached up slowly and tucked a strand of hair behind her ear, fingertips grazing the edge of her jaw. He let his thumb trail across her cheek, soft and deliberate. A touch that asked and promised.

"Maybe," he said, low and rough, "I want you to forget."

The air between them snapped tight.

Nora's breath hitched. Her heart pounded. Everything about this felt inevitable and electric. She swallowed, gaze locked with his. "You want to get out of here?"

Simon didn't hesitate. He downed the last of his drink, leaned in like he was about to kiss her then stopped, just short of her lips. "More than I want another lap."

Back at her place, they didn't make it to the couch. The second the door closed, she was against it. Simon's hands in her hair, his mouth claiming hers with a hunger that felt like it had been building since day one. Nora moaned softly into the kiss, clutching his shirt like she needed to hold onto something real.

It was all heat and urgency and unspoken knowing.
He lifted her, and she wrapped her legs around his waist
like instinct. They didn't speak. They didn't need to.

Her sweatshirt hit the floor first. Then his jacket.
Buttons were forgotten. Zippers protested. Her fingers
found the bare skin at his waist and dragged upward,
mapping muscle and intention.

He carried her down the hall, lips locked, hips
grinding with barely-restrained control. Her back hit the
bedroom door. It swung open behind them. They
stumbled in together, tangled in fabric and want.

She pulled him down onto the bed, their bodies
meeting in fevered rhythm, urgent kisses, breathless
gasps, her hands in his hair, his mouth on her neck, her
shoulder, the soft curve of her stomach. Each touch felt
like discovery. Each gasp, permission.

Her fingers slid beneath the hem of his shirt,
tracing the taut skin of his stomach, feeling the sharp
intake of his breath. Then lower until her hand found
the edge of his waistband.

Simon's body jerked like a live wire, his mouth
crashing to hers, all teeth and tongue and desperation.
She could feel his want now, hard, urgent, impossible to
mistake. His hips pressed into hers, and her body arched
up to meet him, a gasp slipping from her lips as heat
bloomed deep and fast.

She was gone. Floating. Anchored only by the
weight of him, the sound of his breath, the way his hand

fisted in the fabric of her shirt like he was barely holding on.

But just as her palm slipped lower, Simon froze. Not fully. Just a pause. His body trembled with restraint. One muscle twitch away from losing control.

His forehead dropped to hers, breath ragged.

"Fuck," he whispered, voice wrecked.

She stilled, pulse pounding in her throat. "What?"

His hands cupped her face, reverent and shaking. "If I keep going..." His voice cracked. "I won't be able to stop."

Nora searched his eyes dark, dilated, unguarded and that's when she felt it. Not just arousal but reverence. Need, yes, but also depth. He wasn't just holding her. He was offering something, and suddenly, she knew this wasn't about hesitation. It was about intention.

Simon's jaw clenched. His hands flexed against her skin, his body straining with restraint.

"Nora..." His voice was hoarse, tight. "Say the word."

Her chest rose sharply against his. She was trembling now, and not from fear but from how much she wanted this. Wanted him.

"I want you," she breathed, voice thick. "I just... I don't know what I'm doing. I don't know if I can be the kind of person who does this and doesn't fall apart afterward."

His fingers tightened at her waist, anchoring her.

"You don't have to know," he said quietly. "Just… don't pretend it's nothing. Because it isn't."

Her eyes stung. She nodded, barely.

"I don't want it to be just a memory," she whispered. "Even if I'm scared."

His thumb brushed the edge of her jaw, reverent. "Then we wait."

They stayed tangled like that, foreheads pressed, breath uneven, hearts thundering. Not pulling away. Not rushing forward. Just holding the space between want and readiness. She exhaled into his shoulder, lips curving against his collarbone. "Next time."

Simon huffed out a breath half laugh, half agony. "That's the cruelest promise I've ever begged for."

She lay on her side in the quiet dark, sheets twisted around her waist, one hand still curved in the ghost of his touch. The silence wasn't heavy, it was humming. Her body ached in the best way, muscles alive and wanting. It wasn't just the physical that left her breathless. It was the way he'd looked at her. Not just with heat but with care. As if he wanted all of her, not just the version she'd rehearsed.

She pulled the blanket tighter, heart still racing. They hadn't crossed the final line. They'd come close, so close it left her shaking. With want. With wonder. With the raw terror of being wanted back.

Her phone buzzed softly on the nightstand.

Simon: Still breathing?

Nora stared at the screen for a beat, heart hammering in her chest. She ran her thumb over the edge of the phone, as if she could feel him through it.

Nora: Barely. You?

Simon: Haven't stopped thinking about you.

Or how close I was to losing my mind completely.

Her breath hitched.

Nora: You and me both. I'm still shaking.

A pause.

Simon: I should've stayed.

She swallowed hard, heat rising in her cheeks even now.

Nora: If you had... I don't think I would've let you leave.

The dots appeared. Paused. Reappeared.

Simon: You wouldn't have had to.

She sat up, phone in hand now, pulse thudding at her throat.

Nora: It scared me. How much I wanted to forget everything else. Even just for a night.

Simon: It scared me too. Not because I didn't want it. Because I've never wanted anything that badly and still walked away.

She stared at the screen, every word landing in the hollow behind her ribs.

Nora: Next time...

Another long pause. Then:

Simon: *I won't stop.*
Nora: *Then don't.*

Her thumb hovered over the send button for a long moment. She didn't delete it. She hit send. Set the phone down and let herself feel what she wasn't ready to name.

***

Simon sat in his car outside her house, engine quiet, hands still gripping the steering wheel. His lips were swollen. His pulse still thrummed in his neck and the scent of her, lavender and heat and something wholly Nora—clung to his shirt like a challenge.

He could still feel the way she moved under him. The urgency. The restraint, the whispered *not just tonight*.

He'd wanted her, but what wrecked him wasn't the wanting. It was the way she'd trusted him enough to stop. No games. No shame. Just truth.

He let his head fall back against the seat, eyes closed. This wasn't going to be simple. He didn't want it to be. He didn't want easy. He wanted real, and Nora? She was the realest thing that had happened to him in years. His phone lit up again. Her last message glowed on the screen.

Nora: *Then don't.*

Simon exhaled hard.

"Next time," he whispered into the dark. "There will be a next time."

***

Lane 4 Group Chat – Coach McDimples

Rina: Nora. Spill. Immediately.

Vanessa: You disappeared faster than Rina when she hears dryland training is optional.

Rina: I was stretching. Spiritually.

Nora: We grabbed a drink.

Rina: Define "drink."

Vanessa: And define "grabbed."

Lulu: Was his shirt still on when said drink occurred?

Nora: You're all monsters.

Rina: Horny monsters who root for your happiness.

Vanessa: So… breakfast debrief? I'll bring muffins if you bring details.

Rina: And coffee. For hydration. Post-game recovery.

Nora: Fine. But only if someone brings Advil and no one brings judgment.

Rina: Deal.

Lulu: No promises.

Nora tossed her phone on the bed and stared at the ceiling. She was smiling wide and unguarded and for once, not trying to analyze every beat, every breath. She didn't know exactly where things were going but she knew she wanted to find out and she wasn't doing it alone. Whatever was next, it was going to be hers.

Old Worlds, New Fire

Nora told herself it was just a party. A few hours, some snacks, a reason to celebrate Vanessa's promotion and prove, mostly to herself that she could still walk into a room and not disappear. She'd almost backed out twice, but then she remembered the note in her journal:
Show up, even when you want to shrink.

So she came. The house pulsed with string lights and curated playlists. Lulu had outdone herself: artisanal cheese boards shaped like anatomical hearts, drinks named after Vanessa's moods (The Spicy Softie, The Quiet Crisis), and a glitter piñata full of compliments and ibuprofen.

"I swear to God, if Lulu tries to make a toast, I'm leaving," Vanessa muttered, scrolling through the group text from across the kitchen.

"She already wrote one," Rina said. "It rhymes. There's a metaphor about scalpels and emotional growth."

Nora laughed, but something inside her stayed tight.
This was familiar territory, small talk, curated perfection, people who knew versions of her she didn't claim anymore. Then she saw the invite list. David's old

coworker. Someone from their couples book club. It was a reunion of ghosts she hadn't invited.

Still, she stayed. Black dress. Sharp smile. Glass of prosecco held like a shield. She mingled and laughed at all the right places. Answered questions about work and hobbies and whether she was still "doing the swim thing."

Everything felt one breath too shallow. Like she was wearing someone else's confidence, and it didn't quite zip in the back.

"Nora, isn't that Kristen from your old team?" someone said.

She turned...and there she was. Flawless. Sculpted. Sauvignon Blanc in hand, wearing judgment like lip gloss.

"Oh," Kristen said. "I didn't realize you were still in town."

Nora smiled, teeth sharp. "I didn't realize I needed to submit my travel plans."

Kristen blinked, caught off balance. "You look good."

"I am good." For a second, it felt like armor. Then the air shifted. The music blurred. The lights felt too warm. She turned, glass raised and saw him.

David was standing like a punctuation mark in the doorway. Same watch. Same detached ease. Same unreadable gaze. Her spine went stiff. Her pulse, erratic.

He smiled, polite. "Nora."

Like he hadn't left her in pieces. Like she was someone he could still greet without consequence. She held his gaze for a beat too long, then turned, heart thudding, glass too tight in her grip.

Simon arrived forty minutes late. Dark jeans. Navy henley. Six-pack in hand. He looked like trouble wrapped in ease, and Nora's breath caught like she hadn't expected him even though some part of her had hoped.

"Oh look," Lulu whispered. "A surprise guest."

Nora nearly spilled her wine. He moved through the room like he'd always belonged. Hugged Vanessa. Dodged Rina's commentary, and then he found her.

"Hey," he said softly.

She turned. "Didn't think you were coming."

"Didn't plan to. Lulu guilt-texted me with six emojis and a quote about destiny."

She smiled. "Sounds like her."

They stood just outside the circle of party noise. Close enough to feel the bass underfoot, far enough for privacy.

"You look... good," he said.

She exhaled. "I'm trying to feel it. This used to be my world."

He nodded. "Is it still?"

"I don't know."

"You didn't look like you belonged to it."

She looked up. "Then what do I belong to?"

Simon's eyes softened. "Maybe something better."

The playlist shifted. Slow. Sultry.

He held out a hand. "Do you want to?"

She hesitated. "I'm not good at this."

"It's just a song."

It wasn't. They both knew it, but she took his hand anyway. They moved slowly, surrounded by laughter and light. He didn't pull her close. She didn't lean in. It was tension and suggestion and a rhythm that belonged only to them. The song ended. The moment didn't. She stepped back just enough to look up at him. For the first time that night, it felt like hers.

Behind her, the party buzzed like static. Familiar voices. Loud laughter. More champagne but the space around her felt… thinner. Then, David stepped in like he'd been circling, waiting for the right moment to strike. He smelled the opening and took it.

"Nora," he said, too familiar. "Didn't expect to see you. Thought you were still in your post-divorce reset era."

Simon's hand, resting lightly at her lower back, tensed. He didn't move. He didn't speak, but Nora felt it, the ripple of readiness.

She turned. "I didn't realize you were invited," she said coolly.

David gave a half-smile. "Mutual friends. Still have a few, surprisingly."

She raised a brow. "They'll grow out of it."

He chuckled, like they were just two exes exchanging harmless barbs. Like he hadn't gutted her and moved on without blinking.

"You always had a flair for drama," he said. "Still intense, I see."

Her laugh came out sharp. "God, you love that word."

Vanessa noticed. Rina stopped mid-conversation. Lulu turned down the playlist.

David kept going. "It's not an insult. It's just who you are. Some people find that hard to live with."

That did it. Nora stepped forward, wine glass in hand, fury and clarity rising like heat in her chest.

"You don't get to narrate me anymore," she snapped, voice rising. "You don't get to rewrite who I was just because it's easier than facing what you did."

David blinked.

"I wasn't too much. I was unsupported. I wasn't emotional. I was ignored and I wasn't impossible to love. You were just incapable of loving anyone who didn't orbit around you."

The room fell fully quiet now. Someone gasped. Vanessa muttered, "Wreck him."

David's expression faltered, but she wasn't done.

"I shrank myself for you. Over and over. Tried to be more palatable, more pliable. I edited myself until there was barely anything left—just silence and smiles and anxiety I mistook for love."

Her voice cracked—but she kept going.

"And still—you left. Not because I was too much. But because I finally started to wake up."

She didn't cry.

She didn't flinch.

She burned.

"And for the record?" she added. "I like my intensity. It means I feel. It means I care. It means I've lived through your mess and still have something left to give—to myself, not to you."

David's mouth opened. Closed. Nothing. Then Vanessa stepped up beside her, arms crossed. "You should leave."

"Now," Lulu added, deadly sweet.

"Before she says something that makes your dick fall off," Rina said, sipping her drink.

David looked at Simon—who stood there, unreadable, tall and steady behind the crowd.

He said nothing.

But his presence was enough.

David turned and walked out.

Not a word. Not a backward glance and when the door shut behind him, it was like oxygen returned to the room.

Nora stood in the center of it all, chest heaving, every muscle still vibrating. She felt stripped down. Scorched. Free.

Simon didn't rush to her. He didn't have to. He was just there. Steady. Watching.

She met his eyes and for the first time in a long time, she didn't feel too much.

She felt right-sized. Like a woman who had finally stopped asking for permission to exist.

Sink or Swim

By morning, the adrenaline had curdled into something heavier. Nora's voice still echoed in her own head— sharp, unfiltered, impossible to take back. The party had ended in a kind of surreal haze: glitter in the air, awkward goodbyes, and the stunned silence that follows when someone dares to tell the truth too loudly.

She hadn't looked for David as she left. She hadn't needed to. Her words had found him.

Lane 4 had closed ranks around her without hesitation—Vanessa flanking her like a bouncer ready to throw arms, Rina tossing a string of profanity like confetti, Lulu launching into a speech about divine rage and the goddess Kali. They didn't need a plan. They *were* the plan.

But the next morning, the pool deck felt... haunted. The silence was louder than the splash of diving blocks or the steady churn of arms through water. Something had shifted. Like the team had exhaled too hard and forgotten how to breathe back in.

They were all off. Vanessa veered into the lane rope during a drill and shouted "I'm fine!" before anyone could ask. Lulu false-started twice and then blamed her chakra alignment. Rina got lapped and flipped off the clock like it had insulted her ancestors.

Even Simon seemed brittle. Focused. Too focused.

"Longer strokes, Vanessa," he said, voice flat. "Reset your kick, Nora."

No smile. No wink. No glimmer of the man who had kissed her like she was gravity and fire combined.

Nora's muscles screamed through every lap, but her brain was louder. Spinning, looping, dissecting every second of the night before—the party, the dance, the kiss, the fallout. Her body was in the pool. Her heart was somewhere else.

And Simon? Simon was all clipped commands and distance. Like nothing had happened. Like she was just another swimmer in a cap and goggles. A ghost of chlorine and regret.

The final relay imploded spectacularly. Vanessa fumbled the turn. Rina nearly lost her goggles. Lulu did a dramatic dolphin dive at the wrong time, swearing it was "interpretive relay." By the time Nora hit the wall, her lungs were on fire and her throat felt tight.

They all floated there—silent, breathless, defeated.

"Okay," Vanessa gasped. "Raise your hand if you've personally been victimized by the universe today."

Lulu raised both hands. "Mercury's not in retrograde. Mercury's in the microwave."

Rina slapped the water. "I swear to God, if we do that at the meet, I'm going to fake an injury and become the emotional support manager."

But Nora didn't laugh. She didn't even look up.

She climbed out of the pool, each step feeling heavier than the last. The towel was scratchy against her skin. The locker room lights were too bright. The air too thick.

She stared into her locker, hoping it might hold some kind of answer. All she saw was her reflection— blurred, tired, unraveling at the edges.

Had she imagined it? The spark? The fire? Had she misread him—again? Maybe that night had been a kindness. A moment. A mistake, because now, he was gone without going anywhere and the ache of that absence made her wonder if she'd stepped too far out of her lane.

The heat of the parking lot clung to Nora's skin, thick and unrelenting. Her towel hung limply over one shoulder, and her bag thudded against her hip as she walked toward her car, head down, breath shallow. She wasn't expecting company, which made the sight of Vanessa leaning against the driver's side door all the more jarring.

Vanessa didn't move. Just tilted her head slightly. "You looked like you needed a minute. Or ten."

"I'm fine," Nora replied, though the words tasted thin.

Vanessa opened the car door and nodded toward the passenger seat. "Hop in. I've got air conditioning and pretzels that expired last week. We'll live dangerously."

The car was a welcome reprieve—cool, quiet, and far enough away from the echoes of the pool deck. Nora sank into the seat, dropping her bag between her feet.

"It was easier to pretend it didn't matter," she said eventually, voice low. "Before last night."

Vanessa handed over the pretzels. "What happened between you two wasn't nothing."

"I thought we were finally on the same page. Then today, he barely looked at me."

"That's not about you, Nora. At least not entirely."

Nora stared straight ahead. "It felt personal."

"Of course it did. You let someone in. You let him in. That's not something you do lightly."

A breeze slipped through the cracked window, but it did nothing to ease the pressure building behind Nora's eyes. She blinked hard.

"I keep wondering if I imagined it," she said. "The connection. The way he kissed me."

"You didn't," Vanessa said with certainty. "I saw his face last night. That man was gone for you. He just hasn't figured out what to do with that yet."

"So, he shut down."

"It's what people do when they're scared. Not everyone's used to something real."

Nora looked down at her lap. Her hands had started to tremble again. She curled them into fists. "I don't want to be someone who scares people off."

"You're not," Vanessa said softly. "You're just not making yourself small anymore. Some people can't handle that. Doesn't mean you shrink back down to make them comfortable."

The silence stretched; but it didn't sting.

Vanessa nudged her shoulder. "You're not invisible. Not to us. Not to me. Definitely not to Simon. I think he just needs to catch up to the version of you that finally showed up."

A laugh escaped Nora—unexpected, wobbly, but real. "You're weirdly good at pep talks."

Vanessa grinned. "Don't tell anyone. I've got a reputation to maintain."

They sat like that for a few more minutes, the sun sinking low and the edges of the sky burning gold. Something in Nora settled, not entirely soothed, but steadier. Like maybe she didn't have to hold everything alone.

"Thank you," she said, voice barely above a whisper.

Vanessa smiled, warm and certain. "Anytime. You're one of us now. We don't let our own sink."

Later that night, the house was quiet, except for the soft whir of the fan and the faint, rhythmic tick of the clock on her nightstand. Nora sat cross-legged on the bed, a blanket draped over her shoulders like armor she wasn't sure she'd earned. Her muscles ached—not from the laps, but from holding herself together all day. From the aftermath. From the raw silence that followed too much truth spoken too fast.

She opened her journal. The same one from the wellness retreat. The same page with the faded prompt written at the top in loopy, lavender ink:
What are you carrying that no longer serves you?
At the time, she'd wanted to write:
The feeling that I need to be small to be loved.
But she'd written:
The idea that I'm too late to begin again.

Now, with her breath shallow and her heart still tender from the weight of what she'd finally said out loud, she added a third line beneath both:
The fear that one bad day means I was never enough.

Her pen hovered after the last word.

She stared at it—long and hard—like it was a confession she hadn't realized she'd been circling for years.

Then, slowly, deliberately, she underlined it. Once. Not to believe it, but to name it. To face it without flinching. Because if she could write it, she could carry it, and if she could carry it, she could swim through it.

She closed the journal and exhaled. Tomorrow, she would show up again. Not because she felt brave, but because the version of her who stood her ground last night deserved to keep going. Even with shaky hands. Even with a tired heart. Even on a bad day.

***

Simon sat in the empty locker room long after the others had gone, elbows on knees, forehead resting in his hands. The hum of the fluorescent lights overhead buzzed like static in his chest.

The practice had been brutal—not just in performance, but in mood. Everyone was off. Even Nora, whose strokes had sharpened these last few weeks, had moved like she was carrying something heavier than water. And him? He'd said maybe five words to her.

"Keep it long. Reset your kick. Good hustle."

Coach speak. Safe. Impersonal. Necessary. Except it didn't feel necessary. It felt like retreat.

His fingers curled into fists, nails pressing half-moons into his palms. He could still feel her from the night before—her breath against his collarbone, her voice in his ear, the way she'd kissed him like she didn't want to come up for air, and he'd let her go. Because of rules. Because of lines. Because losing control felt more dangerous than losing her.

But as he sat there, watching the condensation on his water bottle bead and slide like time he couldn't hold onto, Simon realized something else. He knew that look Nora wore today. The strain behind her smile. The tension in her shoulders. He'd seen it before—in the mirror—during the worst stretch of his life. When he was barely staying afloat, pretending everything was fine.

When the only thing keeping him from falling apart was the lie that he didn't care about losing control but he did care. He cared about her and he wasn't sure how much longer he could pretend otherwise.

***

Somewhere across town, Nora was curled up with that blanket again, trying to quiet whatever was still rattling inside her. Willing herself to keep going, and here he was, in this hollow locker room, willing himself not to go to her.

Two people with the same ache, treading the same water alone—close enough to feel the pull, far enough to pretend it wasn't there.

Open Water

The air at the pool felt charged—thick with leftover storm heat and something else Nora couldn't name. Thunder had rolled through at dawn, and the humidity clung to the rafters, beading on the tile, turning every breath into steam. The water should've felt like relief.

Instead, it bit. Nora slipped in and gasped, letting the chill lance through her chest, a wake-up call she hadn't known she needed. Her pulse was jumpy. Her thoughts louder than her kick.

"Build sets today!" Simon barked from the deck, clipboard already fogging in his hands. "Push the last ten meters. Make it burn."

Lane 4 groaned in harmony.

Nora ducked under and pushed off. Her arms cut the surface clean, strokes practiced, efficient—but not hers. Not today. Her body felt foreign, like it belonged to someone going through the motions, not someone chasing fire. The last practice had rattled her more than she'd admitted. She still heard the echoes of that disastrous relay. Still felt the awkward distance Simon had kept ever since.

Not rude. Not cold. Just... calibrated. Professional. Like he'd re-tightened every screw between them overnight and left no loose ends to follow.

She caught a glimpse of him during a flip turn— arms crossed, jaw set, eyes fixed on her with a tension that didn't match the rest of his body. He gave a small nod.

A pulse of connection. A silent: I see you. Keep going. She held his gaze a beat too long, then pushed off. The water stung her eyes. Her lungs burned. Her thoughts spun.

Was he pulling back? Was she imagining it?

She'd let herself fall—just a little. Into something that felt alive. Into heat and hunger and a kind of safety she hadn't realized she craved. But now?

Now, the rhythm was off. The intimacy replaced by an ache she didn't know how to name. She tried to swim through it, to sweat it out through effort and grit but it clung to her like the humidity and it wasn't her stroke that was breaking.

It was something deeper.

The sun had begun its slow descent, painting the wet tiles in streaks of gold and blush. The air shimmered with post-practice haze—chlorine, sweat, effort. Nora moved slowly, toweling off as Lulu groaned about her hamstrings and Rina unleashed a string of profanity about the last sprint set loud enough to earn a warning from the lifeguard.

Vanessa leaned in, brushing hair off her damp shoulder, her voice just above a whisper. "You good?"

Nora hesitated, pressing the towel to her face to hide the flicker of uncertainty. Then nodded. "Getting there." Maybe.

She looked up and her breath stalled. Simon was walking across the deck, clipboard tucked under one arm, a towel slung low around his waist. He moved like he always did—unhurried, solid, like the pool belonged to him and he didn't have to prove it. Water clung to his skin in silver beads, catching the sunset like glass. Nora couldn't look away.

He passed closer than necessary. Close enough that the heat rising off him mingled with the damp on her skin, close enough to feel like static in the space between them.

"You held the last split like a pro," he said quietly, voice low and just for her.

She turned, pulse quick. "Trying to keep up with your expectations," she replied, forcing lightness into her tone.

He stopped. Looked at her and this time, he didn't hide anything.

"You're not behind," he said, softer now. "You're setting the pace."

The words hit her like a dive into deep water. Not praise. Not flattery. Something else. Something truer.

Her throat tightened, but she held his gaze. Because what else could she do?

He didn't smile. Didn't back away. His eyes stayed on hers, steady and unreadable—until finally, he gave the smallest nod. Like he knew what that look had done to her. Like he felt it too. Then he turned and walked off. His footsteps a soft echo on the slick concrete.

Nora's fingers shook as she tied her towel around her waist. That wasn't just encouragement. That was a line drawn in steam and sun and want and if he could shake her like this with one look and a few words— what would it feel like to fall completely?

***

Simon sat on the bench, towel slung around his shoulders, pretending to review split times on his clipboard. He wasn't. His eyes kept drifting to the far end of the pool—where Nora had just disappeared into the women's locker room.

She looked wrecked tonight—exhausted, maybe even hurting—but still she showed up. Still, she swam. There was something defiant in the way she moved through the water, like she refused to let the weight of everything sink her, and watching her, Simon felt that ache again. Not just attraction, but recognition. Something deeper.

He'd been distant all day. He knew it. Not because his interest had faded—God, no—but because the closer he let himself get to her, the more the walls he'd spent years building began to crack. She wasn't just a swimmer on his roster anymore. She wasn't even just someone he kissed in a moment of stolen heat. Nora had become something else. Someone who saw him. Who stirred up old wounds he hadn't named in years. Who made him want more than just control and solitude.

He remembered what it felt like to lose it all. Not just the race. Not just the dream. But the people who walked away when he wasn't enough. He'd spent years telling himself that staying guarded was safer. That not letting anyone close was the cost of staying afloat. But today, seeing her fight through the water like it was her battlefield too—he realized she wasn't asking for safety. She was asking for honesty.

Maybe she didn't need saving, but maybe she deserved someone who didn't run.

He picked up his phone. Fingers hovered for a moment, unsure. Then, for once, he didn't overthink it. He just typed:

Simon: *Are you free tonight?*

Pause. Then—

Simon: I don't mean for a drink.
I mean... Just us. No distractions. No goggles.

He hovered over send. Then added:

Simon: I want to be where you are. Not just on deck.

He hit send before he could overthink it.

For once, he didn't brace for the crash. He just hoped she'd say yes.

***

Nora sat behind the wheel, damp hair pulled into a knot, windows cracked, the scent of chlorine still clinging to her skin. The ache in her chest wasn't from the workout. It was from not knowing where she stood—with Simon, with herself, with all of it.

He'd been distant. Not cold, but... quieter. Careful. Maybe she had been too. Afraid to want too much. Afraid it had already passed.

Her phone lit up.

Simon: Simon: Are you free tonight?

Simon: I don't mean for a drink.
I mean... Just us. No distractions. No goggles.

The breath hitched in her throat. She stared at the screen, the message settling over her like warm water. Calming. Inviting. A little dangerous. Her fingers hovered, then tapped.

Nora: Yes. But only if you're ready to see the messy parts too. I'm not good at pretending anymore.

The three dots blinked. Paused.

Simon: *I see you already. Tonight, I want more.*

Nora exhaled, pulse racing. She didn't turn the key in the ignition. Not yet. She just sat there, the last of the daylight sliding across her windshield, her phone warm in her hand and something new cracking open in her chest.

She wasn't unraveling. She was unfolding. And tonight—whatever it became—wasn't just a maybe. It was a beginning. One she was finally ready to step into without looking over her shoulder.

The city lights cast soft halos through the blinds as Simon opened the door. Nora stood there in a hoodie and jeans, hair still damp from practice. Simple. Electric.

Simon didn't speak. Just looked at her like he'd been holding his breath all day and could finally exhale.

She stepped inside, the door clicking shut behind her like it sealed something in place. The space smelled like cedar and something clean and masculine. Low lights glowed from the kitchen, casting long shadows and golden warmth. It was quiet, private—their world for the night.

Neither of them made a move at first. Until Simon reached out, gently brushing her cheek with the backs of his fingers. "Hi," he said, like it meant more than hello.

"Hi," she whispered, and then the space between them vanished.

The kiss started slow—like they were remembering how—but deepened fast, fast enough to steal the air from her lungs. His hands slid to her waist, pulling her closer, until there was no mistaking how badly he wanted her. How badly she wanted him right back.

He walked her backward through the living room, lips never leaving hers. Her fingers tangled in the hem of his shirt, pulling it over his head with one motion. She traced her hands across his chest like she needed to memorize him.

"You're sure?" he asked, breath ragged.

"I'm here," she said, voice low. "I'm not leaving."

That was all he needed.

He lifted her effortlessly, urgent—and carried her to his bedroom, setting her down like something sacred and inevitable.

Clothes disappeared in stuttered, heated movements. Her sweater. His jeans. Her bra hitting the floor with a whisper that felt loud in the quiet. His hands skimmed her bare skin with a reverence that made her ache. Then there was nothing between them but heat and want and the weight of everything unsaid.

He kissed down her throat, over her collarbone, down the curve of her ribcage. "Tell me what you need," he murmured.

"You," she breathed. "Now. All of you."

And she got it—him.

The first touch was slow, teasing. The second made her gasp. The third had her hips arching to meet his.

He worshipped her like he'd been waiting a lifetime for permission. It wasn't sweet. It wasn't careful. It was raw and real and earned.

They moved together, bodies tangled and wild, breathing each other in. His name spilled from her lips like a song she couldn't stop singing. Her nails dug into his back. He grunted her name like it was the only thing that mattered.

He pushed her to the edge, again and again, until she finally shattered—mouth open, eyes locked on his. When she did, he followed, lost in her, undone by her, grounded and set free all at once.

They collapsed in a tangle of limbs and laughter and silence. Eventually, Simon pressed a kiss to her shoulder. "You okay?"

Nora turned her head, cheeks flushed. "I don't think I've been this okay in a long time."

He smiled and pulled her closer. "Then stay." and she did.

The sun filtered through the curtains in slow, honeyed rays. Nora stirred, wrapped in a tangle of sheets and warmth. Her legs brushed against Simon's. His breathing was steady, peaceful. She blinked at the ceiling, smiling before she even remembered why. Then it hit her. Last night.

Him. Her. Them.

She turned on her side, studying the way his chest rose and fell. There was something so grounding about the sight—like waking up next to trust.

Eventually, she slipped out of bed, pulled on one of his shirts, and padded into the kitchen.

Her phone buzzed.

Lane 4 Group Chat "X Rated"

Vanessa: So… did Coach put you through some "stroke correction"?

Lulu: Was there a whistle involved or just heavy breathing?

Lulu: Blink twice if you need electrolytes.

Vanessa: Did he shout "last set, best set" at any point?

Lulu: On a scale from "warm-up lap" to "full-body cramp," how are you feeling this morning?

Rina: Did you stick the landing or DQ on the turn?

Lulu: We need stats. Duration. Intensity. Any bonus rounds?

Nora: You're all feral and should be studied.

Vanessa: And yet… you're the one who disappeared with a very smug-looking swim coach.

Vanessa: Brunch. Noon. Wear SPF and bring a diagram.

Nora stared at the screen, cheeks burning and stomach sore from laughing. She glanced over at Simon—shirtless, asleep, and entirely unbothered.

She snapped a pic of her legs tangled in a blanket next to his very male foot and sent:

Nora: *Let's just say… I worked on my core and I'm gonna need a floatie to walk.*

Lulu: *Bitch.*

Vanessa: *Queen.*

Rina: *Legend.*

Behind her, arms slipped around her waist. Simon, still drowsy, whispered into her neck, "You texting your fan club?"

She leaned back into him. "Something like that."

He kissed her shoulder, slow and warm. "Good. Because I'm not sharing you at practice today."

She turned just enough to raise an eyebrow. "Possessive, Coach?"

He grinned against her skin. "Motivated."

She laughed—low and lazily rolled toward him, sheets tangled at her waist. "Then I better bring my A-game."

"You already do," he said, voice rough with something deeper than desire. "But watching you want more… that's what wrecks me."

That quiet settled between them again—not awkward, not uncertain. Just full. Of something forming. Of something that didn't need a label yet.

He pulled her in, like her gravity was the only thing he trusted and she let him. Not because she needed the comfort, but because it felt right to take up space in someone's arms… and not apologize for it.

Maybe this wasn't the finish line. Maybe this was the start of something wild and finally hers.

Rip Current

The pool was dark when Nora arrived—just a low hum from the overhead lights and the sharp scent of chlorine hanging like a promise in the air.

She wasn't supposed to be here yet, but her mind wouldn't quiet. Not with the meet creeping closer like a rising tide. Not with old doubts nipping at her heels. So she came to the only place that ever made sense. The deck was cold beneath her feet. The water, still and glassy, waited like a blank page.

She dove in. Not for speed. Not for points. Just to remember who she was when no one else was watching. Stroke. Flip. Breathe. Push. Her muscles burned in the best way, like they were shaking off the weight of everything she'd been carrying—fear, failure, the echo of David's voice, the ghost of expectations she'd never asked for.

Then, she wasn't alone. She surfaced and caught movement on the deck. Simon. No clipboard. No whistle. No carefully measured distance. Just him. Hoodie slung over one shoulder. Hair still damp from a too-early shower. Eyes locked on her like she was the only thing in the room worth noticing.

"You too?" he asked, his voice low and scratchy with sleep.

She nodded. "Couldn't stay in bed. My brain's doing cannonballs."

He smiled, kicked off his shoes, and dropped into the lane beside her.

They swam. Not for form or feedback, just the rhythm. The quiet. Two bodies slicing through water, finding something like peace in the repetition. Stroke for stroke. Turn for turn. It felt like a pact, silent but unbreakable.

At the wall, they stopped. Hands braced on the edge. Foreheads almost touching. Steam rising around them like fog.

"You're not just ready," Simon said quietly, voice edged with awe. "You're dangerous."

Nora looked at him, her chest tight, water streaming down her spine.

"Then I guess I should stop being scared of myself."

He didn't speak. Just reached out and gently tucked a wet strand of hair behind her ear, and in that moment—no audience, no adrenaline, just the two of them treading the thin line between fear and fire—Nora finally believed she wasn't just showing up for the meet.

She was about to own it.

Practice – 8 Days Out

The deck thrummed with energy, part nerves, part adrenaline, all teeth. Simon paced like a man with something to prove. His clipboard slapped against his thigh, and his voice cut through the humid air like a whistle.

"Time trials are tomorrow," he barked. "No excuses. No coasting. If you're not ready to bleed for your lane, stay in the locker room."

Lane 4 exchanged looks. Tension rippled through their huddle—nervous laughs, bounced knees, the kind of charged silence that came before thunder.

Nora rolled out her shoulders, trying to shake off the static building beneath her skin. Her pulse drummed at her collarbone. It wasn't just the pressure of performance. It was the weight of what she hadn't said. Of everything she felt—for the team, for herself, for him.

Simon stood near the block, clipboard clenched like it might snap in half. His gaze found her. Again. And again. Not overt. Not indulgent. Just steady—like a lighthouse in a storm.

"Lane 4," he called, voice clipped. "Hit the water."

They dove. The cold shocked the breath from her lungs, but it cleared her head. Each stroke cut cleaner than the last. Her arms burned. Her legs screamed, but she welcomed it. Because pain was real. Pain was proof she was here.

At the wall, she flipped hard and surfaced gasping.

Simon was crouched at the edge, the world behind him blurred and irrelevant. "Whatever happens tomorrow," he said, voice low and raw, "you've already won something bigger."

She blinked up at him, the words lodging in her throat.

A beat passed. Two.

"I want to believe that," she said finally, breathless—not just from the swim.

Simon's jaw flexed. "Then let me believe it for you, until you can."

Just like that, she wasn't sure what hit harder—the lactic acid in her legs or the way he looked at her like she was more than potential. Like she was already enough.

The truth was, the stakes weren't just in the lanes anymore. They were wrapped in every unsaid thing between them and she was about to dive in anyway.

The team was buzzing post-practice, the kind of energy that came from anticipation mixed with exhaustion. Lulu was rifling through her bag like a woman on the brink, muttering something about her "lucky cap" and threatening to hex anyone who touched her gear. Rina had one leg propped on the bench as she attempted to stretch her hamstring while devouring a granola bar, crumbs clinging to her hoodie like glitter.

The Masters Club

The locker room smelled like chlorine, citrus body wash, and nerves. It was chaos—but it was their chaos.

Vanessa caught Nora's eye in the mirror. She was already dressed, applying mascara with the precision of a sniper.

"You okay?" she asked, not casually, but carefully—like she actually wanted the truth.

Nora hesitated, then gave a half shrug. "Float and flail."

Vanessa didn't blink. She reached into her bag and held out a protein bar. "That's just nerves talking. Means you give a damn."

Nora took it, the foil cool against her palm. "I really do."

In the background, Rina muttered through a mouthful, "God help us all if Lulu explodes tomorrow."

"She's one chlorinated eyebrow twitch away," Vanessa added, deadpan.

Lulu popped up from behind a locker, goggles askew. "I heard that! My chakras are aligned, thank you very much. This is focus. Not rage. Focus."

The girls burst into laughter, the kind that loosened something tight in Nora's chest. But even in the joy, she felt the undercurrent—the quiet pressure thrumming through all of them. They weren't just showing up for practice anymore. They were showing up for each other. For something bigger.

And Nora? She didn't just want a good swim. She wanted to prove that she belonged, not just in the water, but here, in this circle of mismatched women with messy buns and big hearts and fierce loyalty. She wanted them to see her as one of their own.

She glanced back at the mirror, caught her reflection mid-thought. The woman looking back wasn't the same one who'd tiptoed into this locker room weeks ago. She looked flushed, yes. Tired, maybe. But steadier.

Present.

Part of something.

Vanessa leaned over, nudging her shoulder gently. "You've got this."

Nora didn't answer right away. But this time, when she smiled, it reached all the way to her eyes.

"I really hope so," she said softly. "Because I don't want to go back to floating."

Later that night, as rain tapped against her window, Nora stared at her phone. Her finger hovered. Typed. Deleted. Typed again.

Finally:

Nora: *You meant what you said today?*

It took a moment. Then:

Simon: *Every word. You're leading now. The rest of us are just catching up.*

She stared at the screen, the glow lighting her face in the dark. Her throat tightened. Her pulse pounded louder than it had in days.

Nora: *I'm scared.*

Nora: *Of wanting this much. Of what it means if I don't make it.*

The dots blinked. Paused. Blinked again.

Simon: *You don't have to be unafraid to be unstoppable.*

Simon: *Wanting it means you're alive.*

Simon: *Meet me early again tomorrow?*

She stared, thumbs hovering.

Nora: *What time?*

Simon: *Whenever you need it. I'll be there.*

She set the phone down, her lips parting on a soft exhale.

Not because Simon believed in her, but because—for the first time—she wanted to rise to meet that belief. Not to prove herself to him but to be herself, fully and maybe, finally, that was enough to start.

Time Trials – 7 Days Out

The air inside the rec center buzzed with a low, electric tension. Chlorine clung to every breath, and the echo of whistles and splashdowns ricocheted off the walls like the prelude to battle. It wasn't a meet. Not officially. But the stakes were written on every swimmer's face.

Nora paced the length of the bleachers, headphones in, the steady beat of music pulsing through her—more heartbeat than song. Her stomach twisted and coiled, a restless thing she couldn't soothe. She kept her eyes low, her breathing slow, but the nerves throbbed just beneath her skin.

Lane 4 sat nearby, but they weren't their usual selves. The energy was fractured, refracted through each of their own pre-race rituals. Vanessa sat with eyes closed, whispering quiet affirmations like a mantra. Lulu bounced one knee at a speed that defied physics, earbuds in, lips mouthing what had to be the chorus of her pump-up playlist. Rina stood by the mirror, braiding and unbraiding her hair like the strands held some kind of magic.

Then Simon appeared beside her, silent but steady. His presence hit like a jolt and a balm all at once.

"Your heat's posted," he said. "You've got two sprinters from Lane 2 and the girl from Eclipse Club in three."

Nora pulled out one earbud. "Got it."

"You know what to do."

She looked up at him, and her voice cracked more than she intended. "Do I?"

Simon didn't blink. Didn't flinch. "Yes, and the only person you need to beat is the one who thought she couldn't get here."

The words landed like a stone in a pond—rippling through every layer of doubt.

She held his gaze for a beat longer than she should have, then nodded. Not because the nerves had vanished, but because she didn't want them to win.

She peeled off her warm-ups, her Lane 4 suit hugging her like armor, and walked barefoot to the starting block. The cool tile beneath her feet made her flinch, but she stood tall.

This is yours. Own it.

She stepped onto the block. The world narrowed. The buzz of the crowd faded to static. Her breath synced with the beat that still echoed faintly in her ears. Knees bent. Fingers curled over the edge.

The buzzer snapped like a whip.

She dove.

There was no room for fear now. No space for what-ifs. The water wrapped around her like a second skin, and her body moved on instinct. Stroke. Breathe. Kick. Turn. Again. The rhythm took over, each movement a testament to every hard practice, every early morning, every time she'd chosen to try instead of quit.

She hit the wall with everything she had left.

Her chest heaved as she surfaced, water blurring her vision. She didn't look to either side. Didn't search the faces of her competitors. She looked up.

The scoreboard flashed.

A new personal record—by more than a second.

Her hand flew to her mouth, half-laugh, half-sob, as cheers erupted around her. Lane 4 was on their feet, screaming, splashing the surface like they were baptizing the moment. Even Lulu launched into a pirouette and shrieked, "Our girl's a missile!"

Then she saw Simon. He stood at the edge of the deck, arms crossed, expression unreadable. But only for a second. Then his eyes softened, his jaw loosened, and a slow, brilliant smile stretched across his face. The kind that made her knees weaker than any swim ever could.

She reached the wall and pulled herself up, legs trembling, lungs burning, pulse still caught somewhere between disbelief and joy.

Simon stepped forward with a towel, and for a second, he looked like he wanted to say something more. But instead, he handed it to her gently.

"You did it," he said.

Nora looked up at him, eyes shining. "No," she said, voice breathless but sure. "I'm just getting started."

The team exploded out of the rec center like a firework at full bloom—legs jelly, lungs burning, but hearts ridiculously high. They were flushed from chlorine, adrenaline, and the undeniable rush of knowing they'd nailed it.

Vanessa popped the trunk of her car and immediately pulled out a speaker, cueing up Lizzo with the precision of a woman who'd clearly planned this. The first notes blasted into the parking lot, bold and joyful. Rina, still half-wrapped in her towel, threw her arms into the air and launched into a dramatic gold medal ceremony—complete with a fake tear and an imaginary bouquet. "I'd like to thank the clock, my goggles, and the gods of hydration!"

"Who the hell packs cupcakes for time trials?" Vanessa asked, as Lulu appeared beside her with a Tupperware container, grinning.

"Champions," Lulu replied, solemn as a priest. "Champions pack cupcakes."

Nora blinked at the frosted treats. "Did you—did you frost them in the locker room?"

"Don't ask questions you don't want the answer to," Lulu said, handing her a cupcake with a tiny edible glitter heart on top.

They were loud, giddy, limbs tangled in half-hugs and bad dance moves. The adrenaline had shifted from pressure to pride, and it bubbled out of them in bursts.

"I told you!" Rina shouted, flinging an arm around Nora's shoulders. "You were straight fire, girl."

"I almost puked," Nora said, breathless with laughter.

"But you didn't," Vanessa countered, grabbing her other shoulder. "You held it together and burned the whole damn pool down."

Lulu raised her cupcake like a toast. "To Lane 4: Queens of controlled chaos and chlorine couture."

They whooped and spun, jumping in a loose circle like a bunch of overgrown kids at summer camp. Someone tossed a towel. Someone else dropped their goggles. A bottle of Gatorade exploded mid-shake, soaking Vanessa's sneakers.

No one cared. For a moment, it wasn't about splits or nerves or even the looming meet. It was about joy. Earned joy. The kind that came not just from doing well—but from doing it together.

Nora stood in the center of it all, cupcake in one hand, heart thudding not from fear but from something fierce and full and bright. She belonged. Here, in the chaos. In the circle. With them.

Back home, Nora had just stepped out of a steaming bath, towel twisted in her hair and skin flushed from heat, when her phone buzzed.

Simon: *You were electric today. I can't stop thinking about it.*

She smiled, heart skipping, skin still flushed from more than just hot water.

Nora: *That workout? Or the part where I nearly passed out trying to impress you?*

Simon: *Both. But mostly the part where you made the water jealous.*

She laughed, dropping onto the edge of her bed.

Nora: *I'm officially sore and maybe a little smug.*
Simon: *Good. Now come over. I'll cook. You relax. No goggles required.*
Nora: *If this is another excuse to feed me protein bars and stare at my legs...*
Simon: *Steak. Roasted potatoes. Charred broccolini if you must know. And if your legs are involved, I won't complain.*
Nora: *I'm not above being seduced by carbs.*
Simon: *Then I hope you like dessert.*
Because I've been craving your lips all day.

Her breath caught. She stared at the screen, heat blooming low and wild. No reply. She was already out the door, towel abandoned, heart racing like she was chasing gold.

He greeted her at the door barefoot, sleeves rolled up, kitchen behind him glowing with warm light and the buttery smell of garlic and rosemary.

"Chef and coach," she teased, stepping inside. "What don't you do?"

He leaned in, kissed her cheek, lingered for half a breath too long. "Still working on restraint."

They ate at the kitchen island, legs brushing under the stools. Nora wore the sweatshirt she'd "accidentally" stolen from his bag last week. It smelled like chlorine and cedar and comfort. She fed him bites off her plate, daring him to say something cocky. He wiped butter from her lip with his thumb, eyes not leaving hers.

They didn't talk about the meet. Or the team. Or what this was. They just… were.

Between bites and sips of red wine, the tension simmered—unspoken but alive. Her laugh turned into a sigh when his hand rested lightly on her knee. His gaze dropped to her collarbone and didn't rise again for a long time.

When dinner was over, she stood to help with dishes. "Leave it," he said, coming up behind her. "I didn't invite you over for your scrubbing skills."

"Oh?" she asked, turning slowly in his arms.

He didn't answer. He kissed her instead, and that was all the answer she needed. They didn't make it to the dessert.

Simon lifted her onto the counter mid-kiss, the clink of a fork falling to the floor lost beneath the sound of her laugh breaking into a gasp. Her legs wrapped around his waist on instinct, and he pressed forward, hands gripping her thighs like he was afraid she'd vanish.

"I missed this," he murmured against her neck, voice rough, reverent.

"It's only been a few days," she breathed, already breathless.

"I know," he said. "Not enough." The second time wasn't careful. It was need.

It was Nora pulling off her borrowed sweatshirt like she was shedding every fear she'd carried all day. It was Simon gripping her hips like an anchor and kissing her like he was already halfway drowning.

When they made it to the bedroom, it wasn't neat or patient—it was all collision and craving. Clothes hit the floor like confessions, fingers dragging, trembling, urgent. Her laugh turned breathless when he backed her toward the bed, his mouth claiming hers mid-smile, swallowing the sound as they tumbled down together.

Simon kissed her like he was starved for every inch of her. Like each freckle, each gasp, each shiver was a secret he'd been aching to learn. His hands mapped her like a man retracing a familiar coastline after years lost at sea—her jaw, the slope of her breast, the dip of her waist where her breath caught and her hips bucked toward him instinctively.

She matched him, heat for heat, desire for desire. Her mouth found his neck, her teeth scraped gently at his collarbone, and the groan he let out made her body ache in reply. His control, always so measured, unraveled thread by thread in her hands—and it was beautiful. He didn't just want her. He needed her. Recklessly.

When he entered her, there was nothing soft about it. It was desperate and deep, like he was trying to memorize the shape of her from the inside out. She cried out—raw, unfiltered—hips lifting to meet him, eyes locked on his like a challenge and a surrender all at once.

They moved together in a rhythm that wasn't just about sensation. It was release. Redemption. Her fingers tangled in his hair as his thrusts grew faster, harder, deeper. Every moan, every whispered name was a promise: I see you. I want you. I'm still here.
No holding back.
No rules.
No pretending.
Just Nora and Simon, coming apart and back together, over and over again—like they were rewriting every scar with every touch.

After, they didn't speak for a while. Just lay there— sweat-slicked, breathless, still humming with each other's pulse. Nora didn't tuck herself into him like before. She sprawled across the bed, bare and bold, her skin still glowing, her eyes heavy-lidded but clear.

Simon reached over, brushing a damp strand of hair from her cheek, then dragged his fingers slowly down her arm, like he couldn't stop touching her even if he tried.

"I don't think I'll ever get enough of you," he murmured, voice rough with everything he still hadn't said.

She turned her head, found his mouth with hers, and kissed him with the ease of someone who finally knew her own power.

"Then don't," she said against his lips.
And he didn't

The sunlight hit the sheets like it had plans—bold, golden streaks cutting across the tangled duvet and the bare skin underneath. Nora blinked into the brightness, her body slow to wake but already humming with the memory of the night before. Her muscles ached in the best way, and for a heartbeat, she wondered if it had all been some delicious dream.

Then she felt it—the warm, steady weight of Simon's arm draped over her waist. His skin against hers. The rise and fall of his breath at her back.

Not a dream. Not a regret. Just morning. Real and still buzzing.

She turned carefully, not wanting to wake him, though part of her wanted nothing more than to trace her fingers along the line of his jaw just to prove he was really there. He looked younger in sleep, softer. The perpetual crease between his brows had eased slightly, the tension she'd grown used to seeing in his shoulders now unraveled across the sheets.

He had held her like she wasn't a mistake, kissed her like he meant it, moved with her like he knew the language of her body better than she did.

And now? He was here. Still here. Sleeping beside her like it was the most natural thing in the world.

For the first time in a long time, she didn't want to overthink it. Didn't want to dissect every glance, every word, every 'what now'. She just wanted to hold on to the quiet. To the certainty that, for once, she hadn't run. She'd stayed, and it felt like the start of something.

Carefully, she slipped out from under the sheets and padded across the room, gathering her jeans from the floor and pulling them on quietly. Her thighs ached. Her lips were swollen. Her hair looked like she'd wrestled with a tornado and lost. But when she caught her reflection in the bathroom mirror, she paused.

Something in her face had changed.

She looked... claimed. Not by him. Not in the way she used to belong to someone else, losing herself piece by piece. This was different. She looked like a woman who had chosen something. Something bold. Something good. Maybe even someone.

Her phone buzzed on the counter.

Vanessa: *Café in 20. We're ordering pancakes... and judgment if you're late.*

Nora smiled, thumb hovering over the screen. She tucked the phone into her bag instead, then walked back into the bedroom and leaned down to press a kiss to the space between Simon's brows. He shifted slightly under her touch, murmured something she couldn't quite make out, and settled deeper into sleep.

She left quietly, closing the door behind her with care. Her body was sore, her heart full, and her friends were waiting. But as she walked out into the sunlight, one thing echoed above the rest. She didn't feel like she was leaving something behind. She felt like she was bringing it with her.

The café was chaos—mimosas clinking, toddlers screaming, someone in line demanding to speak to a manager about the "aggressive chia pudding." Lane 4 had crammed into their usual booth like a feral brunch coven, plates loaded with carbs and judgment.

Vanessa looked up from her syrup waterfall and immediately narrowed her eyes. "She's late. And glowing. Like... suspiciously dewy."

"She's glowing and smug," Rina added, sipping her mimosa like she was auditioning for Real Housewives of the Rec Center. "This is not a moisturizer situation. This is a multiple-orgasm situation."

Nora slid beside Lulu and reached for coffee. "I'm not even fully awake yet."

"You're not awake because someone kept you up swimming laps," Lulu stage-whispered, scandalized. "I can feel it radiating off you. It's giving 'exerted in ways we can't put in the team group chat.'"

Nora nearly snorted her coffee. "I'm literally just tired."

"You're tired because your legs are Jell-O and your soul left your body sometime around round three," Vanessa said.

"Round THREE?!" Rina gasped. "Oh my God, he has stamina. I knew it. His shoulders scream endurance athlete."

"Please stop talking about his shoulders," Nora said, burying her face in her hands.

"Did he do that thing where he kisses your collarbone like it's a sacrament?" Lulu asked. "Because I've fantasized about it at least twice during warmups."

"Oh my God," Nora groaned.

"Just say yes or pass a napkin," Vanessa said. "Blink once if he made you breakfast. Blink twice if you were breakfast."

Nora silently slid her plate in front of her and shook her head. "You're all deeply unwell."

"But are we wrong?" Rina asked, twirling her straw.

"No," Nora muttered. "And that's the worst part."

They all cheered and clinked coffee cups and juice glasses like she'd just gotten engaged to a Jonas Brother.

"Just one request," Vanessa said, pointing a fork at her. "Do not become one of those couples that stretch together on deck. If I see you foam rolling each other before practice, I'm quitting the team and taking up jazz flute."

"You've been threatening jazz flute for months," Nora said.

"I mean it this time," Vanessa replied, dead serious.

They all broke into laughter, Lulu snorting green juice and Rina pretending to dab away happy tears with a napkin.

Nora looked around the table—at the chaos, the teasing, the sheer joy of it all—and let herself sink into the moment. These women had dragged her out of the wreckage, fed her carbs and hope, and refused to let her shrink. They saw her happy. Which meant—maybe— she actually was.

Heat Check

6 Days to Regionals

The heat assignments dropped just after sunrise. Nora saw them the moment she opened her phone, still cocooned in sheets and sleep. Her eyes scanned the screen, brain slow to catch up.

Top three swimmers: bolded. Her name... wasn't. She was seeded fourth. She stared at the number. Refreshed the page. Checked again.

Still fourth. Not shocking, but sharp, like a paper cut on her pride. Not terrible. But not there either. Close enough to taste it, not close enough to touch...almost.

She lay frozen under the covers, heart thudding like she'd just sprinted laps. The number sat heavy in her gut, louder than it should've been.

Her phone buzzed again.

Vanessa: *4th isn't bad. It's fuel. Burn it.*

Rina: *You're going to pass at least two of them. One of them eats pizza...poolside...during warmups.*

Lulu: *Rankings don't know what the hell is coming. You're a secret weapon.*

Nora smiled faintly at the screen. But it didn't stick, because fourth wasn't fuel right now. It was fear. What if this is it? What if all the fire and work and want still wasn't enough? What if she'd already peaked and missed it—because she was too late, too broken, too much?

She tossed the phone aside and stared at the ceiling. The crack in the paint above her head looked like a lightning bolt—sharp and fractured, frozen mid-strike.

A metaphor? Probably.

She exhaled hard through her nose, chest tight. Maybe this was the punishment for believing she could change everything in one season. Reinvent herself in a few pool lengths. Maybe you don't get to outrun who you used to be. Maybe fourth place was someone's way of reminding her that she would always be, almost.

Simon stood at the edge of the pool deck, arms crossed over his chest, whistle swinging loosely from one hand. His clipboard sat forgotten on the bench behind him, half covered by a towel, like he couldn't be bothered with logistics anymore. His voice rang out across the tiles—clear, firm, but rougher than usual, like something was unraveling just beneath the surface.

"You've seen the heat assignments," he said, scanning the team. "Let them go. The rankings aren't a prophecy. Swim your damn race. No one else's."

The words landed with weight. Not just instruction—conviction. A message meant for all of them, but if Nora let herself believe it, maybe also for her.

Lane 4 gave a collective nod, half nerves, half performance. Lulu bounced in place, mumbling something about manifesting gold energy. Vanessa rolled out her shoulders like she was heading into a fight. Rina cracked her knuckles and muttered, "Let's make some chlorine cry."

Nora didn't move. Her gaze stayed fixed on the pale blue floor tiles, even as her heart pounded like it might bruise her ribs from the inside out. Fourth place. Close enough to taste it. Close enough to hate it.

She hadn't swum poorly—but it wasn't enough. Not for the board. Not for herself. Not for whatever had cracked open inside her when she kissed Simon like she wanted to rewrite every boundary between them.

But he'd kept his distance. Coaching like a pro. Detached. Disciplined. Professional to the point of cruelty.

She didn't blame him. She hated that she understood. Still, she could feel it—that shift in the air. Like static. Like breath held too long. That uncanny sense that someone was watching. Not the crowd. Not the other swimmers.

Him.

She looked up.

Simon was watching her. Not speaking. Not smiling. Just there. Still and intense. Not hiding anymore. His gaze was steady—sharp and unreadable. No pity. No soft landing. Just heat. Pressure. A kind of silent dare: Break apart or burn through.

It didn't soothe her. It ignited something. She yanked her goggles into place—too fast, too tight. She needed the sting. Then she stepped onto the block. Breath shallow. Muscles coiled. When the buzzer hit, she dove like it could wash everything clean.

The water was ice against her skin. A slap of clarity. No room for doubt here. Only stroke after stroke, lap after lap. Her arms cut through the silence, her legs kicked with fury. She didn't swim for the scoreboard, or for Simon's eyes across the lane. Not for redemption. Not even for revenge.

She swam for herself. For the girl who used to shrink into corners. For the woman who now dared to take up space. Every turn was a reclamation. Every breath a refusal. Her doubts tried to cling to her like drag, but she kicked harder, sliced deeper. Not today. Not anymore.

When she touched the wall, she didn't glance at the clock. She knew it had been good. She felt it in her chest, her arms, the shake in her legs as she surfaced.

Simon was already there—just a few paces away, towel in hand, his face unreadable beneath the sharp angle of his jaw. He didn't move. Didn't speak. But something in his stance had changed. Less guarded. Less sure.

Maybe that was the point.

She didn't wait for a verdict. Didn't chase his approval like she once might have. Instead, she climbed out on her own, dripping and breathless, heart hammering like a drumbeat of defiance.

He stayed silent.

So did she.

Because comfort wasn't what she needed from him—not now. She didn't want a soothing pat on the back or a whispered you did great. She didn't want to be reassured.

She wanted to be undeniable, and that? That was for her to claim. Not for him to give.

Everyone scattered to showers or smoothies or both. Nora sat on the bumper of her car, toweling her hair and breathing in the thick heat. The tension in her chest hadn't eased. If anything, it pulsed stronger with every passing minute.

Simon appeared, hair still wet, clipboard under his arm, t-shirt damp against his shoulders. He didn't speak at first. Just looked at her—longer than usual. Like he could see past the exhaustion to the fire she was still trying to reignite.

"You swam angry today," he said.

"Is that bad?"

"Not if it's focused."

She snorted. "It didn't feel focused. It felt like I was clawing at something I couldn't quite reach."

He lowered the clipboard, stepping closer. "You're seeded fourth, not last. This isn't a setback. It's your runway."

Nora let her head fall back slightly, eyes closed. "You say that like you're sure."

"I am."

She opened her eyes again, voice quieter now. "And what if I'm not?"

Simon moved in, close enough that the air between them all but vanished. "Then you lean on me. Borrow my belief. Until yours comes back."

Their eyes locked. There was nothing casual about it. Not anymore. Not after nights in his bed, mornings tangled in sheets, secrets shared between breaths.

Yet in this moment, it was about more than want. It was about worth. Her throat tightened. "You're really not going to let me spiral, are you?"

"Not a chance."

"Even when I'm a pain in the ass?"

He smirked. "Especially then."

She didn't say thank you. She didn't have to. He knew.

She nodded—small, but certain.

He reached out, just briefly, to tuck a strand of wet hair behind her ear. His fingers lingered just long enough to make her breath catch. Then he smiled, low and knowing, before turning and walking away. She watched him go, the air still buzzing from where he'd stood. Her body still tuned to the heat he left behind.

The living room that evening was quiet, the kind of quiet that settles when the world outside is moving too fast. Nora sat curled on the couch, journal open, pen tapping against the page. In the center, she'd written one number.

4

She circled it. Then again. Then stared. It meant two things.

Lane 4 — the misfit squad that had held her together when she was ready to fall apart and fourth place — the ranking that felt like a ceiling slammed down on her confidence.

One reminded her who she was. The other whispered who she might never be. She drew a line beneath the number and started to write.

Lane 4 saved me.

Fourth place dares me.

I don't back down from dares anymore.

Her phone buzzed on the table.

Simon: *Early swim tomorrow? Just us.*

Nora: *What time?*

Simon: *Whenever your fire shows up.*

She smiled. The kind that wasn't for anyone else. Then typed back:

Nora: *Then expect sparks before sunrise.*

She closed the journal, fingers still pressed to the cover. She didn't want to beat the top three. She wanted to beat the version of herself who ever believed she couldn't. Maybe—just maybe—burn down everything that tried to box her in.

With Lane 4 behind her and Simon exactly where she needed him— Not carrying her but watching her rise.

The pool was still asleep when Nora walked in. The overhead lights buzzed quietly, casting reflections that danced like ghosts across the tiles. The air was thick with chlorine and calm.

Simon stood at the far end, hoodie zipped up, coffee in one hand, eyes already on her. He didn't wave. Just smiled like he'd known she'd come.

Nora dropped her bag and pulled off her sweatshirt in one motion. "I told you I'd show."

His smile deepened. "I never doubted it."

They dove in. For the next twenty minutes, they didn't speak. Just moved—lap after lap, the silence between them turning from awkward to intimate. Stroke. Breathe. Turn. It wasn't training. It was something else. Something quieter. More honest.

After a final set, Nora grabbed the edge, breathless, adrenaline buzzing in her chest. Simon swam to the wall beside her, shoulders glistening, hair slicked back. He rested one hand on the ledge near hers. Their arms didn't touch, but the space between them felt charged.

"You swam like you meant it," he said.

"I did."

"You still thinking about that number?"

She nodded. "But not in the same way."

He tilted his head. "How's that?"

"I was looking at it as proof I wasn't enough." She looked down at the water, then back up at him. "Now I see it as a starting point. Not a ceiling."

Simon smiled, soft and sure. "That's what I see, too." The way he looked at her—it wasn't just admiration. It was recognition. Of the fire. Of the fight.

She leaned in, just slightly. "You believe in me, don't you?"

"I do," he said. "But more importantly—you believe in you."

She let that sit between them, the truth of it warming her more than the water ever could.

Then, like gravity finally won, she closed the space. Their lips met, not with hesitation, but with certainty. A kiss that didn't ask permission. A kiss that didn't apologize. When they pulled apart, her breath was shaky, but her spine was straight.

"Okay," she said. "Now I'm ready."

"For what?" he asked, voice low.

She turned back to the water and smiled. "To burn that number down." Then she pushed off the wall—fast, fearless, free.

By the time the rest of Lane 4 wandered onto the pool deck yawning, half-dressed, and still arguing about whether protein bars counted as breakfast, Nora had already knocked out a thousand meters and was wringing water from her hair like she'd just emerged victorious from a mythical sea quest. She stood tall, towel slung around her neck, the faintest smirk playing on her lips.

Vanessa froze mid-step and narrowed her eyes. "Okay, but why do you look like a goddess who just tamed a kraken and made it say please?"

"Because she did," Simon said as he passed behind them, clipboard tucked under his arm, smirk dangerously close to a grin. His tone was dry, but there was a spark in his eyes. One Nora felt all the way down to her still-tingling toes.

Rina gave Nora a suspicious once-over. "You were here early. Like... weird early. Like morning make out early."

"Just wanted some extra laps," Nora said innocently, dabbing her face with her towel.

"Right," Lulu deadpanned. "Is 'extra laps' the new code for 'horizontal cardio'?"

Vanessa gasped theatrically. "Oh my God, Lulu."

"I'm just saying," Lulu shrugged, eyes wide with fake innocence. "She's glowing. Like, post-yoga and a good cry glowing."

Rina leaned in, whispering loudly, "I think she's high on endorphins and... something else."

Nora laughed, deep and bright. She tossed her towel over her shoulder like a cape. "You're all deeply unwell."

"But like," Vanessa added, looping an arm around her, "unwell with love."

Simon blew his whistle, short and sharp. "Lane 4. Water. Now. Sass later—preferably after no one drowns."

They all groaned theatrically as they shuffled toward the blocks. Lulu mimed a funeral march. Rina saluted dramatically before diving in. Vanessa lingered just long enough to nudge Nora with her elbow.

"Whatever pre-practice ritual you've got going on, do it again tomorrow."

Nora grinned, stepping to the edge. "Oh, I plan to."

She caught Simon's eye as she slipped into the water, just a second, just enough and the heat in his glance told her they were both thinking the same thing.

Morning laps might just become her favorite new tradition.

By mid-morning, the team group chat was already buzzing, final taper schedules, uniform fittings, last-minute hype. Emojis flew. Memes were dropped. Someone suggested matching glitter scrunchies again. The usual chaos.

For Nora, everything felt sharper. Quieter. Clearer. The nerves were still there—but they hummed beneath the surface like power, not panic.

Six days out from the biggest race of her adult life, and she wasn't unraveling. She was ready. Not because of a ranking. Not because of Simon. But because she'd fought like hell to find this version of herself—fierce, focused, unflinching.

She wasn't swimming alone anymore.

Not in the lane.

Not in her head.

Not in her life.

She had fire in her lungs, steel in her bones, and Simon's quiet belief echoing in her bloodstream like a drumbeat: Wanting is the start of everything and now... She wanted it all.

The Push

Five Days to Regionals

The pool was louder now. Tighter. The energy around Lane 4 had shifted into something sharper—less jokes between sets, more staring at the clock. The sound of slaps on water, the echo of breath. It all meant one thing: they were getting close. Taper week was always strange. The workouts got shorter, but the pressure got louder.

Nora arrived early. She wasn't the only one. Vanessa was already stretching with headphones in. Rina bounced on her toes, muttering her splits from memory. Lulu adjusted her cap with a scowl.

Simon didn't have to say much that morning. Just a few quiet directions and a raised eyebrow when Nora lingered by the kickboard stack. He didn't smile, but his eyes were warm. Focused. Steady.

She needed that steadiness. Because inside, she was all nerves. Her muscles still ached from the early morning swim with Simon the day before, but it was a good kind of sore—a reminder of momentum. Of movement. Her body felt different now, more hers. Stronger.

She slid into Lane 4 and let the water swallow the noise. They started slow. Loosening up the joints. Easy 100s to reawaken the rhythm. Nora exhaled underwater, bubbles trailing along her cheekbones, before breaking the surface and catching her breath. The pace gradually picked up. She fell into rhythm quickly, letting the water cradle her into focus.

Stroke. Breathe. Kick. Flip.

Every time she surfaced, she caught glimpses of her team—each of them locked into their own orbit of determination. Lulu, fierce and controlled. Vanessa, churning water like she was born in it. Rina, teeth clenched, laser-focused on the clock. Lane 4 didn't talk much that day, but they moved like one. Four bodies, one will.

Her own breath came cleaner now. Her flip turns hit sharper. Her catch stronger. The tension of the week hadn't vanished. But it was channeled—transformed into speed.

Simon blew the whistle. "Sprint pyramids. Full throttle. Rest is earned." Groans, but no one argued.

Nora pushed hard. Harder than before. Even when the lactic acid burned in her legs. Even when her shoulders screamed. She thought about that number 4. She thought about every version of herself she'd buried under doubt and she swam through them all.

They gathered at the end of practice, towels wrapped and hair dripping. Breathless. Spent. Sharpened.

Simon walked the deck slowly, clipboard in hand, eyes moving from swimmer to swimmer like a laser beam. He gave feedback like a scalpel—precise, fast, cutting through excuses.

"Vanessa, fix your entry angle. Lulu, your third lap needs more discipline. Rina, breathing pattern's off. Nora—"

He paused.

Everyone turned.

He looked at her for a beat. "You're holding back at the wall. Don't. Not this week. Not ever again."

The words landed like a body check.

Nora nodded, jaw tight. "Got it."

Lulu elbowed her as they headed toward the locker room. "Why do I feel like that was coaching foreplay?"

"Don't encourage her," Rina muttered, already smirking.

"I'm just saying," Lulu went on, towel slung over her shoulder like a cape. "If my ex-husband talked to me like that, we'd have three more kids."

Vanessa sipped from her water bottle with dramatic flourish. "That man says 'breathing pattern' like it's dirty talk."

Nora rolled her eyes. "You're all ridiculous."

"But you're glowing," Vanessa sing-songed. "Like a woman who's been thoroughly… coached."

Nora tried to bite back her grin. Failed.

"Let's just focus on the meet," she said, tugging her swim bag higher.

Rina snorted. "Oh we are. We're just not sure which event you're training for—100-meter freestyle or Olympic-level tension."

Lulu wagged her eyebrows. "Either way, we better win gold."

Later, Nora doubled back to grab her fins. The equipment closet door creaked open and there he was. Alone. Shirt clinging to him in all the right places, damp from practice. Coiling lane lines like it wasn't the single most distracting thing she'd ever seen. The air smelled of chlorine, leather, and him. Music played low, some pulsing beat that felt like a heartbeat beneath the quiet.

He looked up. Didn't say a word. She stepped inside, letting the door click shut behind her. It echoed.

"You scared me a little out there," she said. Her voice was soft, but it carried. "That tone. That edge."

"Good." Still coiling, like his hands needed something to do. "You need to be pushed. You're not here to be comfortable."

She crossed the room slowly, each step a dare. "And if I break?"

That made him stop. The line slipped from his fingers. He turned and everything snapped. Two steps. That's all it took to close the space. His hands were on her hips, her back slamming lightly against the shelving. Fins hit the floor.

His mouth crashed into hers—hot, urgent, unrestrained. There was no teasing this time. No breath between them. Just heat.

She gasped against his lips, fisting his damp shirt, pulling him closer until she could feel every solid inch of him. His hand slid up beneath her team hoodie, calloused fingers grazing bare skin. Her breath hitched as his palm found the small of her back, holding her there like he couldn't let go.

"Nora..." he said against her mouth, a warning, a prayer, a curse.

She kissed him harder in response. Her thigh slipped between his legs, teasing, testing, and the sound he made—low, guttural—shot straight through her.

"Tell me to stop," he rasped.

She shook her head. "Don't you dare."

His hands roamed now, up her spine, along the edge of her ribs, never venturing too far but close enough to make her ache. She tugged his shirt upward, fingertips brushing the ridges of his stomach.

But just when it tipped toward reckless— He stilled. His forehead dropped to hers. "We can't. Not now. Not here."

"I know," she whispered, though everything inside her screamed otherwise.

His hand stayed on her waist, grounding them both. "After the meet," he said. "After you set the water on fire."

She swallowed, breath ragged. "That's a long five days."

He gave a half-laugh, half-growl, brushing her cheek with his thumb. "Then go. Before I stop caring about rules altogether. I'm not going to be the reason you lose focus," he said. "Not when I've never wanted you more."

She stared at him, lips parted, every nerve humming. Then she kissed him one last time—slow and deep, a promise tucked inside a goodbye.

"Five days," she whispered.

He nodded. "And then I'm not holding back."

***

Simon stayed pressed against the shelf, eyes closed, fists clenched at his sides. Her scent lingered—chlorine, skin, and the unmistakable pulse of want—but it was more than that now. It was knowing her. Having her. Remembering the way she'd unraveled beneath him, and how he'd come undone right alongside her.

His heart pounded like he'd just finished a brutal IM set, but this wasn't exertion. It was restraint. Barely.

She'd kissed him like she meant it. Like the water, the world, the risk didn't matter and he'd almost let go. Again.

Training this week had wrecked him. She was laser-focused in the pool, rising to every challenge with that wild, quiet fire he'd come to crave. When she looked at him, mid-set, eyes dark and determined, like he was the current she'd caught hold of—he forgot every line he'd drawn.

The locker creaked under his weight as he leaned back, dragging his hands through damp hair. This wasn't just heat anymore. It was hunger, yes, but also reverence. Respect. Something tender that scared the hell out of him.

He wasn't just risking his job or the team dynamic. He was risking her trust—the fragile, hard-earned thing that mattered more than all the rest.

His phone buzzed on the shelf.

Nora: *Still shaking. Not sorry.*

He let out a breath he hadn't realized he was holding.

Simon: *Still catching my breath. Still pretending I have any control around you.*

A pause.

Nora: *Five days, right?*

He stared at the screen. Five days until the meet. Five days until the rules changed. Until there were no more excuses.

Simon: *Five days. But if you keep touching me like that when no one's looking, I'm not going to make it.*

Three dots. Then:

Nora: *You already didn't.*

He laughed quietly and helplessly. Then slid the phone into his pocket, heart thudding, the ache in his chest shifting into something bold and dangerous and full of promise.

***

The moment still clung to her skin like steam as she stepped under the shower spray. Water rushed down her spine, but it couldn't wash away the heat coiled low in her belly. Not from the kiss. Not from the way his hands had found her waist like they'd always belonged there.

She pressed a palm to the tile wall, chest rising and falling. Her muscles ached from practice, but it was a different kind of breathlessness now. The kind that came from being seen. Touched. Wanted, and not just wanted—believed in. That was what undid her. That was what made her knees still feel shaky.

Five days. Five more days until the meet. Until the line between them shifted again. Until everything either ignited—or fell apart.

She got dressed slowly, grounding herself in small motions—shoelaces, towel, lip balm. The kind of mundane things that felt like armor when the world was tilting slightly on its axis.

Outside, the sun had nearly vanished. The parking lot was quiet. A single moth danced around the overhead light as she slid into her car.

The warmth that bloomed in her chest wasn't just from the kiss. It was from the knowing that he saw her. That she was ready and that maybe, for the first time in a long time—she wasn't in this alone.

The soreness returned that night but it was tinged with satisfaction. She sprawled on the floor, foam roller under her calves, iced coffee sweating beside her.

Her phone buzzed.

Lane 4 Chat: Queens of Chlorine and Chaos

Lulu: Emergency team dinner tomorrow. My place. Carbs + trash TV = peak performance prep.

Rina: Garlic bread or I'm boycotting.

Vanessa: Also, if anyone mentions rankings, I'm bringing a spray bottle.

Rina: Pajamas mandatory. I want maximum comfort and zero bras.

Nora: I'm bringing wine and judgment.

Lulu: Stretch. Rest. Hydrate. Also bring tea. Gossip. Emotional damage. Whatever you've got.

Vanessa: Especially chlorine-flavored gossip

Lulu: NORA, come prepared. I saw that equipment closet linger

Nora: *I'm not the only one making sexy eye contact…*
Lulu, I saw you fawning over the lifeguard!
Lulu: *He has objectively excellent calves. That's just*
science.
Rina: *Save the thirst for tomorrow, squad. I'm bringing my*
emotional support lasagna.

Nora smiled at the screen. Her heart felt lighter than it had in days.

Then a second buzz.

Simon: *Tomorrow. 5:30. Before anyone else arrives. Meet*
me at the pool. No clock. Just us.

She didn't reply right away.

Instead, she closed her eyes, let the ache settle into her bones like music. She was scared. She was tired. She was sore, but she was ready.

The Test

Four Days to Regionals

The early morning light hadn't fully claimed the sky when Nora pulled into the lot. The pool parking lot was empty, dew slicking the windshield like a fresh breath. She sat for a moment, hands gripping the wheel, heart thudding in her chest. It wasn't just nerves. It was anticipation. Electricity.

Simon was already waiting by the door, coffee in hand, hood up, posture casual—but his eyes locked on her like she was the only thing worth watching.

"Morning," he said, voice low and warm, like gravel smoothed by years of tide.

"Barely," she replied, stepping past him, pulse ticking up.

He unlocked the gate, held it for her.

They walked the deck in silence, footsteps echoing like something sacred. The air inside was thick with chlorine and anticipation. The pool lay still—glasslike— waiting.

Simon set his coffee down, took her bag gently, like it was something precious.

"We're not tracking splits today," he said. "This isn't about numbers."

Nora peeled off her sweatshirt, revealing a navy training suit and skin still marked faintly from yesterday's pull set. She adjusted her cap, her gaze steady.

"Then what is it about?" she asked.

Simon met her eyes. Steady. Calm. "Trust."

Her breath hitched. She nodded. Stepped to the edge. The water shimmered and she dove in. There were no whistles, no shouted intervals. Just breath, movement, and silence. She swam until her shoulders burned and her lungs ached, and then she swam harder. Not to win. Just to feel the fight.

Simon moved beside the water like a shadow, never too far, crouching now and then to murmur in her direction:

"Lengthen your reach."

"Hold your core."

"Let it flow."

Every word skimmed the surface between them, gentle and anchoring. When she finished her final set, she floated at the edge, chest heaving. Simon crouched beside her, eyes locked.

"You weren't holding back," he said.

"Not anymore," she replied, her voice hoarse with effort.

He offered her a quiet smile. "I saw it. The shift. You're owning the water now."

Nora rested her cheek on her forearm, blinking up at him. "I didn't want to need this so much."

Simon's voice dropped. "Wanting isn't weakness, Nora. It's what fuels us."

Her fingers curled around the edge of the lane. "Even if it scares me?"

"Especially then." He reached down and brushed his fingers lightly over her wrist—just once, but it lingered. "You're not the only one scared."

She nodded. Then pushed off, gliding into another lap—not because she had to, but because she could.

Nora pulled herself out of the water, muscles trembling, chest heaving. She sat on the edge, legs still submerged, as Simon stepped forward and handed her a towel, but he didn't walk away.

Instead, he lowered himself beside her, his presence warm and close but not pressing. Their knees almost touched. Their silence stretched.

"I used to think if I just did everything right— every rep, every drill, every decision—nothing could fall apart," he said, eyes on the shimmering water. "But everything still did."

Nora glanced sideways. He wasn't just talking about swimming.

"I lost Trials by a hairline," he continued. "I blamed the lane, my goggles, the crowd noise, but it was

me. I swam not to win—just not to lose. I locked it all
down. No nerves. No joy. Nothing but tension."

His voice broke just slightly on that last word.

"I thought control would keep me safe. It didn't. It
just made me numb."

Nora turned toward him fully now, her heart tight
in her chest.

He met her gaze. "Then you showed up. With your
fire. Your fear. All of it right there, and for the first time
in a long time, I wanted to feel again." He looked away.
"Which scared the hell out of me."

Nora's throat tightened. She reached out, slowly,
and laced her fingers through his. Not to comfort. To
say: Me too.

"I let someone make me small," she whispered.
"David didn't say the words, but he didn't have to. The
sigh when I spoke too long. The way his eyes glazed
over when I shared a win. The look he gave me when I
cried during a movie. It was death by a thousand tiny
cuts."

Simon's jaw clenched.

"I stopped asking for things," she said. "Stopped
dreaming out loud. Stopped believing I could take up
space and still be wanted."

She looked down at their joined hands, then back
up. "I thought love meant disappearing." Simon's
breath caught. "That's not love."

"I know, now" she said softly. "But I didn't."

Silence fell again, but this time it ached with meaning. He squeezed her hand, his thumb brushing the side of hers like he was trying to memorize it. "I don't want you to shrink for me. I want you to blaze."

Her eyes shimmered. "Then stop holding back."

Simon swallowed hard. "You scare me, Nora."

Her voice was steady now. "You scare me too."

They sat like that for a long time, two people learning to want without apology, to hurt without hiding, to choose each other without losing themselves and in that quiet, something sacred took root. Not a promise. Not yet, but the fragile, fragile start of one.

Tidal Wave

Practice had just ended when Simon's voice rose above the scrape of goggles, the slosh of tired feet.

"Nora, hang back for a sec."

Her pulse kicked. She wrapped her towel tighter, ignoring the way Vanessa and Rina both slowed to glance back. Simon stood alone at the edge of the deck. No clipboard. No backup. Just a look on his face she couldn't read.

"We're shifting you to Lane 2 starting tomorrow," he said evenly. "Coach's call."

Nora blinked. "Lane 2?"

Simon nodded. "We want you pacing against different swimmers—pushing your speed, throwing off routine."

She opened her mouth to respond but stopped. Her breath caught somewhere behind her ribs. Away from Lane 4. from them.

She nodded once. "Got it." It came out flat.

He didn't say anything else. Just gave her a tight smile, the kind that didn't touch his eyes. The kind that meant we don't have a choice.

She turned, towel damp against her shoulders, and walked back toward the team, but the moment they saw her face, she knew the news had already shifted something in the air.

Vanessa stepped forward. "What's going on?"

"They're moving me to Lane 2."

"What?" Rina's voice spiked. "Why? That's—no."

"Some strategy thing," Nora said lightly, too lightly. "Cross-training. Fresh pacing. It's not a big deal."

But no one laughed. Lulu's smile fell off her face.

"It is a big deal," Lulu said. "We've trained together all season."

"You're part of us," Vanessa added. "Lane 4 is Lane 4 because you are."

Nora shrugged like it didn't matter, like her chest wasn't caving in. "It's just lanes. We're still a team."

Rina raised a brow. "It's not just lanes. It's the one place we know how to breathe."

That was the thing. It wasn't about drills or yardage. It was about belonging. Nora looked at them— her messy, mouthy, loyal crew and felt the sting creep up the back of her throat.

"I'll still be here," she said. "Still cheering. Still us."

As she walked to the locker room, the ache in her ribs told her the truth: Sometimes the hardest part of growth wasn't failure. It was being asked to rise... alone.

Simon didn't say much. Just a clipped, "See you tomorrow." No eye contact. No quiet encouragement. No secret smirk that said I see you in the way only he could. Just words. Cold. Spare. All wrong. Nora felt the absence like a slap of chlorine to the face.

***

What she didn't see, what he made damn sure she didn't see—was the wreckage he carried as he turned away. His voice might've sounded detached, but inside, he was fraying.

Simon hadn't slept. Not really. He'd spent the night watching shadows crawl across the ceiling, heart hammering like he'd never touched calm. The pillow beside him still held her scent, like a bruise he kept pressing. Her laugh had embedded itself in the walls, soft and unshakable, and her name, beat behind his ribs like a secret he couldn't afford to say out loud.

She was everywhere. In the water. In his thoughts. In every crack of his composure and now, he had to pretend she wasn't.

He wanted to undo it. All of it. The reassignment. The quiet. The boundary he'd drawn like a coward wearing the mask of a coach. Every instinct screamed to fight for her. Not as her trainer. As her person, but he didn't. Because this wasn't about what he wanted. It never had been.

She'd earned that reassignment. A new lane. A harder challenge. One that could push her even further. Maybe even win her the time she was chasing. And the awful truth? He agreed with it. Objectively. Strategically. It was the right move.

But emotionally? It gutted him.

Because if she swam better without him... If she rose in that new lane, proved to herself and everyone else that she didn't need him to level up—what did that mean for them? What did it mean for everything they'd shared in between the strokes and glances?

Maybe it meant he was just a chapter in her story. Not the climax. Not the resolution. Just the part where she remembered how powerful she was all on her own.

So he stood there, watching her retreat from the deck with stiff shoulders and no glance back, and he forced himself not to follow. Not to reach.

He swallowed the ache, buried the want, and let his silence be the thing that protected her dream. Not because it hurt less, but because loving her meant believing in her, even if it meant standing still while she moved forward. Even if it meant watching her swim away.

***

She slammed the car door so hard the rearview mirror shook. Then she screamed—raw, primal—into the steering wheel, forehead pressed to the leather, fists clenched tight. The sound ripped through the cabin, bounced off the windows, fell back onto her like a second skin.

But it still wasn't loud enough to drown it out.

You don't matter.

You're easy to leave.

You're forgettable.

Her breath caught. Shallow. Fast. Her chest heaved like she'd just sprinted a mile with no finish line in sight. The seatbelt cut into her ribs. Her training bag slumped beside her like a hollowed-out version of herself.

She gripped the wheel like it might anchor her to something real. Something solid. But her hands were shaking. Because this wasn't just about the lane. It was the look on Simon's face—the nothing in it. The clipped tone. The way he didn't fight for her. Didn't even look at her.

It was the silence. The way Lane 4 had fallen quiet, like a party she used to be invited to, and it was David. That goddamn Tuesday afternoon. She'd walked into his office, two coffees in hand, still buzzing from the morning's big win—her idea approved, her pitch applauded. She was proud. Hopeful. Maybe even expecting him to be proud, too.

He didn't even glance up from his laptop. Just muttered, "You're really celebrating that?"

She froze, the door still half-open behind her. He leaned back in his chair, eyes flat. "Nora, let's be honest. You're great at smiling and making people comfortable.

But no one sees you as the one with the answers. You're not the big-picture type. You're... support."

She stared at him, heart dropping in slow motion.

Then he added, with a shrug that felt like a slap: "You should be happy to be in the room. Know your lane."

Know your lane.

It echoed long after she'd left. Long after the coffees had gone cold. Long after she stopped bringing ideas to anyone.

He didn't have to cheat. He just chipped away at her until she forgot she was ever whole and now it was happening again. This ache. This hollowing. This feeling of being shuffled aside, no explanation, no lifeline. Just... forgotten.

The tears came fast—hot and stinging, making her eyes blur before she could even swipe them away.

She looked down. Her phone blinked in the cup holder.

Lane 4 Chat: Lane 4 FAM Dinner

Vanessa: *Dinner tonight? Bring wine or secrets (ideally both)*

Lulu: *do tears count as an appetizer? asking for a friend*

Rina: *only if they're seasoned with drama*

Nora stared at the screen. Her thumb hovered over the "Not Coming" button.

Don't go, that old voice said. Don't let them see
the crack.
Don't give them proof that you were always the weak
link.

Her thumb pressed. Paused. Pressed again.

And then— Another voice. Softer. Deeper. Hers.

You stayed this morning. You swam. You're still
here.

She swallowed hard. Grabbed a tissue from the
glovebox and blew her nose, hard enough to feel it in
whole body. No victory speech. No triumphant music
swelled in the background.

Just breath. Just choice. She wasn't going to run.
Not again. Not because someone else decided she didn't
belong. She wiped her face with the sleeve of her
sweatshirt. Reached for the gear shift. Not whole. Not
yet. But still standing and maybe, for today, that was
enough

***

Simon sat in his car long after the parking lot had
emptied, engine off, headlights dim. His hands were still
locked on the steering wheel like he needed it to anchor
himself—because everything else inside him felt like it
was slipping.

The silence was suffocating. He picked up his
phone. Opened a new message.

Simon [typing]: You okay?

Delete.

Simon [typing]: I didn't want to pull you from Lane 4.

Delete.

Simon [typing]: I can't stop thinking about you.

He stared at that one for too long. Then erased it too. Instead, he opened the Notes app and let his thumb move faster than his breath could catch up.

You think I don't care. But the truth is I care too damn much. That's the problem.

I've never been neutral with you. Not from the beginning. The second you walked onto that deck with that storm in your eyes, looking at the pool like it owed you something, I felt something shift. You weren't just another swimmer. You were a spark I couldn't ignore.

You scare me. Not because you're fragile, but because you're not. You remind me of everything I used to feel before I shut it all down. Before I convinced myself that calm and control were safer than passion. That the clean lane lines and the structured workouts were enough. That if I could just keep everything in order, I wouldn't lose everything again.

And then you smiled at me. And everything cracked.

I've spent years building a life that didn't need anyone. A version of myself I could trust, steady, solid, the guy who didn't screw things up. Who didn't reach too far or let anyone in too close. But you? You make me want more. You make me feel more, and I don't know what the hell to do with that.

I'm supposed to be your coach. That's what I keep telling myself. But that word—it's too small. It doesn't hold what I feel when I watch you fight through doubt, when I see you rise even when you're shaken. It doesn't explain the way my chest aches when you laugh, or the way I can't stop looking for you in a crowded room.

This isn't just want. It's deeper than that. It's the way I respect you. The way I admire the fire in you. I see the way you carry yourself, even when it hurts. Especially when it hurts, and I know that if I'm not careful, I could get in the way of everything you've fought to reclaim.

That's what wrecks me. The fear that loving you might clip your wings. That I'll become another reason you hold yourself back.

So I've stayed quiet. Tried to play it safe. Pretended that distance was noble. That holding the line would somehow protect you—and protect me. But the truth is, I'm already in it. Deep. And silence isn't safety. It's surrender.

I don't want to lose myself in this. I've done that before, and I barely clawed my way back. But with you... I want to figure out how to build something. Something that doesn't ask either of us to shrink.

So no more pretending.

I want to be the man who stands beside you—not in front of you, not above you. Just beside you. Fully. Honestly.

*Without fear. And without losing the pieces of myself I
fought to rebuild.
Because you're not a detour. You're not a mistake.
You're the first thing in a long time that's made me want to
be more.*

He sat back, exhausted, his chest tight like he'd just
surfaced too fast and forgotten how to breathe. He
didn't send it but the truth lived there now etched in
digital ink, raw and exposed, a confession he couldn't
say out loud. Not yet. Maybe not ever.

***

Nora sat cross-legged on her bed, notebook open in her
lap. Her pen hovered above the page. She hadn't
journaled in weeks. Like moving her body had somehow
silenced her thoughts but tonight… she needed both.

She wrote:

**I feel stupid for hoping this would be different.
I thought Lane 4 meant something. I thought he
did.
Maybe I was just a summer distraction in a navy
swimsuit. Maybe I'm not built for any of this—
spotlights, expectations, pressure. I used to be the
one people counted on. Now I can't even count on
myself to not unravel over a lane change.**

She stopped, staring at the words until they blurred.

Then, in smaller handwriting:

But I didn't quit.

Not this time.

I got in the car. I screamed. I broke a little.

And I still want to swim tomorrow.

She drew a shaky breath. Then added:

Because I want to know what happens if I don't walk away. Because something in me is still reaching. Because maybe I'm worth the next lap.

She closed the notebook, slid it beneath her pillow, and turned off the light.

Nora showed up the next day. No tears. No explanations. Just goggles pulled tight, shoulders squared, silence wrapped around her like armor. She didn't glance at Lane 4. Couldn't. Not yet. Her chest felt too tight, her heart too raw. She wasn't sure if she could handle what she'd see in their eyes—pity, disappointment, or worse, indifference.

When practice ended, they were there. Waiting. Rina was the first. She crouched at the edge of the pool like it was the most natural thing in the world, hand extended, palm up. She didn't speak, didn't smile—just steadied Nora with the kind of touch that said: You don't have to do this alone.

Vanessa followed, already unfolding a towel like she'd timed it to the second. "I warmed it on the radiator," she said, breezy but intentional. "So if it smells like singed lint and desperation, blame me."

Then came Lulu, holding a green juice with the solemnity of a priest presenting communion. "Drink this. It's kale, ginger, and probably some trace amounts of lawn," she said. "But also—you know—hydration and rebirth or whatever."

Nora took it with both hands. "Tastes like regret and grass clippings," she whispered, the words catching halfway between a laugh and a sob.

They didn't press her. Didn't ask what happened or what hurt. They just fell into step beside her, forming a loose orbit as they wandered to the bleachers, wet footprints trailing behind them like a constellation. No one led. No one followed. They just moved together.

Vanessa dropped onto the bench and patted the space beside her. "Come sit in your power," she said.

Nora sat. Towel-wrapped, damp-haired, heart still rattling.

Lulu pulled a handful of neon Post-its from her hoodie pocket, each one folded into a tiny paper triangle. "We started a thing," she said. "Mantras. Don't mock them. Or do. But they're working."

Rina rolled her eyes, but her voice was gentle. "They're basically spells, if you think about it."

Nora unfolded hers.

Own the water.

She stared at the words, chest tightening again but not from hurt. From recognition. They were simple, but they were for her.

No speeches. No dramatic group hug. Just the quiet gravity of women leaning in. Shoulders touching. Legs overlapping. Breaths syncing. A constellation drawn tight on a metal bench in the echo of the pool deck. A place to land. A place to rise.

Vanessa's voice was soft but steady. "Being moved doesn't mean being replaced."

"You're not invisible," Rina added. "We see you. All of you."

"You're Lane 4," Lulu said, her voice fierce, "no matter where they put your name on a heat sheet."

Nora blinked hard. The tears didn't fall, but they shimmered. The ache didn't vanish, but it lightened. She folded the Post-it carefully and tucked it into her swim bag.

Then she looked at the women beside her—her people, her sisters, her weird, wonderful lighthouse crew—and for the first time in days, she exhaled.

"Lane 4 is family," she whispered.

The words didn't feel borrowed or brave. They felt true. Not because nothing had changed but because everything had—and they were still here. They weren't just saving her. They were saving each other.

The Countdown

Three Days to Regionals

The meet was close enough to taste. Every breath at practice felt heavier, thicker with anticipation. The usual soundtrack of splashes and casual smack talk was replaced by something quieter, more focused. No more experimental drills. No surprise sets. Every lap now had a purpose. Every stroke was a rehearsal for war.

Nora stood at the edge of Lane 2, one arm slung across her chest, stretching slow. Her muscles ached, but it was a good kind of ache—the kind that said she hadn't backed down. She watched the others in Lane 4 warming up across the pool. Her lane. Her people. Still joking, still chaotic, still wrapped in the kind of comfort that only comes from knowing exactly where you belong and yet here she was, two lanes over. Not unwelcome. Just... unrooted. Like being at a party where you used to live.

She pulled her goggles down, the plastic biting into her skin. Her hands trembled slightly. Maybe from adrenaline. Maybe from the quiet whisper inside her head that still hadn't gone completely silent.

What if you peak too early? What if Lane 2 is where they put swimmers who don't deliver when it counts? What if they were right about you?

She blinked hard and shook it off. No, she'd earned her spot. Not just in this lane but in this sport, in this version of herself.

No one else had come into this pool gasping for breath and clawed their way forward lap by lap. No one else had crashed, burned, rebuilt, and come back sharper. She wasn't here by accident. She was here because she refused to let anyone—Simon, David, her own shadow—decide she was done.

She adjusted her cap. Breathed in. Counted to four. Exhaled.

On the deck, Simon barked out a split time. His tone was all business now. The clipped consonants. The zeroed-in gaze. She could feel his presence like a current in the water—even from across the pool. He didn't look at her. Not directly. But she still felt watched. Seen.

They hadn't touched in days. Barely spoken. Whatever quiet thing had bloomed between them had been pruned back to something professional, restrained, strategic.

But Nora knew what lived beneath that clipped precision. She'd felt it. Against the shelving. In the stolen minutes between sets. In the way he said her name like a confession. She dove in, and in that moment, there was no more room for doubt.

There was just water and her and the fire in her lungs saying: Go.

Nora dove in and gave the water everything. It wasn't just practice anymore, it was a reckoning. Each lap was a trial. A demand. A dare. Her arms sliced through the surface with precision, but her insides were chaos. Fury and doubt twisted in her gut like a rip current.

Her breath stayed even, but her mind was anything but.

Why had he pulled away?

Why now, when she needed him most?

Why touch her like she mattered, only to retreat like she didn't?

The questions stung more than the chlorine. The ache in her chest wasn't from exertion—it was the aftermath of silence. The phantom of a connection he seemed desperate to forget, and every time her face broke the surface for air, she imagined screaming across the pool: *Don't act like I don't mean something. Don't make me the only one carrying it.*

Mid-set, she caught his eyes. A single glance. A single nod. Precise. Measured. Infuriating. A crumb of acknowledgment, like she should be grateful for that scrap. Like she hadn't been in his hands, in his sheets, in his damn heartbeat.

It wasn't enough. She slammed her hand against the wall at the next flip turn, harder than necessary, and powered off like a rocket. Her legs burned. Her lungs protested. But she didn't care. She fed the fire. Let it sharpen her. Let it become something useful.

Her new lane partners were beasts—quick off the block, ruthless in the water, sharp-edged and relentless. There were no glances, no cheerleading, no shared mantras. Just competition. Yet—something in it worked. It forced her to hold her line. Forced her to find an edge that didn't rely on comfort.

She missed Lane 4, but she couldn't deny the steel that Lane 2 forged in her. Then she heard it. His voice. Clear. Singular. "Nora, lead the next set." She blinked water from her lashes and pulled forward. The others followed and just like that—she was in command.

The water shifted around her like it had been waiting for her to take charge. Every movement was smoother now. Cleaner. Her body synced to the current like it was an extension of herself. Every pull stronger. Every breath, precise.

Simon walked alongside the lane, silent but ever-present, keeping stride like he was pacing her heartbeat. He didn't speak. Didn't cheer, but his gaze didn't waver and she felt it. She felt him. Like a tether. Like gravity.

She didn't look at him, but she knew he saw her now. Not just as a swimmer. Not just as the woman who'd kissed him breathless behind a storage shelf. But as a storm.

When she exploded off the wall for the final 100, his voice cut through the air again.

"Hold that pace. Find your fire."

She did. She summoned every ounce of pain, longing, fury, and turned it into propulsion. The pool bent to her will. The world narrowed to a tunnel of speed and silence and flame. And when her hand slapped the wall one last time, she ripped off her goggles and blinked up—

He was there. Already kneeling at the edge, his face unreadable but eyes burning.

"That was it," he said, voice low, steady. "That's what I've been waiting to see."

Nora's chest heaved but it wasn't just air she inhaled. It was pride. Power. Proof. Beneath it, under the glimmer of adrenaline and recognition, was that same heat. That same ache. That same maddening question still unanswered:

Did he pull back because it was too much... or because it wasn't enough?

Still, she didn't ask because this wasn't the moment for begging. This was the moment she proved she didn't need to.

The pool deck had emptied. The fluorescent hum above was the only sound besides the slow drip of water off her fingertips. Nora lingered, stretching out her arms, pulse still thrumming from the final set. She was sore. Spent. Sharpened.

Simon appeared beside her. He didn't speak right away. Just stood close enough that she could feel his presence steadying her, anchoring her like lane lines in rough water.

At last, his voice broke the silence—low, rough around the edges. "You swam like someone who knows who she is."

She turned to him, breath catching. "I think I finally do," she said softly. "Or at least...I'm not afraid to find out."

That was all it took.

He didn't ask. Didn't check the room. He just took her hand—roughly, desperately—and pulled her toward the corridor that led to the storage room.

Nora followed.

The door clicked shut behind them. The air inside was thick with chlorine and heat. Dim light filtered through the cracked blinds. Kickboards, ropes, fins, forgotten towels. A forgotten corner of the world and the only place either of them could finally breathe.

She turned to him, heart pounding. Then he kissed her. There was no pretense, no gentle build. Just all that tightly leashed want breaking open at once. His mouth crashed into hers like he was done pretending, done holding back. Her hands yanked at his shirt. His gripped her hips like he needed to anchor himself or else burn up on the spot.

They didn't speak. They didn't have to. She pulled his shirt over his head. He tugged hers off in one motion. His mouth was on her shoulder, her collarbone, her chest—worshipping and ravenous all at once.

She gasped when he lifted her, pinning her back against the mat pile. Legs wrapping around him. His shorts dropped. Her suit bottoms were gone in a blink. Their skin met in a rush of heat and need and memory.

It was slow at first. Almost reverent. Then desperate.

He moved inside her with a shuddering groan like he'd been waiting for this—for her—for too long.

She met him with every thrust. Every breath. Every inch of herself.

She was dizzy with it.

With him.

"God, Nora—" he said, voice cracking.

She grabbed his jaw, made him look at her.

"I'm here," she whispered.

And something broke in him.

"I love you."

It tore out of him like a truth too big to hold back anymore.

She froze for just a second. Then cupped his face with both hands, eyes burning.

"I love you too."

He kissed her hard, relief and longing crashing together—and then they moved faster, chasing the edge. When they finally shattered—together—it wasn't quiet.

It was fierce. Gasping. Unapologetic.

After, they lay tangled on the old gym mat, breathless, skin slick and sticky. His hand found hers. Their fingers locked.

He looked over at her, eyes unreadable but full.

"No more holding back," he said.

She nodded, chest rising. "No more pretending this doesn't matter."

Because it did. Because they did.

The second Nora walked in, dripping with smug satisfaction and still wearing Simon's hoodie, the locker room went feral.

"HO-LY HELL," Lulu shrieked, leaping onto the bench like she'd spotted a celebrity.

Rina dropped her conditioner bottle in shock. "Oh my GOD. Look at her. She's levitating."

"I KNEW IT!" Vanessa shouted, slapping the locker door. "I told you all when she said 'extra laps' she meant horizontal cardio."

Nora froze mid-step, hoodie yanked halfway over her head. "Can you all not?!"

Lulu practically lunged. "Is that a HICKEY?!"

Nora scrambled to fix the hoodie. "It's from a goggle strap!"

"Oh sure," Rina said, arms crossed. "A flesh-toned, perfectly mouth-shaped goggle strap."

"Tell us everything," Vanessa demanded. "Was it slow and tender or, like, utility-closet feral?"

Lulu gasped. "Wait—was it the utility closet?! THE SACRED CLOSET?!"

Nora turned beet red. "You guys are insane."

"That's not a no," Rina whispered.

Vanessa held up her Hydroflask like a mic. "On a scale from 'chaste forehead kiss' to 'I need physical therapy,' where are we landing?"

Lulu jumped in: "Did he say something emotionally constipated but devastatingly hot? Like 'I can't lose you before regionals' while removing your swimsuit?"

Nora hid her face behind a towel. "This is a hate crime."

"THIS IS LOVE," Rina corrected, shimmying in celebration.

"You radiate post-coital energy," Vanessa added. "Like... your aura smells like chlorine and sin."

"You guys are the worst, in the best possible way" Nora muttered.

There was a pause. Then all three exploded again.

Rina threw a tampon like a confetti cannon. "CONGRATULATIONS ON GETTING LAID...AGAIN...IN THE STORAGE ROOM!"

Nora doubled over, laughing so hard her eyes watered. "I swear to God, I hate you all."

Vanessa grinned. "Shut up. You love us."

And she did. Desperately. Even if she was definitely hiding in the locker stall until everyone left... and possibly sleeping in Simon's hoodie until the end of time.

The automatic doors whooshed open and the they all spilled out of the rec center, still buzzing from practice. Nora was the last to emerge, hair damp, cheeks pink, looking glowy.

Simon walked out behind her. Silence. Like the universe paused.

Then—

"Ohhhh my GOD," Lulu howled. "Is that a post-swim strut, Coach?"

Vanessa shrieked. "No, no, no—THAT is a man who has recently been emotionally rearranged."

"Wait," Rina said, pointing. "Are you two... are you two wearing the same smile right now?"

Simon froze mid-step, clearly debating if he could just turn around and sprint back into the pool.

"Simon," Lulu said sweetly, blocking his path with one tiny arm, "do we need to debrief you on how Nora likes her eggs in the morning? Because we made a chart."

"I hate all of you," Nora muttered, dragging her hoodie over her head.

Vanessa cackled. "That's not what you were saying twenty minutes ago, apparently!"

"STOP," Nora hissed, wide-eyed.

"You guys," Rina said in mock horror, "the utility closet. It's ruined. I'm never going in there again. I'll see a kickboard and think of your… kicks."

Lulu doubled over. "She came out of the locker room looking like she'd seen God and made out with him."

"And Simon," Vanessa added, turning to him with a slow nod, "you look like a man who just saw the light and then immediately lost all structural integrity."

Simon pinched the bridge of his nose. "Please. Please don't say structural integrity."

Nora was walking away now. Power-walking. Speed-walking. Probably considering international relocation. But Lane 4 trotted after her like loyal glittery gremlins.

"You're glowing," Vanessa sang.

"You're limping," Rina added.

"I'M NOT—"

Lulu grinned. "I'd limp too if I'd just been romantically tackled by six feet of pent-up swim coach."

Vanessa pulled out her phone. "This is going in the group chat. Immediately."

Simon looked at Nora, completely undone, completely his and laughed despite himself.

Nora threw her hands in the air. "You people are feral."

"And we're YOURS," Lulu yelled.

"LANE 4 FOREVER," they all shouted.

Simon shook his head, still grinning. "You girls need help."

Vanessa winked. "Nah. We just needed you to finally tap that."

Lane 4 FAM Chat: Lane 4 Forever
Lulu: Okay, taper starts tomorrow which means I'm officially retiring from movement until Regionals.
Rina: We literally have practice tomorrow.
Lulu: And I shall glide through it like a majestic sloth. Respect my process.
Vanessa: Reminder: No boys, no drama, no dairy this week.
Nora: …You brought an entire cheesecake to the pool deck on Monday.
Vanessa: It was emotional support dairy. Different rules.
Lulu: Taper week = emotions are HIGH and our leg hair is LOW.
Rina: Speak for yourself. I'm conducting a science experiment on my shins.
Nora: I'm alternating between feeling like a goddess and crying over an old cereal commercial.

Lulu: That's the spirit. Peak taper behavior.

Vanessa: Nora, if I don't see you strut in tomorrow like you own all six lanes and the chlorine in the pipes, we're fighting.

Rina: Verbal threats = love in this group.

Nora: Love you psychos.

Lulu: Lane 4 is a coven and the pool is our potion.

Vanessa: Now shut your eyes, hydrate, and visualize domination.

Rina: And Lulu—no texting your lifeguard crush during dryland. WE SEE YOU.

Lulu: He said I inspired him to consider sunscreen. IT'S SERIOUS.

Nora: Can't wait to swim fast and emotionally unravel with you all tomorrow

Vanessa: Lane 4 forever, baby. Let's go turn some chlorine into gold.

Nora set her phone down, the glow of the Lane 4 group chat still buzzing in her chest like static and sisterhood.

The house had gone quiet. The kind of quiet that used to feel like absence—but tonight, it felt like fuel. She stood, stretched out her shoulders, and walked to the window. Outside, the world spun on like nothing was about to change. She knew better, the countdown clock was almost out. Just days to Regionals and for the first time, she wasn't counting down with dread. She wasn't unraveling. She was sharpening.

Every lap. Every ache. Every whisper of doubt had been burned away in chlorine and fire. The stares. The reassignment. The silence from Simon. None of it broke her. It built her. She wasn't the underdog anymore. She was the storm, and Regionals? They'd better be ready for her.

The Taper & the Test

One Day Until Regionals

The rec center buzzed with quiet intensity. Regionals were tomorrow, and Lane 4 could feel it in their bones. The air inside was crisp, the pool warm and humming like a live wire. It wasn't just anticipation, it was readiness.

Lane 4 stood together again. Nora planted her feet beside Lulu, Vanessa, and Rina. For a heartbeat, she let herself soak it in. The belonging. The full-circle return. After days in Lane 2 clawing for footing, Coach Patel's reassignment the night before felt like absolution. Or maybe redemption.

Nora knew it hadn't come from Patel. It was Simon. It had to be. No explanation, no ceremony—just a slip of paper on her locker that morning with her name and her lane, underlined once: Lane 4.

She hadn't said a word to him yet. Didn't need to. Not after what had passed between them. Not after everything they didn't say but felt.

"Okay," Lulu said, hands on hips, "we're not starting this last practice without a power pose circle. Non-negotiable."

Rina raised an eyebrow. "Is this the one where we summon inner goddesses or scream into the chlorine fog?"

"Yes," Lulu said solemnly. "Both."

Vanessa rolled her eyes but stepped forward anyway. "Let's make it weird."

They formed a loose circle on the pool deck. Arms up. Chins high. Breathing deep like warriors preparing for battle—or maybe chaos. Nora stood a little taller.

"I swear to God if you make us do interpretive dance again—" Rina began.

Lulu pulled a crumpled note from her swim parka like it was ancient wisdom. "We speak our mantras. We assume our stances and we reject mediocrity in all its beige forms."

They burst out laughing but did it anyway. Each of them calling out their mantra like a sacred oath:

"Fast is a mindset!"

"Flirt with the edge!"

"Hydrate or die-drate!"

"Own. The. Water."

They stood in a goofy-yet-somehow-epic circle of outstretched limbs and powerful declarations, breathing in each other's energy like a collective spell.

"Okay now, truth serum," Lulu said, pulling out her mason jar of green goo.

Vanessa backed away like it was radioactive. "No."

"One sip each. Don't be cowards."

Nora took the jar and braved the first taste. "Tastes like grass and vengeance."

Rina gagged after her sip. "Why does it feel like it's judging me from the inside?"

Lulu nodded proudly. "It should."

As they passed it around, Simon appeared at the far end of the deck, clipboard in hand. He didn't say anything—just paused, watching them, the faintest smile tugging at the corner of his mouth.

Vanessa elbowed Nora. "Your boyfriend looks amused."

"He's not my—" Nora started.

Rina snorted. "Girl, please. That man watched you like you were the Olympic flame."

"Can we not?" Nora said, cheeks pink.

"Can and will," Lulu grinned. "Also, you're glowing and slightly limping. Coincidence? I think not."

Nora threw her towel at her, laughing, just as Simon's voice cut across the deck: "Let's lock in, Lane 4. Time to finish strong."

As they turned toward the blocks, Nora glanced at the three women flanking her. Her team. Her tether.

Vanessa bumped her shoulder. "You ready?"

Nora nodded. "More than ever," and as they stepped up, arms brushing, they didn't just look like teammates, they looked like a unit forged in fire, sweat, and too many green smoothies

The Masters Club

The rec center pulsed with pre-meet energy. Regionals were tomorrow, and Lane 4 stood shoulder-to-shoulder at the edge of the pool—no longer splintered, no longer uncertain. Four silhouettes joined together as one.

This wasn't just a return. It was a reclaiming. Lulu cracked her neck like she meant business. "So. We're gonna scare the chlorine out of this pool or what?"

Vanessa bumped Nora's hip with hers. "You good?"

Nora nodded once. "Better than."

Rina blew a breath out. "Alright, witches. Let's fly."

They didn't need a countdown. They dove in as one—four bodies and one heart. It wasn't graceful. It was powerful. The water wrapped around them like it remembered their rhythm. Like it had missed them.

Nora's strokes synced with theirs like she'd never left. Rina's pacing pulled her forward, Vanessa's underwater kicks lit a fuse, and Lulu—chaotic, fearless Lulu—cackled mid-butterfly and nearly swallowed half the pool. It didn't matter. They were back.

They were Lane 4.

The workout hit hard—sprints, ladder sets, oxygen-starved repeats—but they fed off each other. Each of them pushing the next. They didn't just swim. They hunted. As one.

Simon watched from the far side of the deck, calling intervals, voice low and even. But his eyes never left Nora. Not once.

"Last 200," he called. "Together. Make it count."

They did.

Every turn hit clean. Every pull was deliberate. They moved like a single force cutting through water, leaving only churned-up power in their wake.

When they finally surfaced, panting and laughing and leaning against the lane line like they'd just swum to war and won, Nora felt it all hit her at once: her team. Her place. Her fire.

Lulu slapped the water. "We are a damn unit!"

Rina coughed. "I briefly saw God and she was wearing a glitter scrunchie."

Vanessa grinned and handed Nora a water bottle. "You didn't miss a beat."

Nora took a long sip, cheeks aching from the grin she couldn't stop. "You didn't let me."

Lulu held up her truth serum mason jar. "Victory sip?"

Vanessa recoiled. "Absolutely not."

Lulu shrugged. "More for me. Tastes like kale and revenge."

They circled up right there on the deck, arms touching, heads tilted toward one another in their usual, chaotic constellation.

Then, from behind them:

"You've already finished more than most would dare."

Simon's voice.

They turned. All except Nora. She didn't have to. She felt him.

Rina leaned in, stage-whispering, "Oh my god, he's giving Disney Channel monologues now."

Vanessa added, "We've entered the soft-launch phase of Nora's situationship."

"Hard-launch if she walks back to her locker limping again," Lulu quipped.

Nora buried her face in her towel. "You're all terrible."

Simon, somehow not hearing or expertly ignoring them offered a subtle nod before walking off. Nora, still breathless, still a little stunned—watched him go, her heart full of things unsaid.

The countdown clock ticked toward Regionals. Forged in chlorine, girlhood, grit, and truth serum that tasted like pond scum. Every breath, every bruise, every look from him and every time Lanc 4 stood by her side had carved her into something new. Tomorrow? She wasn't just racing. She was arriving.

Later, after the others had cleared out and the pool noise faded to a distant hum, Nora stayed behind in the stands—still wrapped in her towel, hair damp against her cheeks. She sat unmoving, eyes fixed on the water as if trying to memorize its surface. Or maybe steady herself against it.

Simon approached slowly but didn't sit right away. Just stood there for a moment, holding something between his fingers.

"I found this," he said quietly, "stuffed behind the lockers. Lost and found bin. Figured it was yours."

She blinked, taking the folded slip of paper from him. It was wrinkled and slightly water-stained.

Her breath caught.

A sticky note. Her handwriting faded but unmistakable.

Don't choke. Show up. Finish something.

A laugh slipped from her lips—thin and shaky. "God. I forgot about this."

"I didn't."

She looked up at him, startled.

"I saw it your first week. Before you even made it through warm-up," he said. "You were sitting out front in your car. You looked like you might bolt."

"I almost did."

He finally sat beside her, close enough to feel the heat coming off her skin but still letting her breathe.

"I wrote this after I saw David," she said, her voice flat with memory. "Right before that first practice. He was at the bank, of all places. Just... smiling like nothing had ever happened. Like I hadn't spent years of my life shrinking myself for him."

Simon didn't speak. He didn't need to.

She kept going, her eyes still locked on the water. "I used to call it a bad breakup. Like it was mutual. Like we just didn't work. It wasn't that." Her jaw tightened. "He chipped away at me. Quietly. Constantly. Made me question my instincts, my ambition. Called it love, but really it was erosion."

Simon's hands curled into fists. He forced them to relax.

"He told me once," she whispered, "that I was 'too much to root for.' Can you believe that? Like being proud of me was exhausting."

Simon's throat worked around the silence.

Nora looked down at the note again, fingers smoothing its crumpled edges. "I wrote this in the car. I didn't think it would change anything. Just needed something to hold onto."

"It did change something," Simon said. "You showed up."

She turned to him, slowly. Her eyes glistened, but her chin didn't waver.

"You think I can do this?" she asked.

He didn't hesitate. "I know you can."

A long pause passed between them, quiet but charged. Then his hand slid over hers, warm and certain.

"He didn't break you, Nora."

She looked down, voice soft but steady. "No. But I've been putting myself back together ever since."

"You have." He looked down at the note in her lap. "And every brick you've laid has been yours. Not his. Not mine. Yours."

She leaned into him, her head resting on his shoulder, the note still clutched in her hand like a talisman.

In that quiet space—between old wounds and new courage—they sat. Not as coach and swimmer, but as something steady. Something becoming.

Lane 4 FAM: The Masters Club

(8:37 PM, the night before Regionals)

Lulu: *Just shaved my legs. I am SPEED.*
Also maybe slightly bleeding.

Rina: *Just laid out my suit, cap, backup cap, backup to the backup cap... and 4 protein bars I will not eat but need emotionally.*

Vanessa: *I'm doing yoga to center myself but also scrolling TikTok. So... balanced?*

Nora: *Packing my bag. Realized I still have Lulu's glitter scrunchie from last week. It may now be good luck.*

Lulu: *OMG DO NOT WASH IT. It is marinated in pure victory and vibes.*

Rina: *Also, whoever took my watermelon Nuun tabs, I will find you.*

Vanessa: *That was Nora. She thought it was candy.*

Nora: *IN MY DEFENSE it was pink and I was dehydrated and vulnerable.*

Lulu: If this meet goes sideways, I'm blaming the watermelon theft.

Rina: If this meet goes sideways, I'm blaming Lulu's swamp potion.

Lulu: Excuse you, it's green juice. Cucumber. Celery. Truth. Perseverance. Beyoncé.

Vanessa: I'm bringing sour candy and sarcasm. That's my fuel.

Nora: What if I mess up tomorrow?

Rina: Then we pick you up, shake you off, and reapply glitter.

Lulu: Then we scream "Lane 4 forever" and cannonball into the warm-up pool.

Vanessa: Also we probably cry. But like, hot girl crying.

Nora: Okay but seriously. I love you guys. So much.

Lulu: Ugh gross feelings. But same.

Rina: Die for you bitches. Just saying.

Vanessa: Tomorrow we swim like champions. Or caffeinated squirrels. Either way.

Lulu: Lane 4 is always a vibe. See you at sunrise, mermaids.

Nora: Let's go set the pool on fire.

Nora set her phone down on the nightstand, the glow of the group chat still warming her chest. The girls' jokes, their chaos, their unwavering belief wrapped around her like a favorite hoodie. She exhaled slowly, the kind that empties more than lungs.

As the room settled into silence, a different kind of energy stirred. Not nerves. Not fear. Something... quieter. Sharper.

Then

Simon: *You asleep yet?*

Nora: *Not even close.*

You?

Simon: *Nope. Thinking about tomorrow.*

Thinking about you.

Nora: *Dangerous combo.*

Simon: *Tell me about it.*

I watched you lead that last set like it was war. You're ready.

Nora: *Then why am I so scared?*

Simon: *Because it matters. Because you care.*

Fear doesn't mean you're not ready. It means you're alive.

Nora: *That was almost poetic, Coach.*

Simon: *Don't tell the other swimmers. I have a reputation to protect.*

Nora: *Seriously though... thank you. For pushing me. For seeing me. Even when I didn't see myself yet.*

Simon: *Always.*

(And especially when you didn't.)

...

Simon: *I want to say something. But I'm not sure it's the right moment.*

Nora: *Say it anyway. I can handle you now.*

Simon: I'm proud of you. Not for swimming fast—though damn, you do. But for coming back to yourself.
Nora: Okay, now I'm crying. And it's your fault. Just know that.
Simon: Occupational hazard of falling for someone unstoppable.
Nora: We're still unpacking that clipboard trauma, FYI.
Simon: It's not trauma. It's... structured emotional buffering. That clipboard is a symbol of my deep emotional repression.
Nora: We'll unpack that later. Right now, I'm going to try and sleep, and tomorrow, I'm going to show up and finish what I started.
Simon: That's my girl. Sleep tight. Dream big. I'll see you at the blocks.
Nora: Don't be late.
Simon: Wouldn't dare.

She turned off her phone and set it face-down on the nightstand. For a moment, she just sat there, cross-legged on her bed, the quiet settling around her like fog. No clipboard. No coach's voice. No team chatter or chlorine in her hair. Just her.

Tomorrow, she'd step up to the blocks. Not because someone was watching, but because she had decided to show up. Finally, it didn't feel like proving something to the world. It felt like claiming something all her own.

She pulled the folded sticky note from her bag, the one Simon had handed her like it was treasure and smoothed it flat.

Don't choke. Show up. Finish something.

She smiled, because this time, she would.

***

Simon sat in his apartment, lights low, clipboard tossed on the floor. It was the first time he hadn't reviewed splits the night before a major meet.

Instead, he stared at the empty space beside him on the couch and imagined Nora there. Legs curled under her. Smirking at his annotated heat sheets. Daring him to lighten up. She'd rewired him in ways he hadn't known he needed.

Not just with the way she swam but the way she lived. The way she cracked open hard things and let the light in. Maybe that was why he couldn't sleep, because she wasn't just racing tomorrow. She was arriving and win or not, he'd be there—eyes locked, heart wide open—ready to meet her on the other side.

***

The First Heat

Arrival – Regionals Day 1

The regionals natatorium was a cathedral of chlorine and chaos. Sunlight cut through the high windows in golden beams, illuminating the haze of steam and nerves that clung to every surface. Banners hung like relics from the rafters, each one a testament to swimmers who had once stood on this very deck, lungs burning, hearts thundering.

The bleachers were a riot of sound and movement. Parents held laminated heat sheets like holy scrolls. Coaches barked last-minute instructions. Someone dropped a cowbell. A toddler in a too-big swim cap wandered between the rows, dragging a soggy stuffed dolphin and a trail of Goldfish crackers. The air crackled with potential.

Lane 4 walked in. Not casually. Not quietly. They arrived—like a glitter-drenched girl gang summoned for battle. Navy warmups zipped to the chin. Lightning bolt tattoos stamped on sharp cheekbones. Lulu had wielded her travel-size can of body glitter with religious fervor, misting their shoulders like she was blessing a coven before war.

Vanessa adjusted her headphones and popped a piece of gum with cinematic precision. "Okay, let's go remind people who the hell we are."

"I brought backup tattoos," Rina whispered, rifling through her bag like a magician. "And gummy worms."

"Bless you," Lulu said, already handing out tinted lip balm labeled *Swim Like You Mean It.*

No one said it out loud, but the weight of Regionals pressed at their backs like a current. This was it. The moment they'd trained for. Bled for. Screamed, sprinted, and sweat through a season for. Even so, the Lane 4 energy remained untouchable: bold, weird, ride-or-die.

They moved as one toward their assigned bench, and that's where Simon stood. Clipboard in hand. Polo crisp. Coach Mode activated. He looked like stability incarnate—sharp lines, firm voice, every motion precise. He didn't fidget. He didn't pace. When his eyes met Nora's, something in him shifted.

Not visibly. Not for the crowd, but she saw it. The blink that lingered a second too long. The breath that caught before it could settle. The way his posture softened, like his body recognized her before his brain gave it permission.

He handed out heat assignments, relay orders, and schedule reminders with practiced ease. When he reached Nora, he dipped slightly, his voice low, meant for her alone.

"You look dangerous."

She didn't glance up. Just rolled her shoulders back, the corner of her mouth twitching.

"Good," she said. "I feel like it."

He didn't say anything more, he didn't have to because she was dangerous now. To her competitors. To every version of herself that ever doubted she belonged here and as the whistle echoed and swimmers began warming up, Lane 4 took their place at the edge of the pool—not just a relay team, but a force. The countdown had begun.

The 4x100 relay was up first. Not a warmup. Not a soft start. Regionals didn't believe in easing in. Nora adjusted her cap with shaking fingers, blinking against the brightness of the lights. The air inside crackled— whistles, chants, the slap of water against lane ropes. All of it too loud and not loud enough to drown out the sound of her own pulse.

Lane 4 stood behind the blocks, shoulder-to-shoulder, a wall of glitter, muscle, and quiet fury. No one smiled. Not yet. Vanessa rolled out her shoulders. "Let's wreck something."

"I'm bedazzling my rage," Lulu muttered, holding up a sparkly fist.

Nora's nerves buzzed. She wasn't the first. She wasn't the anchor. She was the third leg. The hinge. The bridge between keeping up and breaking through.

The Masters Club

Vanessa stepped onto the block first. A deep breath. A subtle nod. Whistle blown. Then she launched—arms slicing, legs pounding, all grit and fury. Her tempo was feral and hungry. She clawed through the water like she had something to prove, because she did. They all did.

Nora and the others tracked her every stroke. No one spoke. This was religion now. At the turn, Vanessa clipped the wall—just slightly off. A ripple of panic fluttered in Nora's chest. Lulu hissed. Rina muttered something sharp under her breath but no one fell apart.

Lulu was up next. She bounced once on the block, glitter catching the overhead lights like she'd planned it. Vanessa hit the wall and she dove—not clean, but fearless. Her stroke was a little wild, a little showy, but there was power behind it. Every kick was defiance, every breath a grin she refused to hide. She wasn't the fastest, but she swam like the water was lucky to have her. When she slapped the wall, her eyes were blazing, already looking for the next cheer to throw.

Now it was Nora's turn. Lulu hadn't even looked up from the water when Nora dove in. The water met her like it knew her name. She cut through it clean, all fire and fight. Every kick an answer to every doubt that ever dared to rise in her chest. She wasn't the backup plan. She wasn't an afterthought. She was Lane 4.

She caught the girl in the adjacent lane on the second lap.

Passed her on the third. Behind her, she could feel the others screaming. She couldn't hear the words. Didn't need to. They were in her blood now.

At the final turn, she poured everything into the wall, lungs burning, limbs searing. Her hand slapped the pad and Rina exploded off the block before Nora's body even surfaced.

Nora gasped at the surface, gulping chlorine-laced air, her chest heaving.

Vanessa reached down first, grabbing her wrist. "That's how we fucking swim."

Lulu shouted, "We're still in this!"

Rina blazed through her laps like a comet, closing the gap. The crowd was roaring now, drowning out even Simon's commands. Nora felt her throat tighten, not with fear. With pride. Wild, breathless pride.

Rina touched the wall. They were third. Not first. Not perfect, but united. Lane 4 pulled each other in, arms over shoulders, heads pressed together in a tangle of steam and sweat and glitter.

"We did that," Vanessa whispered.

"No," Lulu said. "We are that."

They didn't need medals to know what they were made of. Nora? She didn't need a hero's moment to feel like she belonged because she had them, and they had each other.

As she was wringing out her cap, breath still ragged from the relay, she heard a voice as familiar as it was venomous sliced through the noise.

"Well. Look who finally figured out how to finish something."

Nora turned slowly, like she already knew. David stood there in a pressed white shirt and smug entitlement, standing just past the barrier like he owned the damn building. His grin was all teeth. Predatory. Polished. Empty.

"What are you doing here?" she said, her voice flat.

He sipped from a sleek paper cup, probably $7 espresso with a splash of judgment. "Saw the meet on the schedule. Thought I'd drop in, I couldn't miss the Nora Comeback Tour. Heard glitter was involved. Very 'look at me', Very on brand."

She stiffened. "Leave."

He ignored her. "Third place, huh? Impressive. Honestly. You're usually better at collapsing under pressure that rising to meet it."

Simon appeared like gravity at her side, silent and still, but the tension in his shoulders was coiled and ready.

David's eyes slid to him. "Ah. The coach. Of course, very cliché." Simon's jaw flexed, but he didn't speak. Not yet.

David turned back to Nora, stepping closer, voice just low enough to cut. "You always did need someone to rescue you, didn't you? I just got tired of holding you together."

Something in her snapped.

Nora dropped her towel, stepped forward, and pointed at him with the full weight of her fury. Her voice didn't shake—it boomed.

"You didn't hold me together. You hollowed me out."

David blinked but she wasn't done. Not even close.

"You chipped away at me—inch by inch—until I questioned my own fucking reflection. You rewrote every win as luck, every dream as delusion. I shrank myself to fit inside your fragile masculinity, and you still called me 'too much.' I gave up promotions, friendships, pieces of myself so you could feel like a king in a sandbox."

Her voice rose. People nearby turned to look.

"You didn't break me, David. You bored me. You drained me. You made me feel like being seen was a burden, like ambition was a disease and when I finally woke up, you were already halfway into someone else's life like I'd been a clerical error."

His face flushed, mouth opening and closing again.

"You don't get to show up now. You don't get a front-row seat to what I rebuilt without you. You sure as hell don't get to comment on it."

She stepped even closer. Inches from him.

"So take your espresso. Take your weak-ass insults and take your spineless little ego back to whatever sad LinkedIn-influencer nightmare you crawled out of. Because this—" she gestured to the pool, the team, the roar of her life behind her "—this is mine now. Not yours. Never again."

She leaned in with a smile that didn't reach her eyes. "You are the least interesting thing about my story."

Then she turned and found Lane 4 standing behind her. Vanessa. Rina. Lulu, and Simon. They'd heard everything.

Rina's mouth was slightly open. "Holy. Shit."

Vanessa let out a slow, impressed whistle. "Someone get this woman a crown and a dagger."

Lulu held up a hand for a high-five. "I felt that in my ovaries."

David tried to salvage what little pride he had left. "Cute little squad you've got there."

Simon stepped forward, flanking Nora like a wall. "Run along," he said quietly. "Before she makes you cry in front of witnesses."

David's smirk faltered. His eyes darted toward Nora, then toward the small crowd forming nearby—coaches, parents, athletes. He turned on his heel and walked off, faster than he probably realized. No one stopped him. Nora stood still, chest heaving.

Did that man seriously just roll up in a button-down and try to rain on your Regionals moment?" Vanessa asked, deadpan.

"He's lucky I didn't throw my Hydroflask at his forehead," Rina muttered.

"You okay?" Lulu asked, stepping closer. Not crowding—anchoring.

Nora exhaled. Her hands slowly uncurled. "Yeah," she said. "Actually... yeah."

Simon was still beside her, his presence as grounding as her team's. He didn't reach for her hand, didn't need to. Just being there was enough. So was the look in his eyes—fierce, steady, unshaken.

Lulu handed Nora her water bottle like it was sacred. "Hydrate, champion."

Vanessa bumped her hip. "And next time your ex shows up, warn us. I've got earrings I can throw like ninja stars."

They all laughed, loud and real and sharp around the edges.

Nora looked at them—her girls, her team. Her chosen family. Then at Simon, who watched her like she was the entire reason he believed in second chances. She didn't say anything. She didn't need to. Because in that moment—with Lane 4 flanking her, glitter still clinging to her collarbones, and Simon at her side—she didn't feel small. She felt unstoppable and finally, finally... free.

Group Chat: LANE 4 LIFE

Lulu: Breaking News: Local man attempts villain monologue, gets vaporized by ex-wife in front of God and a regional swim meet.

Vanessa: I'm still recovering. Nora's "You were just too small" line?? That wasn't a burn. That was a cremation.

Rina: He evaporated. I saw it happen. Just a David-shaped puff of insecurity.

Lulu: Also me, filming from the bleachers like...

Nora: *Stopppp*

Vanessa: No, we will not. You ended him. That was the emotional equivalent of a 400 IM with bricks in your suit and still beating him to the wall.

Rina: Wait wait wait, do we have a nickname for him now? Because I'm voting for: David the Damp.

Lulu: No no, I raise you: Ex-has-been.

Vanessa: The Ghost of Insecurity Past

Nora: *I hate all of you. I also love all of you.*

Simon (lurking the chat for once):
I'd just like to point out: I told him to leave before he cried. He did not listen. He did, in fact, cry.

Lulu: SIMON IS HERE OMG

Vanessa: He speaks

Rina: Sir, thank you for your emotional support silence and post-murder escort. We stan.

Simon: *Just doing my job.*
Also, remind me to never get on Nora's bad side.

Nora: *You're safe.*

Unless you ever say "midlife crisis in spandex."

Lulu: *OOF TOO SOON*

Rina: *Never too soon. But always on time. Like that takedown.*

Vanessa: *We're framing the transcript and hanging it in the locker room.*

Lulu: *LATER, WE SWIM. RIGHT NOW, WE PETTY.*

Nora: *I'm crying. You are all chaos and I love you.*

Vanessa: *We love you more. Now get ready for your next event, Queen of Scorched Earth.*

***

Simon sat high in the stands, elbows on knees, jaw locked so tight it ached. He hadn't moved since the encounter with David—hadn't trusted himself to. His fists still itched. His pulse still throbbed with everything he didn't say.

Not because he needed to defend her but because watching her defend herself—with that unshakable voice, those wildfire eyes, that fury honed like a weapon was inspiring.

She hadn't flinched. She didn't crumble. She had roared and now, there she was again. Standing at the edge of the block, head high, eyes forward.

Nora. Not the woman who'd walked into his pool months ago, trembling with doubt and dripping with questions. But the one who had carved herself out of steel and steam and every scar she used to hide.

He watched the muscles in her shoulders tense, her fingers flex. The quiet inhale before the starting beep. She looked like something forged—not born.

In that moment, Simon didn't just want her. He believed in her. Like faith. Like fact. She wasn't swimming to silence ghosts or prove something to a man who'd never deserved her. She was racing for the woman she'd become and Simon knew, deep in the marrow of his bones, that he would never stop loving her. Not because she needed him, but because she didn't.

She had chosen her lane and he would spend the rest of his life cheering her down it.

***

Back in the far corner of the locker room, Nora sat alone on the bench, towel draped around her shoulders like armor gone soft. Her legs still trembled—not from fatigue, but from the adrenaline crash that follows surviving something brutal and unspoken.

She had faced him. David. The man who once made her question every part of herself. Who had trimmed her down, bit by bit, until she fit the version of a woman he could handle.

Not today.

Her duffel bag slumped at her feet. She reached for it with a steady hand, unzipped it, and pulled out the old, battered notebook—the one that had traveled with her from the parking lot on day one to this moment.

She opened it to a blank page.

The locker room buzzed faintly behind her—showers hissing, swim bags unzipping, someone laughing over a playlist—but Nora sat in her own stillness.

She pressed pen to paper.

I don't need to be understood by people who never tried to see me.

The line came fast, almost violent in its truth. She stared at it like a mirror—one that didn't shrink her or ask her to apologize.

She underlined it. Once. Twice.

Her breath hitched, catching like a wave breaking inside her chest. The memory of David   his voice, his smirk, his sharp little jabs, rose up like bile but she didn't flinch this time.

She didn't cry. She burned. Her hand moved again.

Not fragile. Not too much. Just finished pretending to be less.

Tears pricked her eyes but they didn't fall. Not because she was holding them back, but because they weren't needed anymore. They'd already done their job. Cleansed her. Gutted her. Forged her. She capped the pen and stared at the page for one more heartbeat.

Then she closed the notebook. Set it down gently beside her, like something sacred.

Rising slowly, she walked toward the mirror. The girl who had once stared into this same glass and wondered if she belonged was gone. Nora peeled off her cap, shaking free a wave of damp hair. Water clung to her lashes. Her cheeks glowed from exertion. And her eyes—

Her eyes were electric.

No more folding herself into palatable pieces.
No more silence to protect fragile egos.
No more dimming just so someone else could shine.
She wasn't too much. They were never enough.

She met her reflection head-on and smiled. It wasn't over. It had only just begun. This was Day One. Tomorrow? She wasn't just swimming. She was coming for blood, and glitter, and every single lane, because this time? She wasn't here to survive. She was here to burn it all down!

Fireproof

Arrival – Regionals Day 2

Day two didn't creep in. It came roaring. The natatorium throbbed with noise and nerves. Every whistle a battle cry, every footstep on tile a drumbeat. Chants ricocheted off steel beams like war songs. Chlorine thickened the air, mixed with the scent of ambition and adrenaline.

Lane 4 walked in like they owned the place. Matching braids. Fresh lightning bolt tattoos. Lulu's signature glitter haloed their shoulders like war paint. No one rolled their eyes this time. They weren't trying to sparkle. They were here to scorch.

Lulu struck a pose as they entered. "Let the slayage begin."

Vanessa raised an eyebrow. "We're not Beyoncé backup dancers."

"We are today," Rina muttered, pulling her goggles down with a snap. "Accept your destiny."

Nora followed them, just a step behind but not in their shadow. Her jaw was tight. Her spine was steel. She moved with the coiled precision of someone who knew exactly what she was made of.

Her journal was zipped into her duffel, but the words from last night echoed like a drumbeat: *Not fragile. Not too much. Just finished pretending to be less.*

Simon found her near the stretching mats. He didn't say anything right away. Just handed her a dented black thermos. Coffee. Two creams, no sugar. The good stuff. The real stuff. Her stuff.

Nora took it with a nod. "Thanks."

"Didn't want to risk another vending machine tragedy," Simon said, his voice low, warm.

Their eyes locked. No smirks. No veils. Just truth. *I see you. I choose you,* and for the first time that weekend, before the roar of the crowd and the whistle's shriek, Nora felt it down to her marrow. She wasn't racing to prove she belonged. She was racing because she did. She didn't need to burn for anyone else. She'd already made herself fireproof.

Her first event of the day: the 200 freestyle. Fast. Technical. A razor's edge between finesse and fury. Nora stripped off her warmups with deliberate movements. No hesitation, no pretense. Just the sound of her heartbeat syncing to the pulse of the natatorium. She stepped onto the block, toes gripping rubber, spine tall, breath steady.

A sharp slap to her heel. "Clear the damn lane," Lulu muttered behind her, mischief and menace braided into her grin. Nora didn't flinch. She grinned, shoulders loose, body coiled like a spring.

Her eyes found Simon. He stood by the bulkhead, arms crossed, no clipboard in sight. Nothing to hide behind. Just Simon, calm on the outside, storm in his eyes. There was heat there, pride, and something quieter. Something that made her feel seen in a way no finish line ever had. He didn't speak. He didn't have to.

The horn blared. She dove. The water took her like it knew her. Like it had been waiting. Not to drown— but to crown. She cut through it like a blade, turns tight, pull long, each stroke a vow: I am not here to survive. I am here to rise.

Her lungs burned by the third lap, but she didn't slow. She welcomed the fire, fueled it. Because the only thing she chased was the version of herself that used to hesitate. That used to question. That used to fold to someone else's comfort.

Not anymore. She slammed the wall—second place, but it didn't feel like settling. It felt like owning something.

She climbed out, water slicking down her skin, lungs heaving, and there he was. Already waiting. No clipboard. No coach voice. Just Simon and the towel in his hand, forgotten. He looked at her like she was a solar flare. Like she'd just done something holy. "You didn't hold back," he said, voice low—reverent, almost.

Nora met his gaze, eyes still wild with adrenaline. "I don't have anything left to hold back."

His throat bobbed. He stepped closer. The rest of the world dimmed.

"I felt it," he murmured. "Every damn stroke."

She blinked, something fluttering in her chest that had nothing to do with the swim.

His hand brushed the edge of her shoulder, brief but anchoring. "You didn't just swim it, Nora. You claimed it," and somehow, that meant more than any medal.

Her breath caught. Not from the swim. Not from fatigue. But from that one damn sentence. Before she could speak, his hand brushed the small of her back. Fleeting. Steady. Certain, and suddenly, the water wasn't the only place she could fly.

Lane 4 were chaos incarnate and right now, they were also a pile of limbs and laughter across the locker room lounge. They sprawled on benches and yoga mats, tangled in towels and damp hair, sharing granola bars like communion wafers. The room smelled like chlorine, cocoa butter, and something suspiciously like Lulu's ginger foot balm.

Rina lay upside down against a bench, her legs propped on the wall. "Do we have to swim again today?

Or can we just live here now and become aquatic cryptids?"

Vanessa, perfectly wrapped in her plush monogrammed towel like a Roman senator, held out a thermos. "Only if I get to be the ghost of mid-pack mediocrity. Haunting the heat sheets."

Lulu grinned and reached into her Mary Poppins swim bag. "Speaking of hauntings…"

Rina groaned. "No. No! I swear to God, if you brought that creepy tarot deck—"

"It's not creepy. It's intuitive," Lulu said, already shuffling like she was channeling cosmic truth. "And it's tradition now."

"You made that rule up literally last month," Vanessa muttered, but she still shifted forward, clearly interested.

Lulu narrowed her eyes. "Would you deny the magic of the cards before Regionals Day 2? The audacity."

"I'm just saying," Rina grumbled, grabbing a juice box. "Last time you said I was going to go through an emotional reckoning, and then I cried in the shower because I forgot my second towel."

"Prophecy fulfilled," Lulu said smugly.

"Pick your poison, witches," she added, fanning the cards out like a blackjack dealer in glittery eye shadow.

Vanessa plucked one. "The Queen of Swords. Appropriate."

"You are emotionally efficient and mildly terrifying," Rina said.

"I accept that," Vanessa said, raising her thermos like a toast.

Rina picked next. She flipped her card, and when she saw it, her eyes widened. "Oh no. The Tower. Again. I swear this deck is bullying me."

"Transformation through destruction," Lulu intoned. "Get ready for a breakthrough, babe."

"I'll break through your glitter supply," Rina muttered.

Lulu cackled. "Bring it. I've got backup decks."

Nora picked last.

She hesitated for a beat, fingertips brushing the edge of the spread. Then she chose a card and turned it over.

The Phoenix. The room stilled for a second.

"Oohhh," Lulu breathed. Her voice shifted, less performative, more reverent. "That's a rare pull."

"What does it mean?" Vanessa asked, leaning closer.

Lulu looked up, eyes sparkling. "Rebirth. Power. Rising from ash. It's not a warning. It's a truth. You already burned. Now you build."

Rina let out a low whistle. "Damn."

Nora stared at the image, wings spread, fire curling, a shape made of heat and heart and fight.

"Fireproof," Lulu said simply. "That's you."

Across the room, Simon sat with his clipboard half-forgotten in his lap. He wasn't pretending not to watch. Their eyes met, and she felt it again, that thread between them, tugging tighter.

Nora smiled, slow and sure.

Lulu, not missing a beat, sprinkled a pinch of body glitter over their heads like a blessing. "For luck," she said.

"For battle," Vanessa corrected.

"For glory," Rina added.

"For hydration," Lulu said, throwing a bottle of coconut water at her.

They dissolved into laughter again loud and alive, glitter dusting the floor, hearts beating fast not from fear, but from readiness. Nora held her card like armor. Fireproof and rising.

Nora's last event for the day: 100 fly. Brutal. Unforgiving. The stroke that demanded everything— shoulders, lungs, legs, heart. The one she used to avoid. The one she used to fear.

Not today. She stepped behind the block, goggles in hand, heartbeat a steady war drum in her chest. The natatorium was loud—coaches barking, teammates shouting, horns blaring, but inside her, there was only stillness. Focus. Her body buzzed with anticipation. Not dread. Not panic. Readiness.

Rina leaned in just before they were called to the blocks, muttering, "You've got this. Remember—you're not swimming away from the past. You're swimming into the damn future."

Nora gave her a crooked smile. "Then I better make it fast."

Simon's voice rang out from the side of the pool—not loud, but impossible to miss. "Fly like hell, Nora."

She turned toward him.

He wasn't wearing the clipboard face. No mask. Just him—Simon, solid and steady, but with a spark in his eyes she hadn't seen before. Not just belief. Pride. Hunger. Wonder.

She held his gaze and smirked, all fire. "Watch me."

The whistle blew. She stepped onto the block, rolled her shoulders back once, then dropped into her stance. The buzzer cracked through the air and she flew.

She sliced into the water like a blade—clean, efficient, fierce. The water didn't fight her; it cradled her. Fed her. Every undulation of her body was smooth and sharp, her kick powerful, her arms catching the water like she owned it. By the halfway mark, her lungs were screaming, her shoulders burning. But she didn't care.

She thought of David—scoffing in the stands. Of every voice that said she was too old, too late, too soft. She thought of her own doubts, the ones that used to choke her when no one else could see and she swam anyway.

Harder.

Freer.

Like every breath was a reclamation.

Last stretch. She saw the wall ahead and gave one final, all-out surge—one last act of defiance, of belief. Her fingers smacked the pad and she screamed. Not polite celebration. Not controlled sportsmanship. A guttural, raw, primal cry. The kind that echoed. The kind that turned heads. The kind that meant something had been exorcised.

The crowd blinked in surprise. Then Lane 4 erupted.

Vanessa was on the bench, pounding the wall. Rina screamed like a banshee. Lulu tossed an entire bottle of glitter into the air. "YES, YOU SPANDEX PHOENIX!

Simon was already by the side of the pool by the time she climbed out dripping, gasping, shaking with adrenaline but not trembling. Alive. Triumphant. He didn't speak right away. Just stared at her, breath caught like he'd just witnessed something holy. She wiped water from her eyes, grinning, unfiltered.

"Damn," he whispered finally, voice low and reverent. "That was everything."

She tilted her head, breath still coming hard, chest heaving. "I know."

Then, without overthinking, without checking who
was watching, she closed the space between them. His
hand found her jaw, warm and sure, as her lips found
his—chlorine-slick, breathless, a collision of pride and
relief and want. The deck noise roared around them—
cheers, laughter, a few wolf-whistles, but none of it
touched the heat sparking under her skin.

When they finally broke apart, he was still close
enough for her to feel the smile he didn't quite let show.
She'd risen, heart unbroken, and now the whole damn
world had seen it. She was fireproof now.

She toweled off slowly, still burning from the inside
out. The sound of the crowd dulled around her—cheers
and announcements melting into white noise. Lane 4
had exploded with praise, pulled her into a sweaty,
glittery group hug. Now, after the rush, after the noise,
she needed space. Not an escape, just a moment to
catch her breath.

When the team settled into their hotel rooms or scouted
vending machines for celebratory snacks, Nora slipped
away. She walked the perimeter of the natatorium, the
hush of night soothing against the static in her veins.

The pavement was cool beneath her sneakers. The
chain-link fence hummed faintly when she brushed
against it, the metal warm from the day's heat. Above,
the stars blinked like they knew things she didn't.

She leaned against the fence and exhaled—long and low. Not from exhaustion, but from release. She wasn't unraveling. She was unfolding.

A footfall behind her. Familiar and unhurried. Simon, didn't speak right away. Just came to stand beside her, his presence calm and electric all at once. The moonlight caught the sharp line of his jaw, the quiet intensity in his eyes.

"You okay?" he asked gently.

She nodded. "Better than okay."

There was something unspoken in the space between them—like the energy hadn't left the pool, just shifted here. Into this quiet. Into this moment.

Simon looked at her like she wasn't just the woman who had scorched through the water. He looked at her like she was the whole damn flame.

"I'm in this," he said, voice low but certain. "With you. Not just as your coach. As yours."

Nora blinked, her throat tightening. She studied him for a beat; his sincerity, his steadiness, the way his hand twitched at his side like he was trying not to reach for her.

"Are you sure?" she asked, her voice softer than she intended. "Because I'm not some safe harbor, Simon. I'm wind and waves and wildfire some days."

He stepped closer. Just enough for the heat of him to meet the chill of the night. "Then I'll learn to sail. Or burn. Whatever it takes. You were never too much, Nora. You've always been exactly right."

Tears pricked her eyes, but she didn't look away. She reached for his hand, and this time, he didn't hesitate. Their fingers laced—warm, certain, known. They stood there like that for a long moment. No rush. No rules.

Just breath. Stars. The quiet thrum of a fence and a future unfolding. Tomorrow, she'd race again. Tomorrow, it would all be on the line. But tonight? She was fireproof and found and finally, finally—home.

Final Lap

Morning – Championship Vibes

The natatorium was electric. The kind of buzz that existed before thunderstorms or once-in-a-lifetime wins. Crowds packed the bleachers, waving signs, blasting air horns, wearing matching shirts and war paint. The air smelled like chlorine and nerves, like something important was about to happen.

Lane 4 walked in as a unit—braids re-done, glitter freshly applied, eyes locked on the water. Vanessa had a temporary tattoo that said "Dominate" in cursive across her bicep. Lulu sparkled from hairline to heel. Rina brought noise-canceling headphones she never used. Nora's journal peeked out from her duffel bag, but she didn't need to read it this morning. The words lived in her now.

They were warriors. Messy, loud, brilliant warriors. Not flawless. Not perfect. But forged in something fiercer than polish.

Simon stood near the team bench, clipboard in hand, but his energy was different—coiled, intense, quietly proud. He handed out the heat sheets, voice calm but commanding. "You've done the work. Swim your race."

When he reached Nora, he didn't just hand her the paper. He touched her hand. Brief. Intentional.

"You ready?"

She looked him square in the eye. "I was born for this."

He smiled, the corner-of-his-mouth kind that meant everything. "Then go take it."

Lulu raised a fist in the air, glitter catching the light. "Let's shatter some timelines, ladies!"

"It's records," Rina muttered, already rolling her eyes.

Vanessa grinned. "Timelines, records—just swim like your ex is watching and we're good."

Laughter rippled through the group. The air stayed charged. Something crackled inside Nora's chest. Not fear. Not anxiety.

Focus.

Her first final was the 200 free. She slipped into the ready room and sat in the far corner, stretching, zoning in. The room buzzed with other swimmers—some pacing, some meditating, some whispering with their coaches. Nora closed her eyes and went inward.

She pictured the pool. The turns. Her pacing. The moment her hand would hit the wall. Mostly, she pictured herself—the version of her that used to whisper, "Don't choke." That voice wasn't gone. It had just been rewritten. "Don't hold back," she whispered softly to herself.

When they called her heat, she stepped onto the block like it was a throne. No nerves. No noise. Just Nora.

The horn blared. She flew. Every stroke was a defiance. Every breath a reclaiming. She felt the power in her core, the rhythm in her bones. By the final lap, she knew she wouldn't win gold but she also knew she had never swum like this in her life.

She touched the wall and looked up. Personal best. Third place. Lane 4 screamed themselves hoarse. Simon didn't wait. He was there, hand out, no clipboard, just pride. She grabbed it, pulled herself out, and for a second, their eyes said everything.

There were more events. More races. More noise, but for Nora, that moment—that single swim, that single look—was the medal. The rest? Icing.

The 400 freestyle relay wasn't just another event, it was a statement. A culmination.

Vanessa exploded off the block with her signature fire, setting a blistering pace that pulled the team into the race like a gravitational force. Nora stood at the edge of the block, every muscle vibrating with readiness. Her heartbeat matched the rhythm of Vanessa's strokes—strong, steady, relentless.

As Vanessa neared the wall, Nora rolled her shoulders back, took a breath, and launched. She cut through the water like a blade, fierce and focused. The cheers from the stands faded into a hum beneath the surface. She didn't chase perfection, she chased presence. Every pull was precise, every kick driven by something deeper. She wasn't just swimming for time. She was swimming for self.

She touched the wall, heart hammering, and Rina exploded off the block.

Nora surfaced, gasping, lungs burning—but smiling. It hadn't been perfect—but it had been hers. Still, the race wasn't over.

She climbed out quickly and joined the others at the edge of the lane. Shoulder to shoulder, they screamed for Rina, who sliced through the water with a kind of graceful defiance. Nora grabbed Vanessa's hand. Vanessa grabbed Lulu's. They were linked, breath held, willing every stroke forward. Rina's final flip turn was tight, fast, fearless.

Then came Lulu. Lulu dove in like she'd been shot out of a confetti cannon. A little messy, a little wild, but powered by something no stopwatch could measure— pure, unfiltered heart.

"Come on, Lulu!" Vanessa shouted, her voice cracking.

They were all yelling now—Nora, Rina, Vanessa— so loud it felt like the building might lift off. Even Simon, usually cool and composed, was shouting through cupped hands.

Lulu's arms churned. Her kick was furious. Her glitter scrunchie started to slip but held on, like it knew this moment mattered.

The anchor leg was a blur of effort and heart. Stroke by stroke, Lulu clawed back seconds. When she hit the wall, the scoreboard flickered. They didn't win...but they won.

Nora's throat closed. Vanessa screamed. Rina started crying and swearing simultaneously. Lulu popped up, sputtering.

"Did I keep my suit on?" she gasped.

"Barely," Rina laughed through her tears, "but you stuck the landing."

They wrapped around Lulu in a wet, laughing heap, arms tangled, hearts full.

Simon appeared behind them, holding out towels, but he didn't say anything. He didn't need to, because this wasn't just Nora's redemption. It was all of theirs. This was the finish line. Not the wall. Not the time. The moment they realized they'd done it—together.

Back at the team bench, the adrenaline still buzzing in their veins, the final heat of the meet rolled on. Nora tugged her battered notebook out of her bag and flipped past the pages—the scribbled drills, the anxious notes, the moments she thought she'd never make it through. She turned to a blank sheet and wrote:

I'm done trying to earn my place.
I already have it.

She underlined it twice.

Rina leaned over and read it, nodding solemnly. "That's gold-medal energy."

Lulu was sobbing in earnest, her glitter somehow smudged across three people. "My mascara wasn't waterproof," she wailed. "Nothing prepared me for this emotional arc!"

Vanessa tried to stay composed arms crossed, hip cocked, like it was just another race but her red-rimmed eyes gave her away. "We're never going to shut up about this, you know," she said, voice thick. "Like, ever."

They bounced and shrieked and half-danced in a puddle of joy, spinning in tight circles like a constellation of chaotic stars. Every high-five was a celebration, every shriek a release. It was messy. Loud. Alive.

***

Simon stood behind the curtain of cheers and chaos, just outside the whirlpool of celebration, watching her. Laughing with her team, eyes bright, cheeks flushed, face lit from within. There was something about seeing her like this—undimmed, unafraid—that reached inside him and stayed. Settled somewhere beneath his ribs like it belonged there.

He hadn't just fallen for her. He'd been changed by her. The girl who once doubted she deserved the lane. The woman who now owned every inch of it. He watched as she wiped glitter from Lulu's cheeks with a tenderness that made his throat ache. She high-fived Rina, then turned toward the stands and waved— unapologetically, joyfully. Not shrinking. Not performing. Just… standing fully in who she was.

She wasn't asking for space anymore. She was space. Simon took a breath and stepped forward. Not to interrupt—just to join.

***

When Nora turned—dripping, breathless, electric—and met his eyes, the world narrowed to just the two of them.

He stepped forward, towel forgotten in his hand. His voice was low, but steady. "I've never been prouder of a swim in my life."

She tilted her head, grinning through the fog of adrenaline. "Not even yours?"

He shook his head. "Especially not mine."

Then—he kissed her. Right there on the deck. In front of everyone.

It wasn't tentative. It wasn't quiet. It was a declaration—like planting a flag after the final stroke. Like the last page of a book that had begged to be dog-eared, highlighted, and reread.

The cheers that went up might've cracked the ceiling. Rina screamed so loudly a lifeguard flinched. Vanessa let out a stunned, "Well, okay then!" Lulu launched a literal fistful of glitter into the air like a human confetti cannon.

When they finally pulled apart, Simon leaned in, his voice warm and steady against her skin.

"I see you," he whispered. Nora's whole face lit up. She didn't hesitate. "I see you too."

Behind them, Lane 4 erupted in unison:

"Power couple! Power couple! Power couple!"

It was ridiculous.

It was wild.

It was everything.

In that moment, they weren't just teammates, or swimmers, or coach and athlete. They were equals. Co-conspirators in their own second chance. They were a story that had come full circle. The final lap. The start of everything else.

That night, after the team dinner and the teary formal goodbyes, Lane 4 took over Vanessa and Lulu's shared hotel room with the kind of uncontainable energy only girls who have become can conjure.

There was pizza. Sour Patch Kids. One extremely illegal bottle of "hootch" that Lulu had smuggled in and labeled "vitamin potion." Wet swimsuits hung from lamps. Glitter coated every surface like joy had exploded.

It wasn't pretty. It was perfect.

"To us," Vanessa declared, raising her paper cup like it was champagne.

"To surviving," Rina added from the floor, half-buried in a tangle of hoodies and snack wrappers.

"To glitter and greatness," Lulu shouted, striking a pose that made her fall off the bed and knock over a laundry basket.

"To never swimming fly again," Rina groaned, and the room howled with laughter.

Then Nora stood, cup in hand and the energy shifted—not dimmed, but focused.

"To choosing ourselves," she said. "To not waiting for permission. To walking back into the pool, the room, the world—and saying: I belong here."

A hush followed. Just a breath. A beat.

Then: "To the Masters Club," she added, eyes gleaming.

Rina sat up straighter. "Wait—is that a thing now?"

"It is now," Nora said, grinning. "Mastering our fears. Our futures. Ourselves."

"I want jackets," Lulu whispered.

"Crowns," Vanessa added.

"Legacy," Rina said.

They clinked their cups with more force than necessary. Liquid sloshed. Glitter flew and it didn't matter, because this wasn't just a celebration. It was a revolution. They weren't just swimmers. They weren't just girls. They were the founders of something bigger. A sisterhood stitched together by chlorine, chaos, and courage.

A declaration. A movement. A club where you earned your place not by being perfect, but by showing the hell up. In that wild, glitter-drenched, laughter-soaked room, every one of them knew;

They didn't just take up space. They redefined it, from now on—Lane 4 wouldn't whisper. Lane 4 would make waves.

Simon – Epilogue

Some people don't just change your path—they remind you there's still one worth walking.

For a long time, I believed the best parts of me were in the rearview mirror. I wore discipline like armor. Built a life out of control, predictability, and quiet distance. It was safer that way. Easier to keep people at arm's length than risk being left gutted again.

Then came Lane 4. Then came her. Nora didn't fix me. She didn't try to. She saw me—really saw me—and still chose to lean in. Not in spite of my cracks, but maybe because of them. She didn't ask me to be someone new. She reminded me I was still becoming. Loving her didn't feel like losing myself. It felt like finding my way back.

I used to think coaching was about perfection. That respect was earned through authority. It turns out, the real work—the real courage—is in showing up fully. With your fears. With your flaws. With your heart in your damn hands.

It's in the moments between laps. In the quiet support. The shared glances. The trust that doesn't need to be spoken to be known.

The Masters Club

The Masters Club may have started in the water, but what we built lives far beyond it now. In Nora's boldness. In Vanessa's grit. In Rina's fire and Lulu's sparkle. In every one of us who thought the best was behind us—only to realize we were never done growing.

I'm not perfect. I'm not finished. But I'm here. Loving her. Loving this life, and finally, loving the man I've become.

I'm not hiding anymore and I'm not letting go. I used to think I was broken. Now I know I'm just beginning.

Epilogue – Nora

You don't realize how far you've come until you catch your own reflection— and recognize her.

The pool deck smells like chlorine and second chances. Every Tuesday afternoon, I stand in a worn-out T-shirt that says Coach Nora, a whistle around my neck, teaching beginners how to float. How to trust the water. How to trust themselves. Still, there are moments when it hits me—this is my life now.

Not a placeholder. Not a detour. Mine. I didn't come here searching for transformation. I came because I was unraveling. I'd spent years trying to shrink myself into someone else's idea of love. Someone else's version of enough. I didn't know who I was without the roles I'd played, the approval I'd chased, or the quiet ache I'd carried like a second skin.

But Lane 4 changed that. In that lane, I found breath again. Found women who didn't just see me— they saw through me. Who laughed with me, cried with me, showed up for me, and let me show up for them. Who reminded me I didn't need to apologize for taking up space.

I found Simon, too. Not as a savior. Not as a fairy tale ending. But as a partner in the real, messy, breathtaking middle. A man who didn't ask me to be less. Who never flinched at my strength or my scars. Who met me, exactly where I was, and waited there with open hands and unwavering eyes—until I could meet myself, too.

The Masters Club started as a joke. A sarcastic rebellion against "too late" and "past your prime."

But now? It's a movement. A mantra. A promise that we're not done becoming. That we are allowed to want more, to fall apart, to begin again. That we can be full of contradictions; tender and tough, soft and unshakable, scared and still standing.

It's Vanessa, fierce and unyielding, learning to trust herself. Rina, bold and brilliant, trading performance for presence. Lulu, showing up in glitter like it's her birthright. Simon, steady and storm-scarred, choosing love without losing himself. And me—no longer shrinking. No longer waiting for permission. No longer wondering if I'm too much or not enough. It's all of us.

We're not chasing our former selves anymore. We're becoming people who make ourselves proud— one stroke, one breath, one brave, messy lap at a time. We're not finished. We're just getting started.

This is the Masters Club.

The Masters Club

Author's Note to the Reader

So… you thought that was the end? Please. You've met Lane 4. You didn't think they'd ride off quietly into the sunset, did you? Of course not. They demanded a retreat, matching tank tops, and glitter — so much glitter.

Here's a little extra joy for the road — a glimpse into what happens when badass women (and one reformed coach) trade the swim deck for a lakeside cabin, armed with vision boards, confessions, and love that refuses to quit.

With gratitude and glitter,
Olivia Savage

The First Annual Masters Club Retreat

One month later. A lakeside cabin. One big bag of glitter. Zero adult supervision.

"Okay, but I still don't understand why we're doing a vision board at 8 a.m.," Lulu groaned, flopping dramatically onto a pile of throw blankets in what had once been a peaceful, neutrally-decorated Airbnb living room.

"Because growth requires intention," Vanessa said from the kitchen, her voice muffled by a face mask and total authority.

"And because Rina threatened to make us do sunrise yoga," Nora added, sipping her coffee with a smirk.

"That threat still stands," Rina called from the porch, where she was stretching in a sequined hoodie and pajama pants. "My chakras are crackling."

Lulu groaned louder, pulling a fuzzy blanket over her face. "This retreat is a scam. I was promised snacks and lake selfies. Not emotional homework before breakfast."

Vanessa walked in with a tray of coffees and the kind of calm efficiency that suggested she'd already color-coded the agenda. "For the record," she said, handing out mugs, "this is still better than last year's Girls' Trip when we ended up at a silent meditation retreat and someone got kicked out for whispering."

"That was me," Rina said proudly, entering the room with a Masters Club: Camp Edition tank top and a tiara made of glittery pipe cleaners. "Totally worth it."

Nora sat cross-legged on the rug, cradling her mug, grinning at the beautiful, unfiltered mess that was her chosen family.

Vanessa: composed and competent, wearing under-eye patches while organizing a "feelings folder."
Lulu: loud and lovable, currently buried under three blankets and one decorative pillow.
Rina: chaotic joy personified, radiating glitter like it was oxygen.
And Simon—leaning against the doorframe with a half-smile, arms crossed, watching the scene like he'd won the lottery.

They'd planned this retreat half-jokingly after their last swim meet. What started as a sarcastic group chat called "Camp Masters" had somehow turned into a real weekend: lakeside bonding, too much wine, vision boards, group therapy disguised as games, and one mysterious warning from Lulu: Bring waterproof mascara. You'll cry.

And they had. During the team trust falls.
During the late-night fire pit confessions.
During the moment Vanessa admitted she didn't want
to have to be "the strong one" all the time—and
nobody tried to fix it. They just reached out and held
her hand.

Later that night, they stood by the dock wrapped in
mismatched sweatshirts and oversized sweatpants,
holding paper lanterns like it was a scene from a
coming-of-age movie for grown-ass women.

One by one, they whispered something they were
ready to release. And let go.

Vanessa released guilt.
Lulu let go of pretending things didn't matter when they
did.
Rina let go of fear—loudly, dramatically, with jazz
hands.
And Nora?
She let go of the version of herself who believed she
had to shrink to be loved.

She held her lantern for a moment longer,
fingertips trembling.

Simon stepped behind her, wrapping his arms
around her waist. His cheek brushed her temple.

"What'd you let go of?" she whispered.

He kissed the top of her head. "The lie that I was
safer alone."

Her eyes filled. "You didn't cry during the trust falls."

"I cried internally," he said, deadpan. "Where it counts."

She laughed, turning in his arms to kiss him. Behind them, the others cheered. Or heckled. With this group, it was always a little of both.

Their lanterns floated upward, slow and glowing, carving soft trails into the dark like tiny declarations.

Above them, the stars burned bright. Beside them, the lake held their reflections steady and in that moment, surrounded by these wild, powerful women and the man who met her where she was— Nora thought:

This is what mastery looks like.

Not perfection.

Not control.

Presence.

Joy.

Love—earned, chosen, and held with both hands.

And maybe a tiara made of pipe cleaners.

Because honestly?

Why the hell not.

Masters Club Manifesto

Founded unofficially in hotel room #426 with glitter, sour candy, and Lizzo.

We believe in:

- ➤ Power poses before performance reviews.
- ➤ Glitter as a lifestyle.
- ➤ Showing up, even when it's hard.
- ➤ Choosing ourselves. Out loud.
- ➤ You don't have to swim to join. You just have to jump in.

Book Club Discussion Questions – Masters Club

1. "I choose who gets to see me now."
   What does this line mean to Nora—and how does it reflect her personal growth throughout the story? Have you ever experienced a moment where you made a similar decision?

2. The Masters Club isn't a place—it's a choice. What do you think Masters Club symbolizes? How did the team transform it from a joke into something powerful?

3. Simon and Nora's relationship is full of tension, tenderness, and transformation. How does their dynamic evolve, and what makes their love story unique? Where do you think their balance of fire and vulnerability comes from?

4. Lane 4 is more than a swim lane—it's a sisterhood. Discuss the role of friendship and community in Nora's journey. How does each Lane 4 member support her differently?

5. Failure, anxiety, and starting over are recurring themes. How does Nora's flashback to her image of herself connect to her experience in

the pool? What lessons about resilience and second chances did you take from her story?

6. Humor and heart go hand-in-hand. How did the mix of comic relief (like Lulu's green juice or the group chat chaos) enhance the emotional impact of the book?

7. "You're not just learning. You're leading." How does Nora step into leadership by the end of the novel? What moments mark her transformation from student to mentor?

8. The wall isn't the end—it's the push-off point. Where else in life do we face "the wall"? What does it take to push off and fly, like Nora did?

Thank You for Reading

If Nora, Lane 4, or The Masters Club made you laugh, cry, or feel seen, I'd love to hear from you! Reviews help readers (and authors) more than you know.

Follow along at: www.oliviasavagebooks.com
Instagram: @oliviasavagewrites

About the Author

Olivia Savage is the author of The Confidence Playbook and The Leadership Pivot. With two decades of experience in leadership, reinvention, and creative storytelling, she brings heart and humor to everything she writes.

She lives in Northern Virginia where she swims slowly, dreams wildly, and believes in glitter as a coping mechanism.